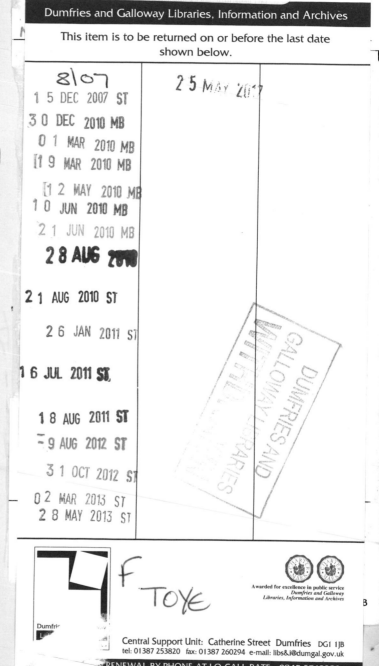

Joanna Toye

Shula's Story

BBC BOOKS

FOR OLIVIA
AND FOR POPPY.

This book is published to accompany the Radio 4 serial entitled *The Archers*.
The Editor of *The Archers* is Vanessa Whitburn.

Published by BBC Books,
an imprint of BBC Worldwide Publishing.
BBC Worldwide Limited, Woodlands,
80 Wood Lane, London W12 0TT

First published 1995
Reprinted 1995
Copyright © Joanna Toye, 1995
The moral right of the author has been asserted

ISBN 0 563 38703 3

Designed by Graham Dudley Associates

Set in Caslon 540 Roman 11/14pt
Printed in Great Britain by Martins the Printers Ltd, Berwick-upon-Tweed
Bound in Great Britain by Hunters & Foulis Ltd, Edinburgh
Jacket printed by Lawrence Allen Ltd, Weston-super-Mare

ACKNOWLEDGEMENTS

I must thank Heather Holden-Brown of BBC Worldwide and my editor, Caroline Plaisted, for their encouragement during the writing of this book. Camilla Fisher, Archivist of *The Archers*, helped me enormously in teasing out details of Shula's early history, and the Editor of *The Archers*, Vanessa Whitburn, has been unstinting in her support, without which I would simply not have been able to undertake the project. Thanks are due also to the wider production team of *The Archers*, past and present, the writers, including Debbie Cook, Mary Cutler, Simon Frith, Graham Harvey, Caroline Harrington, Susan Hill, Peter Kerry, Helen Leadbeater, Mick Martin, Louise Page and William Smethurst, and, of course, the cast, not least Judy Bennett as Shula, who have between them created the very seductive place which is Ambridge.

JOANNA TOYE

The Archers' Family Tree

John Archer *m* Phoebe

John Benjamin *m* Simone Delamain
(Ben)   1900-1929
27.5.1898-2.8.1972

Frank *m* Laura Wilson
1.6.1900 -   29.8.1911-
30.5.1957   14.2.1985

Daniel *m* Doris
15.10 1896-   11.7.1890-
23.4.1986   27.10.1980

(1) John (Jack) *m* Margaret (Peggy) Perkins
17.12.1922-12.1.1972   b.13.11.1922

Jennifer *m* (1)Roger
b.7.1.1945 | Travers-Macy
           | b.9.3.1944
           | div. Feb 1976

Lilian *m* (1) Lester
b.8.7.1947 | Nicholson
           | 7.6.1946-
           | 18.3.1970
           |
           m (2) Ralph Bellamy
           | 26.2.1925-18.1.1980

Anthony William *m* Pat Lewis
Daniel (Tony)   b.10.1.1952
b.16.2.1951

Adam
b. 22.6.1967

Deborah
b. 24.12.1970

James Rodney
Dominic
b. 30.3.1973

John Daniel
b.31.12.1975

Helen
b.16.4.1979

Thomas
b.25.2.1981

m (2) Brian Aldridge b. 20.11.1943

Katherine
Victoria
(Kate)
b.30.9.1977

Alice Margaret
b.29.9.1988

(2) Jack Woolley
b.19.7.1919

William Forrest *m* Lisa

Edward George (Ted)
10.1.1902-17.1.1920

Thomas William (Tom) b.20.10.1910
m
Prudence Harris (Pru) b.27.7.1921

Philip Walter *m* (1) Grace Fairbrother
b. 23.4.1928 | 2.4.1929-22.9.1955

m (2) Jill Paterson
b.3.10.1930

Christine *m* (1) Paul Johnson
b.21.12.1931 | 10.1.1931-10.5.1978

Peter
(adopted)
b.5.9.1965

Shula Mary
8.8.1958
m
Mark
Hebden
20.2.1955-
17.2.1994

Kenton
Edward
b.8.8.1958

David
Thomas
b.18.9.1959
m
Ruth
Pritchard
b.16.6.1968

Elizabeth
b.21.4.1967
m
Nigel Pargetter
b.*8.6.1959*

m (2) George Barford
b.24.10.1928

Philippa
Rose (Pip)
b.17.2.1993

Daniel Mark
Archer
b.14.11.1994

The Archers

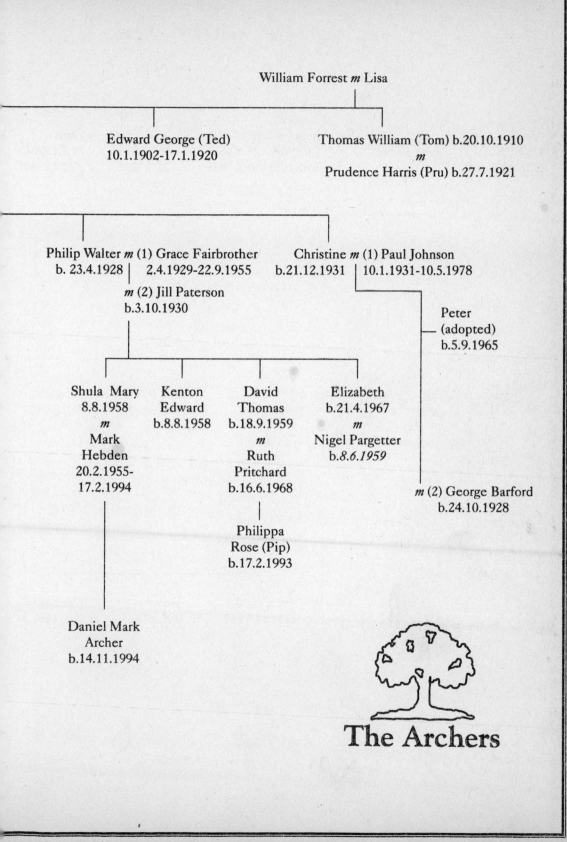

18 FEBRUARY
—— 1994 ——

A LOW MIST lay along the valley, legacy of the previous day's
rain. It was at its thickest down by the river, where it trailed in
the water, and draped the naked trees. Even without the mist,
little could have been seen of the surrounding countryside, as sun-
rise was a long way off on this February morning, and there was
every sign that this would be one of those winter days when it
never seemed properly to get light. But, though it was only just
after six, there were lights on in the village — not the glare of
sodium streetlights (Ambridge had resisted those thanks to a vigor-
ous local campaign) — but lights in cottage porches and farmyards
and milking parlours. For in the countryside of South Borsetshire,
the day starts early.

At Brookfield, a handsome brick-and-timber farmhouse on the
outskirts of the village, milking was already well under way. But for
once it was not Phil or David in charge. Unusually, one of the
workers had been called in to see to the cows — and the reason he
was preoccupied was not because he was calculating his overtime
payments. The anxious glances he cast across the yard at the back
porch of Brookfield farm house, and the kitchen window, where a
light burned behind the gingham curtains, were not because he
had detected clots in the milk or because the teat cup liners
needed changing. They were because tragedy had struck this ordinary village, this ordinary family. And even the shelter of Brookfield's stout walls could not protect anyone inside from the fact that
life would never be the same again.

Bert stepped out of the way as the clusters swung off the last
cow on the right-hand side of the parlour. Wiping her teats with
iodine, he shook his head. Slowly he moved to release the gate

which would let the cows, replete and relieved, back into the yard.

'Get on there!'

Work was supposed to be good for you at a time like this, folk said, to take your mind off things. He slapped the cows' rumps, felt their flesh warm and solid, heard the regular rhythm of the pulsator, saw the milk froth and foam into the glass jars. He'd seen, felt, heard all these things thousands of times before and taken comfort from them but never had they seemed more meaningless than they did today. When poor Shula... Bert sighed. Poor Shula.

Mike Tucker shifted down a gear as he came up to the bend in the road, the milk crates rattling in protest on the back of his Toyota pick-up. But it was a nasty bend and the roads were greasy and he wasn't taking any risks — not when Betty had promised him a nice bit of black pudding for breakfast. He saw the car as soon as he rounded the corner. They'd straightened it a bit, moved it onto the verge, but in the light of his headlamps he could see the gaping wound it had gouged in the tree, and could imagine the force of the impact which had folded the bonnet, splintered the windscreen and crumpled the roof. Some poor devil would have been lucky to get out of that alive. With a new caution borne of the awareness of someone else's misfortune, and even though the road was empty, Mike indicated well in advance of the drive to Nightingale Farm, where Mrs Antrobus' Afghans set up their usual dawn chorus of greeting. It wasn't until he was putting her silver top and her orange juice on the step that he realised whose car it was. Mark Hebden's.

'Shula? Can I come in?'

Jill waited nervously on the landing. It was over half an hour since Shula had gone to have her bath. Jill just hoped she hadn't locked the door.

'Of course, Mum. The door's open.'

Jill pushed open the bathroom door and was cocooned in a womb-like warmth.

'I brought your dressing gown and a clean nightie, love — then you can go straight back to bed.'

Shula lay in the water, her eyes puffy and her mouth tight with tension. Despite the supposedly relaxing effect of the water her mother could see that her body was rigid. Jill sank down on the Lloyd Loom chair which had belonged to Doris and which she had been about to throw out when Elizabeth declared it back in fashion and if Jill didn't want it, she'd have it for her room. So Jill had repainted it, and there it stood.

'I can't go back to bed, Mum.' The degree of control in Shula's voice was unnerving. 'I've got to ring the office and let them know I'm not coming in today.'

'I can do that for you,' said Jill at once.

'No,' insisted Shula. 'I ought to speak to Mr Pemberton myself. There's stuff I was going to get ready for the end of the financial year...'

Her voice trailed off.

'Don't worry about it for now,' soothed Jill. 'Look, why don't you get out, love? That water must be freezing.'

'Hmm? No, no, it's all right.' Shula gave a faint half smile. 'Mark could never understand how I could bear the bath water so hot. Men can't seem to stand it, you know. Must be their pain threshold or something...'

Suddenly her voice was fuzzy with tears.

'Shula —'

'They all said he wouldn't have felt any pain. The sergeant said he would have been dead the second the car hit the tree.'

'Oh, love.'

This was her baby, her first-born. Jill had fed her and changed her nappies, brushed her toddler curls, taken her to have her injections and made her go to the dentist, checked that her wellingtons weren't rubbing her toes, supervised her homework, had her friends round to tea. All that work, all that cossetting — all that love. It wasn't enough. It couldn't spare Shula what she was going through now. So what was it all for?

'Why Mark, Mum? What had he ever done to hurt anyone? So why?'

'I don't know, love. I don't know.'

'Everyone who knew him — everyone — said Mark was one of

the nicest, kindest men they'd ever met. And we were so happy.'

Jill's throat throbbed from the effort of not crying herself.

'Come on, Shula,' she said gently. 'Come on, get out of that bath and let me give you a love.'

'Oh, Mum, I don't want to get out! I don't want to do anything again, ever! Not without Mark!'

Jill knelt by the bath. Wrapping her daughter in her arms, she held Shula's head on her shoulder while Shula cried and cried. And neither of them knew whether the droplets of water running down Shula's back were the bathwater or Jill's own tears.

'I've brought you some coffee, darling.'

Jennifer Aldridge, her Puffa jacket set off with a loosely knotted silk scarf — Jennifer was incapable of looking scruffy, whatever the situation — leant on the side of the pen. Most of the ewes and lambs from Brian's first lambing had been moved out into the paddocks now but there were still a few in the yard — and wherever they were, they all needed feeding until the spring grass started to grow. Debbie released the ewe whose foot she had been examining and straightened. Her eyes were deeply shadowed and her cheeks were pinched and pale, in a way that had nothing to do with the dank February day. Jennifer had protested when Debbie had said she was coming out to the stock but Debbie had said she wanted to keep busy — to give herself something else to think about.

Debbie joined her mother and took the mug.

Jenny unwrapped a foil parcel.

'I brought you some Florentines, too. Look, all warm from the oven.'

Debbie shook her head.

'I couldn't. I just couldn't. Sorry, Mum.'

Jennifer bit back all the things which mothers say about eating and keeping your strength up and instantly regret.

Debbie pushed her dark hair off her face with a gloved hand.

'I still can't get it out of my mind. It's like it's superimposed on everything else. I look at a field of ewes and all I can see is that — that — idiot coming straight towards us and going so fast and Dandy rearing right up and Caroline ... well, she didn't have a chance — Caroline just not being able to hang on ... and ... the terrible thud as she hit the road ... and then Mark's car, coming straight at her. Except — I don't know how he did it, I don't know how he missed her ... he slammed on the brakes, and skidded, and swerved ... and ... smack ... right into the tree.'

Her voice cracked. Jenny took her hand.

'Debbie, why won't you let me ring Richard and ask him to give you something?'

'I'm all right, Mum,' said Debbie.

'But you're not —'

'Maybe I want to suffer a bit, OK? Maybe I ought to. I mean, I seem to have come out of this one pretty well. There's Mark dead and Caroline in intensive care and Shula being so, so brave —'

'So are you.'

Debbie laughed.

'Me? I'm pathetic. I couldn't even tell the police anything about the first car, the one that overtook Mark.'

'Darling, it was dark, it was drizzling —'

'Yes, it was. And I was the one who insisted we stay out a bit longer. We could have come back here for a cup of tea before going to Shula's but no, let's go for a gallop on Heydon Berrow, I said, and Caroline said, why not? Well I know why not — if we hadn't, then we wouldn't have been coming along the lane at the same time as Mark was on his way home from work, and the car would never have scared the horse, and Caroline wouldn't have been in the road for Mark to avoid and —'

Debbie started to cry, great gulping sobs.

'And now Shula's lost him, lost him for good. Now she's got nothing.'

Richard Locke held the syringe up to the light and flicked it.

'Ready?'

Obediently Shula rolled her tights down, exposing warm flesh. Richard stooped. Shula flinched as the needle made contact but the sensation was momentary.

'All done.' Richard hesitated. 'I do think you're right to carry on with the treatment.'

Shula met his eyes. It wasn't so much that she had made a conscious decision to carry on, more that to opt out would have required an effort of will she hadn't the energy to exercise at the moment. And she certainly didn't want to talk about it.

'Look, Richard, let's just leave it, OK?'

'Fine.'

Richard busied himself repacking his bag. He was a good doctor and a good friend. He'd been a good friend to Mark, too. Only three nights ago they'd both been frogmarching Robin across the Malverns for his surprise stag night. It seemed light years away now.

'I'm sorry, Richard. I didn't mean to take it out on you.'

'You take it out on who you like,' he said. 'You've every right to.'

Shula watched the clouds roll past the window. It had never brightened up. Grey from start to finish, today. The bird feeder swung on the rustic arch which Mark had put up for the Albertine rose he'd bought her one birthday — the same variety as the one which clambered over the porch at Brookfield, and which she'd always loved. Often, on summer evenings she'd drag her deckchair right down the garden to be near the arch, just so she could smell that rose — and she'd be sitting there in the half-light when he came in from cricket nets, all sweaty yet sweet-smelling of grass and he'd flop down beside her and she'd run her fingers through his hair and think ... and think ... nothing. Because when you don't imagine anything's going to change, you don't think to yourself — I'm so happy, now, here, here and now with this man who is my husband, who loves me, and I love him, and we have a lovely home, and we have good jobs and friends and a wonderful family and we're so lucky — you don't think it at all. You take it all for granted and he says 'Would you like a drink?' and you say 'I'll get it, you're tired,' and he says 'I wouldn't mind something to eat. I only had time for a sandwich,' and you say, 'There's pâté and Brie and a bit of French onion tart — shall we have a picnic?'. And that's your life.

Suddenly the doorbell shrilled and Tibby twitched awake on

Shula's knee. Sighing, she moved the cat on to the sofa and reached across to switch on the light. The dark shapes in the room leapt into focus — the fireplace with its stripped surround and black grate which Nelson had helped them track down, the Liberty print chesterfield, the balloon-backed chair which Shula had bought for the nursery... The watercolours they'd had from Kenton, the mass of photographs, some framed in silver, some in Thai silk, of their wedding, of little Pip, of Shula and Kenton as babies, of Mark's parents on holiday in Madeira... The Wedgwood candlesticks, the carriage clock and the decanters (wedding presents) and the stuffed frog she'd bought Mark as a joke...

The bell shrilled again. Slowly, testing every step, Shula went to the door.

'Nigel!'

Nigel was crouched under the porch to get out of the wind, his coat collar turned up against the weather. In his hands he held a mass of freesias.

'I had to come, Shula. Sorry, if you don't want to see anyone —'

'Nigel, of course I want to see you. Come in.'

She led him through to the sitting room and drew the curtains. Nigel laid the flowers down.

'I've just dropped Lizzie back at Brookfield. I didn't know if you'd be there or —'

'I wanted to be here. Mum's just gone to get her night things, then she's coming back to stay with me.'

'Good. As long as you're not on your own.'

The words seemed to echo around the room.

'But I am on my own,' said Shula evenly. 'And I always will be, now.'

DECEMBER
——— 1976 ———

Right then Sheila, this will be your desk —'

'It's Shula, actually.'

'It was a choice of either having your back to the wall or being able to see out of the window, we thought you'd prefer — I'm sorry, what did you say?'

Miss Pearson, Mr Rodway's secretary, stopped abruptly in her monologue and scrutinised the new girl closely. Since the window in question looked out onto the dustbins, Shula wondered if there was much in it.

'I said, my name's Shula.'

A frown crossed Miss Pearson's perfect *maquillage*. She was not the frazzled dragon nearing retirement which her name had led Shula to expect. In fact she could only have been in her late twenties — a mere ten years older than Shula — but so far, after nearly an hour's introduction to the wonders of Rodway and Watson, Estate Agents, of Borchester, there had been no invitation to call her by her first name, no promise of shared confidences over the morning digestives, and absolutely no chance, in Shula's estimation, that they would ever nip over to The Feathers for a quick lunchtime drink, and return giggling having given their home phone numbers to a couple of feed reps. Inwardly she sighed. Her father and mother had been so thrilled when the job came up.

'It's only an office junior, Dad,' she'd protested.

But her father had insisted on getting out the sherry, her mother had made her favourite mandarin gâteau and even Elizabeth, at the age of nine, had been moved to make her a card which showed Shula being thrown from a horse in front of a For Sale sign. 'From Horses to Houses' read the greeting, in Elizabeth's just-about-joined-up writing.

'Honestly, Dad, anyone would think you were glad to get rid of me!'

'Nonsense,' her father declared, replacing the stopper in the decanter and passing her a glass. 'You'd be an asset to any business. I was very sorry to lose you from the farm office.'

'Oh yes?' Shula grinned. 'That's not what you said when you couldn't find the latest invoice from Borchester Mills.'

'Oh well, nobody's perfect. And that was about the only thing that went wrong while you were working for me.'

'Come on Dad, I was only your secretary for a couple of weeks. Who knows what havoc I could have created, given time? Ordered pig nuts instead of dairy cake, lost your butterfat premium from the figures, banked the milk cheque in my personal account...'

Her father put down his sherry glass. A log slipped in the grate and the old tabby cat, stretched out on the hearthrug, twitched its ears, still sound asleep. Phil Archer leant forward and took his elder daughter's hands.

'Now look, love. I know you'll say I'm only saying this because I'm your dad, and that's bound to make me biased —'

'I should hope so!'

Here it came. Another pep talk.

'—but you want to stop knocking yourself. Have a bit more faith in your own abilities. And now you've settled on the idea of a business career, I hope you'll give it all you've got. I know you're disappointed you couldn't work with horses but — well, that's life. What we want very often doesn't work out. What marks us out is what we make of what's on offer.'

Disappointed? Well, that went some way to explaining the feeling she'd had all summer. The feeling that said it wasn't worth getting out of bed, the dragging sensation that made her feel as if her feet were made of lead and her head of cotton wool. A feeling that was frightening if she thought about it too hard because it said that if horses (which had been her life until now) were not going to be her career — then what else was there? And Shula had no answer to that.

Her father sat back and took another sip of sherry. She realised with a start that she was expected to speak.

'Um — yes, I'm sure you're right, Dad.'

Phil still looked expectant. What else could she say? How could she tell her parents that no one was ever going to convince her that a job stuck in an office in Borchester would ever be a substitute for the life she had imagined for herself ever since she could remember? How could struggling to remember the shorthand outline for 'thanking you in advance for your kind co-operation' replace soaring over fences on Mister Jones, the chestnut gelding, or even passing on her love and knowledge of horses to pony-mad little girls on Saturday mornings?

Shula had never thought she had it in her to hate a person as much as she hated Trina Muir. If she'd known when she was picked as the pupil for the trial lesson when Trina first applied for the job with Lilian, that as a result Trina would be standing in her way now, she'd have made sure and been even more difficult to teach. Then Trina might not have got the job and it might have gone to someone else, someone who even now might be leaving Ambridge, leaving a vacancy at Auntie Chris' just ready for Shula to step into.

Instead, here she was two weeks before Christmas, on her first day at Rodway and Watson. With difficulty, Shula hauled herself back to the present and Miss Pearson.

'Shula? S-h-u-l-a?'

'That's right,' answered Shula brightly. 'And my twin's called Kenton.'

Miss Pearson raised an eyebrow. She'd already chosen her children's names, though she and her fiancé, Rodney, weren't getting married for eighteen months. Michael for a boy, Sarah for a girl. Naturally they'd have one of each. That was the sort of life Miss Pearson led.

'Where did you hear about the vacancy, er, Shula?'

'The Careers Office sent me.'

'I see. And had you always set your heart on a career in estate agency?'

Shula considered. She could lie, of course. It would save a thousand further questions, and Miss Pearson might even see to it, if she gave the right answer, that she got her own waste paper bin, a plentiful supply of paper clips and an unchipped cup at coffee time. But lying was not Shula's strong point. On the other hand, perhaps diplomacy was.

'I'm sure it'll be very interesting.'

Fortunately, Mr Rodway chose this moment to pop his head out of his office. This was Miss Pearson's signal to drop everything. Another cup of coffee? An expertly typed letter? The immediate collection of his dry cleaning? His wish, as Shula was to find out, was Miss Pearson's command.

Hastily installing Shula at the desk facing the window (her back thus exposed to a draught from the ladies toilet), Miss Pearson glided off, telling Shula to settle herself in.

Shula put her bag on the desk and listlessly opened the drawers, empty save for a box of ring binder reinforcers. She looked at her watch. Half past ten. She wondered how early she could decently go to lunch.

Just then the door from the street opened and an elderly man shuffled in, glad to be out of the December wind. Miss Pearson had already explained that Mr Richards, the Sales Negotiator, was out measuring up a couple of properties this morning, and that Mr Rodway Junior was conducting an auction at Waterley Cross. As Miss Pearson and Mr Rodway Senior were still in conference ... Now was Shula's chance. Perhaps he'd come in to sell his twenty-bedroom mansion? Or, even better, *buy* a twenty-bedroom mansion? He was obviously just dressed in that down-at-heel overcoat for disguise. He was an eccentric millionaire who hadn't been out of the house for years. How was he to know fashions had changed?

'Can I help you?' she asked, as she'd been told.

The old man took off his shiny trilby and brushed the cold rain from his lapels.

'I hope so, my dear. You know those sales particulars? Have you got any old ones I could have to roll up for firelighters?'

Ten thirty-three. The excitement's going to kill me, she thought. All this and twenty pounds a week.

As the morning wore on, Shula did not have much cause to revise her opinion. Even working at Brookfield had been better than this, with her father popping in and out of the office to use the phone, the vet or a rep arriving, the tanker driver to chat to, her Mum bringing her warm scones from the oven, and, of course, the secret satisfaction of knowing that whenever she crossed the yard, Neil Carter her father's farmworker would materialise and strike up a conversation. Still, she had someone rather more interesting than Neil Carter to think about since Charles Hodgeson had been on the scene. Miss Pearson had set her the task of photocopying sales particulars and as she placed them one by one under the lid of the machine, she allowed her thoughts to wander back to Saturday night.

'Charles, stop — stop it — that's enough!'

Shrieking with laughter, Shula flopped down on one of Grey Gables' spindly gilt chairs.

'No more! I can't!'

'Shula — not even the Gay Gordons?'

The little gold chair next to hers creaked ominously as Charles threw his weight on to it as if he were getting into the saddle.

'Why the Gay Gordons anyway? It's a Young Farmers Christmas Dance, not Burns Night.'

'What proof have you got? I've always said Ambridge was in a time warp.'

'Let's sit this one out and have another drink,' Shula pleaded.

'I don't think so,' said Charles. 'Not till you've earned it.'

His dinner-jacketed arm crept round the back of her chair and she felt it drape heavily across her bare shoulders. He lowered his head so that his lips brushed her neck, then nibbled their way up to her ear lobe. His free hand stole round the back of her head and tilted it slightly so that when he lifted his lips their next natural resting place was on her mouth. As Shula's lips parted for his kiss, a feeling more than anything else of triumph was ricocheting round her head. She'd had her eye on Charles from the first time she'd seen him out hunting, straight-backed in the saddle of a beautiful bay mare. It hadn't taken much doing to find herself next to him as the stirrup cup was being poured, still less for Mister Jones to pick up a stone and to have to borrow Charles' hoof pick. From there it was an easy step to a drink in The Bull, Ambridge's pub, the next night, then a meal out in Borchester... Too bad if Neil Carter carried a torch for her. He was a sweet enough bloke, and a good friend, but not boyfriend material. Not in a million years. She closed her eyes to Charles' kiss but it was harder to close them against the sight of Neil in The Bull earlier in the evening, looking somehow shrunken and diminished in his jeans and washed-out sweatshirt, next to Charles. Tall, goodlooking Charles in his black tie, better looking than Neil, let's face it, even if he'd been the one in jeans. As Charles had joked and chatted with Bill Robertson, the vet, Shula had felt Neil's eyes on them. On *her*, watching her every move. When Sid had called her over to the bar, Neil hadn't been able to resist getting a dig in. And something — not guilt surely? — and certainly not a sense that he might be right — had made her spikier than she'd meant to be.

'You don't half find 'em.'

'What?' Shula knew perfectly well what he meant, of course.

'Charles. Mr Lah-di-Dah. So many plums in his mouth it's a wonder he isn't choking on the stones.'

'Look, Neil.' Shula was deadly calm. 'I'm not asking for your approval.'

'Just as well. You wouldn't get it.'

'I'm a big girl. I've got my cycling proficiency badge and my swimming certificate. I don't have to ask your permission to go out with someone.'

Neil studied the pattern on The Bull's worn maroon carpet intently.

'I know you don't,' he said finally. 'It's just — well, does it have to be someone like him?'

'Someone like what?' Now he was really getting to her.

'Shula,' said Neil urgently. 'You know what I mean. Stuck up, posh voice, thinks he owns the place —'

'Neil, if I want a character assessment of Charles I'll employ a psychoanalyst, OK?'

'Shula — I didn't mean —'

'We're going now. So you won't have to put up with him any more. You can have the pub to yourself. And I hope you enjoy your darts match or whatever little excitement you've got planned. I'd call in later to see how you got on but you see Charles'll be taking me home and I might — just might — ask him in for coffee. If that's OK with you?'

Shula was suddenly aware that the photocopier had stopped its rhythmic thumping. The paper tray was empty. She trudged across the corridor to what Miss Pearson had called the stationery store and which was really the cupboard under the stairs. Locating a packet of paper under a ball of string, she returned to the photo-copier, yanked out the tray and laid some paper in it. She pressed the start button and the machine shuddered briefly before the paper jammed. Shula could have kicked it. All she asked was that the wretched thing did what it was supposed to do so that her mind could drift away to more pleasant topics than sales particulars. Or even more unpleasant, but more interesting, like the frequent taking-to-tasks her mother gave her over her choice of men in general and Charles in particular, allied with her supposedly heartless treatment of Neil. Last week's had been typical.

'What have you said to Neil?'

Jill Archer put the big wicker ironing basket down on the scrubbed kitchen table and went to set up the ironing board.

Shula, who was writing to Pedro, a boy she'd met on holiday, and was having rather a lot of trouble finding a suitably flowery Spanish phrase to end with, looked up in indignation.

'What, you mean apart from "Morning" and "How are the pigs today?"'

Her mother erected the ironing board with a clang and smoothed the scorched cotton cover.

'I mean he's got a face like fourpence. I know scraping slurry isn't anyone's favourite task but even so...'

'Oh honestly, Mum, it's not my fault. He found out I was going out with Charles on Saturday night, that's all.'

Jill plugged in the iron and went to fill the water spray.

'You made jolly sure you told him. I know you.'

'I wanted him to know I wasn't free, so he didn't invite me to the pictures or something.'

Jill selected one of Elizabeth's school pinafores, wet her finger and tested the iron. The resulting sizzle was an accusation in itself. Jill knew her elder daughter only too well. Shula enjoyed Neil's devotion.

'You might be grateful for a Neil one of these days, you know.'

Shula laid down her pen.

'Oh Mum, I'd have to be desperate.'

'Neil Carter's a nice boy. And at least he's steady. Look at some of the others you've been out with.'

Shula pushed away her letter with a sigh. Her mother was obviously in for a session on her inadequacies. If she could have left the room she would have but she was waiting for a phone call from Charles and she wanted to be the one to pick it up. She didn't want Elizabeth getting there first and putting him off with her silly playground jokes.

'OK, OK, who do you mean?' she challenged.

'Well — Bill Morrison for a start.'

'Well, don't look at me!' Shula was indignant. 'It was Dad who drove him away.'

Jill gave an incredulous laugh and put the pinafore on a hanger.

'Your memory is very selective at times,' she said.

'Dad took against him practically the first time he came round! I'll never forget that dinner.'

'Only because Bill suggested Brookfield was old fashioned for not having a rotary parlour. You know how sensitive your father is about the cows.'

'Well people aren't going to stick around if all they get is abuse, Mum.'

'Shula. It was whatshername — Sue Warren — who saw Bill off, you said so yourself. Then there was Andy — I thought you had a lot in common. He was very good with horses.'

'Yes, not with women unfortunately.'

'And goodness knows what you got up to on holiday. First there was — who was it? — Dennis?'

'Derek. All he did was teach me to play the guitar.'

'I'm pleased to hear it.' Jill set the iron to 'Cotton' to start on the shirts.

'And I wouldn't call Pedro a boyfriend.'

'He came all the way over here from Spain only last month!' Jill protested. 'Are you trying to tell me he just wanted to see the sights of Borsetshire?'

'Anyway it was Michele he was interested in. It's usually the way.'

Jill turned one of Phil's favourite work shirts over to iron the underside of the collar. Now she was getting somewhere.

'You've got nothing to prove, you know, Shula,' she said gently. 'Michele's older than you.' Michele Brown had come over from New Zealand to work as a sheep shearer at Brookfield in the early summer and stayed on.

'Not much Mum!'

'Not in years maybe but she's had a lot more experience. That counts for a lot at your age.'

'And how am I going to get experience? Sitting around the farm talking live and dead weights with Neil? I doubt it.' Shula picked at a splinter of wood on the edge of the table.

'Shula, I'm not trying to argue.'

'No, you never are, Mum. But I'm just saying. I'm eighteen. If you think I'm going to get my kicks going bell-ringing and helping at the harvest supper then I'm sorry but you're in for a few shocks.'

It was the penalty of being the eldest, she supposed. And a girl. Kenton, who had already escaped to the Merchant Navy, and David, who was a year younger, didn't have to put up with all this well-meaning advice. And by the time Elizabeth started going out with boys, her parents would probably be totally relaxed about it all.

'How's that photocopying coming along?'

Shula was startled out of her reflections by the soundless approach of Miss Pearson. Did she *have* a first name Shula wondered? Perhaps that was why she'd made such a fuss about Shula's own. Perhaps no one here had a first name. Perhaps it was a sort of initiation rite with estate agents — you had to renounce childish things.

'Er, Shula?'

'Yes, Miss Pearson?'

'The machine's out of paper. I saw you fill it up once. How many copies exactly did you do?'

'Gosh, I'm sorry Miss Pearson,' said Shula quickly. Hundreds and thousands, probably. 'I must have lost count. I'll take them back to my desk and sort them out.'

A pulse started to throb in Miss Pearson's neck.

'If you wouldn't mind. And then you can staple them together and file them where I showed you.'

'Fine.'

Still not even twelve o'clock.

She was in the middle of trying to marry-up photographs with the sales particulars when the phone rang. Miss Pearson was dealing with a client and Shula grabbed it eagerly. Perhaps this would be the excitement which had been waiting to happen since she'd stepped through the door that morning.

'Rodway and Watson. Good morning.'

'It's afternoon actually.' There was no mistaking Charles' voice. 'Made a million yet?'

'What, mistakes? I can see I'm going to be banned from the photocopier.'

'Well done, first rule of office life. Muck up everything they ask you to do, you'll never be asked to do it again.'

Shula smiled.

'There won't be anything left. I forgot Mr Rodway's sweeteners in his coffee as well.'

'They haven't got you making the coffee have they? I can see I'd better come and rescue you. And them.'

Thank goodness, liberation in the form of Charles.

'You are still coming in later, aren't you?' she said anxiously. 'About that land you're interested in?'

'I can't wait till half four to see you. How about lunch?'

'Lunch?' Shula looked round nervously. 'I don't know if lunch is in my contract.'

'I'll meet you in The Feathers just before one. Don't be late. We'll start plotting your escape.'

Shula replaced the receiver carefully as Miss Pearson approached.

'Shula. When you answer the telephone, we prefer, if you don't mind, the phrase "Rodway and Watson, how may I help you?" Much more client-friendly you see.'

'Right, Miss Pearson. I'll remember that.'

Miss Pearson waited expectantly. Shula smiled nervously. The pulse started to flicker again.

'Anything you want to tell me?'

'Sorry?' It was a bit early for confidences, surely.

'On the phone.' Miss Pearson enunciated as if speaking a foreign language. 'Anything you should be writing down, on Mr Rodway's message pad? I explained about Mr Rodway's message pad, didn't I?'

Light dawned.

'Yes. You explained. But it was just my, er ... er ... Mr Hodgeson. He's coming in later today.'

'Ah, he was confirming his appointment. Good.'

'Miss Pearson?' Shula hesitated, then took the plunge.

'Will it be all right if I go to lunch a little early? Say about quarter to one?'

Miss Pearson's expression demanded an explanation.

'You see I've got to buy a get well card for my Gran. Bronchitis. Quite nasty.'

Miss Pearson shook her head in wonderment. At home in the bureau drawer she had a stock of cards for every occasion — birth, death, congratulations on passing your driving test ... And here was a girl who on her first day had to leave early for lunch to accomplish a simple task. She'd never last. Still —

'Yes I suppose so. But get those sales details filed first.'

Twenty minutes later Shula burst out into the street, taking huge lungfuls of air. Would she ever get used to being inside all day? Of course, Mr Rodway had suggested that that might not always be the case. If she stuck at it, he promised, she could work her way up to being a sales negotiator and, in the fullness of time, a proper chartered surveyor and even — heart be still — an associate partner of Rodway's. Shula had had to concentrate really hard to stop her eyes glazing over as he had outlined a dizzying whirl of farm auctions, measuring up properties, showing round prospective purchasers — and all on a patch which stretched from Penny Hassett to Waterley Cross. Still, all she had to think about now was getting to The Feathers to meet Charles. He'd never seen her in work clothes before, only in hunting kit, evening dress or something casual for going out in. She hoped her navy blazer and pleated skirt wouldn't put him off.

The lounge bar of The Feathers was already filling up when she got there but Charles had bagged a table and armed himself with a bottle of Beaujolais. Shula, who hadn't intended to drink, found herself pressed into accepting a glass.

'I must have something to eat,' she protested as she took her first sip. 'I can't go reeling back to Rodway's on my first day.'

Charles took a large swill of wine, savouring it before swallowing.

'Shula, can I tell you something.' he said. 'You're taking this job far too seriously. You are going to become very un-fun if you carry on like this.'

Un-fun? This didn't bode well. Shula had only known Charles a few weeks but she knew him well enough to realise that fun was high on his priority list. If she exhibited any more signs of seriousness she ran the risk of being dumped for someone who, in Charles' phrase, knew how to enjoy themselves. And with Charles' looks, there would not be a shortage of replacements.

'Talking of fun, what are you doing for Christmas?' Shula decided the best tactic was to plough on.

'House'll be full of ghastly relatives, I suppose,' said Charles glumly.

'Well, come and take refuge with us. I mean, mine'll be full of my ghastly relatives but other people's are never quite as bad as your own, are they?' Shula took another swig of wine, feeling it rush straight to her cheeks. All this frantic jollity was giving her a headache. But Charles cheered up despite himself at the thought of Christmas and more particularly, the prospect of all the women he would have an excuse to molest under the mistletoe. Something in Shula told her that Charles' general bonhomie over the festive season might be something she found hard to bear. Worse still was a nagging feeling that Neil had sensed this aspect of Charles' character all along.

Trudging back to Rodway's with a heavy heart, she realised she had still not bought the get well card for her Gran which had not just been an excuse. Knowing her luck, Miss Pearson would ask to see it in a show of sudden sisterly solidarity. Fortunately, she was herself at lunch on Shula's return, but both Mr Rodway Junior and Mr Richards had returned from their morning's labours. Mr Richards had recorded onto tape details of the houses he had viewed and which Rodway's was to offer for sale and Shula, it appeared, was expected to turn these into the sort of sales particulars she had been photocopying earlier. She had just got herself wired up to the audio machine and discovered how to set the tabs on the typewriter when she was aware that Miss Pearson, who had returned laden down with Christmas shopping, was gesticulating at her.

Shula removed the headphones.

'There's someone to see you.'

The worst of it was that Miss Pearson looked totally unsurprised. 'I expected no less,' her look seemed to say. 'This girl is obviously going to be a total time waster.' But she limited herself to a 'Try not to be too long,' as she tactfully removed herself to just within earshot of Shula's conversation.

'Neil! What are you doing here? There's nothing wrong at home is there?' The words were out of Shula's mouth before she realised how absurd a suggestion it was. Even if there were, her Mum and Dad would hardly send Neil in as messenger.

Neil looked more pathetic than ever, his work boots leaving muddy marks on the carpet, the collar of his donkey jacket turned up against the rain. He looked so sheepish, in fact, that Shula felt sorry for him. She'd given him a hard time lately and perhaps her Mum was right. She ought to lay off him a bit — he took it all so seriously. But honestly, anyone who drove the tractor into a gatepost because he was waving at her was asking to be teased.

'Are you checking up on me?' It occurred to her as he denied it that it could actually be true. Neil had probably heard talk of Mr Richards and Mr Rodway — both Mr Rodways — and for all he knew they were thrusting young executives with silk ties and crisp striped shirts. If only the truth had lived up to his imagination, instead of both Mr Rodways having thinning hair and glasses, despite being thirty years apart in age, and Mr Richards so busy being young and thrusting he certainly wouldn't have eyes for Shula, having made it quite clear already that he was just serving time with Rodway's before moving on to some bigger, smarter outfit more deserving of his talents.

'I brought you this.'

From inside his jacket Neil produced a crumpled paper bag and passed it over.

'What is it? Oh, thank you.' Shula unwrapped the package to reveal an African violet.

'I thought it might cheer up your desk.'

'That's very sweet of you, Neil. It could do with it.'

Out of the corner of her eye Shula could see Miss Pearson taking in this rather scruffy young man and her new employee. That, some degree of guilt, and some degree of devilment made Shula lean forward and kiss Neil on the cheek. His morning's growth of beard was rough, not smooth like Charles' face had been at lunchtime, and he was searingly tainted with pig manure in contrast to Charles' lemony cologne. Miss Pearson stiffened and applied herself with renewed vigour to her work, making great play of answering the phone and cradling the receiver on her shoulder whilst she swivelled round on her chair to get something out of a filing cabinet.

'I'll have to go, Neil,' Shula whispered. 'I might see you this evening.'

She realised too late that Charles would be giving her a lift home and that this last offer had been somewhat tactless.

Neil brightened perceptibly.

'OK, see you then. I'd better get on, anyway. I've got some fencing wire to collect.'

'Thanks again for the plant.'

Neil was the sort of person who, though he said he was going, always hung around till you literally had to show him the door. Shula started this process by moving towards the plate glass window which fronted Borchester High Street. As she did so, Neil reluctantly behind her, the door opened.

'Christmas? Humbug!'

Tall, handsome, early thirties — he exploded into Rodway's, flapping his umbrella into the street.

'If I have to cover another blasted nativity play —

'Let me take that.'

Shula relieved him of the troublesome umbrella, sliding it neatly into the bucket thoughtfully provided by Miss Pearson against the wintry weather.

'Very kind of you. Sorry, am I interrupting?'

'No, no, Neil was just going.'

'Yeah ... bye, Shula.'

But still Neil made no move to depart. The newcomer had clearly reawakened all his fears about Shula's daily exposure via Rodway and Watson to all sorts of temptations.

'Shula — Archer, isn't it? Didn't we print a story about you? Simon Parker, from the *Echo*.'

As if she could forget. This was the man who had splashed her picture across the front page, headed 'Hunting on the Dole'. Her father hadn't come down off the ceiling for a week. And when he did, it was to insist that he wouldn't have the *Echo* in the house.

'That's right, you printed a story about me. Two actually. But the one that matters isn't the one about the village hall in Ambridge not being available for the Youth Club.'

Simon didn't even have the grace to look shamefaced. He snapped his fingers.

'"Hunting on the Dole". Never forget a headline.'

'I wish my father could,' retorted Shula. 'Do you ever think about the distress your stories might cause?'

Simon Parker smiled, showing even white teeth.

'Come on, I'm a journalist, not an evangelist. Anyway, it was all true, else you'd have complained at the time. I can't be expected to suffer for your guilty conscience.'

Shula, not normally slow to anger, was dumbstruck by his arrogance. If she hadn't been in the office she might have been tempted to make a scene. But perhaps a better ploy would be to get Simon Parker on his own to do that.

Neil, sensing the spark between them which wasn't all aggression, was looking disgruntled.

'See you tonight then, Shula.'

'Possibly,' said Shula pointedly.

Honestly, Neil was his own worst enemy, she thought, as she and Simon watched his retreating back.

'Anyway, Mr Parker, how can I help you?'

Miss Pearson would have been proud of her, she thought.

'It's simple — I'm living in the most appalling digs and I'm desperate to move. I'd really like to move out of Borchester if possible. That village where you live — that's pretty.'

'You'd like to move to Ambridge?'

'I might be persuaded. What have you got to offer me?'

The *double entendre* was, Shula realised, totally intentional. Simon Parker was a very sexy man. And didn't he know it. Shula fixed him with one of her grade one smiles which she only brought out on very special occasions. She could have her revenge later.

'Don't worry. You've come to the right place.'

On her desk, the African violet, which Neil had bought hurriedly at the cheap fruiterers in Borchester and was already past its best, shrivelled a little more.

MARCH
—1977—

'W hat do you think?'

Simon Parker looked up from the Rodway and Watson particulars he'd been studying and took a long, considered draught of his pint.

'Tempting, very tempting. That coach house at Edgeley's beautiful — but £100 a month — ouch!'

'I know it's a bit more than you wanted to pay —'

'I said seventy a month top whack, Shula.'

'Can't you stretch it a bit?' Shula took a final mouthful of cottage pie.

'Oh yes, I could stretch it all right. By living on Marmite sandwiches and never having the heating on, I'm sure I could live like a king.'

'It is fully furnished.'

'Handy. I can chew on a chest of drawers when I get really peckish.'

Shula pushed her plate away.

'OK, OK, you've made your point. But that's all we've got at the moment. Perhaps you should ask Jack Woolley for a rise.'

Simon looked sceptical. He'd had more than one difference of opinion with the *Echo's* proprietor.

'The only rise he'd give me is on the tip of his boot.'

Shula despaired.

'Well if you will tell him that the *Echo* looks as if it's typeset with a John Bull printing set and that he wouldn't know a story if it fell on his head, what do you expect?'

'It's true.' Simon spread his hands in a gesture of innocence.

Sometimes Shula wondered if he really wanted the job on the

Echo. Simon was convinced that he was cut out for better things. He was sure that by now he ought to be in El Vino's, vying for scoops and fighting his way to the phone, not propping up the lounge bar of The Feathers, Borchester and wandering back to the office at half past two for a thrilling afternoon writing up bonny baby contests organised by Underwoods, Borchester's department store.

'You'll find a way to make your mark,' she said consolingly. 'I know you will.'

She just hoped he wouldn't have to leave Borchester to do it. She had long since dropped any idea of getting even with Simon Parker for writing that story about her. Getting on with him was her only intention.

Simon squeezed her hand and drank up.

'I'm glad someone's got faith in me. Got time for another?'

Shula looked at her watch and winced.

'Sorry, I've got to get back. Miss Pearson's out this afternoon, taking her mother to the chiropodist, so I'm holding the fort.'

'You see? That's the epitome of excitement in Borchester. "Something afoot at the chiropodist".'

'Oh you're hopeless. Now you're just wallowing in self-pity.'

'So would you be if you had to go back to my digs every night.'

Simon mournfully lit up a cigarette. Shula, who had been gathering her things together, couldn't help but smile. There was something so very attractive about Simon's melancholy.

'She's definitely a hangover from the S.S. you know, my landlady. She even models her moustache on Hitler.'

'Well, write an exposé on her then. Now I've got to go.'

'See you.' Simon raised a hand in farewell. 'Let me know if you come up with any penthouse flats going cheap to a deserving cause.'

Shula smiled to herself as she walked back to the office. It was early March and the evenings were beginning to lighten perceptibly. The crocuses were not yet over and the daffodils were starting to open. With the worst of the weather behind them, and lambing well underway, everyone was in a better mood at home, too. Her dad hadn't said anything scathing about Charles for at least a week.

If things went on like this she might even be able to reveal that she often met up with Simon Parker at lunchtime and he wasn't the devil incarnate that Phil made him out to be. He might even let them have the *Echo* in the house again.

Later that afternoon, busy watering the cheese plants which adorned Rodway and Watson's window, Shula was aware of someone on the other side of the glass making signs at her. Irritated, she turned her attention to her task. If you weren't careful, the watering can, which had a leaky spout, could allow too much water to gush forth. It then trickled through the cane plant pot holders and stained the carpet. And Miss Pearson was very particular about the carpet. But she could sense that the gesticulations were getting wilder. Then whoever it was tapped on the window and the carpet was nearly a casualty of something much worse than just a few drops of water.

Outside, Simon was engaged in an elaborate pantomime which involved pointing at his watch, then the clock outside the jewellers opposite, indicating five thirty. He then pointed round the corner before flapping his arms like a chicken. He then mimed the action of drinking. Shula shook her head. He was completely mad.

'The Feathers at five thirty,' she mouthed.

Simon nodded, gave her a thumbs up and disappeared. Charles was picking her up at Brookfield at eight to go out for supper. She wondered how her father would react if Simon drove her home ...

Simon was ready and waiting with their drinks lined up on the bar when she arrived. The barmaid who had her eye on Simon was hovering, looking as though she would have liked to join them in conversation, but Simon gave her no chance, steering Shula to a quiet corner beneath a reproduction of two reprobates singing a drinking song.

'Cheers.' Shula gratefully sipped her drink.

'To crime!' proclaimed Simon with satisfaction. He was obviously bursting to tell her something.

'Don't tell me you've found out who did the Great Borchester Mail Van Robbery after all these years?'

Shula was incredulous.

'Better.'

Simon set down his glass.

'Can you keep a secret? There's this guy Tyrell, right — Tom Tyrell.'

Shula recognised the name.

'He's a builder isn't he? They've got that development just off the bypass.'

'That's right. But Mr Tyrell doesn't just want to build houses. He wants to put something back into the community. He's a councillor, right, and a J.P. In fact, he's respectability personified.'

'So? Have you found out he doesn't pay his TV licence or something?'

'Shula, think.' Simon leaned forward, animated, attractive. 'Use that pretty head of yours. If I put the words "builder" and "council" in the same sentence what do you think of straight away?'

Shula frowned.

'Multi-storey carpark?' she hazarded.

Simon shook his head in exasperation.

'It's obvious. Corruption. Tyrell has been using his influence on the council to swing building contracts his way.'

'How do you know?'

'Shula!' Simon looked pained. 'Do I ask you if "pleasant shady garden" doesn't actually mean poky and north facing? We're talking professional integrity here. You can't expect me to name my sources. This is a damn good story, that's all that matters.'

Shula sighed. Simon's enthusiasm was usually infectious but something was worrying her.

'Simon, I don't want to spoil things but I think there may be something you've overlooked. Tom Tyrell and Jack Woolley play golf together.'

Simon's face broke into a broad grin.

'Really? Well that settles it. Hold the front page!'

Shula was glad she wasn't in the vicinity of Grey Gables, the country house hotel which the *Echo's* proprietor also owned, when the paper appeared that Thursday but Neil heard it from Michele who'd heard it from Trudy Porter, the receptionist. Puce was the colour of Jack Woolley's face: blue was the air as he reached for the phone to Simon Parker.

'You've what?'

It was the Friday and she and Simon were again ensconced in The Feathers. Miss Pearson had taken to referring to what she called Shula's liquid lunches in front of Mr Rodway but Shula didn't care.

'I've resigned.'

'Simon, you idiot! Why?'

Simon's bravado slipped a little.

'I could say it was a matter of principle, but you know me too well. Journalists aren't very hot on principle. I resigned before he could sack me. Better for the C.V.'

'But what are you going to do?'.

In the space of one lager and lime, Shula could see it all slip away — the cosy lunchtimes which she had become so used to and which she looked forward to so much.

'Oh, I thought I'd run away and join the French Foreign Legion. I think they're still recruiting.'

'Simon, be serious just for once.'

'I am serious. I'm leaving the *Echo* at the end of the month and I won't be coming back.' Then seeing her face, he added more gently. 'Hey come on, don't look so down. Don't you fancy a holiday in the desert?'

It was all very well for Simon to joke about it, and so typical of him to cause an uproar and then walk away. But there was obviously some truth in what he had found out. In the three weeks before his departure (he'd compromised on Paris as his bolt-hole), Tyrell mysteriously resigned from the council. Though Jack Woolley stoutly maintained that Tyrell would never have let his own firm tender for council contracts, Tom Tyrell did admit to helping other firms get sub-contracting work and pocketing a so-called 'bonus' for it.

'I knew I was onto something,' crowed Simon when Shula ran him down in his office one blustery afternoon when he'd failed to show up at lunchtime. 'That's the second time today Jack

Woolley's been on the phone begging me to reconsider.'

'Are you going to?' Shula perched on his desk, showing what she hoped was just the right amount of leg.

'No way.'

'How about if I asked you to reconsider?'

There was a split second before Simon smiled.

'He's sent you as his agent, has he? The Mata Hari of Borchester High Street? Sorry, Shula, I can see right through it. You've got far too honest a face.'

You don't see anything at all, thought Shula sadly. You just have no idea. Now, perhaps, she knew how Neil had felt all these months while she'd been going out with Charles. Watching from the sidelines, wanting something to happen, wanting desperately to be part of someone's life — while they just carried on regardless, occasionally throwing you a crumb of conversation, a smile, a look, which you could hoard and store away against a future which would never happen. Her mother had always told her that one day she'd understand how Neil felt. Now maybe she was getting there.

'You'll come and have a drink with me before I go, won't you?' Simon was asking. 'The Feathers, Friday, first of April. Appropriate, really.'

'You're going to turn round and say it's an April fool and you're not really going?'

'Sorry Shula. I like a joke but not when it's on me. Anyway, the fleshpots of Paris await.'

Shula dressed carefully for work that Friday. It was an impossibly bright April day, ludicrously blue sky, storybook clouds, daffodils bobbing, buds bursting. Spring, and things starting all over again. Like she'd have to once Simon was gone. She'd have liked Simon's last sight of her to be of her in jeans and a T-shirt, barefoot on the banks of the Am amongst the daffodils, but whilst Simon managed to live in a fantasy world much of the time, Shula was deeply realistic. She couldn't see Mr Rodway, still less Miss Pearson, approving of jeans in the office. She chose a printed skirt and a white blouse with a high ruffled neck.

The Feathers was packed, it being a Friday, and she couldn't see Simon at first. Then she found him, with a couple of *Echo* reporters, clustered round the fruit machine. He bought her a gin and tonic. They found a couple of seats and she tried not to meet his eye.

'Typical, isn't it,' she said brightly. 'Just as you're leaving, I've found the perfect place for you to live.'

Simon looked quizzical.

'The flats over the old Wool Market. Seventy-five a month and they've been beautifully done up.'

'Shula — hello!'

'Neil!'

Of course, she'd been stupid enough to mention that she was going to The Feathers at lunchtime when she'd bumped into Neil in the yard before she left for Rodway's.

In his work clothes, Neil looked out of place among the besuited clientèle of The Feathers.

'I had to come in for your dad - udder wash and lice powder and stuff.'

'God, I'm going to miss all this,' said Simon wryly. 'Look, have my seat, I've got to get to the station.'

'Already?'

Shula could hear her voice going up an octave.

'I'm catching the one forty-five.'

She stood up abruptly.

'We'll come and wave you off.'

'Eh?'

Neil looked flabbergasted, as well he might — but there was no stopping Shula. She just wasn't ready to say goodbye to Simon yet. She hadn't intended Neil to tag along, but perhaps she could persuade him he ought to be getting back to Brookfield.

'We'll use my car,' she offered. 'It'll save you getting a taxi.'

Half an hour later they were on the windy platform at Hollerton junction. The one forty-five, a lugubrious announcement informed them, was running approximately thirteen minutes late.

Neil was unimpressed.

'I'm starving,' he grumbled. 'If I'd known it was going to be late I could at least have had a bag of crisps at the pub. I thought you said there was a buffet here.'

'Well, I wasn't to know it would be closed.'

Shula could feel her blood pressure rising. When it had become clear that Neil was not letting her out of his sight — not while Simon was around — she'd thought at the very least she could get rid of him, park him in the buffet with a sausage roll whilst she said goodbye to Simon, but no, with all the tact of a bad attack of chickenpox, Neil was obviously along for the ride — all of it.

Simon approached from the ticket office, his confident stride eating up the distance between them. For the last time Shula let her eyes rest on his face: the firm jaw, the piercing blue eyes and the Byronic sweep of brown hair which he was constantly pushing back from his forehead. Why not just get it cut? Neil had asked prosaically when Shula had commented on it once. Oh Neil, you just don't understand she had screamed inside. Neil's hair was brutally scissored by his former landlady, Martha Woodford, once a month into the same style he'd had since he was eight. On a good day he looked like a medieval monk. On a bad day he looked like the village idiot.

'Hadn't you two better be getting back?' Simon seemed more amused than touched by their farewell gesture.

Shula did a quick calculation. There was no way she'd be back in the office before half two. Miss Pearson would go bananas — but then, as there was no point in her having a lunch hour ever again, surely she could be late back just this once?

'I'm fine,' she insisted. 'And I love waving people off. It's almost as good as going. Dramatic somehow.'

'The one forty-five to Paddington? It's hardly the Orient Express.'

'Oh it is,' said Shula vehemently. 'If you've got enough imagination.'

Neil's stomach rumbled loudly but luckily his moans were curtailed as the train rounded the bend into the station.

'Simon.' Shula couldn't bear it any longer. 'Can I kiss you goodbye?'

Simon grinned. 'If you think it'll add to the drama.'

Shula leaned forward and kissed Simon briefly on the lips. The train hissed to a halt beside them.

'It doesn't stop long, you know,' said Neil sourly. 'D'you want the buffet car?'

Shula had to bite the inside of her lip very hard as she watched Simon get on the train and find a seat — and harder still when he managed to find one opposite a girl with long blonde hair deep in a Jackie Collins novel — but not so deep she didn't register Simon's arrival.

But she was gratified when, having stowed his luggage, he came back to the door, lowered the window and leaned out.

'Don't work too hard, Shula. I never have. Bye Neil, perhaps see you again someday.'

'Yeah,' said Neil without enthusiasm. Shula waved frantically as the train pulled out of sight then turned to Neil with a sigh.

'Well, that's that.'

'Yes. Um, Shula, you know the Young Farmers' dance?'

'Yes?' Shula could afford to be magnanimous now. It was too late for anything else.

'Well how would you like to go? If you're not already going with Charles that is.'

Charles? What did Charles matter.

'No, Neil, I'm not going with Charles. In fact Charles, I think, is on the way out.'

'Really?'

Hope sprang eternal in Neil's eyes. Why, oh, why had she said that?

'Of course I'll go to the Young Farmers' dance with you, OK?'

'Brilliant, Shula, I'll look forward to it.'

'So will I,' said Shula kindly. 'Now come on, let's get back. Dad must be desperate for that udder wash.'

'Of all the estate agents in all the world you had to walk into this one. Or something like that. Is that the phrase you're looking for?'

All Shula was aware of was that her mouth was gaping open unattractively and that she hadn't brushed her hair since that morning. Barely a month since she'd seen him off to Paris at Hollerton Junction, here was Simon Parker, large as life and twice as tanned, standing in front of her in Borchester.

'What I really wanted to know is: are those flats in the Old Wool Market still going begging?'

The manager of The Feathers was so pleased by the return of one of his best customers that he gave them a bottle of wine on the house. As they drank it, Simon explained: how Woolley had only ever treated his resignation as a joke and had insisted his time in Paris was an extended holiday; how he'd insisted that if he came back Woolley let him write for the *Echo* on his terms; and how (and this was what really pleased him) on his return Woolley had upped his salary — which meant he could well afford the Wool Market flat.

Shula was incredulous with happiness. 'You lead a charmed life, do you know that?'

'You know something? You're not the first person to say that. Now, are you going to help me move in?'

The first casualty of Simon's return was Charles. His amiable upper-class ways and his incessant talk about his father's 800-acre pig farm might have palled anyway, in time, but in comparison with Simon's lively stories about the Left Bank they appeared nothing more than an irrelevance.

Shula hadn't really had to finish with anyone before and she didn't find it easy, especially as Charles had his hand inside her blouse at the time, fumbling with her bra strap. The news seemed to take some time to sink in.

'Not see me any more? Are you giving me the push?'

'It's just — I think we ought to go our separate ways, Charles. I mean, I don't want to get serious about anyone just yet.'

'Who said anything about getting serious? I thought we had fun.'

'We did — I mean — we do but —'

'Well if that's how you feel you've saved me the effort. I was thinking of calling it off anyway.'

Abruptly releasing her from his grasp he stood up with as much dignity as he could muster. Shula, who if anything was in a less dig-nified position, stood up too, hastily tucking her blouse back in her trousers. She knew what he said wasn't true but he had to save face somehow.

'I'll see you around, Shula.'

'Yes, I'm sure you will, Charles.'

Next day, when she casually dropped it in conversation to Simon that she and Charles had finished, she didn't get quite the reaction she'd been hoping for. In fact it didn't even seem to register. They were looking at a hi-fi for his new flat and Simon seemed more interested in the output of the speakers than in what she was saying. At home the news hadn't been received quite the way she'd hoped either. True, her mother had expressed sorrow — Charles was unfailingly polite and was always willing to play Cluedo with Elizabeth — but her father had just grunted that the boy had obviously come to his senses.

'Trouble is it makes you easy prey for anyone else who comes along,' he had muttered, hardly looking up from *Farmers Weekly*. 'Oh, by the way, Jill, I hear that Simon Parker fellow's back. Jack Woolley must be mad.'

Shula consoled herself with the fact that she didn't need her father's approval. She put his antipathy down to the fact that no man would ever be good enough — especially not one who had called the Archer name into disrepute with an article about her sponging off the state whilst riding to hounds. She remembered how she'd sworn revenge for the article that day when Simon walked into Rodway's. It seemed ludicrous now. She'd tried to tackle him about it once but he'd been so persuasive that nowadays she took Simon's point that it was extremely good copy. She was glad though, that it hadn't been picked up by the nationals, which, he confessed, had been his hope. 'On a slack news day...' he lamented while Shula gave thanks for whatever it was which had kept the wires humming and had saved her from tabloid exposure. But even without the article, she knew she would have a hard time persuading her father about Simon. For one thing, he wasn't exactly predictable. Shula understood, of course — she knew about deadlines, and leads, and contacts, and how he just had to go for that drink after work, follow up that phone call, or whatever one of the myriad of excuses it was. But try explaining that to parents. They would just have said he was taking her for granted.

Elizabeth, though, had got Simon all weighed up.

'You're daft, you know. You let him get away with murder.' Elizabeth carried on combing her Sindy's hair. Shula stepped out of the shower and reached for a towel.

'Oh I do, do I?'

'He stood you up again last night. That's twice in a week.'

'Elizabeth,' said Shula with deadly calm. 'You're only ten. What on earth do you know about it?'

'I know I wouldn't let anyone push me around like that.'

'I'll remind you you said that one day.' Shula rolled her hair up in a turban. 'Now shove over. I want to paint my toenails.'

But deep down she knew Elizabeth was right. Simon's excuses did wear a bit thin. He hadn't really given her an excuse as to why he'd stood her up the other night and he hadn't even apologised till she'd gone to seek him out. She'd intended to give him a hard time, but somehow with Simon, all her best intentions came to nothing. And when he'd asked her out tonight — not to a make-it-up-to-you dinner but to a meeting of what he called the Netherbourne Angry Residents Association, campaigning for repairs to their village maypole, she'd agreed straight away. But then again, wasn't Simon on his terms better than no Simon at all? If only she didn't find him quite so attractive. And if ever she ticked him off for his thoughtlessness, he stuck his lip out as if he were three, and then kissed the palm of her hand and all up her arm in a pantomime of remorse. Well — who wouldn't give in?

The evening didn't start well. They arrived on time at Netherbourne Village Hall, a dismal tin shack, to find the protesters outnumbered by the parish Council who, in the space of ten minutes, performed a spectacular U-turn and gave in to all the residents' demands. Yes, the maypole could be made more safe. Yes, it could be repainted. Yes, new ribbons could be purchased for dancing. And if all that did not satisfy the residents – well, the Parish Council was even prepared to buy a brand new one. Simon put away his notebook in disgust.

'Typical Borsetshire,' he remarked. 'Everyone's so bloody nice to each other.'

Shula wondered quite why that was such a bad thing, and suggested they went for a drink. In the garden of The Crown, whose landlord prided himself on the condition of his beer, Simon visibly relaxed. It was the longest day of the year, June 21st, and the evening air hung still, as if waiting for a given signal to get dark. On the far side of the pub garden, wheatfields rippled in the breeze, golden and enduring under a crescent moon. Shula snuggled into Simon's encircling arm and breathed deeply of meadowsweet and new-mown hay. Idyllic.

Later, on the way home, they hadn't gone far when he stopped the car. Shula looked at him, puzzled. His face was in shadow.

'Fancy a walk?'

'What, in the woods?'

'Through the woods.' He turned to her. 'Do you know what I've always wanted to do? Make love to a beautiful girl in the middle of a cornfield on a warm summer's evening.'

'In the *middle* of a cornfield?'

'Yes.'

Here it was. The moment she'd been waiting for — and she felt completely unprepared. She should have had some witty remark at the ready about the alien corn or something, but he had taken her so much by surprise that her senses deserted her. Well, perhaps not all her senses. Her powers of speech and rational thought had gone, certainly. But all her other senses were working overtime — at least she presumed that was why she was getting little electric shocks all over, from the soles of her feet right up to her scalp.

Finally she found her voice.

'I don't think the N.F.U. would be very happy about that.'

'Shula.' Simon took her hand. 'Don't take me so literally.'

Shula swallowed hard.

'You — don't happen to have a rug in the car by any chance?'

'I think I might have.' Simon's teeth were pearly in the moonlight. Of course he had. He'd known she wouldn't refuse.

Shula made a last attempt at levity.

'I don't think the N.F.U. minds too much about the *edges* of cornfields.'

'Come on then,' said Simon softly.

Deep in the woods an owl hooted.

This is bizarre, Shula thought as she followed Simon along the field margin. They were in the lee of a deep hedge heady with elderflowers. Shula felt the sandy soil in her shoes. Dried grasses prickled her legs but she ignored them, her eyes fixed on Simon's back in the washed-out blue shirt, the car rug thrown over his shoulder. A little further on the path widened out. Simon squatted down and spread the rug. Turning, he looked up at Shula and held out his hand. Wordlessly she placed her hand in his and let herself be guided down onto the rug. He made sure she was comfy and his hands were gentle as he started to kiss her but at first she was distracted, which surprised her. It was peculiar down at ground level. She could hear scurryings in the hedge and she wondered what sort of nocturnal activities they were disturbing. Simon raised his mouth from hers and smiled as he moved to unbutton her dress. Shula smiled back and placed both her arms round his neck. The corn swayed softly in the breeze and the last thing Shula saw before she closed her eyes were the ears of wheat nodding as if in blessing.

'All right?'

Shula lifted her head from its comfortable place on Simon's shoulder and smiled down at him.

'Wonderful.'

'It was your first time, wasn't it?'

How could he tell? Had she done something wrong?

Dumbly she nodded. But he seemed touched.

'Silly. You should have told me. Come here.'

He drew her face down to his and kissed her lightly.

'Two fantasies in one. Not bad for an evening that started out at a meeting about a maypole.'

Phil was worried about Simon. With a parent's unerring intuition, he knew at once both how dangerous he was and how much Shula cared for him — and so, inevitably, how she'd be hurt. Every time Simon was late picking Shula up, Phil could see the worry in her eyes that he was not coming at all. With other boyfriends there had been an enviable calm about Shula: sometimes she took their phone calls, sometimes she didn't bother and returned them later, sometimes she even got David or Elizabeth to say she was out. But whenever Jill called 'Shula — Simon, for you!' Shula was there, leaping downstairs two at a time, grabbing the receiver, taking a deep breath before she spoke, trying not to sound too excited. Phil talked to Jill about it but Jill, worried herself, was philosophical — or tried to be.

'I don't like it any more than you do,' she soothed. 'But what can we do? We can't protect her for ever. I only wish we could.'

Later, she remembered a conversation she'd once had with Shula, with her daughter bemoaning her lack of experience. Simon Parker seemed likely to take care of that, Jill mused. And promptly started worrying all over again.

But Shula was entranced — by Simon's worldliness, his world-weariness and at the same time his vitality. At the end of the working day, when they met in The Feathers, Simon would tear off his tie with an animal ferocity and undo the collar of his shirt.

'God! I've been stifling in that rat-run all day! Let's drink up and go and get some air.'

For all that he felt his calling lay in Fleet Street, Simon loved the countryside — even though he didn't really understand it. It pleased him when Shula could explain to him the difference between hawthorn and blackthorn, or argue the merits of winter versus spring barley. Jokingly he offered her a Country Notes column in the *Echo* — 'Pity we've just taken on Gordon Armstrong.' Shula revelled in his admiration for in every other respect she was his pupil. Simon loved making love outdoors. When he laid her down on the banks of the Am or on the damp earth of the woods he taught her with lips and fingers the pleasures of her body and how to pleasure him. Half-heartedly Shula complained that they would be more comfortable in his flat, but Simon always won. He won in everything.

The most unnerving thing for Shula was that in order to please Simon, she turned into a person she didn't recognise. In order to keep up with his more adult and cosmopolitan attitudes, she found herself saying — and doing — things which were totally contrary to her nature. But it was a constant struggle for her, not being herself, pretending not to mind when he was late, adopting an air of enforced casualness when he didn't turn up for a pre-arranged meeting, making out she'd enjoyed spending the evening in The Bull with Neil and Jethro or that she hadn't felt like going out anyway, she'd got a headache. When Simon told her he'd applied for a job in the Persian Gulf, Shula swallowed her pain and told him defiantly that she couldn't promise to remain faithful, rather begging the question — never addressed, never even asked — would he? In the same mood, though she had already drafted the wedding invitation: Mr and Mrs Philip Archer request the pleasure of your company at the marriage of their elder daughter Shula Mary to Mr Simon Anthony Parker (she'd managed to get his middle name out of him without his being suspicious) she found herself telling him, when he scorned the wedding ritual, that she'd rather live in sin than get married. Phil, and more particularly Jill, saw the other side to it, the strained look at breakfast, the circles under her eyes.

'He's taking her for a ride,' Phil warned. 'And it's not going to be a soft landing.'

In the end, the landing was even more bruising than any of them could have imagined.

It was May — May Day, in fact. Odd, really, since it was the Netherbourne maypole which had brought them together. The Morris men were in Ambridge, and were dancing outside The Bull, watched by a throng of villagers and sightseers. Simon had his notebook with him — he was never off duty — but Shula was planning a lazy day, with Simon all to herself, and a picnic on Lakey Hill.

He wasn't even quieter than usual, which upset her later when she thought about it, because it showed how little he thought she'd care — how little he'd even considered her reaction.

As she laid out the Boursin cheese, and the chicken and the French bread, and the black grapes — Simon fancied himself as something of a gourmet — he occupied himself opening the wine. Suddenly he said, as if he'd just remembered:

'Hey! I haven't told you my good news, have I? It's finally happened. I've been offered a job in London.'

Shula continued to unpack the basket. Napkins, forks, mayonnaise. Why was he talking in the passive — *it's* happened? — *been* offered? Surely he'd applied for the job — done it himself — that is, wanted to leave Borchester, wanted to leave her?

Making a scene wasn't going to do her any good, and it wasn't the style of the Shula she had created — the Shula whom Simon knew.

The cork popped out of the bottle.

'Come on then, glasses! I think a toast is called for!'

Shula met his eyes for the first time. She saw in them a brief flicker of guilt — but it quickly passed.

'Hey,' he said gently. 'You can come down and see me. It's not the Persian Gulf after all.'

'Yes,' she said, somehow finding her voice. 'That's right. I can come down and see you.'

But she knew she never would.

M AY
——— 1978 ———

S hula?'
    Jill tapped lightly on the door of Shula's bedroom. There was a momentary silence, then a series of scurryings and an ominous burst of nose-blowing before Shula opened the door. She'd made a cursory attempt, Jill could see, to cover up the evidence but apart from the screwed-up balls of tissues only half concealed under the bedcover, which gave the game away immediately, Shula's nose was red and her eyes dulled with crying.

'I came up for that T-shirt. The one with the beading that needs hand-washing. I thought I could fit it in before lunch — oh, Shula.'

The kindness in her Mum's voice had unleashed Shula's misery all over again. Tears were pouring down her cheeks.

'Love.' Jill enfolded Shula in her arms. 'Come on, crying doesn't do any good.'

Part of Jill was glad that Shula could cry in front of her — much better than hiding it. Part went out to her, hurting for her, hating to see her like this. And another, larger, blacker part — a part Jill had never known she possessed — felt furious with Simon Parker for the way he had behaved.

'Oh Mum!' Shula's tears were warm on Jill's neck. She stroked her daughter's hair.

'Come on love, it's because it's all so new... He hasn't been gone long —'

This, intended to be soothing, provoked a new wail of anguish from Shula.

'He's going further than you think! This came this morning.'

Shula broke away and snatched a postcard from her dressing table. Its crumpled form suggested to Jill that it had been screwed up and thrown in the bin, then hastily been retrieved to be keened over.

Jill took the proferred card. Tower Bridge. Jill wished with unusual venom that beheading was still in fashion. It wouldn't have been too severe a fate for the likes of Simon Parker.

'You can read it.' Shula sniffed and blew her nose loudly on the last tissue in the box.

Jill did as instructed then looked at her daughter in amazement.

'Kathmandu! What's he going there for?'

'I don't know! When he left here it was supposedly because he'd got the job of a lifetime on one of the nationals! Perhaps he's always had a secret hankering to be a Buddhist! Perhaps he never had a job in London! Perhaps he just wanted to get away from me!'

'Now Shula, that's ridiculous.' Jill's common sense swung into action. 'I would imagine that the job he got wasn't all it was cracked up to be and, being Simon, he's not going to stick at it.'

'What do you mean, being Simon?'

Whoops. That had been tactless, Jill realised. Never criticise them, even if they'd broken your heart.

'I mean never settling for something that he wouldn't enjoy. You know how ambitious he was.'

Shula seemed mollified.

'He always did want to travel. When he resigned from the *Echo* he threatened to join the French Foreign Legion.'

Jill gave a cluck of exasperation. All talk, that had been Simon's trouble. She and Phil had seen it from the start. Doris, Phil's mother, had agreed. But Shula had fallen for it.

'You'd thought you could go and see him in London, was that it?'

'Oh, Mum, I don't know.' Shula retrieved a scrap of tissue from the floor and dabbed her eyes. 'I don't think it would have worked. He's probably made new friends already, he wouldn't want me reminding him of what he's left behind.'

'You've thought all round it, haven't you.'

Shula nodded. When she spoke her voice still had a tell-tale wobble in it.

'But to think he won't even be in this country... I just feel so —

so abandoned!'

Jill hugged her tightly.

'I know, love, I know.'

'How am I going to go on, Mum? I loved him so much, I really did.'

'Of course you did.'

Jill managed to stop herself from saying 'Not that he deserved it.' She wondered who would be setting off with Simon Parker on his trip. No doubt there was some other impressionable girl in tow by now. Thank heavens he hadn't come up with his cockeyed plan for world travel while he was still in Borchester. Because if he'd asked Shula to go with him to the ends of the earth, Jill knew the answer would not have been no. Hastily revising her earlier curse, she gave a brief thanks that Simon Parker — though sadly alive — was well away from Ambridge.

And that her daughter was still safe at home.

'You'll never guess who that was on the phone — James Wearing.'

Jill looked up as her husband approached from the house. The evening sun was still pleasantly warm and the tubs she had planted out, vivid with begonias, lobelia and Bizzie Lizzies, were grateful for a drink.

'Who?'

Jill concentrated on not drowning the rich, peaty compost. Phil seated himself gingerly in a striped deckchair which he had never trusted and stretched out his legs.

'Come on Jill, you remember. I was at agricultural college with him. He's got a big estate the other side of Gloucester. Always sends us a bottle of port at Christmas.'

'Oh, him.' Jill refilled her watering can from the tap under the kitchen window. 'What's he phoning you for?'

'He's got a favour to ask.'

'He's one of the biggest landowners in the Midlands, Phil. What favour can we possibly do him?

'Well, not him exactly. Apparently his son left school last year not really sure what he wanted to do. He went up to London, thought he'd do something in the City, but it seems he wasn't really cut out for it. Anyway he's home again, and James has decided to take him in hand. He's got him into agricultural college in September next year— so he's looking for a year's practical work for him.'

'Here?'

'In Ambridge. I said I'd make a few enquiries. He doesn't have to come here for all the time.'

'I should hope not. It'd put David's nose out of joint a bit.'

'It'll be a useful lesson for David. I wouldn't want him to spend all his time at home on his year off. He can start looking a bit further afield himself.'

Jill preferred not to think about David being somewhere else for a whole year. She'd miss him too much. He was so even, somehow, none of the ups and downs you got with Shula and Kenton — or Elizabeth, who looked as if she would turn out like the twins.

'I suppose there are people round about who could use an extra pair of hands.'

Jill finished her watering and sat on the warm stone wall at Phil's side.

'I was thinking of Tony actually. He's always saying how hard pressed he is.'

'That's just Tony isn't it?'

Jill eased her shoulders, luxuriating in the warm sun on her back.

'Up to a point. But with just him and Pat, it's no picnic over at Bridge Farm.'

'So you've said yes to this — whatshisname?'

'Nick. I couldn't very well say no, Jill. And it is jolly good port.'

For the first month or so, deep in her depression over Simon, Shula hardly noticed Nick. Which was quite a feat really, because you could hardly miss him. He roared up at the farm every day in his white Triumph Spitfire, usually with the roof down, his blond hair tousled by the breeze.

'Hi, Shula!' As he unfolded himself — there was at least six foot of him — from the car, Shula wondered how he'd ever telescoped himself in behind the wheel. Perhaps that's why he had to have a soft top — otherwise he'd have had to cut a hole in the roof, like the giraffe in one of her picture books as a child.

'Hey Shula, listen.' Nick leaned against the bonnet of his car. 'If you came to work in Ambridge — if the old homestead wasn't here, I mean — where would you stay?'

'Aren't you happy at the Woodfords?'

Shula answered his question with a question as she was, in truth, feeling a little guilty on the subject of Nick's accommodation. After a fortnight at Tony's, where, it had to be said, he'd been a wild success, it was decided that Nick was to work at Brookfield for the rest of the year. Her parents had mooted that he lived in with them and to her shame, Shula had been the first to squash it. Smarting from Simon's abrupt departure and his lack of remorse, she was still nursing her grief. She didn't want to give up her long soaks in the bath, her evenings in the sitting room listening to Leonard Cohen dirges or her private chats with her mum in the kitchen. It was bad enough having David around, clumping in in his big boots and turning the conversation to crop yields and carburettors without giving him a partner in crime. Nick was probably a nice enough chap. Eva, her cousin Jennifer's au pair, certainly thought so — she was always mooning round after him. She was welcome, Shula thought. Compared with Simon, Nick at nineteen seemed gauche and unworldly. Simon had probably spoilt her for men — boys — her own age for good.

But today she had a couple of minutes to spare and she could at least be pleasant.

'Don't tell me Martha doesn't feed you?'

'Don't talk to me about it,' Nick groaned. 'Every night the table's groaning with pies and cakes. Then there's the homemade bread, the biscuits by the side of the bed... If I refuse as much as a third helping she's mortally offended.'

'Tell her you're on a diet.'

'She keeps telling me I'm a growing lad. I mean, look at me — you'd think I'd stopped growing by now!'

Shula did look at him, properly, for the first time. He had nice eyes, hazel, an unusual combination with blond hair — and a smooth skin which had caught the sun. He was dressed for work in jeans and a faded T-shirt and his olive-brown forearms were dusted with golden hairs. Shula was about to say that she'd have a look through the books when she got to work, to see what might be available locally, when Neil, with the impeccable timing which he had made his own, hailed them from across the yard. It was as if his built-in sensors could scent Shula talking to anything male — even if it was only the most innocent of exchanges.

'Morning!'

Neil approached, also in jeans and a T-shirt but giving a good four inches in height to Nick. Neil had caught the sun, too — the back of his neck was bright red.

'You want to watch the back of your neck, Neil,' Shula warned in what she hoped was a sisterly fashion. You had to be so careful with Neil. Display the slightest interest and he could interpret it as repressed lust. He fixed Shula with a beaming grin.

'Yeah, I'll put me hanky round my neck when the sun gets up.'

'Where do you live, Neil?' asked Nick abruptly, more interested in his accomodation problems rather than the possibility of his co-worker keeling over with sunstroke.

'Me? Nightingale Farm,' volunteered Neil helpfully — not that it would mean anything to Nick who didn't know the village.

'It's a big old place just down the road.' Shula filled him in. 'You went to see it originally to see if it'd be suitable for the Youth Club, didn't you, Neil?'

'That's right. Downstairs, that is, not the flat. Yeah, me and Michele have been there — ooh, eighteen months now.'

'You and — hey, Neil, you dirty dog. I didn't realise it was your little love nest.'

Neil's face suffused with colour to match the back of his neck.

'Oh, it's nothing like that. We're just good friends, me and Michele.'

'Oh yeah? That's what they all say.'

Mortified at the suggestion — in front of Shula, as well — that there was anything improper in his living with Michele, Neil vigorously protested that he was speaking the truth.

'In that case,' rejoindered Nick smoothly, 'You couldn't fit another one in could you?'

'Well...' Neil was nonplussed by the speed at which Nick was moving. 'I'd have to ask Michele,' he stalled.

'Why haven't I met this Michele? You've been keeping her to yourself, that's the trouble, Neil. Tell you what, I'll come round tonight, bring a few cans, give the place the once over and provided Michele's OK about it, I'll move my stuff in tomorrow. How's that?'

Over the next six months or so, as she got more used to having Nick around, Shula realised that his moving in to Nightingale Farm was typical of the way he operated. He was always having wild enthusiasms — not always carried through — but when they were, they were directed with devastating accuracy. It was his enthusiasm which had snapped her out of her torpor over Simon. Nick refused to take no for an answer and when he wanted a partner for the Young Farmers' Treasure Hunt, or someone to play darts with at The Bull, Shula was the obvious choice. As the summer took hold and the evenings stretched out inkily till after ten, she would give in to his requests to go over to The Fox at Edgeley for a drink, or for a walk — more of a scramble as she tried to keep up with him — up Lakey Hill. When the men were working late on the hay or the harvest, Shula found herself offering to take out the flasks and the sandwiches, until one day, she realised that twenty-four hours had passed in which she hadn't thought about Simon with a stab of pain — more a dull ache. And when Nick put his arm round her shoulders as they walked along the Am one afternoon, and kept it there, and when he turned to kiss her, she tried not to make the comparison between the taste of his lips and Simon's, the pressure of his hands or the feel of his hair. Shula tried to be as enthusiastic about their relationship as Nick, in his blissful ignorance of Simon, could be. And if at times she was a little muted, Nick would suggest a Chinese takeaway or a game of Poohsticks and she would put the memory of Simon away until she could take it out and examine it alone later. Nick hungered for life, for excitement, for challenge. That's why, he said, he knew he could never have stuck going to the same insurance broker's office in the City every day. He also had the habit of moving in on half-

formed ideas and situations and making them his own. The overland trip, for example.

Soon after Nick moved to Nightingale Farm, Michele had
returned to New Zealand. But she kept in touch with Shula.

'Come and see me,' Michele wrote. 'And I don't mean for a
holiday. Come and stay a good six months or so. You'd love it,
Shula — and I'd love to see you. I'm dying to catch up on all the
Ambridge gossip and I know you're too busy having a fun time
with Nick, now you've decided he's OK, to write me a proper
letter. There are plenty of sheep so you won't miss Ambridge too
much — it'll feel quite like home. Let me know what you think!'

Shula took the letter round to show Nick. She was cooking him
supper. She had thought she'd be cooking for Neil as well but
when she got there she found out he'd gone down to the village to
play dominoes with Jethro at The Bull.

'But I've brought masses of food!' Shula protested.

Nick passed her a can of lager.

'Does he know something about your cooking that I don't? And
hey, come and give me a cuddle before you get garlic all over your
fingers.'

Shula knew that ever since Nick had talked Neil into allowing
him to move in, Neil had had trouble putting up with Nick and his
girlfriends. Eva had been bad enough but once Nick and Shula had
fallen into going out together it had been more than Neil could
bear. Shula felt bad about it. Neil had already had to stand by and
watch her break her heart over Simon. He'd thought he'd wait on
the sidelines till she was over it, then one day she'd wake up and
notice he was there. But before he'd had chance, in had swept
Nick, all sportscar and signet ring — and Shula was lost again.

Shula tried not to think about Neil as she stirred the bolognese
sauce. Nick was laying the table — his one concession to domesticity.

'I can't go to New Zealand of course,' she confided. 'Mr
Rodway was so pleased when I told him I was going to study and
become a fully qualified estate agent. I can't just give it all up.'

'Why ever not?'

'Oh, come on Nick.' Shula rescued the spaghetti which was
fizzing all over the cooker, and turned down the heat.

'Seriously, Shula. People do it all the time. Take a sabbatical.'

'Sabbaticals are something you have when you've been at work for ages. I've only just started.'

'Well I never intend to start,' Nick declared, refilling their glasses. 'Tell you what. You go, and I'll come with you.'

'What?'

'And I'll tell you what you ought to do. None of this jumping on a plane one end and getting off at the other. Go overland.'

'Nick, there's rather a lot of sea between here and New Zealand.'

'You go overland to the Far East, dummy. Then fly on from there. I don't know — Hong Kong, Delhi, Bangkok — you'd easily get a flight. Think about it.'

Shula did think about it. And the more she thought about it, the better an idea it seemed. There was no doubt, she hadn't really settled since Simon. To her shame, she even got out a dog-eared postcard he'd sent her from Istanbul. She wondered if he'd ever made it to Kathmandu. She might even see him. Trip over him at a temple, stumble across him in the bazaar ...

Luckily her parents never made this connection: they were horrified enough at the prospect of her trip without the added complication that she might just bump into Simon Parker in the crowded sub-continent.

Her mother was concerned about the timescale — since Nick had become enthused he'd taken it over, of course. He'd done a lot of ringing around his London contacts, and had found a trip with two vacant places which departed in just two weeks. Phil was simply dead set against the idea. He couldn't believe that Rodway and Watson were even thinking of letting Shula take a six-month sabbatical and thought it was possitively criminal that they should encourage her, as he put it, by keeping her job open for her when she returned. But when Shula was determined about something, there was no shifting her and her parents soon realised that they'd effectively been presented with a *fait accompli*. Phil had blustered about the money she'd need but it transpired that Shula had been stashing away a fair part of her wages every week and had got most of what she needed.

'And we can always earn a bit along the way,' said Nick airily at the family pow-wow which had been called.

'Doing what?' rapped Phil, having visions of the white slave trade.

'Teaching English, probably,' replied Nick. 'Mate of mine did this trip last year. He had no trouble picking up odd bits of translating and stuff.'

Shula looked admiringly at Nick. It was terribly useful having him around to put the arguments. So many of his public-school chums had spent their year between school and University travelling and had, thankfully, returned unscathed that he had an answer for everything. Gradually she felt the arguments against the trip which her parents had put in their way become less substantial and more far-fetched — that she'd miss her favourite custard creams, for instance — and bit by bit, she saw their resistance worn down. James and Mollie Wearing came to supper. They seemed to be taking a broadminded view — as long as Nick came back to start at agricultural college in the autumn, then they were not averse to him widening his horizons. Shula met Nick's eye over the crown-roast of lamb and winked. It was going to be all right!

The trouble was that Shula had always been Phil's favourite, and she could wrap him around her little finger. Coming in on them in the sitting room one evening, when Shula had her maps spread out all round her and was showing Phil the route, Jill was astonished to learn that Phil had even agreed to give Shula some money towards the trip as an early twenty-first birthday present.

In the end, like all parents have to, they swallowed their fears. Phil had severe words with Nick about how he was entrusting his daughter to Nick's care, and how, if anything happened to her, he would be held personally responsible. Nick assured him that he was in total control. The overland trip to Calcutta would take till September, then he, Nick, would be returning to England to take up his place at college. But not till he'd seen Shula safely on a plane to New Zealand.

Phil said afterwards that Jill had visibly aged in the first few weeks Shula was away, waiting and hoping for phone calls or the thin airmail letters with exotic stamps. Shula was good about keeping in touch, which was just as well, as Nick didn't seem to bother communicating with his parents at all, from the number of phone calls asking for information which they received from the Wearings. These became more frequent and more and more worried as September arrived and there was no news of Nick boarding a plane back to England for the start of his course. Unfortunately Phil and Jill weren't able to be as helpful as they'd have liked as communication from Shula — beyond a letter saying they'd arrived safely in Calcutta and were now flying on to Bangkok with a couple of others from the trip — seemed to have dried up as well. A month later came another letter from Shula saying that Nick had flown on to Australia — not a phone call to James Wearing which Phil relished making. Shula, the same letter informed them, was looking for a job in Bangkok!

Doris, who had never voluntarily left Ambridge, even to go to Penny Hassett, was perplexed.

'A job, Phil, in Bangkok? What sort of work is a young English girl going to get out there?'

And though Jill burbled something about 'translations', Phil thought his mother's was a question best left unanswered.

Then, one wet day in November, Phil was loading hedge stakes onto the trailer with Jethro when Jill tore out from the house.

'Phil! Phil! It's Shula.'

'Jill, what's happened? Is she all right?'

Jill was nearly sobbing with relief.

'It's all right, Phil — it's all right. She's coming home!'

It turned out to be not quite as simple as that, of course. Phil was fast realising that with his elder daughter, nothing ever would be simple. She'd had everything stolen — money, passport, belongings, the lot — from the cheap student room she'd been living in and sharing with another girl. Phil would never forget the shock when they met her at the airport. He'd hardly recognised her. Suntanned, her hair cut short and thin — so thin! After supper, that first evening, she'd lit up a cigarette and told them, among tales of temples and elephants moving teak logs with their trunks, that everyone on the trip had called her Lulu.

'Never mind that,' snapped her father. 'What was Nick Wearing thinking of, leaving you out there on your own?'

Shula shrugged and blew a perfect smoke ring. Phil tried not to notice.

'We only ever agreed to go as far as Calcutta together, Dad. He kept his part of the bargain — and more.'

'And what about Michele? Did you let her know what was going on?'

'I was only going to stay a bit longer in Bangkok, till I'd got enough money for the fare. I thought Christmas in New Zealand would be fun — turkey on the beach, and all that.'

Jill deposited a cup of coffee in front of Shula and hugged her close.

'Well, you'll be having Christmas here now, where you belong. I shall make it my mission to fatten you up, my girl. And don't think I'm ever letting you out of my sight again!'

It took Shula a good three months to settle back into village life. The smoking lasted rather less time. Shula smoked her way doggedly through a third of her duty-free filter tipped (it didn't seem so enjoyable or clever back in England) and gave the rest to Jethro, another of her father's farmworkers, instead of his usual roll-ups. Rodway's said, quite understandably, that as they had not expected her to return until the New Year, there was nothing for her before Christmas and, as the winter months were always a quiet time, it could well be Easter before they could have her back. Shula filled in her time with bar work at The Bull, typing at Grey Gables and helping out in the farm office, but Jill could sense a restlessness in her daughter still. Shula complained about there being no man in her life but Jill thought the problem was that there was no sense of direction. She would have missed the lack of a man less had she had something else to occupy her. And it worried Jill that she didn't talk much about her time away. The person Shula did talk to was Caroline — smart, well-connected Caroline Bone who had come to the village to help at The Bull but had rapidly been spotted by Jack Woolley and gently poached (apt, really, as she was a cordon-bleu cook) to work front-of-house at Grey Gables.

'It was amazing,' Shula told her as they walked in the country park, looking for signs of spring and not finding many. 'I can't tell you how empty England seems.'

'Of people, you mean?' Shula had already told her about the incredible sight of an Indian bus, brightly painted, decorated with garlands, packed full of passengers, with people on the running boards, clinging on to the window sills and climbing on the roof.

'Not just that. Everything. Like they take their religion so seriously — these stunning temples and gold-encrusted Buddhas —'

'There's some lovely church architecture in England,' said Caroline mildly. 'That's the product of the same kind of fervour, surely?'

'You're probably right,' agreed Shula. 'But you don't feel it in congregations today. Richard Adamson's a nice chap and a perfectly good vicar but you wouldn't find people walking fifty miles to go to one of his services, which is what people in the East do all the time.'

Caroline laughed.

'I'm quite the wrong person to talk to about this, you know, I'm a complete heathen.'

'Don't you see? I can't talk to Mum and Dad about it. They're just so terrified I've come back in some way changed and that I'm going to head off there again. Every time I mention abroad they look absolutely paralysed.'

'Would you go again?' asked Caroline gently.

Shula stood for a moment, surveying the green sweep of Jack Woolley's golf course, the flags snapping in the brisk wind. Then she met Caroline's eyes.

'I don't know. What is there to keep me here? Rodway's aren't falling over themselves to have me back. There's no man waiting in the wings, begging me not to go —'

'Well that's no reason not to do it, even if there were!' retorted Caroline. 'But I'd miss you, you know.'

Shula tucked her arm through her friend's and they turned for home — for Grey Gables' warm fireside and the chef's cinnamon toast. But she knew that if there were someone in Ambridge for her — someone she really cared about — then, like her grand-mother before her, she wouldn't look any further.

Finally, in the middle of March, Rodway's got in touch. They would be delighted, they said, to have her back after Easter, but Mr Rodway did want her assurance that her trip had been a one-off and that she would resume her Estate Agency training. With only a tinge of regret, Shula was able to give it. Perhaps in the end, she reflected, the Rodway's offer had come at the right time. If it had come any earlier she might not have been ready for it and her answer might have been very different.

She came into the kitchen where Jill was feeding Qwerty, an orphan lamb whom Shula had adopted. Jill looked up.

'It was Rodway's. I start back after Easter.'

The relief on her mother's face was palpable and Shula had the satisfaction, for once in her life, she thought, of having done the right thing. She took the lamb off her mother and buried her face in the warm fleece.

'That's it then, Qwerty. My adventures are over. Back to respectability for me.'

A couple of months later, Phil and Jill were in the kitchen at Brookfield. The evening sun slanted through the window, glazing the oak dresser laden with its willow patterned plates, glancing off the kettle on the Aga. Phil was opening the post, which he hadn't had time to get to that morning and was not impressed to find it mostly consisted of circulars, unmissable offers on slatted floors for pig units, an electricity bill ('How much?') and a demand for his N.F.U. sub. He had not had time to get to it that morning because Shula, on her way to work, had informed him that Neil had told her it sounded like her exhaust had gone — could he see his way to getting it fixed. This was Phil's cue to hold forth now against the iniquities — real and imagined — of his daughter. Her proclivity for spending money (his money, preferably), her constant occupation of the bathroom and the telephone, her appalling choice of men.

'Just answer me one thing, Jill.' Phil laid aside the last of the letters in disgust. 'When is Shula going to find someone who doesn't spell trouble?'

Jill put a pie into the Aga and straightened.

'I might just have the answer for you there, Phil.'

There was a note of triumph in her voice. Phil could be hard on the children sometimes.

'What, she's taken a vow of celibacy?'

'She phoned about twenty minutes ago. She's bringing someone home for supper.'

'A man?'

'Well I trust he won't be a Martian. He's the solicitor she's been dealing with over that farm sale.'

'What? But he's fifty if he's a day —'

'She thought so too but he's twenty-seven and a bachelor. She's only just met him herself, Phil, and she's bringing him home to meet us! Now you must agree that's a first!'

A batch of biscuits was cooling on a wire tray, and Phil helped himself to one as he considered.

'A solicitor, eh? Well, I suppose that could be an improvement on the rest.' And through a mouthful of crumbs, 'These are delicious, Jill.'

'Thank you.'

Jill thought she'd get out the best glasses, just in case.

Phil swallowed and licked his lips.

'What did you say his name was?'

'I didn't.' And would the best china be seen by Shula as going over the top? She turned to her husband. 'But it's Mark — Mark Hebden.'

AUGUST
—— 1980 ——

It was an incredible feeling. Shula was floating high, high over Ambridge, weightless, limitless, as if she'd taken a huge leap off Lakey Hill but would never, ever hit the ground. She felt emptied of all worry and utterly, utterly happy.

Mark's face was close to hers and his eyes were warm.

'Thank you. Thank you so much,' she whispered.

He smiled back.

'My pleasure,' he said.

In the four months since she had known Mark she had run through every gamut of feeling for him. The problem in the beginning, of course, was that she was still comparing every man she met — unfavourably, of course — with Simon. And Mark was very un-Simon-like. Unfailingly punctual, he rang her if he was going to be as much as five minutes late. Unerringly polite, he always made a point of trying to engage her father in discussion about the farm, though it was something he knew nothing about and Phil, always busy, hardly gave him much encouragement. Still, at least he tolerated Mark's ingenuous questions about silage and sheep drenches — if Simon had ever asked him anything he would have assumed (probably correctly) that it was to be part of an exposé of iniquitous modern farming methods. Considerate to the last, Mark always consulted Shula about where she would like to eat, what film she would like to see — whereas Simon would have picked some violent all-action thriller if that's what he'd felt like seeing and never mind that she was cowering behind her hand half the time.

First impressions of Mark had been good. He had been waiting in his car when she rolled up in her Mini at Hordern's Farm that May morning. Expecting the bald, shrivelled senior partner, she had been amazed when he climbed out, immaculate in his navy suit, his white shirt crisp against his black curly hair.

'You look surprised,' he commented.

'I was expecting — someone else,' she faltered, thinking 'How am I going to keep my mind on the job?'

But they'd managed to arrange the business pretty smoothly. Then, as it was nearly lunchtime and they were both heading back to Borchester, he'd suggested a drink at The Feathers, which was a relief because for the last five minutes she hadn't been listening to a word he was saying, wondering instead how she could contrive to spend a bit more time with him. At the pub, she'd left him ordering the drinks and had escaped to the loo, both to see what she looked like and for a spot of calming deep breathing. She hadn't planned on bumping into Jennifer.

'Shula! How lovely! I'm absolutely gasping for a drink.'

'Mm,' said Shula weakly. 'Me too.'

Jennifer's shiny carrier bags bumped against her legs as a woman squeezed past them in the narrow corridor which smelt of chips and air freshener, both equally pungent and equally unpleasant.

'I've found a fabulous dress,' Jennifer confided. 'You'll have to let me show you —'

'I'm sorry, Jennifer, I'm with someone already,' Shula blurted out.

Jennifer's face registered momentary concern then in her usual way, she overrode the problem.

'Well, I'll join you. Anyone I know?'

'I don't know him very well myself, yet, Jennifer, so if you don't mind —'

'Him? Ooh, where is he? Let's have a look,' Jennifer strained to look out to the bar.

'Jennifer, *please*.' Shula was rigid with embarassment. If she was gone much longer Mark might come looking for her, only to find her lurking furtively in a corridor with a giggling harpie.

'Go on, where is he?' Jennifer pushed open the half glazed door to the bar. Mark had found a table and was absorbed in the menu. 'Is that him by the window? Oh, Shula. He's awfully handsome.'

It took another five minutes before Shula managed to rid herself of Jennifer who promised faithfully to take herself off to the Wooden Platter but there were moments during that first lunch when she would actually have welcomed her cousin's garrulous presence.

That first meal with someone new is always a nightmare. Shula ordered a Ploughman's, then wished she hadn't when she saw the enormous chunk of cheese — he was going to think she was a complete gannet. She was longing to crunch the pickled onions but thought she ought to lay off them, just in case, and Mark always seemed to ask her a question when she had her mouth full. But when at two o'clock he looked at his watch and said he'd have to be getting back, she heard herself asking him to Brookfield to supper that evening. Another meal! She must be mad. And when he accepted her stomach flipped over in a way which made her wonder if she'd ever eat again.

In the end, the evening went well, without too many awkward pauses. Jill established that Mark's parents lived in a rather posh suburb of Borchester, that his father was also a solicitor and that Mark's mother, who for some reason — surely a nickname? — was called Bunty, was a keen golfer. His younger sister, Joanna, was in her first year of an accountancy course. David was out, so he wasn't there to say disparaging things about his elder sister, and Shula basked in the warmth of her parents' approval. Mark didn't kiss her before he left, but he gravely noted down her phone number in his black leather diary and she knew for certain he would phone. She went to bed hugging to herself that warm feeling that comes at the start of a relationship, the feeling that says you are enormous fun, intelligent company, and a desirable sexual siren to boot. Why then, when they met again, did she not feel excited? Mark had phoned when he'd said he would, he'd driven all the way out to Ambridge to collect her, only to take her back into Borchester, to Mario's, where he ordered white wine since she preferred it to red, even though he was having steak.

It was all very thoughtful, but in a way very stifling. Shula felt she'd never answered so many questions about her likes and dislikes, so concerned was he that she should enjoy herself every time they went out. Was she in a draught from the door? Did she like it here? Did she really like Italian food — if she preferred Chinese, he wished she'd said — and so on and so on. Typically, of course, both Phil and Jill thought he was wonderful. Jill, knowing her daughter, knew better than to say so, but Phil was unable to contain his delight that Shula had at last found someone whose presence in the house he could tolerate. And of course he was right. Mark was lovely — but wasn't he, well, just a little bit boring? Shula hated herself for being perverse, but she couldn't help what she felt.

'I can't moan about him at home, Mum and Dad think he's wonderful,' she complained to Caroline as they trotted back from a gallop on Heydon Berrow. 'Dad's even gone and asked him to help with the haymaking.'

'You know your trouble — you're never satisfied,' Caroline smiled. 'You go out with a guy like Simon who treats you like dirt, you manage to get yourself abandoned on the other side of the world by the next one —'

'If you mean Nick, it wasn't quite like that —' protested Shula.

'You just don't know when you're well off.'

Shula hung her head. Caroline was absolutely right.

Mark turned up for his day at Brookfield in his idea of country clothes — olive cords and a checked shirt. You could tell his mother had ironed them that morning specially. He listened carefully as Dan, her Grandad — who could never stay away from the farm during haymaking — explained the procedure.

'Of course it's a lot more mechanised than when I was young — we used to cut the grass with scythes then. And even when Phil was a lad, the mowers were horse-drawn.'

'Yes, thank you, Dad,' Phil chipped it. 'We're not here for a session on "All Our Yesterdays". We mowed at the beginning of the week, Mark, we've turned it a couple of times, all that's left is the baling.'

'And that's where we come in,' added Shula, knowing that she'd do an hour or so in the field before coming back to Brookfield with the excuse of getting lunch together. 'Have you done any bale lugging before?'

'You tell me what you want me to do and I'll do it,' declared Mark.

Out of the corner of her eye, Shula saw Neil and Jethro exchange glances. They knew that pitching bales was hard, hard work — hard work accomplished under a relentlessly hot sun or under a lowering thundery sky with the added pressure of getting the hay under cover before the storm broke. But when they got to the field, Shula had to admit she was impressed with Mark's energy. She had the easier task, on top of the trailer, stacking the bales which Jethro then drove back to the barn. Mark was on the ground, tossing bales up to her.

'Come on, put your back into it,' she chided when he stopped to wipe his forehead with the back of his arm. 'You're not in court now.'

'It's not like this in Laurie Lee,' Mark complained between grunts. 'They stick at it for hours on a crust of bread and a swig of cider. When's coffee?'

By the time Shula drove out to the field again at lunchtime in the Land Rover, the sun was high in the sky. Wisps of cloud had begun to pile up on the horizon, but there was no real respite in sight. Shula could hear the haymaking before she could see it, the insistent beat of the baler's engine seeming to enter her body through every pore.

She drove through the gate and parked on a ridge of rough ground under the shade of a horse chestnut. It was no good calling to the men, so she walked across to the little knot of figures to tell them lunch was ready. She had to smile when she saw Mark. His face was streaked with dust through which sweat had made runnels and he was covered in bits of straw, husks and earth. But, determined not to be outdone, he was pitching bales onto the trailer with Neil whilst Jethro piled them up.

'Lunch,' Shula called as she approached.

Wincing, Mark straightened.

'You knew what this was like,' he said accusingly. 'And still you let me come.'

'Didn't I warn you?' Shula teased. She reached out and took one of his hands. The palm was starting to blister. 'Never mind, thirty years of this and you don't even feel the pain.' Then, softening, 'Come on. Come and have a drink.'

She led Mark over to the shade at the edge of the field. Neil and Jethro indicated that they'd follow in a bit.

Shula spread cold barbecued chicken, her mother's pasties, Scotch eggs and salad out on the rug. She poured Mark a tall ginger beer and he drank it in one and held out his glass for a refill.

Neil and Jethro must have been conferring. After about ten minutes Jethro came over and explained they were going back down to Brookfield after all. There was a cow he wanted to look in on, and Neil apparently had to phone through an order of pig nuts for Hollowtree.

'Do you get the feeling we're being left alone?' Shula lay back on the rug, sleepily shading her eyes from the sun.

'I certainly have the feeling I don't fit in.'

There was something in Mark's tone which made her alert. She rolled over on her stomach and propped herself up on her elbows to look at him. He was sitting on the very edge of the rug, half turned away from her, looking across to where the outline of the Hassett Hills blurred against the sky.

'Mark?'

'You think I don't notice. You think I don't see how some of the things I do or say irritate you. I know I'm an easy target. I cut cheese up into little cubes and break biscuits in half before I eat them. I like my cuffs to show under my suit. I'm interested in finding out about farming from your father. I know you don't like it —'

'Mark, that's not fair,' Shula interrupted

'No, you're the one that's not fair. I don't know whose standards you're judging me against — your own, or some former boyfriend's, but I know I'm being found wanting. And it's not pleasant. You'd better face it, Shula, there's no future for us.'

Shula looked down. An ant was clambering up one of the rug's woolly tassels, bent on sustenance. She didn't even brush it away. Was he finishing with her? This was a new experience. She'd been dumped before by a man who'd run off to the other side of the world, she'd been dumped on the other side of the world by a man who'd run off — now it was happening right here at home. It didn't seem to make any difference. It still hurt — even though she couldn't deny that he was right, that he was voicing things she'd been feeling all along. Maybe her hurt had something to do with the fact that because he seemed so eager to please, she'd thought that this was one relationship she was in control of. Yet again, it had proved not to be the case.

'The funny thing was,' she told Caroline later, 'I liked him at that moment more than I had since we first met.'

Which was probably why, barely two months later, they were high over Ambridge in a hot air balloon, savouring the stillness and the silence, feeling utterly removed from the world, weightless, perpetual. Because what Mark said had made Shula think. It wasn't fair to blame him because he wasn't Simon. If you looked at it logically, the affair with Simon hadn't ended very well. It hadn't, if she was honest, always been that good even while it was going strong — so surely the fact that Mark was different had to be a good thing? And anyway, wasn't the problem as much her attitude as his character? She wouldn't have admitted it to him, of course, but she admired the way he had raised the subject. Now she knew that there was more to him and that he was prepared to stand up to her, she actually found him more attractive. It was clear that neither of them really wanted it to end — as Neil and Jethro must have noted when they returned from lunch to find them intertwined on the rug. Jill noted it too and made a point of inviting Mark to Shula's birthday supper at Brookfield — which was where he had presented her with an enormous bottle of expensive perfume — and produced his surprise about the balloon trip.

Shula focussed the binoculars and gave a little squeal of recogntion.

'Mark — look, down there! I can see Aunt Laura in the garden at Ambridge Hall!'

'Aunt who? Are you related to everyone in Ambridge?'

'No, it just seems like it,' Shula smiled. She paused. 'Would you like a big family, Mark?'

'What — you mean in terms of cousins and aunties, or children?'

'Children.'

'Excuse me, m'lud, Miss Archer is attempting to lead the witness,' intoned Mark in what Shula called his court voice. But he pulled Shula gently against him. She snuggled comfortably against his shoulder. 'I s'pose I'd like a couple,' he said casually. 'Have to be boys, of course, because of the cricket.'

Shula sighed contentedly. Perhaps it was going to be all right after all.

'Just don't let your father see it, Elizabeth.'

'I can't believe he said those things! Mark, of all people!'

Elizabeth spread the *Echo* on the kitchen table and poured herself another mug of coffee. Jill turned from the sink.

'Elizabeth — I said put it away.'

'"Socially accepted amateurs." That doesn't sound like Mark.'

'And I don't think Shula will want you commenting about it, either.'

Jill rinsed the potatoes under the tap and placed them in a pan on the Aga. She'd been so pleased when it seemed that Mark and Shula were going to stay the course after all. He was such a nice boy, steady, reliable, quite the opposite of Shula's previous boyfriends. Even Phil couldn't find a bad word to say against him. After a shaky start, it had all been going so well, until this business with the Jarretts...

Of course, the hunt saboteurs had had to target the South Borsetshire Hunt. Jill checked the casserole and put the potatoes on to boil. Of course Shula had had to be there that Saturday. Gerald Pargetter would have to be drunk — though that was nothing unusual. Had he really knocked Mrs Jarrett down deliberately and had other members of the hunt actually ridden at the couple? More to the point, out of all the solicitors they could have chosen, did the Jarretts have to go to Spencer and Holden, and specifically to Mark, to act as their defence? And did it really have to be Phil who was Chairman of the Bench the day their case came up in the Magistrates' Court?

As if there wasn't enough to think about, thought Jill, taking flour and sugar out of the cupboard, with mince pies to make for the W.I. Christmas party, cards still to send, presents to buy and wrap, and a bundle of holly waiting to be made into a wreath for the front door.

'Elizabeth. I won't tell you again. Get that paper off the table, please. When I've weighed this out I need to lay it for supper.'

The magistrates had found the Jarretts guilty of causing a breach of the peace and Mrs Jarrett guilty of criminal damage for spraying a fencepost. But Mark couldn't let it rest there. Jill let the slippery sugar slide through her fingers. What was it he'd said? Something about the bench representing the bias of a Borchester high class Mafia? One minute Shula wasn't talking to Mark. Then she wasn't talking to Phil. And Mark didn't seem to be talking to any of them — in fact Peggy, Phil's sister-in-law, had told Jill she'd seen him coming out of the wine bar in West Street with Jackie Woodstock, one of its best customers. Now apparently Mark was taking the Jarretts' case to appeal at Felpersham Crown Court. And Jill had let herself be talked into giving a New Year's Eve party for all the family...

The door was flung open and Shula staggered in under a pile of parcels.

'I am never, ever going to leave my Christmas shopping this late again,' she said, dumping them down on a chair.

'Anything for me?' asked Elizabeth, trying to peep.

'Nothing,' snapped Shula.

'Did you find anything for your father?' asked Jill. She knew just how torn Shula's loyalties had been between Phil and Mark.

'I couldn't find a thing. Why are men so difficult? It'll have to be another classical album, I think. Or some sheet music. '

'A *Bluffer's Guide to the Law* might come in handy for his stocking,' offered Elizabeth, helping herself to a glacé cherry.

Jill smacked her fingers and glared. Elizabeth seemed to spend her entire school holiday winding Shula up. As a result everyone else got wound up as well.

'What's happened now?' said Shula wearily.

'It's in the paper, that's all,' said Elizabeth, gleefully passing it across. 'I can't see Dad getting Mark a Christmas present at this rate.'

Shula sank into a chair as the full horror dawned on her.

'Dad is going to go berserk,' she whispered.

'It's all right Shula, he already has,' confided Elizabeth. 'He saw the *Echo* at lunchtime. He's probably lodged a complaint against Mark at the Court of Appeal by now.'

Elizabeth's grasp of the law was hazy to say the least but Shula knew what she was getting at.

Wearily Shula climbed the stairs to her room. She flung her parcels on the bed and sank down beside them. Why was everything such a mess? Back in the summer she had thought Mark too mild-mannered for her. That was before she'd found out about his Gladstonian social conscience and sense of fair play. He didn't care whom he crossed to get the right verdict. But to go into print insulting her Dad... She wondered if he'd phone that night, or if she should phone him. If she didn't, he might take Jackie Woodstock out again. He said they were only friends and he'd only done it because Shula was siding with her Dad, but everyone knew Jackie Woodstock's reputation. Well if that was what he wanted ... It was going to be a miserable Christmas.

And the Jarretts' appeal was on New Year's Eve ...

'I've never seen you in your gown before.'

'You've never seen me at the Crown Court before.'

Shula could tell Mark was nervous from the way he kept tugging at the folds of material.

'You're making it all skewiff.' She stood facing him and smoothed out the shoulders.

'Thanks. You can't get to the mirror in the robing room.' Mark smiled briefly, a tight, nervous little smile.

'Oh, hang on, they're calling us in. See you later.'

'Mark — good luck.'

He grinned at her briefly. Shula made her way through to the courtroom: it was very modern, all panelled in light oak. The Jarretts were down in front, looking very respectable. Mark was talking to them and smiling. Shula felt a surge of feeling for him. He looked so right in these surroundings, so confident and confidence-inspiring. She hadn't been sure if she was going to come today. Christmas had been so awful, after the row with Mark on Christmas Eve — and all over that stupid Jackie Woodstock giving him a lift... But then he'd come round in the evening on Boxing Day, when she was slumped alone in front of the television, having politely refused to go to Aunty Chris and George's for supper. They'd — well, made it up would be the official term — but it was better than that, because she knew the family wouldn't be back for ages and the fire was warm and afterwards they'd opened a bottle of wine and lain close and then it had happened all over again.

Shula found her nails were digging into the palms of her hands as Mark got up to speak. And when the judge granted his appeal, it was all she could do to stop herself from rushing forward and hugging him.

It didn't make things any easier with her father.

'I can't wait — never mind the Jarretts, blood sports right here in our own sitting room! What a way to see in the New Year!'

Elizabeth pouted into the mirror. At thirteen she had been experimenting with makeup for years and was in her Clara Bow phase.

'Just because I've asked Mark to the party this evening ... ' Shula wished Elizabeth would use her own room. 'They can both be civilised, surely?'

The phone rang.

'That'll be for you,' said Elizabeth.

'No, it won't,' replied Shula. 'You get it.'

'Shula, I'm doing my mascara!'

Sighing, Shula shrugged on her kimono and went to the phone. A few minutes later she returned triumphant.

'It was Mark. He's rung to speak to Dad. He wanted to get it out of the way before the party. So it really is all going to be OK.'

'More punch, Shula?'

Shula's head was already feeling distinctly light. She shook it, tentatively, both in a negative reply to the question and to see if she could clear it a bit. It didn't seem to have much effect, but Mark took her hand and that made her feel a bit more steady.

'Shall we find somewhere quiet for a bit?'

'Mark, it's nearly midnight!'

'I know. Come on.'

She followed him out of the room, squeezing past her cousin Tony. His wife Pat had been bearded by Aunt Laura who seemed to be carrying on about mechanical hedge trimmers.

The hall was no less crowded: Elizabeth was deep in conversation with George's son, Terry, and little Kate had fallen asleep on a pile of coats.

Mark tugged gently at Shula's hand and pulled her towards the stairs.

'I want to talk to you.'

Shula followed mutely. After all this, surely he wasn't going to tell her he'd decided Jackie Woodstock was more his type? She couldn't see it herself. When they got to the half-landing, he stopped and turned to face her, taking both her hands in his.

'Your hair looks nice tonight. Have you done something with it?'

'I had it cut about two weeks ago.'

'I know that. You've sort of pushed it back on the side. It suits you.'

'Thanks.' I wish he'd get to the point, Shula thought.

She noticed that one of the bullrushes had fallen out of the copper jug of dried grasses which stood on the little sewing table in the recess. The curtains were open and through the leaded window she could see a sickle moon. Mark pulled her towards him, their hands clasped at their sides. His face was serious. They stood for what seemed like an age, just looking, eyes locked, hovering on the edge of a kiss. Shula felt a warm desire uncoil in her stomach and without moving her eyes from Mark's face, leaned fractionally forward to touch her lips to his. But he pulled back abruptly. She realised with a profound and painful shock that she didn't want to lose him to Jackie Woodstock — or anyone come to that — ever.

'There's something I want to ask you. I perhaps should have asked your father first —'

'Mark, it's all right, it'll all be forgotten, this business with the saboteurs. He'll forget it —'

Mark smiled suddenly, a great grin relaxing his face, making him look quite boyish.

'Shula, it's nothing to do with the Jarretts.'

'Oh.'

So it was about Jackie Woodstock. Mark was speaking again.

'I love you. I want to spend the rest of my life with you. I want to marry you. Will you marry me — please?'

JANUARY
—— 1981 ——

The rest of that New Year's Eve passed in a daze for Shula. She knew she had said yes, before flinging her arms round Mark's neck and giving him one of the many kisses she had been wanting to give him for weeks, she knew they had told — told, rather than asked, her parents — but beyond that, the evening, and the days which followed, were a blur. There was the memorable evening when she and her parents had gone to the Hebdens' for dinner. Mark had been to Brookfield several times but Shula had only been to Mark's once before. Then the occasion had been Sunday tea, and she had sat primly in the Hebdens' lounge. Unlike the sitting room at Brookfield, which was a motley collection of family pieces, veterans of generations of boisterous children, everything at the Hebdens' either was, or looked, brand new, and everything had been chosen to go with everything else. The curtains picked up the blue in the three piece suite, the cushions picked out the salmon pink. The gas log fire flickered against the cream carpet, not that they needed its heat, for the modern house was fully centrally-heated and double-glazed, as Mrs Hebden had pointed out, as if Shula were there on a professional visit. She fully expected to be asked to measure up the spare bedroom and examine the 'well-appointed' downstairs cloaks.

So, one dismal evening in January she and her parents set out for the Hebdens again. Shula realised how long it was since she had sat in the back of the car and been driven by her parents. It made her think of long car journeys when she and Kenton were small, squabbling over games of I-Spy and eating too many toffees. Now, in less than a year, she was going to be a married woman, a wife, not just a daughter, and a daughter-in-law not just a girlfriend.

To say the evening was awkward would be to grace it with a description when no word really exists which would sum it up. Reginald Hebden was a solicitor like his son: a member of the Round Table, a golfer and fisherman. Phil was a farmer whose main interests off the farm were musical. Bunty Hebden had originally learnt golf when Mark was away at school, to give her something to do rather than to enable her to spend more time with Reg. She had quickly become rather more proficient at it than he was, and was now a mainstay of the Ladies' Committee. In fact, she seemed to be on every Committee going: the Bridge Club, the Flower Club, and the Womens' League of Health and Beauty. Jill was someone who'd never had time to think of her interests in terms of hobbies — they were her life: the W.R.V.S., the W.I., the church fête, her children, the farm... Most chilling of all for Shula, as she tried to fill in the gaps in the conversation with bright little observations about the light fittings or Mrs Hebden's shoes, was how remote the Hebdens seemed with each other. Instead of the jokey shorthand for affection which existed between her own parents there was — not a chilliness exactly, but a distance which seemed unthinkable to Shula, especially after so many years of marriage. She wondered what the Hebdens talked about when they were alone, and wondered if part of Bunty's reserve towards her, which was a tangible force, was because with their daughter Joanna away at college, she and Reg would only have each other when Mark had left home. What on earth would they find to talk about?

'It wasn't too bad, was it?' Mark whispered as he and Shula walked out ahead to the car.

'Oh Mark, it was awful. They've got nothing to say to each other,' hissed Shula. She meant both Bunty and Reg and the respective sets of parents, but how could she possibly tell Mark she thought his parents' rather formal relationship odd?

'Well, we don't want the mothers to get on too well, they'd only start running our lives,' Mark smiled. He kissed her gently. 'And I want you all to myself.'

Shula laced her fingers behind his head and pulled his mouth down to hers. What did it matter? She wasn't marrying the Hebdens, she was marrying Mark.

'Suits me,' she murmured.

Uncle Tom – actually he was Shula's great uncle, her grand-mother's brother – always made a gloomy prognostication about 'February fill-dyke' and this year looked like living up to his expectations. It was an awful day when Robin Catchpole breezed into Rodway's. Shula was involved in drafting a rather difficult letter to a vendor whom she couldn't raise on the phone about the dry rot which the purchaser's survey had revealed in their cottage, and the consequent 'adjustment' in price which would have to be made. Alison, the new junior, got up from her desk to see to him but Shula gestured that she'd deal with it. The likelihood was that the query would be referred to her anyway.

He was busy looking at the 'Executive Homes' section of the houses on display, though Shula thought from his appearance – jeans and a padded jacket, dark hair curling over his collar – that this was surely wishful thinking.

'Good morning. Can I help you?'

'I'd better not answer that.'

When he turned he had a lazy smile and soft brown eyes which looked her up and down. He looked familiar.

'Robin Catchpole, *Borchester Echo*.'

He held out his hand. Shula smiled inwardly. She'd had her run in with *Echo* journalists. She felt immune. She extended her own hand.

'Shula Archer.'

'Pleased to meet you. I saw you the other night, didn't I? At the Landscape Survey exhibition in Ambridge?' He held onto her hand just fractionally too long. She remembered him now. He'd been staring at her all evening. He had nice hands. Long, thin, fingers — artistic. Shula wondered if he played the guitar. It would suit him.

'Yes, that's right.' Shula seemed to have spent most of her spare time for the last six months crawling through hedge-bottoms under the supervision of her cousin Jennifer and John Tregorran, the local amateur historian. The results had finally been put on display in

Jennifer's studio, much to Brian's disgust. 'What did you think of it?'

'Were *you* involved?'

Shula explained about the hedge-bottoms.

'In that case — brilliant. I told Mrs Aldridge she might even get a vanity publisher interested in producing a book. Her husband — what's his name — Brian — didn't seem very keen though.'

'No — well, Brian's a very busy farmer. He doesn't really want Jennifer distracted.' That was the least of it, she thought, since the whole village seemed to think that Jennifer and John were on the brink of, if not actually having, an affair.

'You'll be working with Jennifer,' she went on, trying to guide the conversation away from the status quo at Home Farm. 'She does a column for the *Echo*. She's my cousin.'

'Oh yes, I'll be working with her.' He didn't sound impressed. 'I've come here as a journalist, right. Come to the cutting edge of reporting: rural crime, pesticides in waterways, deprivation in the countryside. What does my Editor give me to do? Features.'

He sounded just like Simon. Shula smiled inwardly.

'This is Ted Pierce, I suppose?'

'Oh no, he's a relative of yours as well. Your Dad. Your Uncle.'

'Not exactly,' Shula smiled. 'It's just I — well, I used to know someone who worked on the *Echo*.' She took a deep breath. It had been years since she'd even spoken his name. 'Simon Parker.'

Robin registered recognition.

'Oh right, I came across one of his articles the other day. Didn't seem too bad. What's he doing now?'

'I'm afraid I don't know.'

'Great. Today Borchester — tomorrow nowhere in particular.'

'You're all the same.' Shula couldn't help laughing. 'All Simon wanted to do was get away.'

'You're a local girl, are you?'

'That's right, sir,' replied Shula in her best Borsetshire accent, bobbing a curtsey. 'I don't reckon as I've been outside the county boundary — ooh, these twenty years.'

'OK, OK, so patronising's my middle name.' Robin Catchpole laughed. 'How was I to know? I've come from Tipton.'

'Where?'

'Oh, so you are a country bumpkin. It's in the Black Country.'

'If you've quite finished insulting me, I have got work to do.'

He was very, very like Simon. She'd better be careful.

Robin stood up straight and took out his notebook.

'You're absolutely right. It's nearly lunchtime and us journalists have a responsibility to the local licensed trade. You tell me what I need to know and I'll buy you a drink in return. Deal?'

'Go on then.' Shula was both charmed and exasperated. 'I can see I'll never get rid of you otherwise.'

Robin did his best to look wounded which with his liquid brown eyes he did rather well.

'It's all your cousin Jennifer's fault. She's done a piece about cottages and Pierce wants a companion piece on unusual country homes. You know, follies, converted chapels, that sort of thing. So I was wondering...'

'You want me to do your research for you.'

'Hey,' said Robin admiringly. 'For an estate agent you're very sharp. Go on. Never mind the drink, call it lunch. I hear there's actually a decent wine bar somewhere round here.'

Of course Mark had to choose that day to visit Nelson Gabriel's winebar himself, with a client for whom he was drawing up a will. Robin was just regaling her with the stories he would devise to fill up the inside pages of the *Tipton Trumpet* on a slack news day when Shula caught sight of him at the bar. She waved frantically to attract his attention but he was studying the wine list. Finally Nelson pointed out her windmilling arms. Mark looked at first, she was interested to note, slightly irritated, as if his client might withdraw his business because of Mark's obvious connection with this unseemly behaviour. But when he had installed the elderly gentleman at a table he came across. Then he registered Robin.

'Shula! Liquid lunch?'

There was an edge in his voice Shula had not heard before.

'Well hello Mr Pot. My name's Mrs Kettle,' she replied, trying to make light of it. 'Anyway, Mark. Can I introduce Robin Catchpole. Robin's just joined the *Echo*. I'm helping him with a feature he's working on.'

'Pleased to meet you.' Mark's handshake was formal. Mark's hands were squarer than Robin's, Shula noticed, with neat, clean nails. She'd always admired how neat Mark was.

'Mark's a solicitor.'

'Brilliant — handy when those libel suits start flooding in. I'll remember that. Drink up Shula, I'll get you another.'

There was a tension about Mark's back as he walked away to rejoin his client but instead of feeling sorry for him Shula felt resentful. Why shouldn't she have a drink with someone who just happened to be male? Mark didn't own her. Anyway, Robin might be married with three kids for all she knew — but she didn't somehow think so.

The example of the Hebdens still imprinted on her mind, she didn't let it drop when she saw Mark that evening. They went for a pizza before the cinema. The latest blockbuster had finally arrived in Borchester and Shula been nagging about seeing it. Mark was less keen — he'd got a big case conference next day and had said he ought to be working but strangely, that evening, he had caved in. Guilty conscience perhaps? thought Shula uncharitably. She was still cross about lunchtime.

'What are you going to do?' she demanded, stabbing at her salad. 'Ban me from ever taking single male purchasers round houses? Stop me going to conferences because I might meet someone unattached? Don't you trust me at all?'

And Mark had backed off. It was all his fault, he said, he had reacted badly, he apologised unreservedly. Two weeks later he took Shula out for dinner somewhere rather posher than the pizza place and when the waiter had poured the wine produced a small leather box. Inside was a three-stone opal ring which he said had been in his family for a hundred and fifty years.

'Let's set a date for the wedding,' he urged. 'I don't want to wait.'

But as he pushed the ring on her finger — typical Mark, he'd checked with her mother about her ring size and had had it altered to fit — she realised, through the wine and the romance, that it also marked her out as his for all to see.

Not that it made any difference to Robin, anyway. She'd told him the very first lunchtime that she and Mark were engaged. He'd made no comment apart from a wry 'congratulations' but once she'd got her ring and they'd set the date — September 26th — he teased her mercilessly about how she'd soon be an old married woman and how he'd look forward to writing up the account of the wedding in the *Echo*: 'The bride wore white slipper satin and a delicate blush, whilst the groom wore a self-satisfied smile. And, hey, I'm not getting at Mark. Any bloke who'd persuaded you to marry him would have the right to look smug.'

Somehow, Shula did not find this reassuring.

As soon as she had the ring on her finger and the church was booked, it was as if Shula wasn't her own person. All Shula's fears that her mother and future mother-in-law had nothing in common proved to be groundless: Jill and Bunty spent hours on the phone to each other discussing details of the arrangements. There was a lot to be decided — marquees and bridesmaids' dresses and cake and champagne and invitations and hire cars and morning suits and wedding present lists. ('Garlic press? Can't I just use the back of a knife?' asked Shula, amazed. 'Bath towels and bath sheets? What's the difference?')

Then there was the issue of where they were going to live.

'Well, that shouldn't take long,' soothed Mrs Hebden. (Bunty still didn't exactly trip off Shula's tongue.) 'You're both of you in the right business.'

She made it sound as if was some sort of dynastic liaison, Shula thought, as if she and Mark were right for each other because of their complimentary professions, nothing else. But when she repeated Bunty's comment to Robin, he actually agreed.

'She's quite right. Estate agents and solicitors are the people who've got most to make out of marriages. Because what happens to one in three couples? They divorce. Cue the estate agents and solicitors.'

'I don't think that was quite what Bunty meant,' Shula admonished. 'Honestly, Robin, don't you take anything seriously?'

'Not if I can help it,' he said. 'Good grief, Shula, you'll be asking me if I believe everything I read in the papers next.'

So Mark and Shula started house hunting. Her Grandad had tried to persuade them to move into Glebe Cottage, which her Gran had left to Shula in her will, saying he could move back to Brookfield to make way for them, but Shula wouldn't hear of it. Mark thought a flat in Borchester would be practical, and even wanted her to look at one in the Old Wool Market, where Simon Parker had rented his, but Shula managed to dissuade him. Cunningly she drove him out one evening to see a property which was just about to come on the market through Rodway's — a terraced cottage in Penny Hassett. It was only small: two square rooms downstairs and a kitchen and bathroom built on the back, but it was the upstairs which had sold it to Mark: the original black grates in the two bedrooms, the view over the Hassett Hills, the old lilac tree in the somewhat overgrown garden. And best of all, a tiny box room over the stairwell which Mark earmarked for a study. While Mark went around testing the floorboards and tapping the walls, Shula stood in the back bedroom imagining a big brass bed — a four poster, perhaps, with white cotton sheets and lace-trimmed pillows, and a Wedgwood blue wash for the walls.

'A four poster?' Mark was incredulous. 'How in earth would you get it up the stairs?'

'You don't bring it up the stairs, you take out a window,' Shula explained. She'd seen it done often enough.

'Shula, love, you'd have to demolish a wall to get a four poster bed in this cottage. And then you wouldn't have room to swing a cat.'

He was about to produce his tape measure to prove it, but Shula got a fit of the giggles about how serious he looked. She slid her arms round his waist and untucked his shirt so she could feel his warm back.

'We are going to buy it, aren't we? I can see us here, Mark, eating breakfast in that little alcove in the kitchen, pottering in the garden, putting up the Christmas tree by the fireplace ... '

'Well,' said Mark cautiously, 'you'll have to give it a proper survey, of course, and I'd want to get up in the loft but — yes, it's a distinct possibility.'

'Mark! Have you ever done anything impulsive in your entire life?'

'Um — I'll have to think about that one.'

'You like it really, don't you?'

'Yes, OK, I do.' He looped a strand of Shula's hair tidily behind her ear. 'But you're the last person who ought to be carried away by a nice view and a bit of original coving. Is it a sound investment? Will we have to spend a fortune on a new damp course within five years? That's what we've got to ask ourselves.'

'Oh, I give up!' Shula squeezed his waist in mock exasperation. 'I thought I was practical till I met you. Come on, do your last bit of tapping and prodding and let's go for a drink.'

The whole country was smitten with wedding fever that spring. Prince Charles and Lady Diana Spencer were to be married at the end of July and the papers were full of astrological predictions about their compatibility, artists' impressions of the dress she would wear and supposed seating plans for the various dignitaries in St. Paul's Cathedral. Robin told Shula she should be grateful that the only media spotlight she would suffer would be a hack like him from the *Echo* and tried to cheer her up (so he said) by telling her about his sister's wedding. Apparently the groom's father had had a heart attack two days beforehand and the whole thing had had to be cancelled and restaged six months later. Shula spent an entire week following her father around, checking he was not lifting heavy bags of feed and urging him to put his feet up in the evenings.

Shula never sat down and analysed why she was still seeing so much of Robin. It wasn't as if he was still working on features and, even if he were, surely the *Echo* readers' appetite for articles about the architectural heritage of Borsetshire had waned by now? Through a combination of Robin's persistence and Ted Pierce's desire for an easy life, Robin had rapidly been moved to cover the news stories he was desperate for, though from his complaints about the level of excitement in Borchester in a typical week, Shula wondered sometimes whether features had actually been that much worse. He was new to the area, it was bound to take him time to settle in and make friends — that, at least, was how she justified to herself the fact that they tended to meet two lunchtimes out of three in Nelson's. Shula also tried to rationalise it by thinking about all the journalists on the *Echo* she had not got involved with — but part of her wondered why and how this particular profession exercised such a strong fascination for her. She didn't go out of her way to mention her lunchtimes with Robin to Mark, but she told herself she wasn't keeping anything from him — she and Robin were just friends. Like she was friends with Neil.

Well, maybe not quite. There'd been that evening at the flat — for Robin too had ended up at Nightingale Farm, sharing with Neil. Robin was flippant, arrogant — and very, very charming. He'd told her that he loved her. Shula was flattered, but frightened. She'd avoided him for a while after this but after a week of flowers and poems and Robin besieging the office, she gave in. He never mentioned his feelings again and Shula didn't encourage him to.

Mark knew, anyway. Whether it was because of what Shula didn't tell him, or what Nelson or, more likely, Jackie Woodstock did, he asked Shula about Robin. It was at that point that Shula knew she had something to hide, because she was instantly defensive.

'Look, if I wanted a secret liaison with Robin, I'd hardly go to the wine bar, would I? The very fact that I meet him there means it's innocent! It's got to be!'

'It'd be rather more innocent if you didn't meet him at all, Shula! Look, you've got me, you're going to be my wife. What have you got to say to him, anyway? Things you can't say to me?'

Shula was silent, thinking of all the things she'd told Robin about Bunty, and even, on occasion, about Mark. It was really hard to explain. She just felt comfortable with Robin. He'd been around a bit in a way that Mark hadn't. She liked trying ideas out on him to see what he'd say. Was that so awful? Did it point to a real void in her relationship with Mark?

That Sunday, she and Mark went to St. Stephen's with both sets of parents to hear the banns read for the first time. It was late June. The Vicar, Richard Adamson, caught Shula's eye and smiled before reading out:

'I publish the banns of marriage between Shula Mary Archer, spinster of this parish and Mark Charles Timothy Hebden, bachelor of the parish of St. Bartholomew, Borchester. This is for the first time of asking. If any of you knows of any just cause or impediment why these two people may not be joined in holy matrimony, you are to declare it.'

Shula looked at Mark and gave a little smile. She saw her Mum squeeze her father's arm. Bunty, on the other hand, was looking straight ahead. Reg was looking up at the roof buttresses. It was going to happen then. It was real. In three months' time, in this church, she and Mark would be married — man and wife together. To have and to hold, to love and to cherish, from this day forward, forsaking all other — forsaking all other — as long as they both should live...

Back at Brookfield, where the Hebdens had been invited for lunch, her mum showed Bunty the pattern Shula had picked out for her wedding dress. The men had been banished variously to the garden (Reg), to mix a jug of Pimms (Mark) and to check on a possible case of mastitis (Phil).

'You've decided on cream, not white, then?' Bunty asked sweetly. Rather too sweetly, Shula thought.

'Yes, because I'd like the bridesmaids in cream, you see and it'd look funny if I was in white,' Shula replied. There were to be three bridesmaids: her sister, Elizabeth, Mark's sister, Joanna, and Jennifer's younger daughter, Kate.

'It's a very demure style,' Bunty continued, as if this too was a surprise, and she had expected Shula to wear something backless and slit to the thigh.

'Shula's always suited a high neck,' Jill volunteered, 'and of course at the end of September... I think long sleeves are safest.'

'Well, I'm sure it'll look very pretty,' Bunty conceded. 'But you're going to have to get a move on, aren't you, Shula, if you're making it yourself? All those little covered buttons down the back are more than an evening's work!'

'Mark and I have been rather busy with the house,' said Shula in her own defence. 'Now we've exchanged contracts we can start decorating. Once we've got the painting done, I can leave Mark doing the woodwork and start on the dress.'

'I'll make Elizabeth's and Joanna's dresses,' said Jill swiftly. 'Jennifer thinks she can cope with Kate's. You'll have to let me know when Joanna will be home to come for a fitting.'

'It's very good of you, Jill,' Bunty purred. 'I made a lot of things for Joanna when she was small but I'm afraid I'm rather out of the habit. And I'd be loathe to give up my golf during the summer ... '

'Drinks are ready!' Mark called from outside the door. 'Can I come in or are you still in a coven?'

'That's no way to talk about your mother-in-law!' Relieved to be released from Bunty's rigorous assessment, Shula stuffed the pattern and fabric samples into her mother's sewing bag. 'I'll go and look at the potatoes, Mum. See you!' And with that, she was able to escape.

But any respite was only temporary. The Royal Wedding was now just a month away and everyone seemed obsessed. Whenever Shula picked up a paper she was confronted with it: one evening she turned on the television hoping for a distraction and there were Prince Charles and his future bride being interviewed about what they wanted from the day.

In the end of course it was poor Neil who got the brunt of it. When he asked her an innocent question in the yard about wedding preparations which must have been pretty hard for him to ask in the first place Shula was appalled to find herself bursting into tears. Neil was both embarassed and understanding.

'It must be a lot of pressure,' he said.

'Oh, Neil — I don't know,' sniffed Shula. 'There's the house to get right, and the dresses to make, and the invitations to send, and I've got exams at the beginning of August and I've hardly done any revision —'

'Sounds like you could do with getting away for a bit,' suggested Neil.

'Getting away? I've got trouble just getting through the week! Anyway, I'm sorry, Neil. It's just me being silly.'

'No you're not.' Shula knew he couldn't make himself ask about Mark. 'Does — does your Mum know you're feeling like this?'

'Mum?' Shula shook her head. 'She's loving every minute. I couldn't let her see —'

'But you should. She wouldn't want you to be unhappy.'

'Oh I'm not unhappy, Neil,' said Shula quickly. 'Don't get me wrong. Things have just got a bit on top of me, that's all.'

'Oh. Right.'

Shula put away her hanky and tried out a smile.

'I'd better get to work. I've got to make an early start because at lunchtime Mark and I are going to Underwoods to decide on what crystal we want. Then this evening we're going to a warehouse in Felpersham to look at carpets.'

'Very nice.'

'I hope so. You'll have to come over and see the cottage when it's finished.'

'You'll have to have a housewarming,' Neil suggested.

'And ruin all our lovely new things? I don't think so!'

'No, maybe not. Well, I'll let you get on. Take care, Shula.'

'Thanks, Neil.'

Shula carried on, of course. They sorted out the crystal and the cutlery, and the colours for the bath towels. Mark added garden tools to the list: Shula put down a Meissen dinner service and a handwoven silk carpet.

'No one's going to buy us those!' Mark protested. 'It's not fair to ask.'

'I shouldn't think anyone's going to buy us a power saw, either, but you put that on,' retorted Shula.

'That's different,' replied Mark.

'Yes, it is, because you're not joking about it and I am about the carpet and the dinner service. Don't you see?'

Mark was silent. They were walking down to see Richard Adamson about their choice of hymns for the service. It was late July. The creamy elderflowers — the ones which had escaped picking for wine or cordial — were turning dry and brown in the hedgerow. Overhead swifts somersaulted in the sky. Shula shivered.

'They're moving south already, you know, the swifts. Uncle Tom says so.' Uncle Tom had been a gamekeeper all his life. He knew everything there was to know about the countryside.

'Mmm.'

'This is the very start of autumn really. The trees look tired, don't you think?'

'What? I don't know.' Mark was distracted. They were nearly at the vicarage. Shula waved to Sid who was watering the hanging baskets at The Bull.

'Seen anything of Robin lately?' asked Mark suddenly. If he was trying to get onto safer ground than the wedding present list he could have chosen a better subject. But maybe there wasn't any safe ground any more. They seemed to manage to bicker over the silliest little things: the paint roller, the buttonholes, the way Mark always made Shula's tea too weak ...

'No. He sent me a picture of Tiddles in his washing basket,' said Shula dully. When one of the Brookfield farm cats had produced a litter, Shula had persuaded Robin to have one of the kittens.

'Very enticing,' said Mark. 'I'm amazed that cat's still alive. I wouldn't have thought he was organised enough to feed it. I don't know what possessed you to give it to him.'

'Perhaps I thought Robin needed the company,' said Shula rather more sharply than she meant to, 'Since you made it perfectly clear you didn't like him spending time with me. Anyway, we're here now. Don't let Richard hear us arguing.'

'Who was arguing?' asked Mark as Shula, sighing, rang the bell.

But they were arguing, more and more. Suddenly nothing Mark did was right for Shula. Nothing Shula did was right for Mark. Her birthday was approaching. Shula didn't particularly want to celebrate it, beyond the usual supper at Brookfield with the family, but Mark wanted to treat her.

'We can't afford it!' she protested.

'You're determined to get that silk carpet somehow, aren't you?' he teased. Except it didn't seem like teasing, it seemed like a reminder of their disagreement about its place on the list.

Without telling her, Mark booked a table at Grey Gables anyway. Shula thought afterwards she might, just might, have got through it, had not Jack Woolley, trying to be kind, sent over a bottle of champagne 'for the happy couple'. Champagne always made her weepy but that was usually when she'd had a few glasses: now she dissolved in tears before it had even been opened. Mark took charge of the situation, calling for the bill and hustling her out before Jack could see.

Shula managed to contain her sobs until Mark had unlocked the car and they were both safely inside. Then she turned to him, buried her face in his neck and wept. Mark stroked her hair, pushing it away from her hot, red face, wiping her eyes with his hanky.

'It's all got too much for you. Look, no pressure. Let's call off the wedding, if that's what you want.

'No!' Shula's voice was panicky.

'I'm not saying we won't ever get married, but we haven't got to do it now. We can give ourselves another six months to get the house straight, calm you down — what's the rush?'

'I'm frightened, Mark.'

'Of course you are. It's scary, getting married. It's a big thing, like Richard's been telling us in all these preparation class things.'

But that wasn't what Shula meant. She didn't contradict him but what really frightened her was — if she didn't go through with it now, if she gave herself time to think, would she still want to do it in six months' time? So she fought it. She wiped her eyes, blew her nose loudly, took a deep breath. She told herself she was looking away from Mark because she didn't want him to see her looking such a sight, but it was easier to talk to the glove box than to look at his face when she said she did want to marry him in September — she wanted it more than anything. He pulled her towards him and kissed her gently.

'That's what I want too,' he said. And drove her home.

That night, Shula lay awake for a long time. What was the matter with her? Mark was everything she had ever wanted. She loved the feel of his body, his long eyelashes, the far away look in his eyes when he made love to her. She loved the fact that he was so dedicated to his work, that he was good at it, that she could respect him for it. She tried to think back to all the good times they'd had, the hot air balloon, that New Year's Eve when he'd proposed, her delight that Mark had won his case with the hunt saboteurs. She tried picturing Mark in his gown at court, she pictured him in his office with the picture of her in its silver frame, or at home mowing the lawn for his father. She could see the two of them at things they had done in the past: but what she could not picture any more was waking up with Mark on every morning of her future, having breakfast with him, having supper with him, going to bed with him. In those pictures he was always insubstantial, faceless. But she knew that the thought of not being with him — and him being with someone else — was dreadful too.

The worst thing was not being able to tell anyone how she felt. Mark was so understanding she could have screamed. She never seemed to have long enough with Caroline to talk about anything serious and anyway, she feared she had allowed to happen what she had sworn she would not: she had let herself drift away from Caroline and become wrapped up in Mark, in being a couple.

Closing her eyes to how she was feeling they resolutely went on with painting the cottage. Caroline came round and approved of their colour scheme: the soft blue she had imagined in the bedroom, fawn for what would be Mark's study and magnolia everywhere else. They told her they hadn't mastered wallpaper yet but agreed that would come in time — by the time of their silver wedding perhaps. Shula didn't meet Mark's eyes. How long can this go on? Shula screamed in her head. And all the time the twenty-sixth of September was getting closer.

The end when it came was sudden and unexpected. Shula was bashing in a nail to put up a picture over the fireplace in the little sitting room. Mark had been painting the bathroom and came downstairs to wash his brushes.

'Can I do that for you?'

He came and stood behind her, watching her at work. Shula tensed immediately.

'No thanks, I can manage.'

'Try and hit it square.'

I'll hit you in a minute, she thought.

'I am!'

'Shula, let me do it.'

He was smiling. Kindly if you like — or patronising, superior.

'I was doing fine till you came along! You're putting me off!'

'Oh, so it's my fault. Well if you want your picture to fall down within a week—'

'I don't care about the blasted picture! I'm just sick and tired of having to do everything the Mark Hebden way! It's got to be straight, it's got to be perfect, put those brushes in the turps, Shula, try not to get paint on the glass — have you ever listened to yourself? And you're so impatient! If it isn't right the first time —'

'Impatient? Me?' Mark had heard enough.

'Yes. You are.'

'I don't believe you. I've been so patient with you over the last few weeks — I've bent over backwards to understand what you've been going through, being sympathetic — haven't I?'

'Yes.' Shula could not deny it.

'I've stood by like a spaniel while you dithered over something that affects my future as well as yours, and you jump down my throat because I offer to help you bang a nail in straight. I don't think you understand what you're saying half the time.'

'I'm sorry.' And she was.

But he wasn't listening. All the accumulated injustice was pouring out.

'What do you want from me, Shula? Well? Do you know?'

She couldn't answer his questions. Things had been said now which couldn't be unsaid. Which showed them just how far apart they were.

'It's not going to work, is it?' said Shula finally, her voice seeming to come from miles away.

'I don't know.' Mark had turned away from her. He was staring out into the garden which was still a thicket of knee high weeds, picking spots of paint off the French windows. It had taken her ages to paint all the wood. Two doors, each with eighteen individual panes... 'It's not for lack of wanting it to.'

Shula's throat hurt from trying not to cry.

'I know,' she said quietly. 'I've tried. And I do love you.'

Mark swallowed hard.

'I really didn't think it would ever come to this.'

'Look at me,' Shula begged. 'Please Mark!'

'Why?' He was as remote and distant as he could possibly be.

'Please! I can't bear it ... '

'Just leave me —' Then he relented. 'Oh, come here.'

'Hold me, please.' She reached for him. 'Just hold me.'

He put his arms round her. Their hurt was a physical pain.

'I'm sorry, Mark,' she said. 'I'm so, so sorry.'

Even then it wasn't over. They had to tell her parents, they had to tell his parents.

'Shula, please, don't keep going on about the money!'

'But Dad, even if the marquee people let you cancel, there's the dresses all made, and Mum's outfit, and the cake's made —'

'Shula, I couldn't care less! All I care about is that you're happy.'

'Oh, Dad, don't be nice to me. Everyone's been so nice to me and I don't deserve it!'

'Well I'm going to be nice to you whether you like it or not.' Phil sat down by his daughter on the sagging chintz-covered sofa and hugged her close. 'You're very precious to me and your Mum. You've done a very brave thing — of course you deserve it.'

'But have I done the right thing Dad? That's all I want to know?'

'You won't know that now, Shula, you can't. It'll take years before you know. But if you and Mark had doubts you've done the right thing for now. And that's about as far as you should be looking.'

'You're postponing the wedding?' Bunty pushed her glasses up her nose and laid aside the crossword she had been doing. Reg, as usual, stared awkwardly out of the window. All this emotion.

Mark put down his tea cup, one of the best teacups with the gold rim which Bunty always got out when Shula came round.

'No, Mother, we're cancelling the wedding. We don't think we should go ahead with it.'

Shula looked at the floor. Bunty wouldn't be that sorry, she knew. She had never thought she was good enough for her precious Mark.

'Well, I must say I'm surprised, Mark — and very sorry. Are you both absolutely sure?'

'Absolutely. Aren't we, Shula?'

Shula nodded mutely.

'But — the wedding's barely six weeks away — all the arrangements have been made.'

'I hardly think that matters, Mum, if Shula and I don't want to go through with it.'

At least, thought Shula, I'll never have to pretend to like her awful flower arrangements again.

November
——1983——

'Nigel, wouldn't you be more comfortable if you took your head off?' Jill sounded concerned.

'Uh?'

'Take your head off, Nigel.' Shula pointed at her own head to explain.

There was a short pause, then a nod, then a great amount of anguished writhing before Nigel finally wrenched off the head of his gorilla costume to expose his own face poking pinkly out of a furry ruff. He let out a deep breath.

'I'm glad you said that. It's jolly hot in there.'

'Have a drink, dear. Shula, get Nigel a glass of orange juice.'

As Shula went to the fridge, her progress somewhat impeded by the curly-toed slippers and rustling silk pantaloons of her harem girl costume. Nigel sat down with difficulty on one of the Windsor chairs and rested his chin on his paw. They were going to a fancy dress ball organised by the League of Friends of Borchester General.

'You know Mum's got a point,' Shula observed, returning with his glass. 'Aren't you going to have a hard time eating and drinking this evening?'

'Ah, well.' Nigel rummaged in his capacious fur belly and produced a curly red plastic straw. 'I've bought myself this for the occasion. Look.' He demonstrated. 'It slots in nicely between the canines.'

'So it does,' said Jill, secretly impressed at his foresight.

'Not that I'm going to drink terribly much anyway,' Nigel added hastily, for her benefit.

Jill smiled indulgently. Nigel's reputation was not as bad as his father's — Phil maintained Gerald Pargetter was the last man in the county to suffer from gout — but Jill somehow doubted that Nigel would be quaffing orange juice all evening. Still, at least he made Shula laugh — and he made *her* laugh as well, as she told Phil when Nigel and Shula had roared off into the night, looking forward to stopping for petrol on the way to Borchester and scaring the attendant.

Phil laid aside his *Farmers Weekly* where he had been enjoying a rather thought-provoking article about potato storage.

'Jill, I know what you're going to say — that it's nice to see Shula getting out and about again. I know what she went through with Mark, and she's had a miserable couple of years. Bumping into Mark all the time with his latest girlfriend, and now he's got this new fiancée ... But really — Nigel Pargetter, of all people.'

'I'm sorry, Phil, but he seems like a very nice boy.'

'Boy being the operative word. He's younger than Shula, isn't he?'

'Only a year or so, not that it matters. I just want her to have some fun, Phil. She's been so sad lately. Depressed. She doesn't seem young any more.'

Phil picked up his reading glasses, a sure sign that conversation was closed.

'Nigel Pargetter's the right choice then. He must have a mental age of about ten. What's he doing with himself these days, anyway?'

Phil stopped talking, his glasses suspended in mid-air over the bridge of his nose.

'Well?'

Jill took a deep breath.

'He sells swimming pools,' she said.

'Swimming pools?' Phil repeated as if this was a totally alien concept.

'They're very popular, apparently. I mean, Brian and Jennifer have got one, haven't they?'

'I hope you haven't told him we'd be interested!'

'Of course not, Phil. The poor boy's not having much luck at the moment, though.'

'It's hardly the time of year to think about swimming, is it?'

Outside the November rain pattered skittishly against the windows.

'It's always the time of year to think about swimming, Phil.'

Even to herself, Jill sounded as if she was parroting something Nigel had been taught on his salesmanship course. Phil's eyebrows went up accordingly. Still the glasses hovered, though they had been lowered to Phil's lap again now.

'There might be work to be done,' Jill improvised. 'Holes to be dug, liners to be put in — I don't know. Then it'll all be ready for spring.'

Phil sniffed. The glasses were raised again, and this time settled firmly on his nose. He eased himself in his chair and picked up his magazine.

'Swimming pools. In this country. He'll be selling ice cream next.'

Jill put down her knitting. She was making a cardigan for her great niece Helen's Sindy doll and it really was very fiddly. She could do with a break and she clearly wasn't going to get anywhere with Phil tonight.

'I expect you'd like a cup of coffee, would you, dear?' she asked. 'With a couple of gingernuts?'

Shula hadn't thought for a moment that Mark would be there — fancy dress wasn't his sort of thing at all. Perhaps his fiancée, Sarah, had persuaded him. Whatever the reason, he looked very dashing. They both did. Sarah was in one of those big dresses with a laced bodice which pushed her breasts into a proper cleavage. She had a white wig and a fan and a beauty spot painted on her cheek. Mark told Shula, without a hint of irony, that she had come as the Wicked Lady.

'And you're Dick Turpin, I presume?' Shula asked, trying to hold her tummy in. Whatever had possessed her to expose so much flesh?

'More a sort of all-purpose highwayman, I think,' smiled Mark. 'The costumes aren't bad though, are they? We hired them from Borchester Little Theatre.'

Shula nodded and smiled. If she'd known Mark was going to be there she might have made a bit more effort than just blobbing a tub of glitter onto an old bikini top and borrowing some harem pants which Caroline's brother had brought back from his holiday in Turkey.

'Oh, Nigel, what have you been doing?' She was grateful when Nigel joined them, his fur spattered with luminous spray string.

'It was Tim Beecham that did it,' he complained, removing his head and plucking at his chest. 'I was going to save it till later. He always has that effect on me.'

'Well, you sit here and pick your fur in peace,' said Mark. 'I'm going to dance with Shula.'

She followed him onto the dance floor: Sarah, he said, was having to dance with her uncle. It was a four-piece band — a drummer, a bass guitarist and a saxophonist fronted by a woman in a leopard-print dress who played keyboards and, if you were exceptionally unlucky, sang. Fortunately she was giving her vocal chords a rest. They were playing Moon River. It was that sort of band.

'So, how long have you been going out with Pargetter?' Mark asked casually as they swayed.

'Hmm? Oh, not long,' said Shula. There was a pause as she listened to the music.

'You've gone quiet,' said Mark.

'No, I haven't.'

'You're thinking. I can tell. You always go quiet when you're thinking.'

Shula wondered whether to tell him. Oh, what the hell. It wasn't as if it was going to change anything.

'It's just — well, this tune, I suppose.'

'Ah.'

'Silly, isn't it?' she said brightly.

'No.' Mark moved his hands at her waist and she could feel his fingers in contact with her bare flesh. Stop it, Shula, she thought but she said it anyway.

'D'you remember that night we went over to Edgeley and there was that old boy in the pub —'

Would he remember she wondered?

'With a mouth organ.'

'That's right.'

He remembered.

'And he couldn't get it right for love or money,' said Mark.

'We were all singing it to him.'

'And then on the way home...'

Mark didn't need to finish.

'Yes.'

They both remembered.

When the song finished she didn't think they should dance any more. Mark gave a little wave as he went back to join Sarah and her parents and her uncle and aunt and their friends. Shula waved back. Now she knew where they were sitting it was going to be really hard not to keep looking over there all evening. Nigel was dancing with Pat which meant, of all people, she'd have to go and talk to Tony.

'Honestly, Shula, your boyfriend ought to be locked up!'

Tony was not amused. With his pigeon chest and skinny legs he hadn't ever been a convincing Superman. Now that Nigel had managed to spray him with champagne and his crêpe paper emblem had disintegrated and the dye from his T-shirt was running down his arms, he looked as though he had been in contact with a family-sized lump of Kryptonite. Nigel was still cavorting on the dance floor with Pat over his shoulder. She was dressed as Bo Peep and was pretending to thump him with her crook — in fact, Jethro's crook, which Shula had spray-painted silver and had wound around with ribbons. On Monday she'd have to explain what had happened to it but, for tonight, oblivion seemed the best way. She emptied her glass and refilled it from a nearby bottle.

'That's the way to treat them, Tony,' she said. 'Bundle them over your shoulder and away you go.'

'He's an oaf. A degenerate oaf.'

'Just because nobody's bundled you over their shoulder — champagne?'

Unusually, Tony ignored the offer.

'I don't know what's got into you, I really don't. There's Mark, a nice reliable, responsible sort of bloke —'

Shula turned away, only partly alerted by a shriek from Pat

whom Nigel was lowering to the floor.

'Shula, do something with him before we all get thrown out,' Pat pleaded, laughing.

'Come on, Nigel,' said Shula. Oblivion, remember? 'Let's show these boring old farmers how it's done.'

It was dawn — well, it was struggling to be dawn — a dull, November dawn. And cold. But Nigel wouldn't be put off.

'There are always bluebells in these woods,' he declared, dragging Shula in her curly slippers through brittle bracken which caught at her filmy trousers.

'Not in November,' said Shula wearily. It was five to six. 'Can we go home now, please?'

'I promised that I would deliver you over your doorstep at dawn with your arms full of flowers and I never break a promise,' said Nigel. 'Never.'

'I really don't mind,' said Shula. She was wearing Nigel's Barbour but underneath her skin was a mottled purple and her fingernails had gone blue. 'I'm freezing. I'd really rather you took me home.'

'Really? Oh, all right,' conceded Nigel. He wrapped her in his big furry arms and cuddled her. 'Did you enjoy yourself tonight? Last night?'

'Very much,' said Shula warmly. He was so sweet.

'I thought...' Nigel hesitated. 'I thought I saw the odd quavery look in Mark Hebden's direction.'

Shula looked into his honest eyes.

'I didn't know you were watching.'

'Mark wouldn't have carried you over the doorstep with your arms full of bluebells,' said Nigel simply.

Shula gave a little laugh.

'No,' she said. 'He wouldn't.'

Then Nigel drove her home.

'So you see Mr Archer, they really do come in all shapes and sizes. We can meet your every requirement.'

Phil rubbed his eyes wearily. Nigel had arrived for supper at about six thirty. It was now nearly ten o'clock. He had missed an excellent early music concert on Radio Three, and the nine o'clock news, or more specifically, the weather forecast, and still the boy did not seem able to interpret his polite indifference as a 'get lost'. If he'd had his way it would have been impolite indifference, but Jill and Shula had made it very clear that this was not an option.

'Nigel doesn't really expect you to buy a pool, Dad,' Shula hissed later when he escaped for five minutes on the pretext of having to phone Brian about the beet at Home Farm. 'But please let him carry on. He's got to try out his sales patter on someone.'

'Why me?'

'Because. Look, if he can't send Head Office some "Calls made" sheets soon, they'll make him go back to sales school and that ghastly Jerry will tease him about what a comedown it is for a virtual member of the aristocracy to be rubbing shoulders with people from comprehensives —'

'That's not teasing, it's the truth,' said Phil. 'Can't he get a proper job?'

'Selling is a proper job, Dad. It takes a lot of skill.'

'Skill that Nigel evidently hasn't got — oh no.'

'Mr Archer, there you are! I found it! This is what I wanted to show you. Look, the Kaliph. Isn't it stunning?'

Nigel came into the kitchen brandishing a glossy brochure in which a swimming pool, its improbable azure hue rivalling an even more improbably azure sky, was being marvelled at by a father armed with barbecue tongs whilst mother and armbanded children frolicked within.

'It's this sort of Moorish shape, you see — fun, don't you think? Shula could dress up in that stunning harem costume again and sort of undulate out from the house with glasses of mint tea. Mr Archer?'

The door to the farm office slammed as Phil, speechless, left the room.

'He's — just got to make a phone call, Nigel. Hey, have you shown Mum the Pompadour? Come and tell her about it. You're really good on that bit where you say "let them eat crisps" —'

'—Because the unique water filtration mechanism will remove

anything and everything from the water.' Nigel finished the sentence, then went on. 'Oh, Shulie, thanks. You've no idea how much this is helping me.'

Shula kissed him affectionately on the lips. Nigel put his arms round her and gave her a squeeze.

'You are wonderful. Have I told you that today?'

'Several times.'

Nigel kissed her again. He was nothing if not good for her. Not only did he not mind when she pinched his chips but, unlike her brothers, he never made the unkind connection between this act and the flabby bits which she knew were there, especially in the harem costume. If anything, Nigel seemed to find her flabby bits rather exciting, if the way he had grabbed at them enthusiastically at the Fancy Dress ball was anything to go by. True, this might not have any sexual or even romantic meaning, because, especially after a few drinks, he was rather like a not-very-housetrained puppy, or a small child who'd had too many sweets and been allowed to stay up late but it was nice to feel that someone was interested in her again. Things had been so dismal after Mark. Two years' worth of dismal.

'Now then Nigel, put my daughter down.' Jill approached with a loaded tray.

'I'm sorry, Mrs Archer. She's just so gorgeous.'

Jill laughed her infectious throaty laugh. This was just what Shula needed. 'Another cup of tea, Nigel?'

'Oh, yes please, Mrs Archer. Let me help you. Will your father be long, Shula? If he doesn't like the Kaliph, perhaps he'd be interested in the Atlantic — though it is rather big ... '

In the office, listening whilst doodling a gibbet with a dangling figure on his blotter, Phil heaved a heavy sigh.

Shula stretched luxuriously in the bathwater. It had been raining when she left the office — cold, December rain — and raining even harder when she got home. She had got drenched just running from the car. Still — another day closer to Christmas which, since Nigel, she was actually looking forward to. Another day at the office over, and Mr Rodway had actually praised her work on a rather complicated catalogue for a dispersal sale at Waterley Cross. She stretched her toes and twizzled the hot tap, a trick she was rather proud of, enjoying the growing warmth of the water. She was going out with Nigel later. They'd probably go to Nelson's wine bar, have a laugh and a few drinks, then he'd bring her safely home, kiss her in the car with his usual eager ardour, then walk her to the door and kiss her rather more chastely in case Phil was watching — or worse still, listening. She knew her father didn't approve, but let's face it, which of her boyfriends had he liked? (Don't answer that, she thought to herself). All right, maybe Nigel was a bit young sometimes, but at least he knew how to enjoy himself. Unlike — Ouch! That water was definitely too hot now. Gingerly Shula negotiated the flow to turn off the tap and eased her shoulders under the water level. Steam rose from the surface. Shula took her hands out of the water and examined them. No nail polish. No rings. Just rather red, and hot.

She could have had a ring. She could have been Mrs Mark Hebden for over two years now. Her wedding band would have lost that new shininess. It would probably be scratched where the opal engagement ring rested against it. Would they still be in the house in Penny Hassett or would they have outgrown it? She might have got tired of tripping over his cricket gear in the bedroom, or his legal boxes in the hall. There'd be splashes up the back of the sink and down the side of the cooker. That bit of thin carpet they were going to put down in the bathroom would be worn through, probably. Mark lived there on his own now. But not for long. He was going to marry Sarah Locke in the summer. Blonde-haired, suntanned, rich, young, clever Sarah Locke — who just happened to be the daughter of the senior partner at Locke and Martin's. How convenient. How very like Mark to assure every aspect of his future in one sensible move. Pretty young wife, safe old law firm, partnership prospects. Bunty must think she'd died and gone to heaven. Shula reached for her bath mitt and began to scrub her arms vigorously.

Of course it was always the way things happened. No sooner had she decided that she fancied Mark again, after the terrible time when he was living with that ghastly Jackie Woodstock who sort of sneered every time she saw Shula in the wine bar, than he'd asked her out — come into Rodway's specially and asked her to go for a drink. Shula had tried to be cool about it, telling herself in Underwoods next day that she needed a silk shirt anyway, of course she wasn't buying it just to go to The Griffin's Head with Mark — but as soon as she got to the pub, he told her he'd got something to tell her. What he told her was that he was engaged to Sarah Locke. Trust Mark to do the decent thing. He wouldn't let her hear from someone else. But it wasn't really the decent thing. The decent thing would have been to say he still wanted to marry her. But he hadn't. He didn't. So now, there was Nigel.

In her frenzy of punishing scrubbing, Shula hadn't heard the phone. Her mother tapped on the bathroom door.

'Darling, that was Nigel. He says he's got some good news and he's taking you to Grey Gables to celebrate with a few others. Oh, and can you wear your red dress. The short one.'

'Da da da da da *da*-da, let's all do the conga, da da da da, da da da *da*...'

Shula tried desperately to hang onto Nigel's jacket as he wove in and out of the furniture in the Grey Gables bar, a task not made any easier by the fact that she had to keep taking one hand away to remove Tim Beecham's paw which roved round the front from her waist and when removed from there, found its way up her skirt. Behind Tim came half of Borchester Young Conservatives, in various states of drunkenness and undress, all following Nigel who, as the leader, had seized the stag's head from the wall and was holding it aloft, its antlers grazing the chandeliers.

'OK, Nigel! *Nige*, that's enough!' called a voice from the back. 'Polly's fallen over — uh-oh, there goes a table.'

Nigel stopped abruptly, causing Shula to cannon into the back of him, and Tim into her, in Tim's case rather more enthusiastically than was strictly necessary. Nigel lowered his arms and hugged the stag's head to his chest as Shula turned and surveyed the carnage. The tables were strewn with empty glasses and bottles. There were peanuts and crisps all over the floor following a boisterous food fight between the 'wets' and the 'dries'. Polly, who admittedly had cracked her elbow rather nastily as she fell, was being given the kiss of life by the Membership Secretary, a hirsute individual called Lucian.

'Oh Nigel,' whispered Shula in awe. 'Shall we do it again?'

'Yes!' Tim took up the cry but Nigel shook his head.

'Only if someone else carries this thing, my arms are nearly dropping off —'

'What on earth's going on?' asked a voice from the doorway, appalled.

'Caroline! Come and join us!' Tim detached himself from Shula and crunched across the carpet to put his arms round the totally bemused Caroline, who was very much on duty. 'Come and do the conga with me. Or the rumba? Or the lambada?'

'No! Where's the barman? What are you doing here — it's after hours!'

'Oh, we're not drinking, he wouldn't serve us any more,' Shula put in.

'I can see why — and what's happened to the blackboard? *Old* game pie? Chocolate *mouse?*'

'Old game pie!' chortled Tim. 'I didn't see that one! Was that you, Shula?'

Shula could see that Caroline was not impressed and that Tim trying to nuzzle her neck was not helping the situation. Swiftly distracting his attention with a couple of party poppers from Nigel's pocket, and the promise that if he was good, she'd give him a kiss under the mistletoe before they went home, she drew Caroline on one side. But Caroline had found something else to worry about.

'Shula, this is Mr Woolley's Chrysanthemum Society Challenge Cup, why's it all sticky inside?'

'Ah well — we were making a sort of punch, you see and we needed —'

'A receptacle,' Nigel chimed in. 'Mr Woolley won't mind.'

'Oh, won't he?' said Caroline crisply. 'I don't suppose you're the one who's going to have to explain the mess to him. Or to the cleaning staff, come to that.'

'Oh, no, you don't understand. Me and Mr Woolley, we're on great terms. He's going to buy a swimming pool off me. Hence the celebration.'

'Nigel, I'd be surprised if Mr Woolley ever gives you the time of day after the mess you've made in here tonight — what are you doing?

Nigel was concentrating hard, his arm round Caroline.

'Got it!'

'Nigel!' Caroline pulled herself sharply out of Nigel's grip.

Somehow Shula sensed Nigel had chosen the wrong moment for his party trick of undoing girls' bras through their clothes. She didn't think it actually influenced anything Caroline said to Jack Woolley — they helped her clear up and she promised not to say a thing — but sadly, next day, it appeared that Nigel had got hold of the wrong end of the stick. Jack didn't in fact want a pool at all. The celebration had been for nothing. The only good thing that came out of it was that Polly paid her up her Y.C.'s membership and rapidly got engaged to Lucian's brother Tarquin. But that was no consolation to Nigel.

Christmas came and went. All through January and February Nigel didn't sell a single pool. Shula tried to cheer him up. She knitted him mice warmers for his racing mice in the Pargetter colours. They had fun squeezing into the child-sized beds in the old nursery at Lower Loxley, Nigel's home, and reading Paddington bear books. Nigel took her to dinner at the Connaught to celebrate another nearly-sale and she brought the next day's newspapers back to Brookfield with her at four in the morning, which puzzled Phil at breakfast. But that sale fell through as well. By March, Nigel was desperate. One Saturday, as they waited for the hounds to pick up a scent near Lyttleton Covert, Nigel confessed that if he didn't sell a pool soon, he'd get the sack.

'Then my father will throw me out for good and I'll spend the rest of my life sleeping on Tim Beecham's floor in that God-awful flat of his in Borchester. There ought to be a skull and crossbones on the door.'

'Oh, Nigel.' Shula took a sip from his proferred hip flask and passed it back. Nigel took a long swig, then another. 'I hate to see you like this. And you must never go to Tim Beecham's. There's always a bed for you at Brookfield.'

'Ah, but would it be yours, Shula?' Nigel was in a very melancholy mood. Luckily, before Shula could reply, the horn sounded and they were off.

Nigel seemed a little better, Shula thought, for a good gallop. The fox had gone to ground but they'd had a good chase and as they sat by the fire at Brookfield, resting their frozen feet on the fender and eating scrambled eggs, she dared to suggest tentatively that he approach Jack Woolley again.

'Let's face it, he's the only person round here with enough money and you're right, Grey Gables is crying out for a swimming pool.'

Nigel popped a square of buttery toast into his mouth and chewed thoughtfully.

'You're right. I'm right. I'm going to tell him he needs two. An outdoor and an indoor one. You watch me. I'm going for Salesman of the Month from a standing start.'

Maybe all the practice with Phil and Jill had improved Nigel's technique, maybe he was heartened by his sale of a kiddies' paddling pool masquerading as a fishpond to Derek Fletcher at 11, Glebelands — but by April, Nigel was actually looking as if he might achieve his target sales for the first month ever. Shula breathed a sigh of relief and insisted, superstitiously, that because the last two celebrations of sales he had planned had gone horribly wrong, this time she would treat him and pay for his ticket to the Hunt ball. Even Phil was disposed to smile on Nigel — but only briefly. Sadly the incident after the ball, when Nigel ('Of course he was looking for the bathroom, Dad, what do you think I am?') mistakenly tried to get into bed with Phil and Jill, most unluckily on Phil's side, rather soured relations for a while.

'I shouldn't worry about it,' Shula reassured Nigel, as he tried for the umpteenth time to work out his commission on Jack's pool with the aid of David's calculator. 'Dad's only really happy when he can disapprove of my boyfriends. That's why it would never have worked with Mark. They got on far too well.'

But a little hollow voice inside her told her she was lying. She liked Nigel a lot, of course she did, he was the best fun you could have without taking your clothes off — although there was quite a lot of that, as well, on their more drunken evenings — especially if Tim Beecham was around. But, well, he wasn't all that grown up. When she had had a grown up — a very grown up — relationship with Mark, she hadn't felt ready for it. Now, perhaps, she was. Or had Mark become more attractive since Sarah was on the scene? Was she — and this was really hard to admit — using Nigel to make Mark jealous? If so, it wasn't working. Only that day Mark had phoned her at Rodway's to ask her to sell the cottage in Penny Hassett. He'd been very understanding, of course.

'I mean, if you don't want to do the measuring up, is there anyone else you can send? Or perhaps you don't want to handle the sale at all.'

Shula had laughed, a false, squeaky laugh, and her voice didn't sound like hers at all when she replied.

'Mark, don't be silly. I can be professional about this.'

'Good. When would you like to come round then?'

When the appointment was fixed she put the phone down very carefully as if it, or she, would break. So the cottage she and Mark had been going to live in wasn't good enough for rich, young, clever, blonde, suntanned Sarah Locke. She wanted a smart new house on a Georgian-style estate in Borchester, no doubt, with 2.4 garages for their 2.4 cars and, later, the buggies and bicycles of their 2.4 children. Shula felt tears sting her eyes and she looked down fiercely at her desk, blinking. On her pad she had written: '16.5.84. 7 p.m. Measure up our cottage.'

When the evening came, it was just as ghastly as she expected. She knew exactly which were Sarah's touches to the kitchen — the clutter of spice jars and — horrors — a mug tree on the worksurface, neither of which Mark would ever have introduced by himself because he liked all the kitchen surfaces kept clear. Shula wondered whether, in time, she'd have been able to influence him and make him ease up as Sarah obviously had. It hurt her that he had done for Sarah what he wouldn't do for her. She could remember having an argument — one of their last, bitter, silly arguments, about a parsley pig which she had wanted on the window ledge. Mark said it made it impossible to open the window. Shula said she didn't mind moving it every time, and as she was the one who did most of the cooking, and she was the one who wanted the parsley, she would take responsibility for it. 'And what about when I want to open the window?' Mark had said. 'Then I have to move the blasted thing, or am I supposed to call you from upstairs to do it?' Shula had given up, because by then she was giving up very easily but she remembered it now and it rankled.

In the bathroom she didn't like the sight of Sarah's toothbrush twinned with Mark's, or her camomile shampoo — well she doesn't *look* a natural blonde, thought Shula meanly — still less did she like the sight of Sarah's dressing gown hanging silkily on the back of the bedroom door.

Mark followed her round solemnly.

'It wasn't really a good idea for you to do it, was it?' he said gently, when she'd snapped her tape measure back in its case and put her folder away. 'I'm sorry.'

'It's not your fault,' said Shula brightly. 'I could have sent some-one else.'

She hadn't realised how the details of the life Mark now shared with someone else would hurt her. It was a big step forward, realis-ing that it wasn't just the big things that hurt. The little ones did as well. Ridiculous, though. Whoever heard of being hurt by a mug tree. Unless it fell on your head.

'Coffee?' Mark asked.'Or are you seeing Nigel?'

Touché, thought Shula. She did of course, have Nigel. She didn't know it, at the time, but he told her later he'd driven over to Penny Hassett because he couldn't stand the thought of Shula seeing Mark that evening. He'd hidden in the bushes outside the cottage for what seemed like hours till Caroline, who was taking her old English sheepdog Charlie for a walk, had found him and dragged him off to The Griffin's Head for a drink.

'Coffee would be nice,' she said to Mark. She leaned against the sink and watched him make it, his dark head bent over the mugs. One was new, and one she remembered, the one with Mark's birth sign, Pisces, on it. His hair was shorter now, and it suited him. She wondered if she could tell him so without it coming out wrong. This was dreadful. Why had she thought she could do it? She hadn't spent this much time alone with Mark since they were doing up the house together. It had been a really stupid idea. She should have sent someone else. She just had to concentrate on getting out of there without crying.

She managed it, but only just. And in bed that night she cried and cried, at first noiseless tears which slid out of the corners of her eyes, then great tearing sobs into her pillow. Wouldn't it ever stop hurting?

July

——1984——

Shula turned from the filing cabinet, wearing the falsest of smiles. In her hand she held the particulars of No 10, Foster's Row, Orchard Lane, Penny Hassett. The couple waited expectantly. They were young, early twenties perhaps. She was wearing an engagement ring and an eager smile. He was wearing a look of scarcely-contained impatience. They were the perfect purchasers. They had a mortgage facility sorted out, they were first time buyers so there would be no chain. What was the matter with her? Someone was going to buy the cottage and it might as well be them — at least they looked as if they might like period features and a pine kitchen. If she let them go who knew who might come along? People who'd spill coffee on the carpet and flush cigarette ends down the loo? This was ridiculous. It was one thing having an opinion about prospective purchasers when the house was yours, but it wasn't hers. It was Mark's. It was absolutely nothing to do with her who bought it — except it was. She and Mark had chosen that house. To Shula, it remained theirs until it was sold.

Gathering herself together, because increasingly these days, she expected to look down and find herself in several small pieces on the carpet, she held out the photocopied sheets.

'It's really very good value for the price,' she heard herself saying. 'The present owners — owner — has had a lot of work done. New roof and everything. Anyway if you want to go and view it, Mark's — the — er — vendor's number's on the back. He's in most evenings — except when there's cricket nets, that's Wednesday I think. Oh, and which night's the Round Table — is it still a Thursday?'

She knew she was babbling. She saw them exchange glances,

wondering, probably, how much detail Rodway and Watson required of their clients. Did vendors have to fill in a questionnaire about their hobbies?

Smiling a thank you, they left. Shula knew they'd go straight over to the Copper Kettle and mutter about how odd she'd seemed, before driving over to Penny Hassett to look at the house from the outside, wondering how much under the asking price they could offer if they liked it. She would have done the same herself.

The phone made her jump and she picked it up nervily after only one ring.

'Rodway and Watson.'

'Shula? Are you all right?' It was Nigel.

'Fine.'

'You don't sound very fine. In fact you sound like a person who needs cheering up. There's a dance tonight at the County Hotel. Can you make it?'

Shula knew instantly that she didn't want to go. She was tired, she had nothing to wear, and she didn't feel like talking to people. She also remembered after Nigel had persuaded her and she'd put the phone down that Caroline was coming back from a conference in London on the late train and she'd said she'd meet her at Hollerton Junction. She rang Nigel back to tell him, thinking she had the perfect excuse, but he wouldn't be deflected. They'd both go and meet Caroline, he said. They'd probably have had enough of Tim Beecham's 'Knock Knock' jokes by half ten, anyway. (Half seven, more likely, thought Shula). And so she went. And really, looking back, it changed everything.

'Mark! Oh, Mark!'

Shula ran into the room and flung her arms round his neck. Gently he disentangled himself and indicated to the police constable that they should be left alone. The policewoman withdrew, closing the flimsy door, and left Mark and Shula alone in the interview room.

'Oh, Mark, I'm so glad you're here.' Her voice wobbled in relief.

Mark led her over to the table and pulled out a chair.

'Sit down,' he said kindly.

Shula obeyed. She'd only been inside Borchester Police station once before, when she was about fifteen, to hand in a purse she'd found in the street. She'd never imagined she might spend time in one of their cells, with Nigel in the one next door, banging about and making a fuss.

Mark sat down on the other side of the table and took a ruled notebook out of his case. He unscrewed the top of his fountain pen, before writing the date and time at the top of the page, along with her name. Shula slumped back in her chair. She felt ridiculous in these surroundings in her evening dress. She didn't even have a coat to put round her shoulders. Mark was in a jacket and tie even though it was nearly midnight and she must have got him out of bed. A bit of his hair was sticking up at the back where he'd combed it too quickly. Shula wondered if Sarah had been with him, if he'd left her sleeping, her golden head on her equally golden arm, up in the brass bed in the blue bedroom at Penny Hassett.

'Right, then. Tell me all about it,' he said calmly.

He was obviously going to treat it as a case like any other. Like she had stupidly thought she could treat the sale of the house. How was it that men could be so much more detatched? He tapped his pen on his pad in a gesture she suddenly remembered with frightening intensity. How many times had she seen him do that over lists of stuff from the supermarket or the builders' merchants? She'd found it irritating then. Now it seemed measured, thoughtful, patient. Mark was patient. She'd accused him of being impatient when they broke up. She'd known at the time she was being unfair. Stumblingly, she started to tell him.

'Well, we'd been to a dance at the County Hotel — me and Nigel. When we came out Nigel couldn't find his car. I didn't know where it was parked because David had dropped me off. We looked round the Market Square for a bit —'

'Hang on, hang on. OK, you didn't know where it was parked but are you telling me Nigel didn't either?'

'Well, he did, of course, but he couldn't remember,' Shula explained as she leaned closer to Mark across the table.

'I see. Any particular reason why he couldn't remember?'

'Well he — he'd forgotten.'

'Nothing to do with the amnesiac quality of rather too much to drink, I suppose?' Mark's voice sounded sarcastic.

'Mark, whose side are you on?' She knew he didn't like Nigel. She knew it had been a stupid thing to do. She didn't need him making her feel small. Mark met her eyes. He was judging her and as usual she was being found wanting. She subsided.

'OK, he had had quite a bit. Which is why I said I should drive.' Shula moved back in her chair.

'But you hadn't found his car at this point?'

'No. But I would when we did.'

'Right. Good. So?'

'Well, after we'd looked for a bit, Nigel decided Tim Beecham must have taken his car for a joke, because Tim had borrowed it before Christmas and still had the spare set of keys.'

'Ye—es.' Mark sounded cautious but incredulous.

'So Nigel saw one parked on the Market Square which he thought was Tim's — and the keys were in the ignition.'

'So he took that as an invitation to drive it away.' Mark looked Shula straight in the eyes.

'Well that's what made him sure Tim had taken his — and left his own for us. All ready and waiting.'

'I see.' Mark wrote something down in his notebook.

Shula could tell Mark was not going to say anything that wasn't impartial but she could tell from his tone how improbable it all sounded. Two years ago, even a few months ago, she'd have accused him of being pompous. Now she had a nasty suspicion that his point of view was perfectly justified and it was what any reasonable person would have thought. Any reasonable person — wasn't that what the law was all about?

'So he got in?' Mark continued.

'Yes. He got in the driver's side. And I was still saying I should drive, but he said not, so I got in the passenger side and Nigel reversed and ... that's when he hit the lamppost.'

'And then he drove off?'

'No, no.' Shula spread out the fingers of both hands on the table emphatically. 'We got out and looked at the damage and then I said it proved he wasn't fit to drive and I was taking over. So I got in the driver's side and he got in the passenger side and we drove off. We were in a bit of a hurry, because we were supposed to be meeting Caroline at Hollerton Junction. Anyway, we hadn't even got to the bypass when Nigel suddenly said it couldn't be Tim's car because there weren't any old sandwich packets and Mars bar wrappers on the floor and it hadn't got the furry dice which Nigel gave Tim for his birthday. And I was still driving and that's when I saw the police car behind us. So I pulled over.'

'Well, that was sensible anyway.' Mark sighed.

'Oh, Mark, don't say it like that. I'm sorry. I know it sounds stupid and incredible now — '

'Don't go saying that in court, for goodness' sake.'

Shula bit her lip.

'Are we going to have to go to court?' she said in a small voice. 'Can't you get me off?'

'It'll have to go to court, Shula,' said Mark gently. 'They're charging you with taking and driving away.'

Shula settled back in Mark's car. When she'd been to see him the next day, he had recommended that they opted for trial at the Magistrates' Court rather than the Crown Court and at the preliminary hearing, the date had been fixed for August 23rd. With that settled, and the sale of the house at Penny Hassett which she was still supposed to be handling going through, Shula had jumped at her Mum's suggestion that she should go and stay with her cousin Lilian Bellamy in Guernsey for a while. She honestly didn't think she could face any more reproachful looks from her Dad, let alone from Nigel, who obviously found every consultation or phone call she had with Mark about the court case the equivalent of a stake through the heart. It also meant that it would fall to Mr Rodway to dot the i's and cross the t's on the house contract, to oversee the haggling over carpets and curtains and to nag about the survey. To say she had not been looking forward to it would be to call Tim Beecham merely high-spirited. Every day when she had had to deal with a niggling enquiry about Foster's Row she had wondered when her mask would slip and show what she was really going through. She felt Saint Shula was about to take her place along with the others in her Sunday School picture book, wearing a beatific smile as she held out the fragments of her broken heart.

She had agreed eagerly when Mark had offered to drive her to the airport. She'd always loved being driven by him. In the old days, she would reach over and take his hand and hold it in hers and when he needed to change gear they would do it together. She would watch his eyes in the driving mirror watching the road behind and his profile as he turned this way and that at a junction. She'd better make the most of it today. Soon he'd be married to Sarah and she'd have no excuse to travel in a car with him ever again, unless perhaps he saw her in Borchester one wet winter night in years to come. She'd be a miserable spinster waiting at the bus stop because her car had packed up yet again, on her way back to the cheerless flat which she'd have been shamed into buying because she couldn't decently live at home any longer. He'd be in his big shiny partner's car, and he'd whirr down the electric window and offer her a lift. And she'd have to give him directions to where she lived, and she'd get in with her lonely frozen dinner and tin of catfood bumping against her legs. He'd be going home to supper, lovingly cooked by Sarah, who hadn't gone back to work after having the babies, but kept her figure in trim with aerobics, drove to the supermarket every Friday in her nippy Fiesta, and was a wow at the pre-school playgroup parties. She'd have to stare very straight ahead so as not to see the baby seats in the back, his wedding ring, him.

'You're very quiet.' Mark's voice made the fantasy horribly real for a second.

'I'm thinking.'

'Oh, Shula,' said Mark reproachfully. 'Haven't you grown out of that yet?'

But he was quiet as well. The countryside was anything but quiet: where they weren't harvesting they were baling or hauling straw, where they weren't baling they were taking another cut of silage. The roadsides looked dry and brownish under a white August sky. Shula saw a large flock of swallows on a barn roof, a horse rolling in the grass, before the suburbs of Birmingham reached out to draw them in.

He chose a funny moment to tell her, she later thought, given that they'd had nearly an hour in the car. They were at the traffic lights, waiting to cross the dual carriageway into the airport. The airport hotel, one of those 1930s buildings with glittering metal windows and flat roof, had the Union Jack flapping for some reason and a banner which announced a 3-course businessman's lunch (Mon-Fri). The lights seemed to stay on red for a long time. Shula had fallen completely silent. Now it was almost time to leave him, she didn't know how she was going to do it. She was meant to be staying with Lilian for two weeks. Perhaps she and Mark could just drive round for a fortnight. Would anyone miss them?

'I — um — there's something you ought to know.' Mark was staring straight ahead. 'Sarah and I have decided not to get married after all.'

Shula waited to feel some emotion but she was too stunned.

'Not get married? Not at all?'

'I don't seem to be very good at engagements, do I?'

Mark released the handbrake as the car in front moved off.

I don't want to go, thought Shula. Now especially I don't want to go. What am I doing going on holiday when I could be here with Mark, who's not going to marry blonde, suntanned, clever, young, rich Sarah Locke? Why is he telling me now? How long has he known? Is it him? Is it her? All the questions she couldn't ask, but most wanted to. He and Sarah had parted. He was on his own again. And she was going to Guernsey.

She didn't hear a thing from Mark when she was away. Nigel wrote every day and sent a dozen long stemmed red roses on her birthday. 'Coals to Newcastle!' laughed Lilian, meaning Guernsey's flower industry, but Shula was too busy searching her post for the envelope with Mark's writing. It wasn't there. When she got home she found he'd delivered her card to Brookfield but before she could phone him to say thank you, Nigel arrived with even more flowers and a reservation at Redgate Manor for a belated birthday celebration. When she rang Mark's office next day, the secretary he shared said he was with a client. When he returned her call, she was out on a viewing. Shula gave up, but she didn't give in. She felt she must be the only person in the world who was looking forward to going to court — at least she'd see him there.

A week later she stood in Borchester Magistrates' Court in a grey linen dress which she'd bought specially for the occasion, because she thought it looked demure, and heard Nigel fined £200 for taking and driving away, plus £200 costs, while the charges against her were dropped.

'Champagne!' she cried as soon as she and Mark were out of the courtroom. 'You've earned it.'

Nigel and his parents were in conference with their barrister. Gerald Pargetter had insisted on getting his old Etonian chum Sir Michael Sturdy to represent Nigel — not, as Mark had predicted, that it had done much good. If anything it seemed to have irritated the bench.

'I'm sorry, Shula, I can't.' Mark seemed preoccupied. 'I've got a lot of work on. There's a big case come in and I'm expecting a call from abroad.'

She was unreasonably disappointed. Of course she shouldn't have expected him to clear the whole day for her, though she knew deep down she had.

'Well, when are you going to let me thank you?' she insisted.

Shula could feel Nigel's eyes on them as he was borne away by his parents but she couldn't even make herself turn and wave.

'You still love Mark, don't you, Shula?' he asked when he phoned that evening.

'Don't be ridiculous!'

But she knew it was true.

She persuaded Mark to go to Nelson's with her the following night. It was an awkward evening. Despite the champagne, Mark didn't seem at all relaxed. He didn't even seem very excited by the thought that completion on the cottage was only days away.

'Shula, I've got something to tell you.'

'Oh, Mark, what now?' Shula was determinedly cheerful. 'All

these years you've been a woman trapped in a man's body?'

Anything. Just don't let his wedding to Sarah be on again.

'The thing is — it's all come about rather suddenly — but I'm going to Hong Kong. There's a case coming up and they need an assistant, it's commercial, rather complicated — '

Anything. But not that sort of anything.

She felt drained of all energy and all emotion when she called in at The Bull on the day Mark was due to leave. Joe Grundy and his son Eddie were in there, looking rather the worse for wear, but that was nothing new. Joe slurped his cider and wiped his mouth with the back of his hand.

'We was talking to a friend of yours last night,' he volunteered. 'That po-faced solicitor, Mark Hebden.'

'Down The Cat and Fiddle,' added Eddie.

'Really?' said Shula coolly. 'Have you heard from Clarrie? How's Rosie's husband?'

Eddie's wife Clarrie had been summoned to Great Yarmouth to stay with her sister, Rosie, while her husband Dennis was in hospital.

'Eh? Oh, all right, I reckon.' Joe was dismissive, more interested in the exploits of the night before. 'We was all paralytic by nine o'clock, him and all. We all got round the piano and had a sing song.'

'Yeah, if he wasn't off on a slow boat to China I might have signed him up with the band,' offered Eddie. 'He'd have to loosen up a bit though. Wanna crisp?'

Shula shook her head. She remembered suddenly how she and Mark had sat in a pub garden once and he had told her he had been slung out of the church choir for smoking, and how she hadn't believed it of him.

'Still,' intoned Joe. 'He's a broken man, isn't he?'

'Yeah.' Eddie tipped the final crumbs of his crisps from the bag into his mouth. He crunched and swallowed. Shula stared at the floor. 'Is it true what they say about how you drove him to it?'

Which was how Shula found herself making the journey to Birmingham airport again. Sid, who had tactfully interposed himself into the conversation, had suggested gently that she had nothing to lose by trying to catch Mark at the airport. Only my sanity, thought Shula as she tried to park. She thumped the steering wheel in frustration as the car in front halted to allow a Maestro to attempt to reverse into a space which was far too narrow. Oh come *on*!

Outside, jets revved their engines and she could hear the tannoy bonging in the distance through the car's open window. It was hot, it was sticky, she had a headache. She wanted desperately to go to the loo but she knew there wasn't time — at this rate she'd be pressing her nose against the glass as his plane rose into the sky. When she finally found a space, she parked at any old angle, thrust a fistful of change into the machine and tore towards the terminal. If he'd gone through passport control she'd had it. Frantically she scanned the crowd. Where were all these people going? Was that him? No, too fat. She ran up the escalator. He might be at the bookstall. It was a long, long flight to Hong Kong and he couldn't read his legal papers all the way, not even Mark. No. No one who looked like Mark, just a harassed mother trying to stop her toddler ripping the magazines to shreds and a bald businessman furtively glancing at the top shelf titles. Shula slumped against the till dejectedly. As she looked up she saw a sign for the coffee shop. It was worth a try.

There were no words to describe the look in Mark's eyes when he looked up from his paper to see her standing there. He just got up and took her in his arms and kissed her in front of the whole restaurant. Not a very Mark-like thing to do at all. And she kissed him right back.

'I'm glad you made it,' he said. 'I was beginning to give up hope.'

Shula kissed him again. He tasted of coffee.

'I was about to go through,' he said. 'Two more minutes and you'd have missed me. Where were you this morning? I was looking all over for you.'

'I'm sorry,' she said, her arms round his neck. 'I didn't know. You've got me now.'

He sighed and pulled her against him, stroking her back.

'I'm sorry about everything that's happened,' he said. 'I've made a mess of it. As usual.'

'You haven't made a mess,' said Shula. 'It's me. I keep messing it up.'

He touched her lips with his finger.

'Will you be all right?' he asked.

'Now I've seen you, yes.' Shula leaned her head briefly against his shoulder then looked up at him. 'I was just so scared that you were going to go away without knowing — you don't hate me, do you, Mark? I'm not driving you away?'

'What?' She obviously wasn't making sense.

'Oh, never mind. Just please come back. Promise.'

All that remained was to sort out Nigel. Shula hadn't been feeling good about Nigel for ages. Knowing how much he cared made it harder but it had to be done. It took her another week to pluck up courage. She told him in the rose garden at Brookfield. It was a soft September afternoon, the shadows lengthening on the grass, the sun kind on the mossy paths, the toiling bees. She sat him down on the wooden seat which her Mum and Dad had bought each other for one of their anniversaries and took his hands in hers.

'I know what you're going to say, Shula. Please don't.'

'I'm sorry, Nigel.'

'Just tell me what you want, and I'll do it. Look, we won't hang around with that boring Tim Beecham any more. We'll be just you and me. It'll be good, Shulie. We've had such fun.'

'I know. It's been lovely. But I don't feel about you the way you feel about me and I'm sorry — it's just not fair to you to carry on.'

'But I don't mind if you don't love me like I love you. I'd rather have that than not have you at all. How can you think this is kinder?' Nigel squeezed her hands.

'I didn't say it was kinder. But it's the only thing I can do.'

'It's Mark, isn't it? He's half way round the world and you'd rather have the memory of him and the promise of a postcard of Kowloon than me who's right here.'

'Don't make me answer that, Nigel. Please.'

Shula could tell he was going to cry because he got up abruptly and stumbled his way towards the house. She stayed, with the sun on her back, until she thought it was safe. Then she went into the house, locked her bedroom door and sobbed.

Jill always found the hum of the milk tank and the swish of milk into the jars in the parlour soothing and she needed soothing today. Phil was down in the pit, wiping the cows' udders before the clusters went on. She signalled to him and when he had finished all the cows, he climbed up the stone steps and followed her into the yard.

'I've just come to tell you to go easy on Nigel, if you see him.'

'Me? I'm never hard on the boy.' Phil was indignant.

'I don't think that's strictly true, Phil,' Jill corrected. 'Anyway, Shula's finished with him and he's feeling rather bruised.'

'Oh.'

Phil's 'Oh' spoke volumes — relief, mostly.

'I suppose he's been bending your ear about it?' he queried.

'He did come in and have a word, yes, but I've sent him off home. Funny, his car's still in the yard. You don't think ... '

'No, Jill, I don't think we're going to be fishing him out of the slurry pit. He's probably just gone for a walk.'

To wait till his eyes weren't so red, thought Jill. She could imagine what Gerald Pargetter would make of a son who shed tears.

Five minutes later she popped her head round the door of the milking parlour again.

'It's all right, Phil, you needn't worry, I've seen Nigel. He's in the orchard with Elizabeth.

'With Elizabeth?' Phil stepped back to avoid being hit as Number 18's clusters swung off.

'I think they're playing Scrabble.'

'Good,' said Phil, distracted by a cut he'd just noticed on 54's hind leg. Barbed wire, probably. He'd have to get Jethro to have a look at the fencing. 'That's nice.'

OCTOBER
——— 1984 ———

'Thank you,' said Shula taking the impossibly fluffy cloud of candy floss from the woman and handing over her money. She loved watching, fascinated, as the stuff was spun from nothing in the big revolving drum, loved the wiry texture of it on her tongue before it dissolved away. She had promised David a toffee apple, but she'd lost him in the crowd: perhaps he'd gone on the Waltzers again. It was years since she'd been to the Mop. Uncle Tom said it wasn't what it was. Even he couldn't remember it as a hiring fair, but before the war, apparently, there had been more traditional entertainments like the Bearded Lady and the Rat Woman who sat with rats swarming all over her instead of all these new-fangled 'rides'. In the place of hamburgers and hot dogs you could get an ox sandwich for threepence. 'Everyone had a marvellous time,' Uncle Tom had reminisced. 'Except the ox,' added Elizabeth under her breath: she was not so strictly vegetarian these days but could still be pious about meat-eating when she chose. Shula had said she probably wouldn't bother with the Mop but David, not noted for his fellow-feeling, had taken pity on his sister since Mark and Nigel's dual departure and had forced her into coming with him.

'Hey, watch it!'

Shula had been so lost in thought she hadn't seen the tall blond young man stepping backwards to get a better aim at the shooting gallery. Now he had candy floss all over his jacket. Luckily he seemed to have sense of humour, too.

'This never happens to Clint Eastwood.'

'I'm sorry,' Shula said, trying to scrape off the worst of the pink foam from his sleeve. 'It's awfully sticky. I wasn't looking where I was going.'

'Don't worry, it was due for a clean anyway. I had a dog throw up on it earlier.'

'Eurgh. Not your day is it?' said Shula.

'Oh, that's par for the course,' he replied. He held out his hand. 'Martin Lambert. I'm Bill Robertson's new assistant.'

Shula had heard her father discussing the imminent arrival of a new vet.

'Tell you what, help me win a teddy bear for my little god-daughter and I'll buy you another.'

'I don't think I could eat another one,' Shula exclaimed.

'Oh, so you wiped it all over me deliberately — you'd gone off it had you?' he grinned.

Five minutes later they were the proud owners of a lime green furry gonk with bulging orange eyes.

'Well worth £3.50 of anyone's money,' said Martin, stuffing it in his pocket. 'Right, are you game for the Big Dipper?'

'I don't know how you do it,' said Caroline when Shula told her about Martin. 'You only have to venture outside the door and you're tripping over men who want to take you out.'

Shula protested that this was hardly true, but Martin was a welcome distraction and over the winter they drifted into going out together. If it hadn't been for the certain knowledge that she was still in love with Mark, Shula might well have enjoyed Martin's company more. He was good fun, sporty, hearty, liked rugger and real ale, went rock climbing in Cumbria, wanted to take her home to meet his Mum and Dad. But Shula was only really living from one of Mark's letters to the next. They were not as frequent as she would have liked. She had no trouble in finding the time to write to Mark every week or ten days, passing on the trivia of Ambridge life — how Clarrie Grundy had had another little boy, Edward Junior, or how Jethro was predicting a poor lamb flock next spring for some complicated reason to do with what David had been feeding the ewes. Mark's letters were rather slower to arrive. She told herself it was because it was all new and different and he was ever so busy, of course. Gradually, she built up a picture of his life there

— the tennis club and the horse racing (Mark, betting on horses! She must tell Kenton!), the visits to Stanley market on Sundays and the lightweight suits he'd ordered from the little tailor in Kowloon. He sent her a postcard of the Great Wall when he took a few days off to go to China, and in another letter he said he wanted to go to Malacca and buy a cane like a character out of Somerset Maugham. He signed his letters 'Love, Mark,' but he didn't write 'I love you' or say he was counting the days till he came home again. He had originally said he might be back by Christmas. Then it turned into six months. In February he told her he'd accepted another six month contract. That would mean he'd been gone a whole year.

Shula didn't mention Martin in her letters. It wasn't as if it was a grand passion on her part and it couldn't be for him either, she told herself, because he seemed to accept her keeping him at arm's length. He certainly never pressured her, never seeming to expect more than a friendly kiss in the car. Shula was grateful to him, glad to have the winter evenings filled with mindless activity, so that she didn't sit in her room re-reading Mark's still-too-infrequent letters and worse still, reading things into them. She mentioned Mark from time to time in conversation with Martin, but she didn't know how much he knew. Then one night when her parents were out and they'd been watching the late night film, he pulled her towards him on the sofa. Shula lifted her face for the usual, almost brotherly, kiss and was shocked when Martin's lips came down hard on hers. For a moment she was too shocked to respond, but when she tried to pull away his arms went tighter round her. She struggled but it only seemed to arouse him.

'No, Martin, please!'

He went on trying to kiss her. She turned her face away and his kisses landed damply on her cheek.

'I'm sorry, but no — I don't want this.'

Why was she apologising? Anger gave her strength and she pushed him off. His hair was ruffled and his tie askew. And his pride was hurt. He pushed his hair back with both hands and stood up.

'You know your trouble, don't you? You've living in the past,' he said accusingly. 'I've heard all about your fabulous fiancé who's on the other side of the world. Mark, wasn't it? Well, I suggest you call him, and get on with it, because you're obviously saving yourself for him. And you'd save the rest of us a lot of trouble if you'd just get back together with him and have done with it.'

He left abruptly, slamming the front door behind him and roaring off in his Volvo with the dog grille and drug case in the back.

Shula sat there, staring unseeing at a lacklustre chat show. He had a point. She knew she loved Mark — and properly now, not in the romantic 'I'm getting married, someone's actually proposed to me' way of four years before. What she felt now was real and solid and enduring. She couldn't have felt it, she was sure, if they hadn't broken up: it came from realising what she had lost. For the last year, every time she'd thought they'd had a chance of getting back together, something had got in the way — a plane to Guernsey in her case, a jumbo jet to Hong Kong in his. After they'd said goodbye at the airport before he left, after the relief and passion of his kisses, she had thought he'd write straight away, saying he couldn't wait to come home. But two weeks had gone by without a letter till finally she'd had to write first, keeping the tone bright and friendly, not wanting to give herself away. And when he'd written back he was bright and friendly too. They both seemed to be dancing round each other, neither wanting to make the first move, the fear of what had happened before tripping them up. She'd got to give it one last go with Mark. She'd got to make the move. Otherwise she'd never know.

Hong Kong had one of those airports which stuck way out into the sea. They always made Shula nervous — why had Kenton ever told her that you'd have a harder landing on water than on the ground? — but she forced herself to keep her eyes open. She didn't want to miss a moment. Mark might ask her if she'd noticed something spectacular as the plane banked and descended and she didn't want him to think she wasn't open to the cultural as well as the romantic possibilities of her holiday. It had been hard enough to gauge from Mark in the couple of phone calls they had had since she first rang announcing her trip quite what he made of her intention to come and visit. He had explained that he would try to take some time off to show her around but he would have to go to the office some days. He said she could of course have the run of his flat and that he'd made a lot of friends who would be only too happy to look after her. Shula fell a slight chill of fear. Did he mean *girl*friends by any chance?

If she had been looking for nothing more than a holiday, it would have been idyllic. Mark was the perfect host. He was often working during the day but he arranged for the wife of one of his senior colleagues to take Shula shopping or to the club to play tennis or swim. He would join them with the other men in the late afternoon, and Shula would squint into the sun and sip her drink and watch him dive and wonder how she'd like the life of an expat wife. At the weekends he took her round the markets, where the herbalists ground their powders, where snakes writhed in cages ready for the pot, and where to her horror, tiny songbirds chirruped, blithely unaware that they too were on someone's dinner menu. She bought silk pyjamas and pearl earrings and a beaded cardigan, rice bowls and spoons and a teapot with a bamboo handle. They went up from Garden Road by funicular and criss-crossed the harbour on the Star Ferry. On her last night Mark took her to eat on board a floating junk which was supposed to have the best food in the city. They had birds nest soup and duck with shredded spring onions and plum sauce in tiny pancakes, and lychees and a sort of rice pudding to follow. All evening Shula wanted to say 'Marry me, Mark,' and all evening she didn't. Next day at the airport, they were constrained. Mark had taken an hour off but a case was coming up to a crucial hearing and he had a lot to do. Shula felt she was taking up his time — and for what? She was just living in the past. They had nearly married, once. She had been naive and stupid and spoilt and she had ruined everything. Last year it had seemed that there might still be something there. When she had seen him off for Hong Kong at the airport she hadn't mistaken the force of feeling behind his kisses. But that was nearly a year ago. It seemed that perhaps he had moved on, literally, and she hadn't. Maybe she should just go home and get on with her life and forget him after all. She'd be twenty-seven this year. She'd known Mark since she was twenty-one. That was a long time with nothing to show for it.

She didn't think she'd sleep on the flight (she hadn't on the way out) but exhausted by the emotion of it all she closed her eyes somewhere over India and when she opened them again they were over Turkey. After that she dozed fitfully, reliving every moment of the last two weeks, first wringing every last drop of hope from their better times, then torturing herself with the times when they hadn't seemed to have anything to say to one another or had been talking at cross purposes. She got off the plane like a zombie, hardly bothering to straighten her clothes or check her make up, too tired to think of putting on an act for her parents who were meeting her. As soon as she saw them she burst into tears. Jill wasn't surprised. She had seen Shula's face before she caught sight of them and the droop of her head had told her all she needed to know.

It was a bit like when she came back from Thailand, Shula thought. Her mother fussed around, wanting to feed her up, discreetly not asking the questions she most wanted to. Shula wished she could tell her but she didn't dare broach the subject, fearing her mother's kindness would be more than she could bear. The person she talked to and wept with was Caroline, in her room at Grey Gables.

'I wish I'd never gone,' she wailed. 'Before I did I could kid myself he was thinking about me. After the way we said goodbye before he left I really thought there was still something there.'

'Maybe there is,' soothed Caroline. 'Maybe he just couldn't show it. He's been hurt once, Shula.'

'Don't remind me! I've been so stupid! What am I going to do?'

Caroline sighed.

'Well if phoning's no good, and going to see him didn't do any good — could you write to him? Just let him know once and for all how you feel. You've really got nothing to lose, have you?'

But before Shula had got much past 'Dear Mark', there was a phone call. David took it, so the message he scrawled for Shula was short to the point of brutality. 'Mark coming home tomorrow. Meet him at Birmingham airport 5.p.m. Check beforehand in case of delays.'

'Mark? Why are you dragging me all up here?'

Shula panted behind him as Mark strode on ahead up the lower slopes of Lakey Hill. It was only an hour and a half since she'd met him at the airport: he hadn't even phoned his parents to tell them he was safely back. He'd insisted on her driving straight to Ambridge and there, refusing Jill's offer of tea, he'd told Shula they were going for a walk. He didn't answer her question until they were right at the top. You could see for miles and miles through the cloudless blue of July. Brian's two brand new combines crawled up and down his fields, the barley falling beneath their blades. At Brookfield, too, the combine was still out. The grain had been coming off the field dry all day: her Dad had hardly needed to get his moisture meter out. Directly below them on the hillside the Brookfield ewes, shorn of their grubby fleeces, were compact and curly, cropping the short grass. Bees droned in the clover at their feet: only the birds were silent.

'Well?' asked Shula. He looked so handsome, she was going to fall at his feet in a minute. He'd torn off his tie and left his suit jacket at the farmhouse. He'd got on one of those handmade shirts in a light cotton which she'd chosen with him in Hong Kong, in Nathan Road, palest pink. The old Mark would never have worn a pink shirt.

'I just wanted to see it again. The view.' Mark pivoted around, arms outstretched, taking great gulps of air. 'Oh, that's wonderful.'

'There's a pretty good view in Hong Kong,' said Shula mildly.

'Not like this.' He turned to face her. They were still standing far apart.

'So that's it, is it?' she asked. 'An Englishman's dream of home?'

He held out his hands for hers. Moving closer, knowing and not knowing what was coming, she gave them to him.

'Not exactly. I brought you up here because it seemed like the only place — the right place. That's why I couldn't say anything in Hong Kong. It had to be here, Shula. It's where you belong.'

It was going to be all right. After all this time, it really was.

'You know I love you,' he went on. 'More than ever. And I want to marry you more than ever. Do you want to marry me?'

'Oh, Mark!' She flung her arms round his neck. 'Oh, yes! Yes, please!'

Shula woke very early and lay still. There was not even a second before full consciousness and the immediate realisation that this was the day of her wedding. With a lurch that was half-thrill and half-fear her stomach vaulted purposefully over her diaphragm. Her eyes slid to her bedside clock. Half past six. Dad or David would already be out in the milking parlour, wiping teats and dispensing feed as the cows munched to the sound of the pulsator's rhythm and the local radio news. Her mother, she hoped, had turned over and gone back to sleep, but more likely Jill was sitting up in bed, longing for a cup of tea but not wanting to disturb the rest of the house, making one of her famous lists of 'Things To Do'. The wedding was at twelve. Over five hours and nothing to do in them except get up, have a bath, have a cup of coffee, pick at breakfast, not get dressed, wait for the flowers to arrive, have another cup of coffee, and another, wait for the hairdresser, get dressed and made up, wait for the cars. Shula had never been very good at waiting. But after five years of waiting for Mark, she supposed another five hours wasn't really all that long.

From the quality of the light coming through the pale curtains, she could tell that there was sunshine outside, but sunshine with the fresh edge of autumn. She could hear the woodpigeons calling from the orchard and could see in her mind's eye the starlings busily feeding on the grass among the windfalls. Later in the day there would still be bees nuzzling the honeysuckle but the trees were on the turn, the oaks bronzed and the rowan berries vivid orange. Calving was in full swing and her Dad and David had been busy for the past fortnight ploughing, working the land down and beginning to drill the next season's crops. Shula remembered her Grandad telling her that he always felt that this was when the new year really began — 'Never mind all that Auld Lang Syne rubbish'. He was so thrilled that she and Mark were back together again. 'Never did understand why you called it off in the first place,' he'd said gruffly. He wished, as Shula wished, that her Gran had lived to see her married. 'She's been gone nearly five years,' he'd said to her as she'd walked back with him to Glebe Cottage after Evensong the previous Sunday. 'And I still find myself talking to her. Even now, I sometimes come in the house and almost call her name.' Shula squeezed his hand. Gran and Grandad had been married almost sixty years. Shula could hardly imagine living that long, let alone spending all that time with the same person in the littleness of daily life and the enormity of loving them only. But here she was, about to try it for herself.

She'd allow herself another half-hour. Then she'd get up and make her Mum a cup of tea for once, as a final gesture. Everything had happened so quickly this time round that she hadn't had much time to get sentimental about leaving Brookfield.

'It says here the minimum time for organising a church wedding is six weeks,' she'd told her mother, quoting from one of the bridal books which were again cluttering the kitchen table. 'That means the middle of September.'

'Shula, that's impossible!' said Jill.

'Not if we do it all simply. No messing about with making dresses, and you doing the catering. We'll buy my dress and have the reception at a hotel.'

Shula had no qualms when Richard Adamson offered them a cancellation on September 21st — almost four years to the day since the wedding she and Mark had called off.

'If I was superstitious, Sophie, I'd hardly be accepting someone else's cancellation, would I?' she said when questioned by David's latest girlfriend. 'In fact someone else's cancellation seems rather appropriate for me and Mark.'

Sophie, though in many ways a pain, not least because she was so besotted with David, had really taken Shula's wedding to heart and had even offered to make the bridesmaids' dresses. As she was a fashion design student this was not an offer Shula felt she could turn down.

'Why did you agree? You know what she's like, she'll have us in bin bags and bits of chiffon!' Elizabeth had moaned.

'Of course she won't. She's following a pattern and I've given her the material,' said Shula.

'It's all right for you, you're getting your dress from a shop,' Elizabeth came back at her. 'And I suppose Bunty's getting hers from Rent-A-Tent.'

Bunty Hebden had certainly not got any slimmer in the past four years. Reg had developed high blood pressure — the result of living with Bunty, most people assumed, but in general Shula was surprised at how warmly the Hebdens had welcomed the news of the wedding. Mark said it was because after two false starts — with Shula and with Sarah Locke — Bunty was beginning to think Mark would never make it down the aisle.

'And she's just dying to be a Granny,' Mark had smiled.

'Give us a chance! We're not even married yet!' Shula protested.

They were addressing the invitations.

'We can have fun practising, though,' Mark said, his hand creeping up Shula's thigh under the table. Shula slapped it away.

'That one's for your friends Rory and Belinda. Get on with it!'

'Listen to the nagging wife,' said Mark. 'What am I letting myself in for?'

Shula and Jill went together both to choose Jill's classic cream suit and Shula's white high necked dress. Shula would never forget her mother's face as she stepped out of the changing room in the big bridal shop in Borchester High Street.

'Oh Shula!' Jill's face had creased as it always did when she was trying not to cry.

In the car on the way back, with Shula's dress in an enormous box and Jill's suit in another, Shula begged Jill to tell her again — it was a story Shula loved to hear — about her feelings when she had first held the twins in her arms.

'I'd known you were going to be twins, but I couldn't visualise you as actual babies. There weren't any scans or anything then — the nearest you got to an actual baby was bathing a plastic doll at the hospital in the preparation classes.' Jill eased the car out into the flow of traffic on the bypass. 'I can remember Phil coming in looking all embarassed and out of place but pleased as punch as well and when he saw you both in your little cots — well, his eyes just filled with tears. He put out a hand to your cheek and it was as if he hardly dared to touch you. Then a nurse came in and gave you to him and Kenton to me and we just sat there, gazing, and we couldn't take our eyes off you both. We didn't think about all the work! We didn't know then that you were never going to sleep at the same time or eat at the same time or even wet your nappies at the same time!'

Shula was always moved by the clarity of her mother's recollection. More than anything — more, almost than Mark — she longed for the day when she would feel that special, complete, one-sided love without asking for its return.

Phil and David managed to stay out of the house for most of the morning of the wedding, finding urgent jobs about the farm which needed doing.

'Why they had to leave fixing that gatepost till today, I'll never know,' said Jill, exasperated.

'I think it's deliberate, Mum,' said Shula, smiling, waggling her toes to dry their pearly varnish. 'It's too much like a company of women in here.'

'If you ask me, they're avoiding Kate, and who can blame them.' Elizabeth came into Shula's bedroom, looking disgruntled. 'Have you seen her blooming elephant? She says she wants it.'

'I think it's by the loo. She's not getting her dress creased, is she?' Jill was putting lipstick, glasses and tissues — lots of tissues — in her bag.

Kate was a pain, of course, as everyone had predicted she would be. Mark's sister Joanna had plucked up courage to admit this time that she didn't really want to be a bridesmaid, she'd be far too self-conscious, which left just Elizabeth and Jennifer's Kate, who would be eight in a week's time. However, Shula reflected, as Elizabeth tried to persuade her that putting nail varnish on was not a good idea at this late stage, for all that she was a spoilt little madam, Kate did look the part of small bridesmaid to perfection in her pale blue satin with a garland in her hair. Elizabeth agreed to yet another game of snap as they waited for the car which would take them and Jill to the church. Shula was leaving getting into her dress until the last moment possible.

Now it was time. Jill spread a big sheet on the floor of Shula's bedroom. Shula stood on it in her bra and pants. Her legs were bare and she had bought low heeled white leather pumps. Jill took the dress, all its filmy layers of ribbon and net, off the padded hanger. She placed it on the sheet and Shula stepped into it.

'I hope it still fits!'

'Shula, you've hardly eaten a thing all week,' Jill reproached.

Shula drew the long transparent sleeves up her arms, rested the frill on her shoulder and hung her head obediently while her mother fastened the back and caught the fiddly hooks and eyes at the neck. She turned to look in her wardrobe mirror and didn't recognise herself.

Her father was waiting at the bottom of the stairs as she came cautiously down ten minutes later.

'You look beautiful,' he smiled, taking both her hands. 'I'm proud of you.'

Jill, Elizabeth and Kate had already left, Elizabeth making strangling motions behind Kate's bobbing head.

'Don't you go all soppy on me, Dad,' said Shula.

'Of course not,' said Phil. 'Do you want a drink or anything?'

'I'm perfectly calm!'

'You can help me up the aisle then!'

She knew her father wasn't finding this easy. Emotions weren't really his thing.

'Dad,' she began, 'I want to say thank you. For putting up with me. And all this. I know I'm doing the right thing. I'm just sorry it's been so long drawn out.'

'Shula, what did I say before? As long as you're happy, that's all that your mother and I care about.'

And Shula was happy. Happy to see Mark standing there, tense and straight-backed in the church with Nigel beside him as best man. Happy to see the love in his eyes as he turned to acknowledge her arrival at his side. Happy, happy, happy to say after Richard, as they had practised:

'I, Shula Mary, take thee, Mark Charles Timothy, to my wedded husband, to have and to hold, from this day forward, for better, for worse, for richer, for poorer, in sickness and in health, to love and to cherish, till death us do part ... '

'Enjoying yourself?'

'Oh, Mark, yes. I'm loving it. I don't want it to end.'

'I don't know about that. I'm quite looking forward to our honeymoon, too.'

Shula reached up and kissed him.

'So am I.'

Around them in the Long Gallery at Netherbourne Hall the reception ebbed and flowed. Waiters circulated with trays of canapes and bottles of champagne in starched white bibs. With utter unconcern for her dress, Kate was sliding along the polished floor on her bottom with Tommy, Pat and Tony's youngest. The waiters negotiated them with practised ease.

'They make it look so simple, don't they?' Mark said. 'Like Lord Lichfield taking the photographs.'

When Caroline had airily offered the services of her cousin as photographer they had hardly expected him to be the Queen's cousin as well.

'He was just brilliant,' said Shula. 'Dad hates having his photo taken but he was like putty in his hands. And did you see Clarrie's face when he took her arm to move her in the group shot? I thought she was going to pass out.'

'As bad as my Auntie Ivy,' grinned Mark. 'She got him to autograph her Order of Service. Hey, shall we sit down for a bit?'

'Are we allowed? Have we talked to everyone?'

Mark pulled her, still protesting, onto a crimson damask sofa.

'They can always come and talk to us,' he pointed out reasonably. 'We're not going to start rolling around on the floor or anything.'

'Not yet, anyway,' Shula giggled, cuddling up. 'And it is our day, after all. I do love you, Mark.'

'And I love you, Mrs Hebden,' he replied.

JANUARY
—— 1988 ——

She wanted this evening to be special. Shula let herself in through the front door of Glebe Cottage, juggling keys, handbag and supermarket carriers. It was a brisk January night but the light in the living room which Mark had timed to come on at three thirty had beckoned her up the path: the heating, similarly, had been warming the rooms since late afternoon, teasing creaks out of the wooden floors and hissing in the pipes as the cottage eased its elderly joints. Shula dumped her bag and keys on the oak table in the narrow hall and carried her shopping through to the kitchen. She and Mark had moved into Glebe Cottage a year after they got married and they'd been here nearly eighteen months. She knew exactly what her Grandad had meant when he said it was as if her Gran was still there. She and Mark had decorated. They had, after much deliberation, swopped the old enamel sink for a modern one with a double drainer. They had put in new cupboards. But the old dresser was still there against the back wall: the window was still as poky, and the catch stuck. Shula had begged a rag rug from Brookfield, the one Doris had made, and the 1930s teaset with the peculiarly bright blue and orange flowers. That way there was enough of Gran in the room for her still to be able to see her turning from her geranium cuttings on the window sill, or straightening from the Rayburn (now replaced) her flowery pinafore speckled with flour, her round moon face beaming a welcome. How many times had Shula sat at her Gran's table either here or at Brookfield and eaten scones fresh from the oven or drunk her home-made lemonade, confiding her latest trauma: the teacher who picked on her, the best friend who wasn't, the new dress she just had to have. Shula shook her head. She was getting sentimental. Mark would be back in an hour. She wanted to have a bath, change, lay the table, pour the wine — and have him come through the door to the delicious smell of dinner and a wife who had some news for him.

She was just chopping the mushrooms — having measured the white wine, and added another glug for luck — when she heard his key in the lock.

'In the kitchen,' she called. She had changed into her jeans and a soft blue denim shirt which he liked. He didn't reply but went straight upstairs. Shula frowned. It wasn't like Mark not to come and say hello before he changed. She put the kettle on to boil for the rice, poured two glasses of wine and carried them upstairs.

Mark was sitting on the edge of the bed taking off his shoes. She loved him most at those vulnerable moments when he didn't know she was watching him and he was absorbed in some everyday activity. She loved the intensity with which he addressed everything. The previous summer he'd decided they were going to compost all their garden rubbish. Shula had watched, amused, as he brooded over his compost heap, adding activator, testing the temperature. In the end something had gone wrong, and instead of a rich heap of mulch they had ended up with a damp heap of stinking grass clippings and eggshells but for the time it had taken, Mark had been as intent on his task as a six-year-old with a project on the seashore to hand in before the end of term.

'Drink?' Shula asked, offering the wine.

Mark straightened. He looked tired and more than that he looked worried. Shula sat down beside him.

'Come on,' she said, holding out the glass. 'I'm trying to lead you astray.'

He put his arm round her, pulled her to him and kissed her hair. Then he took the glass she offered and drank.

'What's the matter?' Shula sipped her wine. It was a white rioja she had chosen specially for tonight.

'I'm afraid,' he said, 'that I've been a very bad boy.'

He explained over dinner. He explained it all, in a lot of detail, but all Shula retained was that there had been some problem over a shop lease. There had even been the possibility of Mark being sued for negligence though luckily this had never materialised.

Mark had thought it was over and done with but he had been called in that afternoon to see Howard Jenkins, the senior partner. In the course of their not very cordial conversation it had emerged that Jenkins had known all along. The upshot was that he had been well and truly told off — and the firm was not going to offer Mark the partnership for which he had been waiting for over a year. That was going instead to George Goodwin, who was younger than Mark, smarmier than Mark and was learning golf just to impress.

'I'm being penalised for one small mistake,' Mark said bitterly, pushing his rice round his plate.

'What can you do?' Shula asked. She didn't feel hungry any more, either.

'I don't know yet.' Mark pushed his plate away. 'Anyway, how was your day?'

Shula smiled and told him about Aunty Peggy and the photocopy paper rep. She didn't somehow think this was, after all, the evening on which to tell him that she wanted to talk about starting a family.

Mark had hardly slept that night, tossing and turning, and neither had Shula. She knew he was going over the encounter with the senior partner again and again, rehearsing the cutting things he'd say the next day to Goodwin, cursing himself for how he hadn't adequately marshalled his defence in front of Jenkins. By the time he reached out to pull Shula against him in the five minutes before the alarm went off, he'd made up his mind, he told her. He was owed some time: he'd take a few days off.

'Let them manage without me for a bit!' he said. 'Goodwin can handle that compensation claim for the canning factory and see how he gets on with Sir Sydney breathing down his neck!'

Shula managed to get a day and a half off too. They took the phone off the hook and stayed in bed all morning and after lunch went out for a walk. Without ever deciding on their route or their destination, they found themselves taking the footpath past the Brookfield sheep pens which led across the fields to Lakey Hill. Hands laced together, they followed the edge of the ploughed field. Sparrows darted in and out of the hedge as if they were playing hide and seek. From the old rookery in Cuckoo Covert they could see the comings and goings as the rooks chanced their luck among the furrows.

'You know what you need, don't you?' said Shula, as they crossed a stile. 'You need a distraction.'

'What, like a hobby?' Mark jumped down on to the path. 'Not if you're going to laugh about it the way you laughed about my compost.'

Shula stood and faced him. She unzipped his Barbour and snuggled into his chest. He folded his coat round her, enclosing her in its warmth.

'I mean,' she said, 'A baby.'

Mark looked at her for a moment.

'Come on,' he said. 'Race you to the top.'

When she arrived puffing on the summit he was spreadeagled on his back on the damp ground, watching the clouds chase by overhead.

'It's really weird,' he said, pulling her down beside him. 'It's like those times when you're on a train in the station and there's another one alongside and you don't know which one is starting to move. I can't tell if I'm moving, or the sky.'

'Yes, yes, very poetic,' said Shula. 'Now what about my baby?'

'What, here and now?' Mark groaned. 'What was wrong with this morning? Most women would be pleased to have their husband home on a weekday and settle for that.'

'We're ready, aren't we, Mark?' Shula leaned over him, watching the clouds reflected in his pupils. She loved him at that moment with a fierce lurching pain.

They had already been married for over two years. A lot had happened. Her grandfather had died and Shula had taken up her inheritance of Glebe Cottage. She had moved to a job managing the one thousand acre Berrow estate, owned by her cousin Lilian, on behalf of Rodway's. It was wonderful because she spent two or three days a week in Ambridge. She could call in on her Mum and Dad for lunch, swop gossip with Jennifer or meet David in The Bull. It also meant she had to work with her Auntie Peggy, who ran the office for her daughter Lilian, but, as Nelson said, into every life a little rain must fall. Auntie Peggy meant well but she was set in her ways and utterly resistant to change. Mark said she just needed managing but Shula found it tiring to have to dress up her suggestions for the office so that Peggy thought she'd thought of them. At least Shula wasn't there all week. Just when she was feeling claustrophobic in the estate office, it was time for a day at Rodway's in Borchester. If she had a bad day in Borchester, she could vary her routine with a day at the estate office. Meanwhile Mark had been making good progress at Spencer and Holden: he had been there there for over ten years. He moved up a notch on the car list and was allowed to choose a BMW. He was elected to the Council. He made great play of how he'd converted Shula from her days as scion of the Borchester Young Conservatives, and if she found his fellow S.D.P. members just a little dull, she never said so, entertaining them to fondue or bœuf bourguignon — with claret, of course.

Just when she might have begun to feel all settled and married and just a tiny bit predictable, Nigel had bounced back into their lives, burnt out by the job in the City his father had forced him into, and ready to take control at Lower Loxley. He drove Mark mad with his noisy parties at Woodbine Cottage which he'd persuaded Phil to rent him — but Shula saw a sadder, more grown up side of him when he asked her over to the big house for her professional advice. What she saw made her think of her A level set texts — *Brideshead Revisited* and Tennyson and Yeats.

'The woods decay, the woods decay and fall,' she murmured as Nigel walked her round the sad remains of the arboretum which his ancestor Sir John Pargetter had planted on his return from India in the nineteenth century. The house was no better. The roof had let water through into the Blue Bedroom where Mrs Keppel was said to have stayed during a shooting party and the conservatory was only held onto the back of the house by the ivy which swarmed all over it, poking through the window frames to cover both sides of the glass. The staircase had dry rot and death watch beetle. All the paintings needed cleaning and the curtains in the library were in tatters.

Nigel was determined to get it in hand. Gerald Pargetter had finally succumbed to his sixty years of reckless living. He was barely conscious half the time, either through alcohol, medication or both. Nigel's mother wasn't much better. It was clearly going to fall to Nigel to sort things out.

'I can do it if you'll help, Shulie,' he told her, pouring tea into Sèvres cups from a pot-bellied brown earthenware teapot. (Domestically things were chaotic too). Shula had said she'd be delighted — Nigel was, after all, her oldest friend.

So — she and Mark had their jobs, their home, their families, their friends. They were more than well-off — unlike most young couples they were not struggling with mortgage repayments each month. All they needed was a baby.

'Mark?' He still hadn't answered her question. Now she saw her own worried face reflected in his eyes.

He pulled her face towards him and touched his lips to hers.

'What are we waiting for?' he said. 'Let's go home, shall we?'

It was wonderful to have an excuse to make love with Mark.

'Shula, no! I've got a headache!' he'd cry as she came and stood behind him as he worked in the evenings, sliding her hands over his shoulders, loosening his tie. Then he'd turn in his chair and pull her, laughing, on to his lap. Later, Shula would find she'd got a pink legal ribbon in her hair or that they'd been lying on Exhibit A which was needed for court tomorrow.

'Perverting the course of justice, definitely.' said Mark.

So the phone call from Sonia came as a total surprise. Shula had met her once or twice at Law Society dos. She was a barrister — older than they were — in her early 40s — well respected and very high-powered, which some said came from her addiction to diet cola.

'Mark not back yet?' she enquired in the way she had of doing without verbs. 'Thought he would be by now.' So she could do without pronouns as well, thought Shula. 'Ask him to call me, would you?'

'Why does Sonia Carmichael want you to phone her?' she teased Mark when he got in. 'Is there anything you'd like to tell me?'

'I've no idea.' Mark was already dialling the number Shula had written on the pad. When Sonia was waiting for you to return her call, you didn't bother about niceties like kissing your wife, asking what was for supper or even taking your coat off.

Shula went through to the kitchen. It was Mark's turn to cook. He was the one who had insisted on the division of labour, which, apart from calling off the wedding, was apparently another thing Shula had to thank Sarah Locke for, or so Mark said. She might as well make a start. Sonia, though clipped in her delivery, could be loquacious when she wanted, as many of the Recorders and Judges on the Borsetshire circuit would testify. Shula was on her second glass of wine and had turned the heat down under the potatoes when Mark returned.

'Do I get a drink?' he asked. 'We could be celebrating.'

Sonia, he explained, was ringing to tip him off about a job she'd heard about in a firm of Birmingham solicitors.

'Not too big, not too small — 20 partners,' Mark enthused. 'In the commercial department. That was why I was so long. She gave me the home number of one of the partners and I had a long chat with him. He wants me to go in and see them. I've got to phone in the morning to fix a time.'

Shula smiled, she must have done, because Mark didn't notice anything amiss. But later when he was doing the washing up — really it was her turn, but she'd ended up cooking — she wandered through to the sitting room. She stirred the fire into life and sat down with her tapestry. She was making a cushion with a garland of roses on the front. As she poked the needle up and down and up and down through the canvas she thought about the last time she had driven into the centre of Birmingham. An hour, it had taken her, and that wasn't in the rush hour. It would surely take Mark an hour and a half each way. Three hours a day in the car. Leaving earlier in the mornings — well before it was light, in the winter, getting home later in the evenings, even in summer, when they liked to sit in the garden or walk by the Am. What about his beloved cricket? The season would be starting in a month. Nets would start at Easter. But he was very keen on this job. She hadn't realised — perhaps neither had he — just how unhappy he was until there was the prospect of something different.

They didn't talk about it any more. He came through with coffee and put the television on, then turned that off and read the paper. Shula stabbed at her tapestry. They didn't make love that night for the first time in a very long while.

Soon Shula couldn't remember a time when Mark didn't get up at six thirty and leave the house at seven, day in, day out. He could have left half an hour later but then the traffic was that much worse and, he said, if he got to the office at half eight, he had half an hour without interruptions before the phones started ringing. He claimed he got through an enormous amount of work before most people had even arrived. Shula wondered how much work one person could possibly be expected to do. Mark never left the office before half past six in the evenings, often later, so was never home before eight. Even then, he would gobble down supper and set to work on bundles of papers — and not just for an hour or so. Shula was used to that from his days at Spencer and Holden. These days he would sometimes work till midnight.

'The more he does, the more he seems to want to do,' Shula complained to Caroline as they bobbed about in the shallow end of the new Grey Gables indoor pool.

'You're casualties of the 1980s, aren't you,' Caroline sympathised. 'Dinkies — dual income, no kids.'

And no chance of any, thought Shula, as Mark, after cuddling her sleepily, turned on his side and went to sleep.

The answer, he said, when she protested, was to move closer to Birmingham. She spent the most miserable May Bank Holiday Monday she could remember being dragged round show homes and residential roads in Birmingham.

'Now Harborne's meant to be nice.' Mark peered at his A to Z. They were parked on double yellow lines outside a fishmongers. 'Good schools, state and private, and a good mix of housing. It's not far. Want to have a look?'

When she couldn't drum up any enthusiasm, he accused her of being frightened to leave Ambridge because she didn't want to leave her parents. Shula sulked all the way home in the car. They had promised to call at Brookfield for a cup of tea, to let Phil and Jill know how they'd got on, but she insisted they went straight home — 'I'd hate you to think I can't go a whole day without seeing them' — then she went out in the garden and weeded and dug until dusk.

'I'm sorry, I'm sorry,' Mark said when they were in bed. 'I didn't mean it. Sometimes the drive gets me down a bit, that's all, especially now the summer's here. It seems such a waste.'

'You're telling me,' thought Shula unfairly.

Mark made love to her that night, gently and carefully, with thought only for her pleasure. Shula smiled distantly as he kissed and stroked but she felt nothing.

'Just my luck to be pregnant tonight,' she thought when Mark had snuggled into sleep. 'After a day I'd rather forget.'

But she wasn't pregnant, not that month nor the next.

'You told Matthew?'

Shula was sweeping up the leaves in the front garden. Mark was stooping, putting them into the wheelbarrow. They were going to have a bonfire. He didn't have time for compost now. Matthew Thorogood was the new village G.P. He also happened to be going out with Caroline.

'It's no big deal, Shula.' Mark straightened up, feeling at a disadvantage crouched at her feet. 'I just said we'd been trying for a baby since the beginning of the year and nothing had happened yet. He suggested a Well-Woman clinic.'

'Oh, great. And I suppose the whole pub heard — Tony and Eddie and Sid?'

'Yes, I thought I'd put it on Radio Borsetshire as well — of course they didn't.'

'And if you say why am I so sensitive about it —'

'We agreed, you said so yourself only last week after your Mum and Dad's anniversary do, that we'd get things checked out to make sure nothing was wrong.'

'I didn't agree you could go blabbing to Matthew!'

'The Well-Woman Clinic, Shula,' Mark insisted. 'Why not?'

'If you must know,' Shula started sweeping again, vigorously.

'I'd already arranged to go!'

Shula felt her whole life was ruled by whether her period would arrive or not. Every month as the date approached, she was acutely aware of her body. Did she feel the same as usual? Was there anything different? She'd put on a couple of pounds. Could that mean anything? She felt tired. Could it be? Her clinic appointment fell just before Christmas. Mark had arranged to take the time off between Christmas and New Year, sensing that they had had one too many tiffs over his long hours lately — especially his decision to stay over in Birmingham on the night of the office Christmas party.

'What do you want me to do? Get myself breathalysed? Drink Tizer all night?' he'd snapped.

Shula knew she was being unreasonable but she couldn't stop herself. Because of Christmas, the results of her clinic tests wouldn't be with Matthew till January. Till then she could think about nothing else.

In the dead days between Christmas and New Year, they hung back on one of the inevitable Brookfield walks, throwing sticks into the Am and seeing whose got to the fallen branch first.

'It's nearly a year since we decided to start trying for a baby,' said Shula. 'A year since our walk up Lakey Hill. You do want children, Mark, don't you?'

'Are you trying to suggest I haven't been entering wholeheartedly into the spirit of the operation?' Mark was smiling. In the few days he'd had off he'd visibly relaxed. His shoulders seemed three inches lower and the circles under his eyes were less sharply etched. 'Was that why my sister gave me those ginseng tablets in my stocking?'

'Mark, be serious. If we never had children, would you mind?'

Mark turned and took her face in his hands.

'No. Not as long as I'd got you. You're the most important thing, Shula. I love you. You know that, don't you, even if there isn't much time to show it these days.'

'Yes,' she said. 'I know.'

It was not that Shula wanted the test results to show anything wrong, but when they seemed to suggest that everything was normal, she was in a way disappointed. It either meant that, as Mark said, they just had to go on trying, and not worry about it — or there was something more seriously wrong which these tests could not pick up. To put her mind at rest, Matthew suggested a gynaecologist's appointment. He said Shula did not have to decide there and then whether she wanted to take it that far, which was just as well, because she genuinely didn't know what she wanted to do. I can't walk up Lakey Hill again! she thought, but when she left the surgery she wandered in that direction, zigzagging aimlessly up the slope until she stood on the top.

'I'm on top of the world!' Mark said every time they came up here. She smiled to herself. He never was much good at jokes. She sat down on the damp ground, almost in the identical spot where she and Mark had lain a year before, and hugged her knees to her chest. The stinging wind made her eyes water and hissed in her ears. She and Mark could go on trying — and have lots of fun in the process, as he kept reminding her. But once she went to a gynaecologist, it was like admitting that there was something wrong. There would be more tests. What if they discovered something terrible. What if, like Aunty Chris, she could not have children, full stop. Mark had said not having children was all right if he had her. Well, she had him. Wasn't that enough? Deep, deep down she knew that it wasn't.

She knew she ought to talk to Mark about it. She knew he'd do his best to understand. But there was something about facing the fact that she'd made the most basic of assumptions — that she'd be able to have a child — which made it now seem the most incredibly arrogant attitude. She'd thought she could just stop taking the Pill, wait a few weeks and be pregnant. How could she have made such a presumption? And conversely, perversely, she was furious for all the years that she'd been on the Pill, dosing her body with goodness only knew what chemicals, when perhaps it hadn't even been necessary.

The end of February and Mark's birthday approached. He'd be thirty-four this year. In August, Shula would be thirty-one. If she got pregnant tomorrow, which was hardly likely, she'd already be classed as an elderly mother! What had she and Mark been thinking of, all those years of going out for dinner and lazing around reading the papers and watching black and white films on Sunday afternoons? They'd wasted so much time when they should have been trying to make babies and finding out a bit sooner that it just might not be that simple. Mark, she knew, could sense her turmoil. He was confused enough as to why she'd cancelled the gynaecologist's appointment she'd finally asked Matthew to make for her but he'd sensed he mustn't press her. Now he announced he was taking a few days off so they could spend some time together and talk. It was the last thing Shula wanted. If they started to talk about it she feared what she might say. She didn't think she could look at him as he had done to her and say honestly that he was all she wanted, that children didn't matter. And if *she* couldn't say it, what if he couldn't either any more?

There's always a choice: you talk about things sanely and sensibly, which would have been Mark's preferred option, or you bury things inside, which only works for so long, or you row. Mark wouldn't let her bury it: that was why he'd taken the time off work. The row was therefore inevitable. Shula was almost glad when it came. It started over Nigel. Shula just happened to mention, over supper, that one of the ideas Nigel had come up with, if Lower Loxley were to open to the public on a regular basis, was a butterfly farm. Mark was scathing.

'Butterfly farm! Well, that's typical. Butterfly mind, more like. It's a wonder there isn't a Small Tortoiseshell on the Pargetter coat of arms.'

'It's a perfectly good idea.' Shula instantly defended Nigel. 'Berkeley Castle's got one. It's not enough just to have a stately home these days.'

'Oh, well, with you and Elizabeth puffing up his ideas I expect Nigel will have an entire theme park soon.' Mark took a final mouthful. As usual, he'd managed to end with a bit of everything left: meat, potato and carrot which he stacked up on his fork. Shula seethed.

'Don't complain to me when The Bull's full of coach parties,' he went on relentlessly.

Shula stood up and snatched his plate away as he centred his knife and fork. The fork went flying onto the floor.

'Temper, temper,' he said.

'Oh, you make me so mad!' she cried, slamming the plate back on to the table. 'You always know best. You even know what's best for me. Look how you had the nerve to go to Matthew about my body!'

'Your body, that's all we hear about!' Mark was roused now. 'You, you, you. What you want, what's best for you and we all have to tiptoe around. You've never even explained to me why you cancelled that gynae appointment. Because it doesn't affect me, does it? Not much.'

'Not as much as me, no!'

'That's what you think. Because you never think about anyone but yourself in all this. You say you love me. I don't think you love me at all.'

The words seemed to hit Shula like a physical force. She took a step backwards. She listened to the silence, waiting for his apology as he waited for her strenuous denial. Neither came. Finally he stood up, picked up the plates from the table and the fork from the floor and took them out to the kitchen. For the rest of the evening he shut himself in the dining room with a pile of papers. Shula went into the sitting room and put on the Mozart Flute and Harp to soothe herself. Mark's words were banging in her brain, followed by the emptiness of her lack of response. Did she love him still? If you fell in love, it was surely possible to fall out of it. The more she poked and prodded away at what she thought she felt for Mark the less substantial it seemed to be. She called it love, but perhaps it didn't amount to much more than being married to him and living with him, which were hardly the same thing.

She knew it was a serious row and a horribly close reminder of the time they had first split up. She'd still thought they would make it up before bedtime. She took herself upstairs at ten, having nothing else to do. But when Mark came up he collected the alarm clock and his dressing gown and said he was going to sleep on the sofa. Shula shrugged. She wasn't going to be the first to give in.

Next morning, she still didn't want to talk about it. Mark might have done but she had worked herself up into a state of moral indignation where it was more dignified to wait for his apology than to have to defend herself against his accusation, not least because she was uncertain of how well she would do it. Mark folded the blankets neatly.

'Don't worry about that,' said Shula stiffly. 'You'll be late.'

'I didn't think I'd go in today,' he said. 'Are you going in?'

'Yes.' She had a load of appointments. They could talk — if they had to — tonight.

'What time shall I expect you back?' Mark asked.

'The usual,' she said. And coldly: 'You'll be here, will you?'

He was there when she got back but, to her amazement, he was packing.

'Marion and Johnny said they'd put me up,' he explained. They were friends of his in Birmingham.

'You're leaving me?' Her cold anger had gone, replaced by a giddying mix of dread and humiliation.

'You said you didn't want me here when you got back.'

'I didn't. I asked if you would be here.'

Mark's mouth twitched. It wasn't a smile.

'Cross purposes to the end. After last night — well, it's over, isn't it?'

He'd gone. She hadn't pleaded, though she had said she didn't want him to go. It was Friday evening. There wasn't even work to distract her next day. She moped around the house, too listless to garden. She'd done it. It was her fault. She'd driven him away with her stubbornness. She missed him but she couldn't say for certain whether she missed Mark the person or merely his presence in the house. Kenton, who was now back at Brookfield, seemed to understand. What he called his 'twin's intuition' brought him round that first weekend, and they walked the muddy lanes — avoiding Lakey Hill.

'I really thought I loved Mark when I married him,' Shula said. 'I mean, I had long enough to find out. But — how do you know? You only have your own experience. You don't know if it's the same as what other people call love. Look at Mum and Dad. Can you imagine Dad leaving home if they hadn't been able to have a baby?'

'Is that the only trouble, the baby?' Kenton asked.

'I don't know.' Shula stopped for a moment. 'Look, catkins.'

'Well? Don't change the subject.'

'I really don't know.' Shula started walking again. 'It's been so enormous in our lives for the past year, this business of babies, that everything else has got pushed to the edge.'

She had plenty of time now to try to remember all the other things that she and Mark had done either singly or together and enjoyed. She'd liked reading novels but she hadn't read a book for ages that wasn't about pregnancy or conception. They'd used to go to the theatre at Stratford. They hadn't been for two seasons now, what with him being tired from the commuting and her desire to get to bed. She knew guiltily that though the official reason he'd given was that he found the council meetings too much on top of the travelling to work, *she* was the one who had pressurised him to give up being a councillor. It didn't take many long evenings and lonely breakfasts for her to know that she had to make it up. But it was rather like when Mark had been in Hong Kong. When she went to see him in Birmingham he was polite and formal with her and she came home dejected. She realised how much she had hurt him by not instantly saying 'Of course I love you!' Saying it three weeks later was hardly the same. But, just like Hong Kong, Mark surprised her. Next day he turned up at Rodway's.

'I'm sorry,' he said. 'I was horrible yesterday.'

'No, Mark, I'm sorry. I've missed you so much.'

It was him she had missed, the person, his warm presence in the bed, all his irritating habits, all the love for her which she'd only realised was there when it was withdrawn. He moved back home that night.

'I wanted to come back from the minute I got to Moseley,' he said. 'Marion and Johnny are all right but their house is chaotic. I kept finding cat hairs in the butter and I was doing all the washing for the three of us!'

'Poor Mark! You do like things just so.'

She rested her head on his shoulder. They felt right together. Somehow, it worked. It would go on working.

'I've come to apologise,' Shula said to Matthew before she'd even sat down. He raised an eyebrow in that infuriating, superior way some doctors have. 'You made me a gynae appointment and I cancelled it.'

'I know.' He indicated her notes.

'I didn't feel ready for it. We weren't ready for it. But we are now. I'd like another, please.'

'Endometriosis? How can you have had it and not known about it?' Jill poured Shula a cup of tea. She had taken the day off work. The laparoscopy had only been yesterday and she was still a bit sore.

'Well, I'd been getting a bit of pain, but nothing so dreadful I thought anything of it.' Shula dipped into the proffered biscuit tin, rummaging for her favourite custard creams. 'Anyway they said it wasn't too bad and while they were in there having a look around they sort of burnt away the bits of tissue that had got in the wrong place.'

'Ugh, Shula. I don't know how you can eat that biscuit and talk about it at the same time.'

'Frankly, Mum, when you've had a telescope poked through your tummy button, anything's possible.'

'And they say that'll sort it out?'

'It's the usual story Mum, go home, relax, don't think about it, and see how you go. If nothing's happened in another few months I can go back for more tests.'

'How's Mark?'

'He didn't have to have a telescope through his tummy button, if that's what you mean.'

'Is he being supportive?'

Shula smiled.

'You needn't worry about Mark, Mum. He's being just as lovely as ever.'

Jill squeezed her daughter's hand. She would give anything for Shula not to be going through this. She had seen what her inability to have children had done to Christine. Things were different nowadays of course and Christine maintained she'd come to terms with not having children of her own but Jill never quite believed her. She tried to imagine her own life without her four children and simply couldn't. She just wouldn't be the same person. Shula read her troubled face.

'Don't look so worried, Mum. I was worried. I thought they might say I could never have children. That's why I dithered about the appointment. But they didn't. There was a tiny problem, and they've fixed it. I've got a good feeling about this, I really have. Where are we now — end of April. Hey, by this time next year, you could be a granny!'

MAY
——1989——

But it didn't happen. Shula tried to tell herself — as everyone kept telling her — that their best course of action was to think about other things.

'Relax!' everyone said. 'You're probably getting too hung up about it. Forget all about it and it'll happen when you're least expecting it.'

Some people even went further. Pat Archer, who had no illusions about family life, was brutally realistic.

'Babies aren't the be-all and end-all, you know, Shula,' she advised, ladling out her homemade leek soup into an assortment of bowls for lunch one Saturday. Shula was at a loose end because Mark needed a lie-in. Shula had lain in, wide awake, for as long as she could bear, but then felt she had to be up and doing. 'I could certainly imagine life without my three — and frequently do.'

She crossed to the sink, ran cold water into the pan and opened the back door.

'John! Tommy!' she yelled. Her daughter, Helen, was at Pony Club and Tony was out checking the wheat.

'Help yourself to bread, Shula,' she said, sitting down.

Shula did so. Still the boys did not appear.

Pat took a couple of mouthfuls of soup, then got up with a sigh.

'I don't think I've sat down through an entire meal since I had the children. An entire course, even.'

She repeated her summons and returned to the table shaking her head.

'They know full well lunch is at half twelve on a Saturday,' she complained. 'I've given them a ten minute and a five minute warning, and told them to wash their hands. They'll stroll in at about quarter to and then complain (a) that it's soup and not burgers and (b) that it's cold. I wonder why.'

'It's all very well for you to say, Pat,' said Shula. 'But you haven't not got them. All I seem to hear these days is people moaning about their kids, how much mess they make, how ungrateful they are. It's as if all the wrong people get to have children.'

'Thanks very much!' Pat, who had gulped down her soup, fetched a clean pan and poured the contents of the boys' bowls into it. She put it on the stove again.

'I don't mean it like that,' Shula justified herself. 'But — it just seems that parents are the last people who appreciate them.'

'Yes, well, it's mutual.' Pat was looking out of the window. 'Oh no, look at the state of Tommy's trousers. They must have been playing in the silage.'

In the end, Shula had no alternative but to accept the received wisdom. She told Mark she was going to concentrate on her career, forget about having babies and stop worrying. Work promptly obliged. Mr Rodway made her an Associate and six months later rumours started to circulate that Lilian, who owned the Estate, wanted her money out to put into a yachting marina in Guernsey. Shula was caught in the middle. All the family wanted her inside knowledge — her father and David had their eye on acquiring a bit of extra land if the Estate was broken up — yet she could say nothing. The Grundy gossip machine had it first that a pop star had been seen arriving to view the estate by helicopter, then it was an Arab prince who wanted to start a stud farm, then the Dower House was going to become the nerve centre for one of those cultish religions and all the estate land sold off.

Mark was concerned.

'It's all very well for people to say "concentrate on your career" but you're working flat out,' he said.

'You're a fine one to talk!'

Mark was still commuting to Birmingham. They had both got used to the discipline now and made efforts to make time for each other at the weekends. You get used to anything in time, Shula thought. Like not having a baby, perhaps?

Mark put the last of the glasses he had been drying up in the cupboard. David and Ruth were married now and they had been round to supper the night before.

'You're doing too much, Shula. Your body's got to be in A1 condition to conceive. You've read enough about it.'

Shula's bedside table was groaning with books on 'Pregnancy After Thirty' and 'The Older Mother', along with her basal temperature charts and thermometer.

'I am in A1 condition, I'm always going swimming, I eat all my greens —'

'It's your mental state I'm talking about. You're under a lot of stress at work. Tell Rodway to back off a bit.'

She was encouraged by Mark's concern. It made it more of their problem, and less of hers. He started to spend more time in Ambridge, working from home on the days she was at Rodway's, so that they could have lunch together — and slip upstairs to bed, if it was the right time of the month. In the spring, the village put on a production of *The Importance of Being Earnest*.

'Elizabeth couldn't understand why we had to rush off straight away,' smiled Shula later as she lay with her head fitted into the curve of Mark's shoulder. 'You didn't mind, did you?'

'Shula, when your thermometer calls, I'm ready to do my duty,' Mark replied.

He was joking, Shula knew, but she had to ask.

'Is that what it seems like, a duty? No, I mean it, Mark.' She saw the look of affectionate exasperation which instantly crossed his face. 'I mean, you're the one who has to perform to order ... '

Mark turned on his side so that they lay face to face.

'I love you, silly,' he said.

By May, the Estate had a new owner, who was neither a pop star nor an Arab prince nor a Moonie. He was called Cameron Fraser and he was a Scot with an investment business in Crieff and an estate in Perthshire.

'What's he want another one for?' demanded Joe Grundy when Shula, who had gone round to look at a wall that needed repointing, broke the news.

'Search me. As an investment, probably.'

'Cah. Blooming absentee landlords and I'm here working me guts out —'

Joe broke off for one of his more colourful spasms of coughing. Shula excused herself, saying truthfully that she had a lot to do. Cameron Fraser wanted to look through all the books, the rent accounts, the milk records, the A.I. s for the Estate herd ... present or absent, he was clearly going to make his presence felt. Auntie Peggy, still shocked by Lilian's decision to sell, was not at her most efficient and Shula had a feeling that a lot of the burden was going to come her way. Now she was the one bringing work home at night, toiling away at the little bureau in the sitting room through the summer evenings, while Mark mowed the grass. He would allow her to work till ten, then force her to stop, bringing her a glass of wine or an Albertine rose he had picked from the garden, lifting her hair away from her face and letting it fall back.

'Time for bed,' he'd say and make love to her tenderly, whatever her temperature reading.

They were getting on better than they had for ages. Looking back, Shula saw clearly how their failure to conceive had begun to drive them apart but within the last year, they had come back together again. Now, if she asked herself the question, she could honestly say that even without a baby, their life together was pretty idyllic. She could see that they could be complete without one. It didn't make her want one any less.

'Oh, and I thought he'd forgotten!' Shula raised her head from breathing in the smell of the rustling bouquet of flowers which had just been delivered to the Estate Office. 'Five years on ... Happy Anniversary. I love you,' Mark had written on the card. Auntie Peggy beamed.

'There's another envelope, look,' she pointed out.

Shula ripped it open.

'Tickets for the Royal Ballet in Birmingham!' she cried.

The door was flung open.

'Coffee time already ladies? Shula, did you find those figures I wanted about the repairs to Ivy Cottage?'

'Yes, Mr Fraser. I've got them right here —'

'Bring them through, would you?' Cameron Fraser disappeared into his office.

'I'll tell you later,' Shula mouthed to her aunt, putting the tickets in her desk drawer.

It was a month later, a week before they were due to go to the ballet. Mark had been poring over a complicated property transaction all morning and Shula, coming home for lunch, had dragged him out for some fresh air. They were in their favourite place on the top of Lakey Hill. They had found a little hollow in the side of the hill where they were sheltered from the wind. Huddled together, they were watching the potato harvester making its way along the rows at Brookfield. A flock of gulls, keeping a respectful distance, followed the machine, dabbing at the turned earth for delicacies.

'I get so much more done at home. I feel I've done a day's work by lunchtime.' He kissed her neck. 'Can you skive off this afternoon?'

Shula knew this was the moment to tell him but she couldn't make the words come. Saying it would make it real and she hardly dared believe it herself.

'You've got a one-track mind!' she teased, buying time.

'I have! That's choice!'

'The thing is, Mark ... ' she shifted her position so she could see his face, '... all that may not be quite so necessary in future.'

He looked puzzled.

'I think I'm pregnant.'

'Oh, Shula!'

Mark was crying. He really was crying. They were out of the wind so it couldn't be that. His emotion moved her unbearably. She put her face to his and hugged him tight. They rocked together in the hollow on the side of the hill.

'How sure are you?' he asked after a while.

'I went to see Matthew. My period's late. He can't do a test till I'm quite a bit overdue. He suggested a home pregnancy test. They're much more sensitive apparently.'

'Shula — how long have you known this?'

'I only went today. First thing.'

'And you waited till now to tell me? Come on, we're going into Borchester to get one of those kit things.'

'Mark! I've got to get back to the office!'

'Stuff that! And you can put Cameron Fraser on to me.'

On the way in the car Mark said he didn't know how she could be so calm about it. Because I've had disappointments before, she thought. Because I don't feel any different. I don't feel pregnant. But then I don't know what feeling pregnant's like, do I?

The test had to be done first thing in the morning: apparently the hormones would be at their most concentrated then. Shula had a dreadful night. She'd been so excited at the thought that she might be pregnant, she'd had to share it with Mark, but what if it turned out to be a false alarm? She'd have built up his hopes for nothing. In the morning she felt heavy and tired. Her fingers were clumsy as she fumbled with the testing kit: two little glass phials and a white plastic sampler which would turn blue if she was pregnant, remain white if she was not. Mark made them a tray of tea and brought it up to the bedroom.

'This is it!' he said.

The whole thing only took about fifteen minutes but it seemed like years. Mark was as nervous as she was. When the last minute had ticked by — Mark had brought the kitchen timer up as well — Shula didn't think she'd be able to look. Slowly she drew the small stick of plastic out of the phial. It was blue!

'Yes!' Mark hugged her tightly. 'I said it would be all right!'

'It's a very pale blue, Mark.' Shula still couldn't let herself be sure.

'It's blue, isn't it, that's all that matters.' Mark took her face in his hands and kissed her. 'Oh, Shula, we're going to have a baby!'

The Birmingham Hippodrome was packed and the queue at the bar was three deep. They had had trouble parking so they hadn't had time to order their interval drinks before the performance. Shula stood to one side, by a pillar. It was awfully hot. She wished she'd worn a jacket with a blouse underneath, instead of her black velvet suit.

'Orange juice for madam.'

Mark appeared at her side and held out her glass. Shula looked at him blankly. He seemed to be coming towards her, then going away again. The noise of the room and the bright lights and the smoke were all shifting around in her head. She felt as if her brain had come loose and was shifting round with them.

'Shula?'

'Mark — Mark, I feel dizzy!'

Mark plonked their drinks down on a table and grabbed her arm.

'It's all right, Shula, I've got you. Take a deep breath and we'll try and get you some air — excuse me. Excuse me, my wife's not feeling well.'

He propelled Shula out into the foyer. There were no chairs but he found her a wide window ledge to sit on. The window wouldn't open but she rested her forehead against the cool glass, feeling slightly sick. Mark crouched in front of her, holding her hands.

'Look, let's forget the second half. We know what happens anyway.'

A snooty looking couple nearby, who had been discussing the pas de deux, looked scandalised.

'Oh, Mark — no. I'm feeling a bit better already.'

'You're not just saying that, are you?'

'No, honestly. I'll be fine.'

Mark gripped her hands. She could almost feel his love for her surging up her arms.

'It proves one thing, anyway. You must be pregnant.'

Shula smiled wanly. When the home test had been only slightly blue, Matthew had said that was probably because they'd done it so early. He'd said he'd do a test next week.

'If this is what it's like I think I might be going off the idea.'

Mark raised her hands and kissed her fingertips lightly.

'Sorry,' he said. 'It's too late to change your mind.'

Shula thought her Auntie Peggy would never leave. She had come round to drop in some spread sheets which Cameron was insisting showed a deficit in the accounts for the last quarter but though she kept saying she had to get back to cook Jack's supper, she accepted the sherry which Mark had to offer her, and then seemed to want to stay and gossip about Jennifer. Shula presumed that Mark was taking her own lack of contribution to the conversation as an attempt to get rid of her — he couldn't know that she was having a stabbing pain in her right side which was taking her breath away.

'I'd thought she'd never go!' he exclaimed as he returned from showing her to the front door. 'Right, then, supper.'

'Mark.' It came out in a gasp. 'Can you call Matthew. I've got a bit of a pain.'

'The village bonfire's looking really good.' Even as she spoke Jill could head the falseness in her voice. 'Bert took down some old pallets and he said that the Grundy boys have made a guy that looks just like Jack Woolley!'

I feel such a hypocrite, she thought, trying to cheer Shula up when all I want to do is hold her tight and howl with her. She could hardly bring herself to look at the pinched little face against the hospital pillows with Borchester General stamped in ugly blue down the sides. It hadn't helped that they'd gone and put Shula on a maternity ward to begin with — not, admittedly, a ward with mothers and babies, but one with mothers on bedrest or who'd come in for detailed scans. Shula had been too doped up to realise at first, but when Mark complained they'd moved her to a room on her own. That had advantages and disadvantages, though. As Phil pointed out, she only had her own company and she was clearly not enjoying that.

It was Kenton who'd realised first. Jill didn't know if there was any scientific foundation for all the stories about twins having a sort of extra-sensory perception about each other, but Kenton always knew when something was wrong with Shula. He'd been trying to contact her and Mark for a couple of days.

'They've always got that blasted answerphone on!' he'd complained to Jill.

'Go round,' she'd suggested. But when he did, he said Shula hustled him out.

'There's something going on,' he declared.

'You just called at a bad moment,' Jill had reassured him. 'They're coming to lunch on Sunday. You'll see them then.'

She'd thought Mark and Shula were on good form at that lunch. Shula had been a bit quiet, but Mark was full of life. And they'd been so loving with each other. Jill realised now that they had known of the pregnancy but were wisely keeping it quiet. Not that there'd been a pregnancy for long.

Mark hadn't phoned, he'd come round to tell them face to face. He refused a cup of tea so Jill had nothing to do to take her mind off things. Mark looked absolutely grey. He explained that Shula had had an ectopic pregnancy which had had to be terminated. Worse still, they had had to remove the Fallopian tube in which the embryo had been growing as it was damaged beyond repair. Jill glanced at Phil, her eyes smarting with tears and saw his worry. They all realised the implications. With two tubes it had taken Shula nearly two years to conceive. With one ...

'Anyway.' Jill dragged herself back to the present. 'You'll be out in time to see the bonfire. Oh, I don't mean you'd want to go to it,' she corrected herself, seeing the panic in Shula's face. 'You'll be able to see it from the upstairs window at the cottage, won't you? You love Bonfire Night.'

Shula closed her eyes and a snail's trail of tears ran down her face. Jill chafed her daughter's hand between hers. There was nothing she could say which would have any meaning. Don't worry, there'll be another chance? It wasn't meant to be? She'd heard it all already from well-meaning folk in the village who'd heard Shula was in hospital. She had to listen and nod and seem to accept it. She couldn't insult Shula by passing it on.

'I feel such a failure.' Jill had to bend forward to catch what Shula was saying. 'All I want is to give Mark a baby. He says it doesn't matter, we'll go on as we are but I want a baby, Mum, and I know he does. It's killing me, Mum and it's killing us. It really is.'

Shula thought it was the most miserable time she had ever known. She knew it was her own fault. She knew that Mark was suffering just as much as she was but she couldn't let him get close. She turned in on herself. Even Cameron had to accept that she would not be back at work for a while. Prompted, Shula felt by Caroline, who had started going out with him, he sent a basket of fruit and a card wishing her well. Mark ate the fruit and she chucked the card in the bin. She didn't want to think about work. All she wanted to think about was herself and the baby that might have been. Every morning when Mark had left for Birmingham she would lie on in bed, with a skin forming on the cup of tea he had brought her. Would it have been a boy or a girl? She and Mark hadn't begun to talk about names but it was about time there was another Daniel in the Archer family and she'd always liked Mark's middle name, Charles. Jessica was nice for a girl. Or Emily. Emily Hebden. Emily Jessica Hebden. Yes.

The baby would have been due at the end of June. Such a lovely time to have a baby. She could have put the pram out under the apple tree and the baby could have watched the light and shade of the leaves while she pegged the tiny vests and babygrows on the line. If the blue tits were back in the nest box Mark had put up, the fat babies would be calling insistently, almost ready to fly. In the afternoons, she could have wheeled the pram to Brookfield, along the lanes foaming with cow parsley and spiked with dog roses, feeling the sun on her back and adjusting the canopy to shade the baby's face.

When she couldn't lie there any longer, because the imagining got too real and then it hurt to know it wasn't true, she would get up and run a bath. Every day she would take her nightie off and look at herself in the long wardrobe mirror. Her body looked like anyone else's. Why didn't it work like anyone else's then? Baby girls were born with millions of eggs, all ready to be fertilised. Why not hers?

The worst thing was not being able to talk to Mark. She knew she should but it was just too painful. Sometimes she found herself on the verge of saying what she was really thinking, but her eyes skidded away from his and the words went spinning to the back of her brain. It was hardly surprising that he took refuge in work and when a case came up which necessitated three days in Manchester, said that he really ought to go. Kenton was furious with him, but Shula was almost pleased. It meant she hadn't even got to bother with the minimal effort she was making to be up and dressed and to cook dinner for him in the evenings. She didn't miss Mark when he went. It wasn't like that other, dreadful time when he'd left her to stay with Marion and Johnny. Then she might have been too mixed up to want him back but she missed him fiercely, angrily sometimes. Now she felt nothing. Just tired the whole time. Tired, even, of thinking about babies.

The few days he spent in Manchester seemed to do Mark good, anyway. He'd got on well with the assistant solicitor on the case and they'd had some good evenings, apparently, going to the theatre or out for a meal.

'Well, I'm pleased you enjoyed yourself,' Shula said, her tone conveying the opposite.

'Look, Shula — maybe you think I shouldn't have gone —'

'I didn't say that!'

'—but I did go, and the break did me good. Look...' He came to sit beside her on the sofa.

'Don't move Tibby, he's asleep!'

Just before Shula had found out she was pregnant, Elizabeth, who'd been working on a newspaper in Birmingham, had given them two cats, Tibby and Tiger, which she'd rescued.

Mark sighed.

'You won't let me get close to you, will you.'

'It's only because he's asleep.'

'You know I don't mean the cat. Anyway, I'm taking the rest of the year off.'

'What?' It was only the first week of December.

'I'm going to look after you, properly. Your Mum says you won't commit us to Christmas at Brookfield, and I think you're right. We'll have Christmas here, on our own.'

'I don't want to spend Christmas with you!' Shula thought. She wanted to spend Christmas and every other day hunched under the duvet, preferably asleep. For ever.

Four days before Christmas, when Mark had single-handedly decorated the Christmas tree, put up the holly wreath on the door, bought the turkey and sent out the cards he had chosen and she had said she hated, she was due for her six week check, just as if she really had had a baby. She'd heard women in shops and at the surgery joking about their six week checks and their stitches and how, the day after you'd had the baby, someone from Family Planning came round to talk to you about contraception, and you thought 'What for? He's never coming near me again.' She'd thought she'd be part of that conspiracy of women for whom nothing held any fear — not even, after a few months, the thought of another child, else how come most people had two or three? Now not only did she not feel a woman, she didn't even feel like a complete person. She was useless and empty and dull and Mark must hate her because she'd been so vile. Strangely, he didn't seem to hate her. The nastier she was the sweeter he was in return till she wanted to scream. Couldn't she even be horrible properly? Was that something else she couldn't do?

'That's fine. You can get dressed now.' Matthew turned away from her and peeled off his disposable gloves. He went to the sink and washed his hands.

When Shula emerged a few minutes later he was scribbling something on her notes.

'You've had a rough time, Shula. Try and look forward. Next time I see you I hope it'll be to do another pregnancy test.'

'I'd like you to put me on the Pill.'

Matthew indicated that she should sit down. Shula did so, wearily. She seemed to have spent so much of the last few weeks sitting in different chairs. It was almost less tiring to go on standing, by the time you'd lowered yourself and then dragged yourself up again.

'Have you discussed this with Mark?'

She couldn't lie.

'No, not really.'

'Don't you think it might be an idea? Why don't you both come and see me?'

'Oh, Matthew, I don't know.' Shula fiddled with a thread on the end of her scarf. 'I don't know what I want. I don't know if I want another baby. I don't know if I've got it in me to try. And don't ask me what Mark wants because I haven't a clue. At the moment I can't imagine how we ever cared enough for each other for me to get pregnant in the first place. It's as if we were different people.'

'Look, Shula, I'm not going to insult you by saying it's early days and too soon to make a decision, but you've got to talk to Mark about this. He's involved too. I know he hasn't been through what you've been through physically but I know how thrilled he was about the baby. Going on the Pill isn't exactly a decision you can take on your own.'

Mark hit the roof. He didn't often get angry and he never swore but he did both this time. She was stripping the turkey carcass two days after Christmas — a particularly depressing job and one to which she felt well suited. The cats, who were deeply excited by the proceedings, formed a furry figure-of-eight round her legs. Mark took the knife out of her hand and slammed it on the work-top. He pulled her roughly round to face him as the cats, sensing the change in atmosphere, shot to the cat flap where they both struggled without success to get out at the same time.

'I've had about enough of this,' Mark said angrily. 'Nothing I can do is right, you treat me like I don't deserve to live. It was my baby too, but you're so sunk in yourself that's all you can see. And now you want to go on the Pill!' His hand chopped the air in exasperation. 'We've got to start talking to each other again, Shula, and you've really got to sort out how you feel about having children. We've been backwards and forwards over this, and sometimes I'm enough for you, and sometimes you just want a baby and I don't seem to matter and sometimes — most of the time — you want it both ways. You'd better make your mind up or there just isn't any point in us staying together.'

Then he'd left her and she'd heard him put on his coat and go out. He'd been gone a long, long time. Shula knew he would have gone up Lakey Hill but it was a good hour before she realised that he wanted her to come and find him. Still not knowing what she'd say when she got there, she struggled into her wellingtons and pulled on an extra jersey. As she puffed up the incline — after all the lying around, plus Christmas, she felt more sluggish than ever — she could see him silhouetted at the top. The damp grass pulled at her heels and she thought she was never going to make it. As she drew closer he walked down the last few feet and dragged her up without saying a word. Then he took his hand away and stuffed it in his pocket, staring out over the lifeless village. It was that time of day just before people start putting their lights on when the daylight is almost green. No one was about at Brookfield. Probably all indoors, sleeping off another enormous lunch. Mrs Antrobus was walking two Afghans along a footpath. She had the dogs' leads in her hand. One blue, one red. Mrs Antrobus didn't have children. She had her dogs and the church and the W.I. and a photograph of her late husband Teddy in his uniform on the bureau. Shula had kept a dog-eared photograph of Mark in her bedside drawer the whole time he was in Hong Kong. It had been there ever since they were first engaged. She'd still got it somewhere.

'Whatever happened to that checked shirt of yours?' she asked suddenly. 'The one that was like a tablecloth?'

'What?'

He'd been wearing it in the picture.

'Oh, never mind. Mark, I'm —'

'I'm sorry.' He cut across her. 'It's just ... it hurts so much Shula ... and I can't tell what's hurting more, that we lost the baby or that you won't let me be near you.'

'Oh, Mark.'

She loved him so much and all she did was hurt him.

'It's all right for you,' he continued, staring out over the village, not looking at her. 'People can say they're sorry, and it's awful — and it is — but they don't know what to say to me. They're just embarassed. I feel like nothing. Sometimes I want to shout out loud.'

'I think you should.'

'What, shout?'

'Yes. Perhaps we both should. Like this.'

Shula opened her mouth and let out a yell. Then throwing her head back, another, and another. Mark joined in, tentatively at first, then full-bloodedly so his mouth was a dark circle in his face in the gloomy afternoon. He clenched his fists at his side and shouted and shouted, throwing his pain into the sky so the wind could catch it and move it on. Then somehow they were holding one another and not shouting any more, just holding, and everything seemed unnaturally quiet. It seemed such a daring and unusual thing to have done, like nothing either of them had ever done before. It was as if they were filled with a new respect for each other. Here was an aspect of the other they had not even suspected and which they needed to assimilate into the person they thought they had known.

Shula never mentioned the Pill again. They were careful with each other in private and in public because they had seen the enormity of each other's sorrow and that was a huge responsibility to carry. They got through the period of suspended animation between Christmas and New Year, and managed to get through New Year's Eve at Brookfield. When Underwoods opened its doors after yet another Bank Holiday for its winter sale, Shula spent five hundred pounds in a morning.

She paraded around Glebe Cottage in a cherry red coat reduced from over £200 to £95.

'Now I know you're better,' he said. 'You're spending money.'

'Now I know you're better,' she said. 'You're telling me off.'

DECEMBER
—— 1991 ——

T hey must be in!'
    Mark and Shula stood in the yard at Brookfield, staring up at her parents' unlit bedroom window. There was no sign of life in the rest of the house, which was locked and bolted for the night, so Shula couldn't even use her key.

'They're probably asleep,' Mark shrugged.

'Mark, it's New Year's Eve!'

'The cows don't know that, as your father's always telling me,' said Mark reasonably. 'They'll still want milking at six in the morning.'

'Well, yes, but you'd think Mum and Dad would have made it till midnight...'

Mark shivered. Only the odd rustling of straw and the occasional lowing gave away the fact that a hundred cows were lying in their cubicles nearby, listening. Far away, an owl hooted, its cry flying free on the frosty air.

'Come on, Shula, I'm freezing. These shoes have got really thin soles.'

'You poor thing! I've got bare arms under here!'

When they had met in Pat's kitchen, getting refills of punch that neither of them wanted, and realised that they'd both used the pretext of getting a drink to escape from conversations that neither wanted to have, they'd decided to make their escape from the annual family gathering.

'Let's go,' said Mark, taking her plastic cup off her and putting his arms round her waist. 'What's the point of New Year's Eve if you can't do what you want. I'm giving up chocolate tomorrow, after all.'

'There's a bottle of champagne in the fridge at home,' said Shula. 'We could collect it and go round to see Mum and Dad.'

Phil had come out of hospital after a hip replacement operation just the week before Christmas so Phil and Jill had excused themselves from the jollities at Bridge Farm.

'Whatever you want,' said Mark.

Shula made her way upstairs to find the red coat that she'd bought in the sales a year ago. She couldn't believe that another whole year had passed. It had been a good year on the whole. True, there was still no baby to show for it, but somehow she and Mark had arrived at an understanding about that. It had taken a lot of teasing out, but Mark had got her to talk. He'd talked too.

They'd found a new place for talking, at the expense of the hollow on Lakey Hill — Grey Gables Health Club. Mark had become almost obsessive about keeping fit and ever since he'd picked up one of Shula's many manuals on pre-conceptual care, he'd made sure that she came along with him. Shula protested, but she went — and one day the subtlety of his approach dawned on her. Yes, she needed to keep fit, that was only sensible, but there was more to it than that. She'd told him about how she stood in front of the mirror and her feeling that her body was alien, useless. He thought that if she was in tune with her body, 'listening to it' as Gary, the fitness instructor, always said, she might learn to trust it to hold a baby. She might not be able to love it straight away but she could start to like it.

'No wonder you're such a good lawyer,' she puffed as she turned up the step machine another notch. 'I didn't even realise I was being conned.'

It didn't always work. After another punishing session on the cardio-vascular machine or the weights, she often felt an intense loathing, not just for her body, but for Mark as well, but it was a good humoured loathing, and she told him so. Soon they were in competition — who could do longer on the exercise bike or go further on the running machine. But it got results.

'Look.' Shula flexed her arm. 'No more flappy turkey-skin. And as for my pectorals...'

'I've noticed,' said Mark. 'It's not all self-denial, you know.'

As they stroked lazily up and down the pool after a session in the gym, or sweated in the steam room, Mark talked and Shula listened. She realised that for years she had done all the talking and Mark had done all the listening, and just because he didn't say as much as she did, it didn't mean he didn't feel it.

She loved him more than ever.

'I nearly lost you,' she'd say. 'I nearly drove you away. I was so wrapped up in my misery I couldn't see yours. I let the ectopic push us apart when it should have brought us together.'

'Forget it,' Mark said. 'You've got to go forward.'

As he often said, it wasn't as though they were one of those couples who didn't get on with each other, who needed a family to stick them together, and then fell apart when the children left home. They were both in well-paid jobs which they enjoyed. They had the money to savour their free time. They bought mountain bikes and raced each other round the lanes. Mark relaid the path outside the back door with Victorian blue brick. Shula wondered about an Open University degree. They talked about travelling to the parts of the world neither had seen. Mark wanted to do the West Coast of America and see New England in the fall. Shula said she'd love to go back to India. They started to concentrate on what they had instead of what was missing and instead of yawning emptiness Shula was surprised to find that her life was full.

Somehow during the course of the year they had found a new peace. Her desire for a baby had moved through frustration and disappointment to anger and desperation. Now there was an element of acceptance. Its tenor was not resignation but a sort of benign fatalism. If it happened, it happened. If not, they would cope.

Even more than the training sessions and the Lycra shorts he bought her — ('Black and yellow? Mark, I'm not wearing those!') — the thing which had helped Shula more than anything that year was Mark moving back to Borchester. It had come from him: she hadn't even had to nag. She had got so used to his commuting that she had come to terms with it, and it wasn't as if it stopped her from doing anything. If Mark was going to be late back she saw Caroline or Kenton or her Mum. With the computer screen winking in the back bedroom and the fax machine rasping away, Mark could usually manage to work from home two days a week. So his decision to set up on his own was an unlooked-for bonus.

'There's talk of a merger,' he'd announced one evening in late spring. 'With a big firm from up North, looking for a foothold in Birmingham. I don't know how I feel about it. I like the place the size it is.'

Within a month, having taken advice about the sort of changes the merger might mean, Mark's mind was made up. He left at the end of June, taking four of the firm's best clients with him. He persuaded a reluctant Kenton that the premises of the antique shop Kenton was running in Borchester would be perfect, found himself a partner — a woman, to Shula's slight surprise, Usha Gupta, — and by the autumn, the brass plate was up announcing that Hebden and Gupta were open for business. Shula had no illusions that she'd see any more of Mark — he spent a couple of evenings each week wining and dining would-be clients — but she felt reassured to know he was down the road instead of an hour and a half away. She had always felt that Mark had gone to Birmingham because the change had been forced upon him. He had made it work because he had felt he had to get out of Spencer and Holden. This time it was different. She felt Mark was more in control of it, as they both were in all aspects of their lives. The change felt grown up and mature and good.

'Goodness, I'm smug!' she laughed with her mother. 'How do you put up with me?'

'I'm just pleased that one of my children is settled!'

It was the end of October and they were both making pumpkin lanterns for the Hallowe'en Disco which Robin Stokes, the new vicar, was holding for the 12-16s at the village hall.

'Come on Mum, Ruth and David are happy enough.'

Ruth had joined them for a cup of tea earlier but had disappeared to do the afternoon milking.

'Oh yes, they're all right.' Jill cut a couple of jagged teeth in her pumpkin and surveyed the result. 'But you know Kenton's gone to see an old navy chum this week —'

'He can see his friends, can't he?'

'I wouldn't be at all surprised if he didn't take off again. I don't think the shop's doing very well.' Eased out by Mark, Kenton had gone into partnership with Nelson Gabriel, in a lock-up shop on the Old Market Square.

'No.' Mark didn't think so either, and has always been disparaging about Kenton's business acumen.

'And what do *you* think about Elizabeth and Cameron Fraser?' Elizabeth had been flirting shamelessly with Cameron for months, even while he was still going out with Caroline.

'Oh, Mum, ask me an easier one.' Shula looked at her lantern with dissatisfaction. 'How did you do your teeth so well? Mine are like stumps.'

'Years of practice, dear,' said Jill. 'Give it here.'

She took Shula's pumpkin and set to work on bit of cosmetic dentistry.

'She's going to the opening meet of the hunt with him, you know,' she said as she worked.

'Elizabeth? She hasn't ridden for years.'

'She hasn't read a book for years, and I don't think she's cooked in her life but he got her doing both of those.'

Shula sighed.

'It's very awkward. I find him hard enough to get on with as an employer, let alone as a prospective brother-in-law.'

'Don't say that, dear, please.' Jill flexed her fingers.

'Well, last time I spoke to Elizabeth about it she was fantasising about being chatelaine of the Dower House.' Shula started unravelling the black crêpe paper which was to hang in fronds from the ceiling.

'Cameron can't be serious about her, can he, Shula? He's years older than she is.'

Shula lifted her shoulders in a half-shrug, half question.

'You can't tell with him. He never gives anything away.'

'I just don't want her to get hurt.' Jill turned the last of the pumpkin heads around in final inspection.

'I don't think you should worry too much about Elizabeth, Mum. She can look after herself. We're not babies now, you know.'

After Hallowe'en and Bonfire Night came Christmas, and the New

Year when she and Mark had tried to rouse her parents (they'd been tucked up in bed with a bottle of champagne and the video of *Casablanca*, apparently). Then three months of mud and rain and everyone at Brookfield complaining because the cows were indoors and the yards had to be scraped and they were tired from lambing and just wanted to get out on the land. Easter again, and sitting in St. Stephen's and letting her eyes stray to the font with the carved heads, two of which were supposed to be King and Queen Eleanor of Castille, and praying for the day when she would stand in this church, where she and Mark had been married, for the christening of their baby.

'A baby?'

Shula gripped the edge of her desk. She saw the tendons flex in her hand, noted the grain of the wood, felt the panic rise.

'I'm sorry, I thought you knew.'

Even Cameron Fraser had the grace to look slightly embarrassed. I hate you, Cameron, Shula thought. At least if I can hate you I don't have to hate my little sister who's pregnant by accident, through stupidity and fecklessness, probably, through not taking her Pill. She got through the rest of the day on automatic pilot, feeling as if she'd been sandbagged. That night she phoned Brookfield without even telling Mark and asked Elizabeth to meet her at Nelson's the next day.

'Why didn't you tell me?' she said as soon as they'd sat down.

'Shula, I couldn't.' Elizabeth looked at her sister, then at the floor, guiltily. Nelson had recently redecorated in what he called gentleman's club style — or as Elizabeth called it, poor man's Ralph Lauren. The floor had been sanded and polished a pale blonde. It was like walking over honey. 'It was only to protect you.'

Shula was furious with a boiling anger, the anger of being patronised and felt sorry for and dismissed.

'I'm tired of everyone thinking I need protecting. What do you take me for? Don't you think it was rather more hurtful to hear it from Cameron? In the office?'

'Of course. Of course it was. I'm sorry.'

'No, I'm sorry.' Her anger evaporated as she heard the tremor in

Elizabeth's voice. Shula picked Elizabeth's hand out of her lap and squeezed it. 'Here I am shouting at you, I shouldn't be upsetting you. I haven't even asked how you are.'

'Oh well, you know ...' began Elizabeth. No, I don't, thought Shula, that's the point, but tact had never been Elizabeth's strong suit. 'I'm OK when I get going but a bit grotty first thing in the morning.'

'Well, you must take care of yourself,' said Shula. She was the expert, after all. She owned every book published on the subject. 'What you need in the mornings is a dry biscuit or something. And don't rush to get up. Let Mum look after you. By the way, I've got lots of books you can borrow.'

'Oh — well, thanks, but I don't really want to know all about that stuff. I just want it to be born, so Cameron and I can settle down and be a family.'

You're so young, Shula thought wonderingly. You haven't got a clue. Before the end of the year you'll be a mother and you sound like a little girl. She wasn't at all convinced that Cameron was as delighted about the pregnancy as Elizabeth claimed. In fact he'd been even more preoccupied than usual at work in the past couple of weeks. Shula had caught sight of a couple of cryptic faxes and there had been a lot of insistent phone calls from a particular broker. Fraser was obviously trying to pull off some business deal. Shula hoped for Elizabeth's sake that when it was signed and sealed he would be happy to sink into domesticity but something in her told her that it would require a major character change — and a willingness to make that change on Cameron's part — which in the year she had known him she had never detected. Cameron seemed to like himself the way he was and if others didn't, that was their problem.

Her mother felt the same. They had had to have Cameron round to dinner at Brookfield and the evening had not been an easy one.

'Your father's even begun to appreciate Nigel now he's spent some time with Cameron,' Jill confided to Shula. She gave a deep sigh. 'I just can't warm to him. Elizabeth worships the ground he walks on, but there's something about him I just don't take to.'

'He's slimy, isn't he?' David, who'd been taking his boots off at the door, approached and took his mug of coffee. 'The man's a creep of the first order. And Elizabeth's totally fallen for it.'

As Shula had feared, Elizabeth's plans for a speedy wedding and domestic bliss at the Dower House were soon spiked by Cameron. Having allowed her to raise her hopes, he told her bluntly that, if she wanted to have the baby, he'd support her financially but that marriage wasn't on his agenda and never had been.

'You don't think he's already married, do you?' Shula asked Caroline. 'You went out with him, after all.'

'He never called me by any name but my own, if that's what you mean,' replied Caroline. 'You know, I honestly can't think what I ever saw in him. Poor Elizabeth. What's she going to do?'

'She's going to have the baby and hope he changes his mind, as far as I can tell,' said Shula.

'That's risky,' said Caroline shrewdly. 'I mean, she might get a dear little scrap who sleeps round the clock but she might get a bawling prawn that stinks to high heaven. Babies aren't always that appealing.'

Shula knew why she'd stayed such good friends with Caroline. She always managed to put things in perspective. She was older than Shula. And she hadn't got children. She stopped Shula feeling like a total freak.

But Elizabeth's baby opened up the old wound. Shula had thought the scar tissue was strong enough, but she knew for certain now that it would always be a weak place. She told her mother what she'd told Elizabeth, that she could cope with the news, that the baby would be a Brookfield baby, a lucky baby, and would be loved as such. She told the family that she had come to terms with not having children, that she and Mark had faced the fact that it might never happen for them, and that they had decided that their lives were rich in other ways. It wasn't all true, but she felt she could be fairly convincing while she said it. She only broke at night, with Mark, when they held each other tight and she admitted how it hurt. Her confidence was at rock bottom again.

'Hold me, Mark,' she'd whisper. 'Tell me you love me.'

He always did but she couldn't hear it enough times and it

seemed to wear off quickly. How could he mean it when she was failing him in such a fundamental way?

She couldn't take her anguish to her mother because Jill was beside herself with worry about Elizabeth. For all her determination to have the baby the whole family knew that Elizabeth wasn't a coper. From her trepidation about telling Cameron she had built a dream out of her delight at his initial response and had naively told the world her grandiose plans of how things would be. When it transpired that Cameron's ideas were very different, she was left with an unwieldy situation and the added humiliation of the huge and visible gap between her fantasy and the reality. Nor did she have the maturity to admit it. Though she now declared that single parenthood was what she wanted, no-one really believed it, least of all, as Jill said, Elizabeth herself. But while she was still so valiantly pretending, they had to help her pretend. Jill began to redecorate one of the farm cottages with the idea that Elizabeth and the baby could live there. But even with Brookfield's support, Shula herself had severe doubts about how her sister would manage.

'Mark,' she said cautiously one night as they lay entwined together before sleep. 'I know you'll say it's a mad idea, but what if we were to adopt the baby?'

'What? Shula, love, it is a mad idea.' Mark raised himself on one elbow to look down at her.

'Why?' She hadn't expected him to agree straight away and she'd marshalled her arguments. 'We've talked about adoption, haven't we?'

'In the past, yes, and we ruled it out.' Mark stroked the line of her jaw with the back of his hand. 'You always said you wanted our baby, not someone else's.'

Shula caught his hand and held it there, tight.

'But this would be almost our baby. It's my sister's. You hear about sisters having babies for each other all the time.'

'When they've planned it, yes,' he said gently, 'I know it happens, but that's not what happened with Elizabeth.'

'Please, Mark. Elizabeth's so confused. Maybe this is why it's happened. To give us a chance. Can't we at least talk about it?'

'Darling, you're just setting yourself up to be disappointed. And

I don't think you've thought through all the implications.'

'Mark, I'm not one of your clients to be fobbed off!' She was almost crying now. 'I can't bear this, Mark!'

She heard him swallow his sigh as he took her in his arms. He soothed her and smoothed her hair for a bit, then looked at the clock and groaned.

'It's after twelve. Please, Shula, just forget about it for tonight. We'll talk about it tomorrow.'

Shula didn't bring it up next day, because she knew exactly what Mark would say. But when Elizabeth called at the Estate office on a pretext — really, to try and see Cameron — she couldn't stop herself from asking her if she'd consider letting them adopt the baby.

'You know we'd want what's best for the baby —'

'Shula, it's my baby. I'll decide what's best!'

The phone rang. It was Mr Rodway.

'Elizabeth, wait, please,' Shula begged as Elizabeth left. She dragged her attention back to Mr Rodway, who seemed in something of a state.

'Sorry, Mr Rodway, I didn't quite catch ... I had someone with me ... What?... The Fraud Squad? For Mr Fraser?'

Suddenly Elizabeth and the baby were eclipsed by the side of Cameron's life he had not shown to anyone. Shula's days were filled with investigators and liquidators and calls from creditors. Cameron had gone to ground. The police were trying to pick up a trail which had gone cold and Shula was one of the few known contacts. It was a week until she saw Elizabeth again, when she called round to Glebe Cottage. Shula's heart leapt when she saw her sister at the door. She's had a change of heart, she thought. She's come to tell me we can adopt the baby. Elizabeth refused a drink and sat forward on the edge of the sofa.

'There is no baby, Shula,' she said.

'No baby?'

'I've had an abortion.'

Shula thought her heart had stopped. Then it started up again with a sickening lurch.

'No.'

'Yes, I have. I'm sorry, Shula. But after what you said — I thought I ought to tell you myself.'

'How long have you been awake?'

Mark knelt down by her side. Shula was sitting by the bedroom window, looking out at the May garden. Everything was throbbing with life. The new leaves were so bright in the early sunshine it almost hurt your eyes to look at them. The lawn seemed to have shrunk where the lilac and dogwood and hebe had swelled over its edges. Bluebells blurred the borders. The last of the laburnum blossom drifted slowly down.

'I don't know. Half five — six?' Shula's voice was lifeless.

'I'll make some tea.' He stroked her foot. 'You're cold.'

'Am I? I didn't notice.'

'Shula. Don't be like this.'

'How could she, Mark? How could she?'

They had been through this last night, and late into the night.

'Elizabeth made a choice,' he said simply. 'It's not the choice you would have made, or would have had her make, but it's made now. And it was her choice to make.'

'That's what's so unfair, don't you see?' Shula thought she would burst with the injustice of it all. 'She had all the choices. The choice of whether to have a baby or not in the first place. The choice of whether to keep it. And we were making it so easy for her. She could have had the baby and let us all help look after it. Or she could have let you and me keep the baby, and love it like our own. Instead — oh, what's the point?'

They'd been doing so well. She really had thought she'd come to terms with it. She still couldn't read anything in the papers about children living in poverty or suffering abuse or neglect but these days she could walk past a school playground at morning break or the swings in the park without wanting to cry. She'd even managed to go into Mothercare when she'd first heard about Elizabeth and look at little velour rompers and baby baths. Now she was right back where she'd been two years ago. Wanting and wanting something it seemed she couldn't have.

Robin was a help. She'd always got on well with Robin, the

non-stipendiary minister, right from his first Christmas in Ambridge when she'd had to explain she couldn't do the Christmas reading about the Madonna and child and it had all come out about the ectopic. One night soon after Elizabeth's abortion he came across her sitting in church, wondering, wandering again among all the possibilities and all the apparent dead-ends.

She hadn't meant to tell him. She hadn't gone to church hoping to find him: she'd gone specifically to be alone. But once he was there, she couldn't help herself.

'This — this friend of mine,' she said carefully. 'Well, she's had a pregnancy terminated. And you know, after what I've been through and trying for so long...I just can't come to terms with it.'

Robin gave what she'd said his usual amount of thought.

'I couldn't say this to everyone,' he said finally. 'But I know you're capable of it, so I think you might be able to try. I don't want you to think about it from your point of view, but from hers. And try to think about it, not in terms of judgment for what she did, but in terms of forgiveness. She may seem reconciled to it now, maybe even relieved, but underneath she's probably as confused as you are. She needs all the help she can get and you judging her isn't going to make her feel any better about herself.'

Mark had tried to say the same thing but in a different way, but Shula wouldn't hear it from him. Robin saying it too made her realise that she was allowing the abortion to do what she had sworn wouldn't happen again — to come between her and Mark, with her castigating him for not understanding her point of view when, typical Mark, typical solicitor, he was trying to see it from all sides. With an effort of will that was almost physical — she could feel herself pulling herself together — she tried very hard to do as Robin had suggested. Mark was relieved and supportive. Shula took each day cautiously, anticipating another hurt. When one didn't come, she was more surprised than pleased. It was in this state of fragility that she went to The Bull one lunchtime, invited by David along with the rest of the family, to be told that Ruth was expecting a baby.

Shula had been dreading this announcement ever since Ruth and David had got married. She remembered a conversation she'd had about having children once with Auntie Chris.

'I know I won't be able to look pleased,' she'd said. 'Everyone will be watching me to see how I take it.'

She didn't know if everyone was watching her or not. She couldn't look at Mark, she certainly couldn't look at Elizabeth. She forced herself to look at Ruth, to meet her sister-in-law's nervous eyes and say 'Congratulations'.

With Mark, she was inconsolable.

'It's as bad as it ever was,' she said bleakly. 'How am I going to get through the next nine months, watching Ruth get fatter? How am I going to get through all those years watching her baby grow?'

'Hey, aren't you forgetting something?' Mark said. 'You're writing off our chances entirely. It's not as if we've been told we'll never have children.'

'Oh, Mark, be realistic!' Shula was weeding the border under the kitchen window. It was infested with chickweed. 'I'm nearly thirty-four! That's ancient in gynaecological terms.'

'Rubbish. What about all these women you hear about having their first babies at forty plus.'

'Mark, you hear about them because it's so rare! And I bet they didn't have a history like mine.'

'Shula, if you're determined to be defeatist I can't stop you.' Mark finished his beer and got up from the bench to continue his mowing. 'But I'm disappointed. I thought you'd got over that.'

'I got on with it. I never got over it,' said Shula sadly.

She did have to watch Ruth blossoming, and so did Elizabeth. Shula almost felt sorry for her sister. She knew how hard it was and Elizabeth hadn't had all Shula's practice in coping when everything doesn't go your way. In the aftermath of Cameron Fraser's disappearance Shula was doubly busy on the estate, which was again up for sale. Robin and Caroline started to go out, despite the difference in their beliefs. Shula organised a sponsored bike ride for St. Stephen's. Christmas rolled round again and Shula offered to stage *Mac the Sheepstealer* in church. She had a particularly bad moment when the Sunday school children were putting out the nativity scene which occupied the space below the pulpit every year.

Emma Carter lovingly placed the Baby Jesus in his crib and Shula was reminded of the crib which she and Mark had seen at a house sale. Mark had offered to buy it for her. He had rocked it and she had burst into tears because it was empty.

Ruth and David's daughter, Philippa Rose, was born at four in the afternoon on Wednesday 17th February 1993. Shula had steeled herself to deal with her own feelings. She also had to deal with Elizabeth, who fell apart.

'You've got to go and see Ruth and the baby,' Shula urged.

'I can't! For Heaven's sake, Shula, you of all people —'

'You can,' said Shula firmly. 'You were brave enough to have an abortion. I've thought about it a lot. I'm not saying it was the right thing but it was brave.'

Elizabeth went. Philippa — or Pip for short — was just beautiful. Ruth and David were so proud. Shula went once on her own and once with Mark. When they came back from the hospital, Shula was very quiet. Mark opened a bottle of wine. Out of his briefcase he produced a bundle of property details from some of Rodway's rivals in Borchester and tried to interest her in them. He wanted to move. They had just lost Willow Farm, Matthew Thorogood's old house, to Mike and Betty Tucker.

'Mark, I know what you're trying to do,' she said. 'And I love you for it. It's like when you made me go on that keep fit regime at the Health Club. But in a way it's insulting. I can work it out, you know. You're trying to distract me with a house when what we need is a baby. How is moving to a great big house going to help? Don't you think I'll notice it even more there?'

'I think it's time we made some changes in our lives, that's all,' he replied.

'So do I,' said Shula. 'It's seeing Pip, really. My kid brother a father. And you not. And you'd be such a good father, Mark. I know I've said all sorts of things,' she went on hurriedly. 'That I didn't want to adopt, I only wanted our baby, and I wanted it to happen naturally or not at all. But now —'

'Shula, we've left it a bit late for adoption, you know.'

Poor Mark. He spent his life in — what had Mr Rodway said

about the Cameron Fraser saga? — damage limitation. Calming her down, making her see sense, trying to prevent her from being disappointed. It was all very well, and he had the best of motives, but if she wasn't careful it could stop her from ever doing anything.

'I'm not thinking about adoption, Mark. I mean I.V.F. or something. I just know I'll do anything to have a baby of our own.'

She didn't want Mark to come with her to the doctor. Matthew had been replaced by Richard Locke who was young and keen and had already increased the pulse rates of several of his female patients.

'I'll only have to tell him all about my insides. You've heard it all before. Several times,' she said.

'There'll be a lot of that, won't there, if we go for I.V.F.,' said Mark.

'I don't care.' She hesitated. What was he trying to say? A faint panic fluttered in her chest. 'You do still want to do it, don't you, Mark?'

'Of course I do.' He put down his *Independent* and touched her hand. 'I haven't changed my mind about wanting a child. But it's you who's got to go through all the medical stuff. I can't take responsibility for that decision, can I?'

Thank God. He wasn't changing his mind.

'I'm not asking you to. I've made it.'

Shula stood up, tipping Tiger onto the floor. He stared at her unimpressed with his gooseberry eyes as she brushed cat hair from her skirt.

'Well, I'd better get going.'

Mark stood up and put his arms round her. He kissed her softly.

'I'll call you later. Good luck,' he said.

Shula liked Richard, the new doctor. He was blunt and to the point. Too much so, some said, he'd even had the nerve to criticise Eddie Grundy's style at darts. But that was what Shula wanted. After all the years of being told to go away and hope, a bit of plain talking would be refreshing. Richard didn't disappoint her. Once he'd been through the gynaecological map of her insides, and said her that he couldn't see any reason why she and Mark wouldn't be suitable for I.V.F., he told her straight.

'I just want you to be quite sure you know what you're getting yourself into,' he said, his blue eyes holding hers. 'You know the statistics? A one in five chance of getting pregnant and a one in ten chance of carrying the baby to term.'

Shula nodded.

'I've done my homework. But this is my last chance. I've got to take it.'

APRIL

1993

'So — will you do it?'

It was Good Friday and Shula was picking daffodils for the house. She had to remember to leave some for tomorrow, when Mrs Antrobus would no doubt be in desperate need for the church flowers. Although Marjorie had been the mainstay of the St. Stephen's flower rota for years now, she always underestimated the number of window ledges in the church, or perhaps just got carried away in her enthusiasm and overfilled the vases. Whatever the reason, she often had to call round to Glebe to supplement her displays.

Shula looked up from her frilly bundle of yellow.

'Oh, David, of course I will! Thank you. You surely didn't think I'd say no?'

He looked relieved and embarrassed and Shula saw that he had indeed thought it a possibility. If only people didn't have to tiptoe round her quite so much where children were concerned. Still, it might not be for much longer.

'Well, I can't think of anyone who'd be a better godmother to Pip,' David declared. 'The other two are still up for grabs but Ruth and I both agree, you're our definite.'

'Have you set a date for the christening?' Shula laid the flowers carefully in her basket.

'Don't you start, Mum's already ironed the Archer christening robe. It won't be till the summer. We want to wait till Pip's a bit bigger.'

I could be pregnant by the summer, thought Shula.

'Have you got time for coffee?' she said.

'Love some.'

'We'll have it out in the garden, shall we?' said Shula. 'It's such a lovely day.'

She was grateful for the soft spring weather. Glebe Cottage always seemed to shrink when David was there and he seemed to get bigger and taller. It made her think of the fearful expansions and contractions in *Alice in Wonderland*, a story she'd always found rather sinister. She feared for her bunches of herbs which hung from the beams in the kitchen and dreaded him ever going into the sitting room where she had her enamel boxes and bowls of *pot pourri*.

'Brilliant. This is the life.' David collapsed leggily into a deckchair. The church clock struck the quarter.

'I'll dump these flowers in the sink and put the kettle on,' said Shula.

'Sis?'

'Yes?'

He hadn't called her that for years.

'I just want to say ... well, how brave I think you are with all this I.V.F. stuff. And I hope it works out for both of you. I really do.'

'Thank you. Me too.'

The following week she had her initial appointment with the consultant at the clinic in Birmingham. It was smart and modern and efficient — all plants and prints. The literature talked about 'assisted conception': infertility was never mentioned. The consultant, Mr Gibson, was charming. He was kind and fatherly and had a matching tie and handkerchief and a voice like melting chocolate which Shula could have listened to all day. She didn't even mind running through her gynaecological history yet again. But like so many other times, the first appointment proved to be a false start.

'I can't wait another two weeks for this X-Ray thing!' she fumed to Mark as they inched their way through a dreary suburb of south-west Birmingham on their way home. 'I was all psyched up for something to happen today!'

'Well, what's two weeks when we've waited this long?'

Mark was as infuriatingly reasonable as ever, even about this. Shula sighed and looked out of the window at a particularly scruffy parade of shops. The sky was sullen. Fish and chip papers blew about in the slipstream of hissing buses. Pasty-faced women were dragging toddlers along the pavement. Girls of fifteen or sixteen pushed brand-new buggies looking utterly vacant. Babies and children — everywhere she looked.

'So I've got to go back in two weeks for a hysterosalpingogram,' she told her mother when they got back to Ambridge. 'It can only happen at a certain stage in your cycle, apparently. They inject a dye which shows up on the X-Ray just like bones usually would.'

'How incredible!' said Jill. 'You're going to be a medical expert at the end of all this.'

'Or a nervous wreck,' said Shula.

Knowing they were thinking seriously about I.V.F., Mr Gibson arranged for them to go for counselling sessions. Mark was happy to go along with it: it was Shula who felt she didn't need them.

'I know all the options, I know the success rate — or lack of it,' she said to Mark as they drove to the clinic for the first one. 'I don't know what else they can tell me.'

Richard had said way back in the beginning that she'd need to be psychologically as well as physically strong. After all she'd been through — the disappointments and the monthly failures, the ectopic and Elizabeth's abortion, Shula felt quite strong enough. But the counselling was good. It made them think about questions which they hadn't really fully answered, like just why they wanted a child so much.

'It's not just because it's expected,' Shula said after a long while. 'I mean, expected of me by other people, and me expecting it to happen—'

'Or because we have a thing about — what is it — children being the only real immortality or anything —' Mark added.

'It's more that...' Shula sought for the words. She didn't want to say anything which didn't accurately represent what she thought. 'I think it's partly to do with regenerating yourself. Finding those bits of you that can only come out again through contact with a child. Does that sound selfish?' What if I've given the wrong answer, she thought. It did sound rather self-centred. But it was the truth.

They also started to go to a group with other couples. It called itself a fertility support group not an infertility support group. Most of them were a similar age to Mark and Shula. Many had concentrated on their careers, assuming that as soon as they wanted to start a family, it would happen as naturally and successfully as their promotions and salary rises. They met one couple, Rob and Colette, with whom they got on particularly well.

'I kept putting it off for just one more year,' Colette said when the four of them went out for a drink after the meeting. 'First we were saving up to move house. Then I was offered the job I'd been waiting for for two years. Then Rob lost his job. He got another one, but it was in Cardiff. We hardly saw each other for eighteen months. By the time we started trying seriously, we'd lost six years. Another year before we admitted something might be wrong. I'm thirty-eight next birthday - too old to adopt, even if we wanted to. What do you do?'

It was a huge release to talk to other people who'd been through the same frustrations. Shula realised how isolated she'd become, comparing herself only with mothers when there were thousands of other women in her situation.

Shula was so certain that I.V.F. was the solution. It worried Jill.

'She's pinning everything on this, Phil,' she fretted. She had brought a flask of tea out to the field where he was looking at the lambs.

Phil let go of the struggling lamb whose conformation he'd been feeling and straightened, wincing. The lamb shot off like something out of the Grand National.

'Jill,' he said, 'You're worried, I'm worried but I can't see what good it'll do. We've just got to support her whatever the outcome.'

Jill poured two cups from the flask. She held one out to Phil.

'Don't reckon any of these'll be ready for the butcher for another fortnight at least,' he said.

'Phil! Can't you keep your mind off the farm for two minutes?'

'Two minutes? Was it as long as that? Disgraceful.' He put his arm round Jill's shoulders. 'Now stop worrying. No gingerbread?'

'Of course you must play cricket, Mark.'

It was a bright Wednesday morning at the end of May. The hysterosalpingogram had shown that, as had been suspected, Shula's remaining Fallopian tube was blocked, which meant that I.V.F. was their only option. Shula was delighted. At last something was happening. They were doing something. They were making progress, taking control. She had already started treatment to suppress her own hormone production and prepare her for the implantation.

'You know what they said, we've got to carry on as normal. Your coffee's there.'

'Oh, yes, very normal,' said Mark, gulping it down. He was in court at nine thirty and he had an affidavit to draft before then. 'Ow, that's hot. You've got to go round sniffing like a cocaine addict —'

'How many cocaine addicts do you know?'

'I read the papers!' said Mark. 'Now you've got Richard giving you these nasty injections as well —'

'I don't mind, Mark. You could always do them, you know.'

'Shula, please! Not while I'm having my breakfast.'

Shula laughed.

'You go and play cricket. Or people will get suspicious and I don't want the whole village to know. At least, not till we've got some good news to tell them.'

Mark looked serious.

'You really do think it's going to work, don't you?' he said.

'I wouldn't be doing it if I didn't.'

Now she had started, and was actually doing something definite towards having a baby, Shula felt more positive than she had for years. Ten days later, the clinic told her that her follicles, boosted by the injections, had developed well. After another course of injections to stimulate ovulation, Mark drove her to the clinic early one Sunday morning. There they collected ten eggs from her to be fertilised and incubated.

'They expect me to go home and rest! They'll be lucky!' she said to Mark. 'I'll be on the phone every ten minutes to see if they're dividing.'

Shula spent all day by the phone. Finally, in the evening, the clinic told her the cells were dividing perfectly. She could go back next day to have some of the eggs implanted. Then they would have to go through a two-week wait for a pregnancy test.

'I'm going back to work!' she said. 'I'll go and bury myself in the quarterly accounts and the Grundies' repair bills and see if that takes my mind off whether I'm pregnant or not.'

It wasn't quite that easy. Every time Shula felt the slightest twinge in her abdomen she had to phone the clinic for reassurance. With the pregnancy test a week away, she had to endure Ruth's 25th birthday party, when being sociable was the last thing she felt like. Though all the family knew that she and Mark were having fertility treatment, only Phil and Jill knew the exact timescale.

'I've never known two weeks go so slowly,' she complained to Mark in bed that night. 'Not even at school, in the last two weeks of the summer term when you were just hanging on for the holidays.'

'You ought to plan a little treat every day, something to look forward to,' said Mark. 'Isn't that what they advise on the problem pages of your magazines?'

'How would you know?' Shula pinched him gently.

'I've had to do a lot of sitting round in clinics lately, remember,' he said. 'It's amazing what you learn. I got a very good recipe for Moroccan lamb last time. I'll make it for you at the weekend.'

Mr Gibson came back into the room. His face gave nothing away. Today his tie and handkerchief were not matching, but toning: a maroon paisley and plain silk. He came and sat down and placed Shula's file on the desk in front of him.

'Well, Mrs Hebden,' he began, 'I'm delighted to tell you that your pregnancy test was positive.'

He said a lot more, something about urging her to phone if she needed any reassurance, saying they next wanted to see her in three weeks for the very first scan but Shula didn't hear any of it. She hoped Mark was taking it in. She was sure he would be, he was always so sensible, but when she asked him about it he hadn't a clue.

'I just wanted to get out of there and hold you,' he said as they stood in the car park, hugging and tearful.

'I can't believe it. I can't believe it,' Shula kept repeating. 'I don't feel pregnant. I don't feel any different.'.

'Good, that's good,' said Mark. 'Oh, Shula. I love you.'

'I love you too,' she said. 'So much. Come on. Let's go straight and tell Mum and Dad.'

Jill dropped the sieve with which she'd been sifting icing sugar — she was decorating Pip's christening cake — and flew across the kitchen to hug her daughter.

'Mark, you too! Oh, come here!'

They were both folded in Jill's arms before she broke away, sniffing.

'Oh, it's such wonderful news! Ruth and David are in the garden, why don't you go and tell them. I'll be out in a minute. I must tell your father. Unless you'd —'

'No, Mum, you do it,' said Shula. This was Jill's moment too. She'd been waiting long enough.

Ruth and David were sitting under the apple tree with Pip kicking on a blanket. Pip's christening had been set for the fourth of July. The other godmother was going to be Ruth's Auntie Rose, who had given Pip her middle name. Her little football of a face creased with smiles when she saw Mark and Shula.

'Does Mum know you're here?' asked David. 'Tell her, 'cos she's promised us lemonade in a bit.'

'We saw her, she sent us out,' said Mark, squatting down by Pip. 'Hello Pipsqueak.'

Shula's heart flipped over. She found men and babies even more endearing than women and babies. She suddenly remembered a party, a long time ago, when Mark had had to hold Alice Aldridge, Jennifer and Brian's youngest, and people had said he'd looked like a natural. It must have been a good five years ago. Since then, they hadn't exactly gone out of their way to visit people with babies and she hadn't had much chance to see him in action. He held out his fingers and Pip gripped them. Slowly he pulled her up, then lowered her again. He did it two or three times and Pip gurgled with pleasure.

'I think she likes you, Mark,' grinned David. 'When can you

babysit?'

'That's a point, we haven't been asked lately, have we, Shula?'

Mark released Pip who, feeling abandoned, started to drone. Shula picked her up and she drummed Shula's neck gently with her little fists and blew raspberries in her ear. Shula stroked the perfect head and patted her nappied bottom. Now she could start to get used to the idea that it really would be her turn next. She looked at Mark. He nodded his head.

'We've got some news ... ' Shula began.

Only three days later, Shula stood in the bathroom at Glebe Cottage. She twisted the end of the blind cord neatly round the little brass hook and straightened the carved flying fish Kenton had brought back from his travels, noticing that it needed dusting. Out in the garden she could hear Mark's and Caroline's voices. Caroline must have come round to show them her engagement ring which she and Robin had gone to choose. They'd been secretly engaged since Easter. Shula had been one of the few people who'd known. Just as Caroline had been one of the few people outside the family who'd known about the I.V.F.. Now Shula would have to tell them all, one by one. She'd started bleeding. Not just a spot or two — the clinic had said that might happen. This was proper bleeding. She had lost Mark's baby. Again.

Shula felt heavy and dreary with tiredness. She could hardly make her legs work. Going upstairs to bed required a gargantuan effort. Getting dressed and making the bed the next morning seemed to take every shred of strength. Mr Gibson told her kindly but firmly that her body needed a rest. They would not consider another implant till the autumn. She should just enjoy the summer, take things easy and build up her strength. At least next time the procedure would not be quite what they called 'so invasive'. The embryos which they hadn't used last time had been deep frozen. For the next attempt they would be thawed and placed inside her.

'I'm treating you to an aromatherapy massage at the Health Club,' Caroline announced, arriving with flowers and a pile of *Hello* magazines and finding Shula lying on a rug in the garden, her body in the shade and her legs in the sun. 'Lavender, I think, would do you good, but you'll have to ask the therapist.'

Shula turned her head to her friend.

'Caroline, you are sweet to me. Everyone is. I'm just so tired of people having to be. I keep thinking their patience will run out.'

'It's not a finite supply, you know,' Caroline laughed.

'But it is. People have used up so much on me over the years, haven't they?' Shula said. 'They must be so bored of making the same sympathetic noises.'

'Shula, no one's bored with you. Everyone really admires you for the way you're coping.'

'Well, I'm bored with me,' Shula said. 'Let's talk about you.'

Caroline and Robin were trying to sort out a date for their wedding. It had got to be in the school holidays so that Robin's sons from his first marriage could spend a few days in the village beforehand and be there on the day.

'We can't possibly fit it in this summer because we couldn't organise it in time,' explained Caroline, flicking through one of the magazines. 'Ooh, look, Zsa Zsa Gabor. Mr Woolley would die for a mirror like that. Anyway, October half term's out because the boys are going to the Lake District with their mother. Christmas, which I'd rather like, is ludicrously busy for Robin, so's Easter. Looks like we're left with February half term.'

'I suppose the sun does shine in February. Sometimes,' said Shula.

'Thanks, that's very encouraging,' said Caroline.

'Sorry, I did warn you what a misery-guts I am,' Shula replied.

'Anyway, I don't care about the weather. I just want to be married, like you and Mark.'

'Mark had a chat with Dad, you know.' Shula sat up to rub some more sun cream into her legs. 'Dad called round for some reason when Mark was cleaning his cricket boots and they had this long talk among the rags and the Blanco. It really did him good. Whenever something like this happens, you see, all the attention goes on me and he feels as if no one notices him. It's his sorrow too.'

But she and Mark were solid, she knew that. This time, they hadn't had to go up Lakey Hill and howl. Their grief was quieter and more mature and they were together in it. They were careful with each other and they didn't talk about the future, or another attempt. Negotiating the next day was difficult enough.

The following Sunday it was Pip's christening. It was a glorious July day. After the delicious coolness of the church they went back to Brookfield and stood around in the sunshine, eating and talking. Shula wore a yellow linen jacket, the colour of the daffodils she'd been holding when David had first asked her to be Pip's god-mother. After all the fuss about the Archer family robe and Ruth's own family's robe, Usha, who'd become very friendly with Ruth, bought Pip a simple raw silk christening dress and Marjorie Antrobus, bless her, crocheted a filigree shawl. Pip beamed the whole day long. Jill's cake — iced in palest peach with sugar flowers — was exquisite. It was a perfect day, Shula was sure of it, but it passed her by.

One of the visiting priests to Ambridge had once told Shula that he believed that God only tested people within the limits of their endurance. Shula wondered how much further she'd have to be pushed. It took a real effort of will just to stand in the garden at Brookfield, clutching her champagne flute so tight she thought it would shatter in her hands and talking to Uncle Tom and Auntie Pru, who was out of the Laurels, the nursing home she'd been in since she'd had her stroke, for the day. She knew Uncle Tom hadn't approved of the I.V.F., because Mark had overheard him in The Bull, muttering about meddling with nature, but he took both her hands and held them tight. His old man's eyes filled with tears and he said how sorry he'd been to hear about her 'bit of trouble'. It was almost more than she could take. She excused herself, saying she'd got to find a bit of cool, and fled.

Nigel found her in the rose garden where she'd told him it was over between them all those years ago.

'Cry if you want to, Shulie,' he said, putting his arm round her where she sat on the same bench.

'I can't,' she said. 'I haven't got the energy.'

'What are you going to do?' he asked. 'Are you going to try again?'

'I don't know,' said Shula. 'With the way I feel at the moment...it's just that I've picked myself up and carried on so many times, Nigel. I'm really, really tired of doing it.'

'I bet you will,' he said, then added suddenly, 'Do you know what I admire about you, Shula? It's the way that even after all you've had to cope with, you're still the same underneath. I mean, after everything you've had to go through, most people would be all bitter and twisted but you're not. You're still you. And you're so brave.'

'I feel bitter and twisted,' said Shula. 'Quite a lot of the time.'

'Come on, Shula, don't put yourself down. How many people could have come today, and made those vows for Pip like you did in church? You were just superb.'

Shula managed a faint smile.

'You are sweet to me,' she said.

'It's not difficult,' he replied, squeezing her hand. Shula sighed.

'You know, Nigel, I've thought about it a lot. I think my trouble was I was too loved. Mum and Dad would have done anything to spare me pain. Everything went right — or if it didn't they put it right. Then when you're grown up and things don't go right, it comes as so much more of a shock. I don't know what the answer is, really. You're hardly likely to want to expose your children to hardships to toughen them up, are you?'

'I don't know. Boarding school did it pretty effectively for me.'

'Poor Nigel.'

'I suppose it's something you just sort out as you go along, when you're a parent, how much to protect your children from the world. And you will be a parent, Shula, I know you will. We Pargetters are never wrong. Well, apart from being on the wrong side in the Civil War. According to Richard Locke and his Sealed Knot chums.'

The christening, which was so painful in so many ways, was good in another. It was then that she and Elizabeth finally and properly made up. Elizabeth had come looking for Nigel and found them both in the rose garden. With Nigel dispatched for cups of tea, Elizabeth took his place on the bench.

'I thought I'd escape from the adoring hordes,' Shula said.

'Me too,' Elizabeth replied.

'Are you all right?' asked Shula.

'I'm the one who should be asking you that,' said Elizabeth.

'I was fine,' said Shula. 'Until one of Ruth's cousins asked me when Mark and I were going to start a family. Fortunately Mum stepped in.'

'I know,' said Elizabeth. 'It was probably the same cousin who asked me when I was going to settle down.'

Nothing more was said but the awkwardness and animosity which had been between them for over a year, ever since the abortion, finally seemed to melt away in the Sunday sunshine. Pip was here — a reality — and all the might-have-been babies were not. What had she said to Nigel? She and Elizabeth had both had to pick themselves up and go on. They had to go on going on.

Mark and Shula didn't go for the implant in the autumn. Physically Shula was recovered but mentally she wasn't ready for another disappointment and her previous experience did not lead her to be easily optimistic. Mark understood. He wanted them to take their time. He was busy at work. Among other things, he was defending Neil Carter's wife Susan against a charge of attempting to pervert the course of justice. Susan had been a Horrobin before she married and it seemed her family — her brother Clive in particular — were still getting her into trouble. Clive and an accomplice had mounted an armed raid on the village shop earlier in the year and when Clive escaped from remand he blackmailed Susan into helping him.

Susan's case was to be heard at Felpersham Crown Court on December 23rd. Mark wasn't very pleased.

'I can't even say "at least it'll be over by Christmas", can I? What sort of a Christmas are they going to have, knowing they've got a big fine to find or she's got a hundred hours of community service to do in the New Year?'

The court hearing was early in the afternoon. Mark had said it wouldn't take long, in his opinion, but Shula was not expecting him back much before five. He'd be working on Christmas Eve as well, in the morning at least. Christmas was always a nightmare: everyone seemed to decide they wanted injunctions served and wills drawn up before they settled down to their week of wall-to-wall television. She listened to a play on the radio as she made another batch of mince pies. They had invited all the family round to Glebe at some point in the festivities and, like Jill, Shula had a horror of the cupboard being bare. She and Mark had planned to go to the Crib Service at St. Stephen's at six thirty. When six o'clock came and there was still no sign of him, she rang the office. Usha answered.

'Shula — he hasn't phoned you then? I don't suppose he's had time.'

'Usha? What is it?'

'Susan's been sentenced to six months' imprisonment.'

'What?'

Shula knew that Mark had warned Susan that the charge could carry a custodial sentence, but he had never seriously considered it a possibility.

'Mark's been on the phone for the last hour about an appeal, but it's a long shot. To win an appeal he'd have to convince the judge that the sentence isn't just tough but wrong in principle. And I'm afraid the advice seems to be that even if he stood a chance, by the time an appeal's heard, Susan could be out anyway, with good behaviour,' Usha explained.

Shula told her to give Mark her love, and not to worry what time he got home. *White Christmas* swooned from the radio for the millionth time and she snapped it off. Madonna and child — baby Jesus. Sleigh bells ringing in the snow. Little upturned faces by candlelight. Christmas was about children and babies. One baby in particular. She put her hands to her stomach where there should have been a big bulge by now. So she didn't have a baby this Christmas. Susan had two children, but couldn't be with them. Who was she to complain about injustice?

Only a day or so before, finishing off their Christmas cards, she and Mark had both put down their pens at the same moment and started to speak together. It turned out that they had both been thinking about their next attempt.

'I feel ready now,' Shula said. 'Let's get Christmas and New Year out of the way, then we'll go for it. And before you say it,

Mark, I'm not getting my hopes up. And I've thought a lot about it and I want this to be the last time.'

'I see.'

'Not having a baby pushed us apart, Mark. I feel as if this treatment's really brought us together. But I can't go on being disappointed. This time — if it works — will make three pregnancies. Maybe it's superstitious, but I think that's enough.'

Mark got up and came and crouched beside her and wrapped his arms round her.

'I'm so glad you said that,' he whispered. 'I never thought you would. I thought I was going to have to and it would be rows and I didn't understand and I was holding you back and I'd never supported you like I should. I think you're absolutely right.'

'Good.'

She let her arms fall down his back. She felt utterly comfortable with him. In their disappointments, they had had to show each other the sides of their characters that they would both have preferred to keep hidden. They had had to reveal every insecurity and vulnerability. If they could live with each other after all that, nothing else could touch them. Mark smoothed his thumbs along her eyebrows, round her cheekbones and her jaw. She looked at him looking at her and knew that she trusted him absolutely to want what she wanted and for the right reasons. He tilted her chin and kissed her gently.

'I really do love you,' he said.

'Me too,' said Shula. 'Whatever happens about a baby, it's going to be the best it's ever been.'

Jill waved one last time. Mark and Shula stood in the porch at Glebe Cottage with the light falling on them from behind — one dark head and one blonde. Jill had been watching them all day, had seen them kiss when they thought no-one was looking, had noticed how Mark jumped up to help Shula, opening doors, carrying trays. Phil released the handbrake and the Land Rover moved off.

'You don't think — no, she had a glass of champagne.'

'What are you on about?' Phil was rubbing the windscreen with a duster.

'I was wondering if Shula could be pregnant again. I'm sure last time she didn't drink at all — but it was only a little glass. She didn't have a refill.'

'Don't you think they might have mentioned it?' Phil indicated right at the village green.

'No, I don't,' said Jill. 'I think after last time it would be perfectly natural if they didn't say anything until they were absolutely sure the baby was safe.'

'Well, I'm sure they'll tell us when they're ready,' said Phil.

'Wouldn't it be wonderful, Phil? I thought they seemed happier than ever. We are lucky having Mark as a son-in-law, aren't we?'

'Yes.' Phil turned on to the track where Jill's 'Bed and Breakfast: E.T.B. Commended' sign swung in the wind. 'If only I thought Elizabeth would have the sense to choose a husband like Mark.'

'Do you know, Phil, I can remember you saying the very same thing about Shula.'

'Nonsense!' said Phil. 'Shula's always been fine. She's by far the most capable of our children. Gets it from you, I suppose you're going to say.'

Jill leaned over and kissed him as they drew up in the yard.

'What was that for?'

'Ooh, I don't know. Belated Christmas present.'

'She is the strongest, though, isn't she?' Phil repeated.

'Just as well, isn't it really?' said Jill. 'Now I suppose you're ready for a cup of tea before milking. And if you say you're got room for a mince pie...'

FEBRUARY
——— 1994 ———

'Mum, you can't! Not in here!'

Jill planted her feet a foot apart on Underwoods' sports department's tasteful carpet and took up what she imagined to be the correct stance.

'This feels all right,' she said, chopping the air with the bat. 'What is it they say? Middle for diddle?'

'Mum! We're going to have the sales assistant over here in a minute.'

'How does he know I'm not Captain of Borsetshire Ladies?'

Jill hit an imaginary ball for six.

'Probably by the way you're holding it,' laughed Shula. 'I wish David would hurry up.'

It was Mark's birthday on Sunday and Shula had decided to surprise him with a new cricket bat. David, who had come into Borchester to get some supplies for lambing, had promised to give them his expert advice and was due to meet them in Underwoods.

Shula, normally so organised, had left it later than usual to shop for Mark's present, but then they had been rather busy to-ing and fro-ing to the clinic in Birmingham. Some elements of the now-familiar routine were there: some aspects were different this time round.

Once a scan had confirmed that her ovaries were clear, Shula had started a course of tablets and Richard had begun to give her the painful but necessary injections which prepared her womb to receive an embryo. Three out of the five stored embryos had survived the freezing process. Only yesterday, without telling anyone, not even her parents, as they had promised themselves, she and Mark had been to the clinic to have them implanted.

'Right. What else do we need?' asked Jill.

She reluctantly replaced the bat on the rack.

'I've still got to get him a card — oh, and some wrapping paper.'

'That reminds me, I must get a card for Robin and Caroline,' said Jill. 'You're going to have a busy weekend.'

Robin and Caroline's wedding had eventually been booked at St. Stephen's for Saturday, February 19th, Shula was to be Matron of Honour in bottle green velvet and Mark was Chief Usher, responsible for keeping an eye on Robin's boys, Sam and Oliver, who also had ushers' duties. The timing was a total fluke but Shula was grateful for the distraction. She remembered only too well from last time the two-week eternity between implantation and the pregnancy test. The more she could occupy herself this week and next the better.

'It's a busy week for birthdays, too,' said Jill, fingering a lurid towelling sweat band in fascination. 'With little Pip's on Thursday. Did David mention to you that her party's on Wednesday, though — they're popping up to Ruth's parents on the day.'

'It suits me better, actually,' said Shula. 'Oh, come on, David. I'm planning a little do for Caroline on Thursday. But I'm trying to keep it hush hush. So not a word, eh, Mum?'

It was a time for secrets and surprises. Caroline had said she and Robin were a little long in the tooth for hen nights and stag parties. Shula thought it was a bit of a shame but she'd gone along with it — it was Caroline's wedding, after all. It was Elizabeth who'd been adamant.

'You can't get married without a hen night,' she'd insisted. 'It's just not done.'

'You're very knowledgeable about weddings all of a sudden,' said Shula. They had been browsing through Valentine cards: another date to remember.

Shula wasn't to know Elizabeth's secret which only Jill had guessed: Nigel had proposed to her at the end of January. That too, had to be kept quiet because Julia, Nigel's mother, had finally agreed to seek help for her drinking problem, and they didn't want to do anything to upset her during her treatment. She hadn't always been exactly well-disposed towards Elizabeth and they thought they ought to tell her before their engagement was common knowledge.

'There's nothing here rude enough for Nigel,' said Elizabeth, deftly changing the subject. 'Let's go somewhere else.'

But when Shula had thought about it, she'd decided that Elizabeth was probably right.

'How about a supper for just the four of us?' she'd suggested to Debbie. 'But I need your help. You've got to act as a decoy for Caroline. She'll never agree to it if she knows, especially after what Robin will have been through. Can you get her to go out riding with you? Then just bring her down to Glebe at about half six.'

'Just? How?'

'I don't know, use your initiative,' sad Shula airily. 'Oh, and can you check with Aunty Chris about borrowing a horse.'

Caroline's own horse, Ippy, had been stolen the year before. She missed him dreadfully.

While Shula was planning a sedate supper party for Caroline, Robin's stag night, which would be happening on Shrove Tuesday, consisted of practically kidnapping him for a route march and pancake race across the Malverns.

'I felt so guilty,' said Caroline when she called round to Glebe, having seen Robin dragged off by Richard with some spurious tale about an animal which needed seeing to. 'I'm sure he guessed. He looked at me as if I'd totally betrayed him.'

'At least they've got a doctor with them,' said Shula, thinking of Richard Locke, who had been one of the chief conspirators.

'It's lovely that they wanted to do something for Robin,' smiled Caroline. 'But please don't tell me you've got any surprises for me.'

'If they're yomping across the Malverns, I thought we could perhaps paraglide off Lakey Hill —'

'Shula, that's not funny.'

But Shula wouldn't give anything away. So many secrets.

On Wednesday evening, Shula made a salmon mousse and a chicken casserole and a banoffi pie and a hazelnut meringue.

'What about my supper?' complained Mark, hovering in the

kitchen.

'I thought you'd still be full of pancakes from last night.' Shula was mixing chocolate and chestnut purée to fill the meringue. 'Here, can you draw me three eight-inch circles on this baking paper? If you do it nicely I'll find you a bowl to lick out.'

'Thanks a bunch.'

But he did it good naturedly. They were so much more relaxed these days.

'It's since we decided this would be our last I.V.F. attempt,' said Mark. 'I feel as if we've reclaimed the rest of our lives.'

It was a curiously liberating feeling. It was as if for all these years they had been at the mercy of Shula's body. Now they had said enough was enough. They had done all they could: they were not going to be done to any more. They could both feel a new strength in the realisation that they knew themselves and each other well enough to know when to call a halt. They had taken back control of their lives while they still had some lives to take control of.

Next morning Shula was up early in another frenzy of cooking.

'What is it now? I thought you did it all last night?' said Mark as he edged past her to get to the kettle.

Shula licked her finger.

'Just a few dips and a salad dressing,' she explained, licking her finger. 'Mm, that's not bad. I'll make some toast in a minute.'

Mark spooned coffee into cups.

'Not for me,' he said. 'I haven't got time this morning. I've got an injunction for domestic violence to do first thing. He removed Tibby who was dozing on the morning paper and sat down. 'So are you all set for tonight?' he asked.

'I think so,' said Shula, coming to stand behind him. She leaned forward and looped her arms round his neck, rubbing her face against his newly-shaved cheek. 'The best part of the whole evening is we're having this handsome waiter. Who's going to be charming and efficient. And do all the washing up.'

'Um, yes.' Mark sounded hesitant. 'Look, I'm sorry, love. But there's a chance I might be late.'

'What?' Shula unhooked her arms. Mark looked at her guiltily over his shoulder. 'But I told you about this party ages ago,' she complained. 'You promised.'

'I know.' Behind them the kettle switched itself off.

'All the other nights you've been late and I haven't said a word. And the one night I ask you to be here...'

Mark got up.

'I'm going to have to go,' he said.

'You haven't had your coffee,' said Shula.

'I'll get some in the office,' he replied. 'Look, I'll do my best to get back, all right?'

'Don't put yourself out on my account,' snapped Shula. She knew she was being childish. Mark wouldn't disappoint her unless he had to and she knew how messy, long and drawn out the serving of injunctions could be.

'Shula, please?' Mark appealed.

Shula dumped the blender goblet in the sink.

'Go on, if you're going,' she said unrelenting.

'Yeah. OK.'

She ran hot water into the sink and watched the traces of oil from her salad dressing rise slickly to the top. Mark slid the newspaper into his briefcase and snapped it shut.

'Bye, then,' he said.

Shula turned off the tap. Suddenly it was important not to part like this.

'Just a minute,' she said, turning round. 'I'm sorry.'

'That's all right.' Mark sounded relieved. He hated it when they argued.

'Don't worry about tonight.' She walked over to him and kissed him lightly, her hands going up automatically to rest on his lapels. 'We'll manage. I hope your day isn't too awful.'

She soon forgot the little flurry with Mark. You could hardly call it a row — she just wished it hadn't happened in the first place. She had to spend the morning in Borchester, then the afternoon at the estate office. Aunty Peggy had come back to help out whilst Susan, who had taken over her job, was in prison, and it was hard going. She'd only been gone a couple of years but she didn't have the confidence any more. She got flustered. They'd changed the computer and though Aunty Peggy tried her best, Shula found she had to organise her time so that she called at the estate office for some part of every day. If she didn't, Aunty Peggy had a nasty habit of calling round or phoning during the evening with some inconsequential problem, and Shula didn't want to have to think about anything but Caroline's party tonight. On her way from Borchester she made a detour and called at Lower Loxley. Elizabeth and Nigel were working, as they euphemistically called surveying the proposed point-to-point course for Easter Tuesday. Nigel had already volunteered to organise one of those horse racing videos that evening, which seemed appropriate for Caroline. He jumped at the chance of staying on to serve the ladies if Mark wasn't back in time.

Shula made quite a breakthrough with Aunty Peggy that afternoon, persuading her to try copying a document from the hard disc onto a floppy and back again.

'You see, you can do it!' Shula encouraged.

How awful to be old and slowing down and have everyone think you were stupid. Mark dreaded getting old. He was even dreading his fortieth next year. Aunty Peggy was game to be working at all and she was helping them out of a hole in Susan's absence.

'I'm going to nip off home soon, if that's all right with you,' Shula said. 'I'm not expecting anything dramatic to happen before the end of the day and I've got a surprise hen party for Caroline tonight.'

'Oh, Shula, how lovely! I think secretly she felt quite left out after Robin's. I mean, it's a bit demoralising to think no one's going to miss you enough to bother to organise one.'

'Well, I'll make sure she has an evening she won't forget,' confided Shula. 'Nigel and Elizabeth are coming over early to help me set things up. Mark may not be back till later but I'm hoping he'll wait on us.'

'He is good,' said Peggy indulgently.

'Yes, he is.' Shula felt ashamed of her pique that morning. She'd make it up to Mark. 'If he's really good I might even let him stay the night!'

'Mark's late, I thought he'd be here by now.'

Shula was beginning to get restless but then she always did before her own parties. The dips were in their clingfilmed bowls on the little polished table — pink for the prawn, white for the creamy cheese, with the avocado, which she'd only make when they arrived, still to come. The salmon mousse and the puddings were laid out on the sideboard in the dining room, with the best glasses sparkling under the lights. From the kitchen the scent of chicken and herbs swathed the entire cottage. They had put up the banner reading 'Good Luck, Caroline' which Shula had painstakingly made during her lunch hour with all the felt-tip pens Rodway's could muster. They had sampled Nigel's racing video. Mark had phoned from the car to say he was on his way home, he'd be there in good time. Everything was going to go according to plan. That was how Shula liked her entertaining, planned. It was how she liked her life, really. She'd often said to Mark that that was why she took her failure to have a baby so hard. It was the one thing she couldn't plan. She hated that.

'What time was it when he rang?' Nigel was hanging up a final bunch of balloons round the light fitting.

'I don't know? Ten to?' It was nearly half past six now.

'Where was he phoning from? Apart from the car?' Elizabeth helped herself to a handful of peanuts.

'I don't know. I didn't ask him for a map reference.' Shula could hear herself starting to sound tetchy, like this morning. Surely he hadn't had a flat tyre or broken down or something. The car had only had its M.O.T. last month. She'd have to swallow her irritation with Mark before Caroline arrived. Fine advertisement for married life they'd be.

'Perhaps you'd better get into your D.J. after all, Nigel,' she said.

The doorbell rang, politely but insistently. Twice.

'That can't be them already!'

'It's all right!' said Nigel. 'You delay them at the door, Shula, and I'll slip into the old penguin suit.'

'Ooh, can I help?' asked Elizabeth, mischievously. Shula noticed again how close and happy they seemed. She went and opened the front door.

She often wondered afterwards whether the fact that she had no premonition of what it was going to be meant she was not a very sensitive person. Weren't you supposed to feel a sense of foreboding when something like this happened to someone you loved? She opened the door blithely, smiling, looking forward to seeing Caroline's face when she saw the preparations and saw the policeman and woman. That was when she felt the first giddy lurch of fear.

'Mrs Shula Hebden?'

'Yes?'

It was like every police drama she'd ever watched or detective novel she'd read. Still, that was the point. They had to get these things accurate, Mark always said.

'May we come in a moment?'

'What is it? What is it? Is it Mark?'

She sped them through to the sitting room, where Elizabeth was helping Nigel with his cuff links. Shula saw the officers take in the dips and crisps, the banner, the balloons.

'Would you like to sit down?' the policewoman said. It was the first time she had spoken.

'What is it?' said Elizabeth. 'I'm her sister.'

'Mrs Hebden. I'm sorry to tell you there's been an accident.'

'I can't do it. I can't do it.' That was all Shula thought to herself, all the way along the corridor. She wasn't quite sure how everything had been taken care of, but she knew her parents had been told, and both they and Nigel had said they'd come with her to identify the body — or do it for her, but Shula hadn't wanted that. She didn't want anyone with her when she saw Mark. She certainly wouldn't trust anyone else to do it. What if they made a mistake?

Shula let herself be shepherded through the swing doors, along the side of the W.R.V.S. shop for which her mother was always trying to recruit volunteers, and down another corridor, following signs which said starkly: 'Mortuary'.

She hadn't even cried yet. She was probably too shocked.

When the attendant pulled the sheet back, she'd thought that was when she might cry or cry out or fall down. But she didn't feel like it. She felt — surprised. And curious. It didn't really look like Mark at all. Oh, it was him, but it didn't look like him. People were always saying that dead people looked as if they were sleeping. Mark had never looked like that when he was sleeping. There had never been that stillness about him. This looked like a model of Mark. They had caught some of his features quite well, the eyebrows and the chin, but there was a lot wrong with it. His cheeks shouldn't have been so sunken, for a start. There wasn't a scratch on his face. She'd been wondering about that, dreading seeing him hurt. 'Multiple injuries,' the doctor had said: that would presumably mean head injuries as well. She had supposed they would cover them up, put on one of those little gauzy caps like she'd had to wear for her laparoscopies. But there was nothing to see. His hair sprang up from his forehead just like it always had. It must have been the way they put his head.

'Yes,' she said to the policewoman. 'Yes, that's my husband.'

The police drove her back to Brookfield. Nigel and Elizabeth were there, sitting at the kitchen table, quiet, holding hands. Her mother jumped up as soon as she saw her.

'Shula. Shula, love.'

Shula walked into her mother's embrace. Now she could cry.

From then on it was all a bit of a muddle. Shula knew she'd gone to bed, tucked up by her mother in her old room, but she couldn't sleep. She went through the whole day again from the moment of tasting the salad dressing and Mark boiling the kettle. She tried to remember just what she'd said to him when he'd phoned. She only realised she must have been sobbing when Elizabeth tiptoed in. Nigel must have finally gone home.

'Shula, don't. Please don't. Try and get some sleep.'

Her hopeless little sister telling her to get some sleep. It made Shula cry even more. Elizabeth got into bed with her. Her feet were cold. Elizabeth had never liked wearing slippers: she thought they were middle-aged. Mark needn't have worried about being middle-aged after all. All that time wasted in worrying. Wasted.

Elizabeth put her arms round her and hugged her. Shula lay still and they cried, more quietly, together.

Next morning, she got up because it was what you did in the mornings and went downstairs. Her mother had found her a nightie, but she wore her father's summer dressing gown. The sleeves fell over her hands as she sipped her tasteless tea.

'Oh, Phil,' Jill said thickly when Shula had gone back upstairs for a bath. 'I just want to hold her and take the pain away. Like when she was a little girl.'

'I know,' Phil soothed.

'I really don't think I can bear it. Seeing her hurting so much.'

'We have to bear it, Jill,' said Phil. 'We mustn't let her down. She's going to need us.'

Later that morning, Richard called. Jill showed him into the sitting room. Death was part of his job but even he looked shocked.

'I know words are totally inadequate, Mrs Archer,' he said. 'But I really am so sorry. Mark was a great bloke.'

'Yes, he was,' said Jill quietly.

Shula came into the room.

'I was trying Kenton again,' she said. 'Still no reply.' Kenton who, as his mother had predicted, had left Borchester, was crewing off the coast of Australia.

'Try again later,' said Jill. 'I'll leave you to it.'

Richard had spoken to the hospital before he came round, he told Shula. Caroline was in intensive care on a ventilator. She had a hairline skull fracture though there didn't seem to be any bleeding into the brain.

'I can't go and see her,' said Shula. 'Not yet.'

'No-one expects you to,' said Richard. He unwrapped the syringe in readiness for her daily injection. Shula could feel him looking at her, gauging what to say.

'I want her to be OK, really I do,' she said. 'But —'

'Yeah?'

'Nothing.' She couldn't talk about it.

'You're thinking why Mark and not her. Is that it?'

'Perhaps,' said Shula. 'No, not really.' She shivered. 'To think

Mark and I wanted to bring a baby into this mess.'

'I can understand you might feel that at the moment,' said Richard gently. 'But I think we're right to go on with the treatment.'

Shula shrugged. She didn't care. The thought of a baby seemed utterly irrelevant.

'I just want someone to tell me why, that's all,' said Shula, knowing no one could.

All she wanted to do was to see Debbie. She and Caroline had been coming along the road when a fast car, which must have overtaken Mark, had scared Dandy, the horse Caroline was riding. She had been thrown into the road. Mark had come round the bend, seen the body and had swerved into a tree. That's what the police had told her. That's what Debbie had told them. Shula still wanted to hear it direct from Debbie. Jill reluctantly had to agree to let her go.

Debbie walked back with her to Glebe Cottage. When they got there all the lights were on.

'Must be Mum,' said Shula. 'She's going to stay the night.'

Jill was busy tidying up the kitchen. They said you had to keep busy though that wasn't the reason she was in the kitchen. She always felt happiest in the kitchen, anyone's kitchen. All the keeping busy in the world didn't stop you thinking, goodness knew, she could put away knives and plates and cover food with clingfilm in her sleep, it hardly engaged her brain. Perhaps it just showed you that your body still worked, that your fingers could do things, your feet could cross a room. Perhaps the whole point was just to tire yourself out.

'Jill, what shall I do with — oh, Shula.'

Phil stopped. He was holding Caroline's banner in his hand.

Jill took it from him and shoved it in the dresser.

'"Good luck, Caroline". She still needs it though,' said Shula half to herself. 'Oh, there's something else you can put away, Dad. Down beside you.'

Mark's new cricket bat.

'I had to remember to hide it before he got home.' Shula's voice was dangerously thin and high. 'I shan't need to hide it now.'

'Shula, won't you come back with us to Brookfield? Please?' said Jill carefully.

'I don't think so Mum. Thanks anyway.' Shula picked a browning salad leaf out of the bowl and let it drop back. 'This is my home. This is where I want to be.'

When Shula woke on Saturday morning she was at first so startled to have slept at all that she didn't remember what it was that had prevented her from sleeping. Then she remembered. She lay still. She didn't know what she was supposed to do. She didn't know how to behave. Did it matter? Was she supposed to do anything? She didn't even know what to wear. Did people still wear black these days?

Wearily she swung her legs out of bed and felt for her slippers. She had to feed the cats. She and Mark had tried to train them that weekends were different but Tiger in particular expected feeding at seven, seven days a week. Sometimes on a Sunday they had made him wait until eight but he would come and jump on the bed and circle their heads on the pillow, putting his face right next to theirs, combing their hair with his paw. Nine times out of ten it was Mark who couldn't stand it any longer and got up, cursing. I'll have to do it every day now, she thought. And lug the catfood from the cash and carry. And thinking of breakfast, who was going to eat that huge sack of sugar-free muesli which Mark had bought on his latest healthy eating kick? Shula had said it tasted like a nosebag. What a stupid thing to think about. Muesli.

It was only when she opened the curtains and looked out at the rain that she realised she should have been at Robin and Caroline's wedding. What had happened about that? She remembered her mother saying something about it being cancelled. Marjorie Antrobus had done most of the ringing round. Poor Robin, spending his wedding day at the hospital. She should go and visit. She should.

She heard the bed creak as her mother turned over in the room next door. Gratefully, she went in.

'Mum?'

Jill was instantly awake.

'Can I get in with you?'

Shula had always loved getting into her parents' bed. Once David was toddling around, the boys would have more fun first thing in the morning destroying their bedrooms and making dens but Shula used to listen for her father going out to do the milking. Then she'd creep into the warm space he had left and she and her mother would talk about anything and nothing till the alarm went of again and she had to get ready for school.

Jill moved across the bed to let her in. Shula snuggled into the crook of her mother's arm and lay quiet.

'I don't know what to do,' she said at last. 'Mark would know but he's not here.'

It was all so complicated. She knew there'd have to be an inquest but because the police had not traced the driver of the first car and were still investigating, it was opened and adjourned. They gave her an interim death certificate so at least she could plan the funeral. She wanted hymns that everyone would know.

'I hate it when the organist's practically doing a recital,' she told Robin. 'And I'd like *The Lord's My Shepherd*. It always makes me think of Grandad.'

Robin nodded. He looked grey with tiredness. Caroline had finally come round after six days but she was still desperately confused. Shula had managed to make herself visit whilst Caroline was still unconscious but she hadn't been again since. She knew that Robin was waiting for the right moment to tell Caroline about Mark. She couldn't go before then and she privately wondered whether she'd be able to go afterwards.

Everyone was so kind to her, she felt stifled. On the one occasion she went to the village, she could see people tensing as she approached. At home, people would scuttle up the path and shove a card through the letterbox, hurrying off, grateful not to have to seen her and or to have had to witness her grief. Only Nigel had a knack of calling at the right moment. One day she suddenly felt she wanted to see the place where it had happened. It wasn't far outside Ambridge, she knew. He'd been so nearly home. She mentioned it to Nigel one evening when he called in and he immediately offered to take her the next day.

'What about work?' she asked.

'Lizzie can cope,' said Nigel confidently. 'She's always saying she gets on better without me around to distract her. I'll call for you about eleven.'

The weather couldn't have been more different from the week before. The sky was a vault of blue. Tits and finches twittered in the budding hedges: blackbirds burbled softly to themselves. Where Mark had died the verge was strewn with flowers. The tyres had torn up the grass and the fragile winter aconites but people had brought cellophane and paper-wrapped bunches to lay there in their place. Shula was surprised and touched at how many there were. Even the Carter children had placed a bunch of daffodils there with a card. There were bits of glass and a strip of rubber in the road, too. Shula looked at them, fascinated, and read the police notice asking for witnesses over and over again.

'I wonder if anyone did see anything,' she said.

'If I could ever get my hands on the driver of that other car...' Nigel trailed off.

'Did I tell you your mother sent me a card?' Shula asked. 'I thought it was very kind of her, seeing as she hardly knew Mark.'

'He was well loved,' said Nigel simply. 'Look at all these flowers.'

'I know. Poor tree, though.'

'Well, yes but —' Nigel began. 'Mark was a lucky man,' he said abruptly.

'I think I was lucky to marry him,' said Shula. 'It helps being loved, you know. And having somebody to love.'

As they watched, a blue tit darted down and collected a fragment of torn bark in its beak. All the birds were nesting, pairing, mating, ready to raise a brood. Shula felt the tears begin to slide down her cheeks. There was nothing she could do about it. It happened all the time.

'And now I haven't got anybody to love or to love me.'

'Shula, we all love you.' Nigel was nearly crying himself.

'It's not the same thing,' she said desperately. ' Oh, Nigel. I want him to come back. I just want him to come back and give me a cuddle.'

Nigel put his arms round her and pulled her close.

'I'll give you a cuddle,' he said.

That wasn't the same thing either but it was nice of Nigel to try. As they stood there with her head resting against his, she saw the blue tit again, coming back for another shred of bark. They were so clever. She remembered Uncle Tom telling her about blue tits for her bird project. She must have been about eight or nine. They raised only one brood a year, timed to hatch at the precise moment when millions of caterpillars would be hatching on the late spring leaves. A week earlier or a week later and the chicks' food supply wouldn't be there. Birds were clever in another way, too, and brave. She'd often tried to remind herself of it when Tibby or Tiger struggled through the cat flap with an absurd feathery moustache. Birds raised so many young so that they could afford to lose one of the parents and all but one of the babies.

'Can we go home now please?' she whispered to Nigel. 'I feel closer to him when I'm at home.'

Richard had been coming to Glebe at the same time every day to give her the hormone injections. He was far more committed to her carrying on with them than she was. Her heart wasn't in it any more but she hadn't the heart to opt out. She couldn't face the argument when he tried to persuade her to change her mind: she wasn't up to arguing. On the one occasion she had thought about it, standing at the window on what would have been Mark's birthday, looking at the drenched garden, holding Tiger and tickling him under the chin till he was one big ball of purr, she couldn't believe the time and effort they'd put into having a baby. Why couldn't she just have been satisfied with Mark? She'd been so incredibly selfish. Mark had spent most of his adult life with her. She'd made him take on her concerns. He'd had to live through her disappointments, her tantrums, her failures. He'd even had to make love to her to suit her, not to suit him. A baby? How could she have thought she could cope with a baby? The possibility seemed as remote as them having a pet elephant.

On Friday, a week after Mark's death, Richard arrived at the same time to give her her injection. She submitted to it as usual.

'Shula, I want to talk to you,' Richard began. 'You realise you're due for a pregnancy test today?'

'Am I?'

One day was much like another. No sooner had she got to the end of one than another started.

'I've phoned the clinic and explained everything. Mr Gibson's given me permission to do the test, if that's what you'd prefer.'

'You want to do a pregnancy test?'

'Yes.'

'Oh, Richard, what's the point?' She raised her hands fractionally from her sides. 'There isn't going to be a baby now, is there?'

'Come on, Shula. Just let me do the test.'

So she had. When he showed her the blue colour she shook her head while saying the opposite.

'It's positive?

'Yes.'

'I really am pregnant?

'Yes, you are.'

'I'm going to have a baby?'

'It's wonderful, isn't it?'

Richard smiled encouragingly. Shula remembered those other pregnancy tests. The ectopic. Her last I.V.F..

'Mark always said we could do it.'

'So you hang on to it. For him.'

After all this time. Now.

'Yes,' she said. And she suddenly remembered the blue tits.

NOVEMBER
──1994──

'Caroline?'

'Shula?'

The baby was six days overdue. Shula could tell from the unadulterated terror coming down the line that Caroline knew exactly what she was phoning about. In the background, picking up from Caroline, Shula could hear Jack Woolley beginning one of his low-level panic attacks. Shula heard an 'Oh my goodness' and could almost detect the hand-wringing which would inevitably go with it.

'Are you still there, Caroline?'

There was no answer. Shula could well imagine Caroline nodding dumbly into the phone, speechless for the first time in her life.

Shula eased her position on the bed.

'I need a lift to the hospital. I've gone into labour.'

'Are you sure?'

Only the previous week there had been a panic when what Shula had thought was the baby coming had turned out to be Braxton Hicks contractions. Caroline had been with her when they started, so it was Caroline who got the job of driving her to Borchester General. Though it had turned out to be a false alarm, it was then that Shula had decided for definite to ask Caroline to be her birth partner. Jill would have been the obvious choice, and was, Shula knew, disappointed. She didn't quite know why she didn't want her mother with her when the baby was born: too close perhaps, too much a reminder of who it should have been. Caroline had agreed straight away, doing a good job of hiding her trepidation, obviously mentally trying to work out if Jasper Conran did splashproof co-ordinates for the occasion. No wonder poor Caroline was trying to pretend it wasn't happening now. Shula knew that she'd been jittering quietly ever since she'd agreed: Kathy had told Ruth. Curiously, Shula didn't feel any fear — just an anticipation on the edge of excitement, a keenness to get on with it, a sense of satisfaction that it had happened naturally and she wasn't going to have to be induced, and a conviction that after this day nothing would ever be the same again.

'There's no doubt about it,' she smiled in answer to Caroline's question. 'This is it.'

She'd woken up in a warm puddle and had realised that her waters had broken.

'Oh heavens!' Caroline sounded flustered. 'Look, don't move ... er... I'll be there right away. Just... keep calm, and I'll —'

'Caroline,' interrupted Shula. 'I am calm. I'll put the kettle on.'

'What?'

Caroline, victim of the traditional mythology of midwives always calling for scissors and boiling water, obviously had visions of having to deliver the baby herself on the hall floor at Glebe Cottage.

'For a cup of tea,' Shula explained.

Shula was glad afterwards that she'd taken her time over the tea because it turned into a long day. It took them about forty-five minutes to get into Borchester in the morning traffic, with Caroline torn between creeping along so as not to joggle Shula about and putting her foot down to get her into the safe haven of the hospital as soon as possible.

'Don't do that!' said Caroline jumpily as Shula leaned forward to change the cassette. 'Don't squash your tummy up!'

Shula smiled. She had no other symptoms apart from a low, persistent backache. When they got to the hospital she was admitted and put into one of those gowns which they said did up down the back, but even if it had all its strings left your bottom sticking out so you felt like an overloaded shopping bag. She and Caroline waited in the delivery room, waiting for something to happen. Caroline unpacked the contents of the large bag she had with her.

'Tapes. Right, I've got classical, modern jazz and some Janis

Joplin I borrowed from Pat. I thought it might be good to scream along to. Oh, and I've got Juliet Stevenson reading Jane Austen, and a collection of *Woman's Hour* short stories...'

'Caroline! We'll never have time for all that!'

'I hope not. If you could just try and have the baby by Wednesday, Shula, it would help. We've got a rather important dinner for some steel plating manufacturers that night.'

Caroline had got Jean Paul to pack them a picnic. Shula couldn't eat anything in case she had to have an anaesthetic so at lunchtime she had to watch as Caroline had her smoked salmon tartlet and miniature profiteroles filled with crème pâtisserie.

'It says here "Help her to remain cheerful by chatting between contractions", read Caroline from one of the pile of self-help manuals she had also produced.

'Shut up, Caroline,' said Shula, who was starting to feel an odd cramping pain which was twisting her insides.

'Hang on, Shula.' Caroline was already practically out of the door. 'I'll get a nurse.'

The midwives had changed shift by now: it was after three o'clock. A new one came to examine her.

Shula eased herself up on the bed still feeling more excited than anything else and as she did so felt the griping pain again which seemed to spiral up from her abdomen to encircle her whole body. She let out a gasp.

'Another contraction, my love?' asked the midwife, who was feeling her pulse.

Shula nodded. The midwife jotted something down on a chart.

'All right, you lie yourself back, now. Let me show you how to use the gas and air and then your friend can come back in.'

It took Shula a while to master the gas and air, to start to inhale just as the pain approached so that she could get the benefit whilst the contraction was at its peak. Caroline was mesmerised by the monitor which was graphing the baby's heartbeat in a succession of green squiggles.

'Look at that! Look how it increases when you have a contraction!'

Shula removed the mask and let out a breath.

'I should think my heart rate increases too. That last one... '

It had been a day of pale sunshine, nice for November. Now the colour was beginning to drain from the sky. The clock clunked on another minute.

'Four forty-four,' said Shula. 'That would have been a good time to be born. Very neat. Hey, did you hear that, hint, hint?' she said to her stomach. She sighed. 'Perhaps I'll have a little walk round.'

'Have you got time? If the contractions are coming every two minutes?' Caroline looked agitated.

'Caroline, it doesn't take me twenty seconds to pace round this room!'

'As long as you can get to the gas and air when you need it. They are getting stronger, aren't they?'

Shula laughed.

'Stop worrying!'

'I'm just surprised at how they've left us to get on with it.'

Shula was pleased about it. From the moment she had had her pregnancy confirmed by the clinic, Mr Gibson had told her that in pregnancy and labour she would be looked after by Borchester General, just like any other mother.

'Of course the hospital will know the circumstances, but no one else need know — unless you tell them — how the baby was conceived,' he'd said.

In the event, that hadn't been the hardest part. It wasn't what she had, and how she had come to have it, that took the most explaining, but what, or who, she hadn't got. The hardest part had been going for the antenatal appointments and classes without Mark.

It wasn't till about half past six that she was fully dilated and things really started happening. She still didn't want anything else for the pain. She wanted to be fully aware of what was going on. She'd been waiting for this moment for six years. She hardly wanted to wake up half an hour later and be told what sex it was.

By now there were two midwives in the room, who'd donned disposable aprons over their uniforms. Shula tried squatting for a while but she didn't feel secure enough in that position to push really hard. She knew all about gravity helping the baby but subconsciously she had this image of the baby shooting out fast, and having to be hooked up like a rugby ball in a scrum. No one said birth was dignified but that seemed to be stretching the point. In the end she found herself most comfortable back on the bed, with her legs braced against the midwives' waists to give her something to push against.

'Caroline? Where are you?' she said at one point in a panic between the contractions which were now coming so fast she could hardly tell when one ended and another began.

'Here,' came a voice from her left shoulder.

'No, come where I can see you!'

Caroline obediently came round the bed and smoothed Shula's hair back from her damp forehead.

'Here I am,' she said but Shula was lifting the mask again.

'Come on, Shula, now I want you to use this contraction to really push the baby out,' said the older of the two midwives. Shula groaned as she tried to obey. She felt as if she was going to split in two. Now she understood why one mother had famously described giving birth as being like trying to push an orange up your nose.

She sat forward, grunting with the effort, gripping Caroline's arm, then fell back.

'I can't do it.'

'Yes you can.'

'I can't, I'm telling you!'

'Of course you can.' The midwife was firm. 'Come on now. Is this another one coming?'

With the next contraction the baby's head appeared.

'Reach down, Shula, you can touch your baby's head.'

Shula did so. She didn't really know what she was feeling for. She could only feel a warm hard wetness but it gave her something to focus on. She pushed through the next contraction, and the next.

'Good girl, good girl. Now push! Push! That's it! There's the baby's head out! Pant now, pant it through.'

'Oh, Shula!'

Tears were streaming down Caroline's face. Shula couldn't cry. With the little energy she had left, she was concentrating. With the next contraction, she had to get the baby's shoulders out.

'Come on, now, Shula, this is the last one, I promise you, this baby wants to be born now.'

Shula pushed with all her might, not even bothering with the gas and air. Just let it be over.

'There! There it is! It's a boy!'

Caroline stayed with her up on the ward till her Mum and Dad arrived, anxious with relief. Then she excused herself, leaving Shula with her parents.

'I'd like to introduce Daniel Mark Archer Hebden,' said Shula, her voice wavering. 'Weighing seven pounds twelve ounces. Daniel, this is your granny and grandad.'

Jill's voice was squeaky with tears.

'Oh, Shula. He's perfect.'

'Yes, he is,' whispered Shula. 'And very, very precious.'

Shula didn't sleep that night. It was not one of those hospitals which took the babies to a nursery so Daniel lay in one of those see-through cots beside her. They'd wanted to give her something to help her sleep, they'd wanted to give her paracetamol for her stitches, but Shula still didn't want anything. She wanted to be able to remember every second. For what seemed like all night she lay on her side in the high hospital bed, looking and looking at her baby, falling in love with him. Occasionally she'd put out a hand to his little back to feel he was still breathing. How would she ever dare go to sleep again? God had entrusted the care of this tiny thing to her. Why on earth did He think she could cope? How could she live up to it? But there was an inane grin on her face. She had had a baby.

Coping with the enormity of it wasn't the only problem. It was the little things which rocked her. The first night Daniel slept well: the next night he was wakeful, and fretful. Her milk hadn't come in properly and she couldn't get him to latch on. The nice night nurse said he probably wasn't really hungry, but he might be thirsty. She gave Shula a tiny cup of water to try him with, but he wouldn't open his mouth and it kept dribbling down his face. Then his babygrow got wet and Shula thought she'd better change it because it couldn't be very comfy for him. He didn't like being changed. Few new babies did, the nurses said, but Shula was sure it was because she was doing something wrong. Daniel cried and cried. Shula had to ring the bell for the nurse again because all of a sudden she was crying too.

'What are you changing him for? His nappy's dry,' said the nurse. She was ever so young even in her uniform, with her blonde perm bunched up under her cap. In her leggings and T-shirt, off duty, she'd probably look about fifteen.

'Some water got onto his chest and I thought he might be uncomfy,' said Shula feebly.

'Once you've done a few machine-loads you won't worry about things like that, my love, it's hardly even damp,' said the nurse sensibly. She put Daniel back in his babygrow and placed him firmly back in his fishtank where fell almost straight asleep.

'See? He was tired,' said the nurse gently.

'How do you do it? How did you know he wanted to go down?' asked Shula tearfully, feeling inadequate.

'Practice,' grinned the nurse, who was called Lisa. 'You'll be getting plenty of it.'

The nurses were wonderful. Presumably at every shift change they were reminded that Shula was a widow because not one of them ever assumed that she had a husband. Shula was in a side room, which she had asked for specially. But she still couldn't help seeing and hearing the evidence of family life at mealtimes, in the corridor or in the dayroom.

'"Push!" he says to me,' recounted one mother who looked about twenty and, astonishingly, had just given birth to her third. 'I says "Next time you get up here and do it". Mind you, I don't think he'll want any more now we've got the little lad. He loves the girls but all fellas want a boy, don't they?'

Shula just nodded.

She saw a bunch of red roses on a locker and one of those

padded satin cards which said 'To My Darling Wife on the Birth of Our Son'. It would have been too florid for Mark's taste — they'd probably have giggled about it — but it was the sentiment behind it which moved her. One day she was topping up the water in one of her vases of flowers at the big sink in the corridor when she saw a father leading a tangle-haired toddler away after visiting time. The contrast between the tall male figure and the tiny girl, the way he had slowed his pace to accomodate her, made Shula's throat close up with tears. She'd never see Mark leading their child into the future. She rushed back to Daniel, willing him to wake up so she could hold him for both of them. The nurses had already caught her trying to prod him awake and had told her off.

'You'll be glad enough of him sleeping when you get home,' they'd said.

Home. Shula didn't know whether she wanted to go home or not. In here she was in a sort of no man's land — literally. Apart from the odd doctor and the visitors, it was a company of women. Even for those who had husbands or partners, the men were irrelevant now. There was always someone to turn to for advice about Daniel. At home, even with her mum only a few minutes away, she would be on her own.

She had good days and bad days. Ruth got her on a bad day a week after she came out. Daniel wouldn't settle, nothing seemed to comfort him. Shula walked him up and down. Together they stood at the window looking out at the naked trees, the bare apple boughs, the laburnum under which Mark had had his famous compost heap, the yews and cypresses in the church yard. Shula knew that Daniel couldn't really focus, but she thought he might be able to see general outlines. She found herself superstitiously looking at the clouds in the grey sky, seeing if she could see Mark in them, like some Sunday school representation of heaven. Daniel started to grizzle again and she walked him through to the dining room at the front. And back again.

Ruth found her a while later, with Daniel still crying, and Shula in tears too.

'It was when we stopped by the hall mirror,' she snuffled. 'He looked so sad and I couldn't help it, he's been like this all morning, I don't know what I'm doing wrong.'

'Here, let me have him ... '

Ruth wiped her hands on her overalls and took Daniel. She put him up against her shoulder and rubbed his back. Slowly he soothed.

'He keeps doing that,' said Shula, sniffing. 'Crying for me and then when anyone else takes him ... '

'Tell me about it,' said Ruth. 'Pip was just the same. Your Mum's the worst. Pip would shut up like magic.'

'How does Mum do it, d'you think?'

'I reckon she puts a spell on them,' said Ruth. 'I'll give him a minute then I'll put him down.'

'Oh, Ruth,' said Shula suddenly. She put her hands up to her face.

Ruth placed Daniel carefully in his Moses basket. She sat next to Shula on the sofa and put her arms round her.

'Shh, there,' she said.

'Look at this place, it's such a mess!' sobbed Shula. 'Nappies and jars of cream everywhere and things airing — it's driving me mad.'

'Look, you're hardly talking to the right person about being houseproud but it really doesn't matter you know,' said Ruth. 'Daniel doesn't notice — he wants you that's all.'

'I know.' Shula reached for a tissue. There were boxes of tissues in every room now. She blew her nose loudly. 'That's the trouble. He does want me — and there's only me and sometimes I think I can't cope. It's too much.'

'You want Mark. Of course you do.'

'It's not fair. Daniel's so beautiful. And Mark'll never see him. He never even knew about him.'

'It must be terrible.' Ruth's voice was low.

'People think "oh, Shula's got the baby now" as if that makes it better. I just want Mark, Ruth. I need him, like Daniel needs me.' She gulped and wiped her nose on the pathetically small scrap of tissue which was still dry. 'And then I get so cross with him, Mark I mean. Leaving me with no-one to share this with. I feel so alone. I just don't think I'm up to it.'

Ruth hugged Shula against her.

'Of course you are. Shula, maybe this is the wrong thing to say —' Ruth smiled briefly. 'I'm always putting my foot in it. Look, it's terrible for you of course but — well, Daniel doesn't know Mark's not here. All he knows is that you are. OK?'

It was at that point that Shula decided to let her standards slip a bit. Everyone said she'd been trying to do too much.

'Something's got to go,' she said to Caroline. 'I've decided not to make my own decorations this year. And Mum's going to make me some mince pies.'

'Thank goodness for that,' said Caroline. 'Do you realise how inadequate you've made the rest of us feel all these years?'

Incredibly, it was Christmas again. Last February she hadn't wanted to live another day. Literally. Even when she knew she was pregnant — not when she'd first been told, but later, when it had sunk in and she'd really begun to believe it — even then, she'd just been going through the motions. She said she was pleased, but really she couldn't feel anything. She felt she'd forgotten how to be happy. Every day she cried. She felt utterly alone. Of the two people she might have turned to for comfort outside the family, Caroline was struggling to get better and make sense of what had happened, while Robin was trying desperately to sustain her, run the parish and do his vet job. If it hadn't been for Nigel she didn't know how she'd have got through it at all. He was the only person she could turn to. She limited the amount she let her parents see: her pain grieved them too much and the responsibility for her parents' pain was too much for her to cope with. Nigel suffered for her, of course he did, but somehow he helped her cope where the enormous weight of her parents' sympathy and grief actually held her back. Nigel just got on with helping in any way he could: he took her to the supermarket for coffee and catfood and he mowed the lawn. He also spent evening after evening with her, letting her talk about Mark if she wanted, sitting in silence, holding her, if she didn't. She couldn't have known and still didn't know what her resumed affection with Nigel had done to Elizabeth. She had actually called off the engagement, believing that deep down,

Nigel was still in love with Shula. Nigel had won her back and they too had been married at St. Stephen's in September. Now Elizabeth was mistress of Lower Loxley as well as its Marketing Manager: Nigel's mother had gone to Spain to stay with her sister who had turned up unexpectedly for the wedding, so Nigel and Lizzie were looking forward to spending their first married Christmas alone. The other wedding which should have taken place that year never had. As Caroline slowly recovered, she found herself questioning more than ever Robin's belief in a benign deity who could act so randomly to bring heartbreak to her best friend. Robin tried everything to convince her. He tried to explain the nature of his faith. He wanted them to resume the counselling which they'd been having before the planned wedding. He offered Caroline time — and more time — but she had convinced herself that the accident was meant to happen, that it was preventing her from making a horrible lifelong mistake. Shula was sad when Caroline told her, but not surprised. How could any of them expect to take up where they had left off? Like Robin, Shula had her faith to support her: Caroline did not. Shula helped her pack up and send back the wedding presents. Caroline had decided, she'd said that evening, as they wrapped soufflé dishes and tea trays in bubble-wrap, that she and marriage didn't go. She thought that there were some people who weren't meant to be part of a couple and she was one of them. And some who were, thought Shula. I wasn't meant to be on my own.

The future scared her. Every morning, the first thought she had was that Mark wasn't there. It dulled everything. She was excited about the baby but in a cautious, disbelieving way. She knew the dizzying fear of having everything you trusted taken from you: she knew how tenuous and fragile a thing a pregnancy was. At seven weeks she had an early scan. They showed her the baby's heartbeat pulsing away and she shook her head in wonder. At sixteen weeks Jill came with her for another scan and they brought the X-Rays back to Borchester and showed them off in the wine bar, took them round to show Bunty and Reg. Slowly the baby became real to her. She seemed to be having a textbook pregnancy. No sickness, no swollen ankles, no high blood pressure. But she couldn't enjoy it. She'd waited so long for it to happen and it was tainted with sorrow. As her stomach swelled, and she read through her pregnancy guides month by month, she felt resentful that Mark wasn't there to rub her back and prop up her ankles, like the helpful (curiously, always bearded) partners in the books. Everyone said her anger was good: it was a stage in the grieving process. That in itself made Shula angry. It wasn't as clear-cut as that. How naive to think you could chop something as complicated as losing someone you loved into neat little segments — first you'll feel this: then you'll feel that. Months after it had happened, she was still as shocked and disbelieving as she had been that Thursday night: she was angry and sad and she missed him so much. Guy Pemberton, the new Estate owner who'd lost a wife and a son had told her to take one day at a time. She didn't even feel she had the strength for that. They were all the same, all equally miserable, the next day, and the next. Poor Ruth had tentatively suggested on Usha's behalf that Shula think about what was going to happen to the business.

'I can't,' Shula had sobbed. 'It's all that's left!'

Ruth had stuttered ineffectually, out of her depth, as it all poured out.

'I had to sort out his clothes. That was the first thing,' Shula began. 'I don't know why. I didn't know where to start. Start with his clothes. It seemed ... sensible. Have to be sensible. But nobody tells you what to do with his clothes. When you've sorted them out ... What do you do with them?'

Ruth raised her shoulders helplessly. Shula was crying openly now.

'Mum helped me,' she went on. 'We sorted them all out. I gave some to Bunty. David had his cricket things. Dad had his cap. I put the rest in a dustbin bag, and left them on the doorstep of the Oxfam shop.' Shula took a breath. 'Then I sorted out his books ... and his photos, photos I'd forgotten ... photos that I'd never seen. I found his prep school tie. I gave that to Bunty. A theatre ticket from Hong Kong when I went to see him. His old S.D.P. membership card. Things like that. I sorted through it all. I put it all away. Neatly. Neatly put away. And I answered the letters, changed the bank account ... wrote to ... the electricity company, the council offices, the water board ... I write to inform you that my husband, Mr Mark Hebden...'

'Shula —' Ruth put out a hand but Shula pushed it away. She was alone, wasn't she, beyond help?

'Mr Mark Hebden,' she continued, wanting to hurt herself now, 'died on the seventeenth of February 1994 ... sorted it all out ... drew a line underneath ... tied up all the loose ends ... I did all that ... all that ... all that needed to be done ... and I can't do any more ... I can't face any more ... it broke my heart ... it broke my heart ... because I miss him so much — I miss Mark so much ... '

Only the business was left. Everything else had gone. Mark's life, gone in black plastic sacks down to the Oxfam shop. His gardening trousers, the new suit that he'd hardly worn, his ties, his shirts, they'd all been in one pile, while more painful still in another, a fuzzy photo of Shula by the hot air balloon, the first of her birthdays they'd spent together, the '10 Downing Street' keyring she'd bought him when he was first elected to the council, his old diaries. All Shula kept was his dressing gown, the blue and green towelling one, because it smelt of Mark. She even wore it herself sometimes. It was the nearest she could get to feeling him hold her. Sometimes she would sit and try to conjure up his face, feature by feature, fearing she had forgotten what he looked like. Gradually, when she wasn't trying so hard, it came back to her, and finally, there was one moment she could always recapture: Mark, bringing her tea last Christmas morning, the day they'd had the family round. He'd made it in her favourite mug, the one with the full-blown pink roses on it. He'd put it on the bedside table. She was already awake, but pretended to be asleep, watching out of half-closed eyes as he arranged her pile of presents at the foot of the bed. She wondered what they were. The latest BBC tie-in cookery book, no doubt, and the new Joanna Trollope, the coffee coloured silk camisole, knickers and slip she'd pointed out to him in Felpersham — he'd have gone back for them, she was sure, probably adding in a nightie or something as well — a holdall of Clarins or Clinique, a painted salad bowl maybe or a blown glass jug and a hand-knitted jumper and champagne (there was always champagne) and chocolate mints... He was good at presents. She'd bought him one of those computerised organiser things — not that he needed to be any more organised, it was more of a joke really. And a cricketing autobiography, and a corkscrew shaped like a fish which she'd found in Underwoods, and a mug which played Merry Christmas which she'd found in the market, and some chocolate mints — oh and the dressing gown. If she'd known it was the last Christmas she'd have with Mark she might have tried a bit harder to be original.

'I don't think you could have made him any happier, love,' said Jill as she put the finishing touches to her trifle on Christmas Eve: Shula and Daniel were staying at Brookfield over the holiday. Her mother always knew what she was thinking. Shula had discussed this phenomenon with other people over the years. They said they found it irritating. Shula found it comforting. She wondered if it was peculiar to mothers and daughters, or if she'd be like it with Daniel? 'I remember telling Phil as we drove away last year how happy you seemed.'

'We were.' Shula stroked the soft nape of Daniel's neck as he dozed against her shoulder. 'Sometimes, Mum, that makes it worse. I mean, you look at all the people who struggle on unhappily, who seem to hate each other...'

'No, that must be worse, surely,' said her mother. 'You lose someone you've never really loved: you must think what a waste of both our lives. You know your life hasn't been a waste, don't you? And nor was Mark's.'

In confirmation Daniel snuffled against her shoulder.

'I'll put him down,' said Shula, standing up. 'You'll have to be getting ready soon.'

Lower Loxley were staging *Don Giovanni* and Phil and Jill had been given complimentary tickets. Shula was going to spend her Christmas Eve preparing the vegetables for tomorrow.

'All right love.' Jill blew her grandson a kiss. 'Night, night Daniel.'

Jill grated chocolate over the top of the trifle thoughtfully.

Shula had had the best and worst year of her life. It had been a big year for all of them. Elizabeth and Nigel finally married, after all the upsets, Phil and David still so worried over the T.B. in the Brookfield herd. Jill licked a blob of cream from her finger. Even that, which could be the ruination of Brookfield, seemed insignificant compared with what Shula had gone through. Phil was always saying — it was a saying of Doris' really — that it wasn't so much what life threw at us that mattered, but how we reacted. Phil should know, after what he'd been through with Grace, his first wife, who had also died in an accident. Jill hoped Shula had done her share of suffering. Even if she hadn't, having seen her this past year, Jill had no doubts that she'd cope. She really was the strongest of the children. She was the strongest of them all.

May

——1995——

Now, Mum, have you got everything? Look, there's spare bibs in the side pocket of his changing bag. He's rather dribbly at the moment —'

'Shula, stop fussing!'

Jill smiled. After all the years of looking after her own four children, and plenty of practice with little Pip, she was hardly likely to be phased by looking after her grandson for the day. But Shula's anxiety was only natural. It was her first week back at work and she had, Jill privately thought, let herself in for rather a complicated arrangement whereby on the days Shula was at Rodway's in Borchester, Daniel would go to a day nursery, and when she was at the Estate Office, as she was today, Daniel would be left with Jill.

'Well, you can always change it if it doesn't work out,' Caroline had pointed out reasonably when Shula had been agonising.

'Yes. Yes, you're right,' Shula agreed. They were trotting along a bridle path at the edge of one of Home Farm's fields. Caroline was on her new horse, Maisie, which Guy Pemberton, in a gesture which had got the village talking, had given her as a 40th birthday present. Shula was exercising Guy's horse, Moonlight. It had been her ambition to get back into her jodhpurs since having Daniel and despite the recent attractions of Easter eggs and her mother's Simnel cake, she had finally managed it. She breathed deeply of the sharp spring air. 'And let's face it, I don't have to go back to work at all. If it's all too much hassle I can stay at home and look after Daniel myself.'

'That's not what you really want, though, is it?' asked Caroline gently, pulling Maisie to a halt.

Shula pulled Moonlight up too and turned to survey the green sweep of Brian's wheatfield. Beyond it, the first glimmers of yellow were showing on a vast expanse of rape. The horses lowered their heads to pull at the soft, juicy grass of the verge.

'I can't hide anything from you, can I?' Shula smiled.

'Nope!' Caroline patted Maisie's neck. 'Good girl, Maisie.'

Caroline was not asking for an explanation, but Shula felt she wanted to give one.

'I love Daniel to distraction, of course I do, but that's just what I've got to protect him against,' she said, not feeling as if she was making much sense. 'He needs company of his own age —not now maybe, but he will in a few months. That's why I want him to go to the nursery as well as to Mum.'

'Yes, I can see your logic. And it's very easy to get centred on a baby when you have them all the time. I can see how it happens.'

Since Daniel had been born, Caroline had been almost as besotted with him as Shula, constantly bringing him presents and offering to babysit.

Shula nodded in agreement.

'That's partly why I feel I ought to go back to work. If he has me day in, day out, we're only going to get too wrapped up in each other. Then he won't be able to make relationships when he goes to school, or in later life.'

'Like someone else we know,' said Caroline wryly.

'Simon?'

'Who else?'

Caroline was having a hard time with Simon Pemberton, Guy's son. Her life had taken a surprising turn earlier in the year. After the pain of her break-up with Robin, the last thing she had been looking for was another relationship, but a friendship with Guy had grown out of their mutual interest in horses. When his old hunter, Mungo, had had to be put down, she had helped him choose a new horse, Moonlight, but only a few weeks later, Guy had had a bad fall on Brian Aldridge's off-the-road riding course and had broken his pelvis. Caroline had been doing a perfectly good job of looking after him until Simon had arrived on the scene, bustling in efficiently wanting to hire nurses and companions and threatening to sue Brian. Guy, in his quietly determined way, had gently resisted

Simon's pushiness, backing off from sueing Brian and insisting that Caroline, who had become his constant companion since his fall, was giving him all the care and attention he needed. Simon had buzzed about for a bit without getting anywhere, like a wasp on a windowpane, before admitting defeat — and where Caroline was concerned, not very graciously. Though he didn't even live in Ambridge — he was dividing his time between running the Estate for Guy and his own irrigation equipment business in Leamington Spa — Simon had acquired something of a reputation in the village. Joe Grundy had pronounced him good-looking, which had got everyone guessing, but Joe for once was proved to be right. Villagers who came into contact with Simon reported that he was certainly tall, dark and handsome, with an angular face and such dark hair it was almost black and eyes, according to Sid Perks when pressed, the colour of twelve-year-old malt. Martha Woodford, drawing on her vast knowledge of romantic fiction, said he had a cruel mouth but in the main, it wasn't his appearance but his personality which was the problem. He seemed to be regarded as a cross between Bluebeard and Vlad the Impaler, especially by Susan Carter, who had had more than she would have liked to do with him at the Estate Office.

'I can't wait for you to come back to work!' she'd told Shula when she came round to Glebe Cottage to ask about Shula's return date. She was hoping it would be before half-term as she and Neil were hoping to go on the planned trip to the Ambridge twin-village of Meyruelle in the South of France. 'He just makes me so jumpy!'

If Shula's feelings about returning to work were already mixed, the Simon Pemberton factor, added to the existing ingredients of guilt, panic and inadequacy, threatened to make the entire concoction churn even more. She'd hardly seen the man before her return to work, except once back in the winter when Susan had had flu and she'd gone into the office to hold the fort, taking Daniel with her. Simon had come back from a meeting and had left her with no uncertain impression that babies and business did not mix, that she was deeply unprofessional for taking Daniel to the office in the first place and that she was conniving, along with his father as benevolent despot and the rest of Ambridge as a bunch of peasants stuck in the Middle Ages, to run the village on a feudal system. Shula felt that if she'd told him the Estate was still strip-farmed it would have been no more than he expected. Guy told her later that he'd defended her, telling Simon they were lucky Shula had gone in at all in the middle of her maternity leave.

'The funny thing is, Simon quite likes babies,' he'd explained.

For breakfast? thought Shula.

Now here she was after nearly eight months away, sitting at her old desk again. Graham Ryder, whom Rodway and Watson had put in to cover for her, had left copious notes on what had been going on. 'Good luck — you'll need it' was his closing remark. Thanks, Graham, thought Shula, reaching for the topmost file. The I.A.C.S. forms — so much for easing herself in gently ...

She spent most of the morning ploughing through her 'In' tray with Susan tapping away happily at her wordprocessor. She kept turning round and smiling at Shula as if to reassure herself that she was still there.

'Why did you change the layout of the office, Susan?' Shula asked her. 'It was nice when we worked facing each other. Or did Graham keep trying to distract you?' Ever since someone had misguidedly told Graham Ryder when *Butch Cassidy* first came out that he had a look of Paul Newman about him he'd had a rather elevated opinion of his own attractiveness.

'Oh, no, nothing like that.' Susan looked embarrassed. 'It's so I can see the door. I can't bear Mr Pemberton creeping up on me like he does.'

'Susan! I'm beginning to wonder why I ever came back!' exclaimed Shula. 'To think, Daniel would just have woken up about now, I could have been sitting out in the garden with him — oh, drat!'

'What is it?' Susan looked up.

'I forgot to pack his special juice. Oh well, he'll have to have ordinary fruit juice, I suppose. I'd just better phone Mum and tell her —'

'Tell you what, I'll make us a coffee while you do.' Susan got up and stretched, her hands in the small of her back. 'Oh, Shula, this is lovely. It's just like old times.'

Shula grinned and dialled Brookfield's number. Susan spooned Nescafé into mugs and went to the fridge for the milk.

'Mum? It's me. How is he?' said Shula into the phone.

Out of the corner of her eye she saw the door open.

'Morning Susan,' said Simon Pemberton, behind Susan's back. Susan straightened abruptly from the fridge, turning as she did so. A plume of milk spurted from the carton. Simon stepped back to avoid it.

'Sorry, Mr Pemberton,' gabbled Susan as milk tricked down her sleeve. 'I'll wipe it up.'

'And how nice it is to see Shula back,' he continued.

Shula looked up and smiled falsely as her mother's voice burbled in her ear. With any luck he'd go straight through to his office. But Simon didn't show any inclination to move. Perhaps she could cut her mother off short. But on the other end of the phone Jill had launched into an account of everything Daniel had done, eaten, drunk and regurgitated since Shula had dropped him off and was not to be deterred. Shula was aware of Simon's challenging silence into which her one-sided conversation boomed to the accompaniment of the boiling kettle.

'Did he? Oh, good ... Yes ... Yes ... What? Didn't I put one in? ... Perhaps I could nip home at lunchtime ... No, you've got enough to do ... '

Shula felt Simon's eyes on her.

'Look, Mum, I'd better go ... '

Simon walked across to his office. In the doorway he paused and turned.

'Black coffee for me if you're making some, please, Susan,' he said. 'And ask Shula to come through when she's finished what's obviously an important phone call.'

'It was a nightmare,' Shula told Ruth later when she went to collect Daniel from Brookfield. 'Whenever Simon came through the office I was either on the phone to Mum about Daniel or to Marjorie Antrobus about the Rogation Day service.'

'But apart from that, did you enjoy it?' Ruth asked, pushing her mug of tea to a safe distance across the table as Pip clambered on her lap.

'Well, it's nice to have something to think about that isn't nappies or gripe water,' Shula conceded. 'But with Simon around, I don't know if enjoy is a word I'll be using about my job much in future.'

But as Shula got used to the routine, she was glad she'd made the decision to go back. Since Mark had died, Daniel had been her life. Even before he'd been born, Daniel had been her hope, her purpose for going on. Now that she was back among the grown ups, she could see how she'd come to rely him. Expecting Daniel to be her sole companion was far too much of a responsibility to place on him. It was far healthier this way.

At the end of May she waved her parents off on the coach with the other villagers on their long journey to Meyruelle. Nigel and Elizabeth had already moved into Brookfield to cope with the bed and breakfast guests. Shula knew that Susan had been hanging on for her week off by her fingernails. Susan was normally a perfectly good worker but there was something about Simon which brought out the worst in her. Every letter she typed for him came back with an impatient ring around a mis-spelling, she'd allowed the kettle element to burn out and had overfilled the photocopier with toner powder.

'I know I'm my own worst enemy,' she said to Shula. 'But he gets me in such a state.'

'You go and have a jolly good time,' Shula reassured her. 'Just forget about this place for a bit.'

She didn't tell Susan that Simon had heard on the grapevine about Susan's criminal record and clearly thought the fact that his father continued to employ her was another misbegotten example of Guy's benign disposition.

When Shula got to the office on Tuesday morning, Simon was already there — and with a triumphant look on his face.

'The rent money's forty pounds short,' he announced without preamble.

'What?' Shula hung her jacket on the back of the door.

'I happened to be speaking to the bank this morning — '

'And you just *happened* to check?'

Collecting the tenants' rents was one of Susan's jobs.

'It's rather a coincidence, don't you think, that just when the Carters might have wanted extra spending money for France — ' Simon speculated.

'Susan would never do a thing like that!'

Shula was incensed. Getting at Susan when she was in the office was one thing, running her down when she wasn't here to give her version of events was another. All day Simon wouldn't let it drop. He was due for a meeting with David — her father and David were to start contract farming some of the Estate land in October — but he still managed to find time to check that Susan had, indeed, collected all the rents on Friday. By the middle of the week, Shula couldn't stand Simon's non-stop insinuations any longer.

Ooh, just go back to Leamington! she thought when he asked smoothly if Shula had come across the missing forty pounds yet. When her mother phoned from France she asked her to ask Susan about the discrepancy. That was the afternoon, of course, when her childminding plans, somewhat fragile now Nigel and Elizabeth were in charge at Brookfield, finally fell apart and she had to take Daniel back to the Estate Office for the afternoon. Luckily Simon must have read her mind and had set off for Leamington before lunch. He need never know, Shula thought. She was just typing him a note explaining what she had learnt — that Susan had collected the missing rent on Friday but, too late to take it to the bank, had stowed it in the bottom drawer of Simon's desk, leaving him a note which must have got lost — when the office door opened, crashing into Daniel's chair.

'Careful!' Shula turned from the keyboard.

'What on earth?'

Simon. She leapt to her feet.

'I'm sorry, I'll move him.'

She launched into an explanation but Daniel, jerked out his sleep by Simon's arrival, started to stir. As Shula bent to lift him out, the telephone rang. Hands full of sleepy baby, she dithered.

'I'll get it,' Simon said with hardly any trace of resignation. 'I think he needs his Mum.'

'Are we talking about the same Simon Pemberton?' Caroline was incredulous when Shula recounted the incident later over a glass of wine.

'I know, I was amazed,' Shula agreed. 'But he picked Daniel up and played "This Little Piggy" with his toes.'

After that, Simon often asked about Daniel. And it didn't seem to be an effort, in the way small talk was normally an effort for him — you could see him on a Monday morning forcing himself to ask her and Susan if they'd had a nice weekend. His questions about Daniel seemed natural and unforced but Shula still wasn't very happy about phoning the office one day at the end of June to explain that she wouldn't be coming in.

'Daniel's a bit off-colour,' she told Susan. 'He wasn't one hundred percent yesterday and I felt bad about sending him to nursery. I really think I ought to be with him today.'

It was searingly hot. The flat sunlight glared on the garden, making Shula screw up her eyes. She drew the curtains on the back of the house to keep the rooms cool. Summer was all very well — if you didn't have a sickly baby to deal with. Daniel wouldn't settle. Shula walked him round the garden in the shade, she walked him round the house, she put him in the buggy and took him down to look at the ducks but he was thoroughly miserable. He turned away from food and cried pitifully when Shula tried to get him to have a drink. His little face was hot and cross: his hair lay damply across his head. By the evening Shula was beside herself. When she phoned the surgery they told her that Richard had been called over to Waterley Cross to a man with chest pains. They said he'd be round as soon as he got back. Shula walked Daniel through into the kitchen. He moaned whenever she put him down and her neck was aching with the tension of supporting his weight. Wearily she shifted him onto her other shoulder, his heavy head lolling into the curve of her neck. There was a knock on the door. Richard. Thank goodness. But it wasn't. It was Simon.

'Oh dear, he doesn't look too pleased with himself, does he?' he said, trying to get a reaction out of Daniel.

Shula couldn't keep the worry out of her voice.

'He's not. He's been going on like this all day. Feel how hot he is.'

Then something happened which Shula remembered. She remembered it from when Mark died. Sometimes the grief and the anxiety were too much to bear. You kept it in for days, weeks even, and then suddenly, with the most inappropriate person, it all came out. It didn't matter who — the girl on the checkout at the supermarket, the garage cashier who bothered to smile. Suddenly you were telling them about the awfulness and the loneliness and the heaviness of every day. Now it happened with Simon.

'I'm probably being stupid, I know,' she blurted out, 'but in the shop last week Betty said there'd been some meningitis cases.'

'I can understand you worrying then.'

Shula took a deep breath. 'I'm probably being a silly, hysterical mum. But if anything were to happen to him ... '

'Come on,' said Simon.

'What?' Tired herself, she couldn't keep up with Simon's decisiveness.

'We'll take him straight to casualty. Let's not mess about waiting for the doctor. I'll drive you.'

Grateful to have the decision taken for her after the long weariness of the day, Shula found her bag, locked up the house and followed Simon out to the car. It was a huge silver thing, glittering in the sun. Simon helped her in, took off his suit jacket and flung it on the seat and rolled up his sleeves. Shula hadn't been in a sleek, smart car like this since Mark's. It all came back to her. The smell of the leather seats. The tinted windscreen, the sunroof, the smoothness of the acceleration. She sat in the back, beside Daniel in his carry-seat, grateful that she didn't have to make conversation. Daniel didn't like the motion of the car and kept up a low-level whine all the way, except when he was sick as they swung on to the one-way system in Borchester. Shula mopped at his cotton romper and surreptitiously wiped a thread of spittle off the upholstery. The poor little mite had nothing left to bring up.

Simon wouldn't leave her. They only had to wait about ten minutes till Daniel was seen to — perhaps they always saw the babies first, or perhaps they could see that Shula's distress was by now almost as great as Daniel's. Shula took him through to a curtained-off cubicle where a woman doctor with an expressive face which still managed to give nothing away listened to a list of his symptoms, felt his pulse and took his temperature and said that, for safety's sake, she'd like to do a lumbar puncture. Shula had to hold Daniel, feeling sick, as the needle went in and he screamed in shock and pain. Instinctive tears filled her eyes. But at the same time she was grateful that they were acting so fast, relieved to be in a place where the responsibility for Daniel's welfare was not hers alone, thankful that Simon had turned up when he did. After the lumbar puncture, when they were doing more tests, she realised that she'd better go out and let Simon know what was going on. Even without his suit jacket, he looked absurdly formal in his shirt and tie, sitting on an orange plastic chair while a children's video played luridly on a television placed high up on the wall above his head. Around him parents held their sick or injured children. The fine weather had brought, so the nurse had told Shula, the usual influx of cut feet from walking around with no shoes on, tumbles from bikes and climbing frames, and allergic reactions to stings. Everyone apart from Simon was in summer clothes. Some of the children, siblings who'd had to be dragged out of the paddling pool to accompany an injured brother or sister, were still in their swimming costumes. Shula realised that her pale pink T-shirt was stained with a variety of unmentionable substances and that her long shorts were crumpled. She felt utterly exhausted. Suddenly Simon's presence was just another responsibility, someone else to be considered, someone else's feelings to be taken into account.

'Look, if you want to get off ... ' she suggested.

He shook his head.

'Don't you worry about me. You just get back in there and look after young Daniel.'

Shula felt a surge of guilt for wanting to get rid of him. He had been wonderful.

'I'm very grateful,' she said.

'Mrs Hebden?' A nurse peeped round the corner of Daniel's

cubicle. 'If you could just ... would your husband like to come through too?'

'Er, no, it's ... ' Shula began.

'It's all right,' Simon said.' I'll stay here.'

Shula smiled briefly at him before she hurried away. How embarrassing. How inevitable.

As the nurse lifted the curtain to let her pass into the cubicle she looked back at Simon. He was staring fixedly in front of him, apparently absorbed in a notice about a needle exchange scheme, pointedly ignoring a woman on his right who was unsuccessfully trying to restrain her toddler from untying his shoelaces. She registered that the video playing was *Beauty and the Beast,* one of Pip's favourites.

It wasn't meningitis: Daniel was a victim of some other nasty though unnamed virus. It was nearly ten by the time the tests were finished and the results received from the lab, so the hospital kept him in overnight as he still had a high temperature. Shula stayed too. By the next day he was visibly improved and David collected them and brought them back to Glebe. Daniel slept for most of the morning and Shula dozed too, even more exhausted now as the enormity of what could have been slowly dawned.

She must have fallen asleep because she had this dream about Simon. It was really muddled and confused. Daniel wasn't there, but she was, and David, and Lynda Snell of all people and they were on this huge marble staircase (that bit perhaps came from *Beauty and the Beast*) and someone came and told her that Simon had been in an accident. A car accident. He wasn't badly hurt, but he'd dislocated his shoulder and hurt his foot. (Why his foot?) Then Simon arrived, winched up the staircase in a sort of chairlift and he said his shoulder wasn't all that painful and he had a square gauze pad, brilliant white, on the top of his foot which she couldn't take her eyes off and he kept asking her if she was sure that all the rents had been collected.

The phone woke her and she was glad it did. It was her Mum. Shula could sense Jill's guilt that she hadn't taken Daniel's symptoms of the day before seriously enough.

'It really doesn't matter, Mum,' Shula said. 'He's OK now, that's the main thing. Don't worry about it.'

She replaced the receiver and checked on Daniel. He was still sleeping soundly in his cot, his little fists balled by his head. Shula felt his forehead, which was definitely cooler. His mobiles danced in the faint breeze from the open window. She stood for a moment, gripping the rail of the cot, and whispered a prayer of thanks. Then she went back to her own room and lay down again gratefully on the bed.

From outside she could hear the drone of a mower as someone — Bert, probably, in his lunch hour — cut the grass in the church-yard. Later, if Daniel was better and her Mum could come down, or tomorrow, she would go, as she did once or twice every week, to Mark's grave. She had had a simple headstone erected. She'd had to wait till a year after his death for the grave to settle, which was good in a way, because she'd been able to have carved 'Beloved husband of Shula and father of Daniel'. If only he'd known. If only he could see Daniel just once. She remembered, as her mind drifted away again, walking up Lakey Hill with Caroline on what would have been Mark's fortieth birthday at the end of February. She'd told her what a special place it had been for her and Mark. His silly joke about being on top of the world, how they had stood at the top after the ectopic and yelled and yelled into the wind, each trying to out-shout the other.

'Sometimes, when I look at Daniel,' she'd said, 'I miss Mark more. I look forward to ... his first words ... his first steps ... and then I think I'll never be able to share those moments with the only person who ever could share them ... and I think ... '

'Go on,' said Caroline softly.

'I know I shouldn't and I know it's selfish ... but I just think ... it's not fair.'

Caroline said nothing but she reached out and took Shula's hand. She understood. The last few days had been difficult for her, too — the anniversary of the accident, then the anniversary of her cancelled wedding.

'Go on,' she said. 'We're at the top. As loud as you like.'

But Daniel stirred against Shula in the baby sling and she knew she couldn't yell, much as she wanted to. She wrapped her arms round him and cradled him to her. She pressed her face into his woolly hat. 'Oh Daniel,' she whispered. 'It's not fair!'

Shula turned on her side and bunched up her pillow. She had never thought she would get used to sleeping in this bed without Mark. She still longed to curl herself round his broad back in the mornings, to sense the sleepy smile unfolding on his face and to feel him turn over and move against her. Strangely, she hadn't moved to the middle of the bed, still keeping to her side, closer to the door, closer to Daniel should he wake in the night. But she often awoke to find herself slewed diagonally across the bed and enjoyed stretching her toes down to the cool, furthest corner across all the space which was her own. Now her worry was that she would never again be able to get used to sharing a bed. Not that she wanted to. Not that there was the remotest possibility of it. Shula closed her eyes again. For Caroline, it was not only a possibility but shortly to become a reality. At the beginning of the month, she and Guy had announced their engagement. They were to be married in September. Simon had not taken the news well. Shula remembered the day in the Estate Office when he had told her that he had only learnt of the engagement minutes before the party at which the public announcement was made. Shula had been shocked by the hurt in his eyes. She knew that Guy and Simon didn't have an easy relationship. From the bits and pieces she had gleaned from Caroline, and things Simon had let slip, she knew that Simon had felt ousted by his elder brother Andrew, who took Guy's preferred path for his sons into agriculture, whilst Simon followed his own head and studied engineering. Then Simon had gone and worked abroad before setting up his own company, while his brother managed the family farm. In a way, it was rather like Kenton and David. Shula had often sat up late into the night while her twin confessed to the sense of inadequacy he felt because he didn't get turned on by sheep dipping and pneumatic seed drills. At least her parents had never made Kenton feel guilty for choosing a different way of life. Instead they had tried to understand his love of the sea and his desire to travel. But Guy, it appeared, had closed down on Simon. His brother Andrew's sudden death in a car crash, and later his mother's rather more pro-longed one, had widened rather than breached the distance between father and son. Neither Guy nor Simon relished talking about intimate matters and when they did work themselves up to it, one or other always seemed to pick the wrong moment or get off on the wrong foot and something would be said which pushed them even further apart. It worried Caroline.

'I'm beginning to realise what I've got myself into!' she said wryly to Shula. 'When I think of Sam and sweet little Oliver ... now I'm going to be stepmother to Simon!'

Shula felt for Simon. Yet again, at a time of family crisis when he might, just might, have found some common ground with his father, he had arrived in Ambridge after his father's accident to find Caroline firmly ensconced and his concerns pushed to the side-lines. As they worked together throughout the summer, she found herself instinctively trying to modify his behaviour, urging him to talk to Guy about things which bothered him and not to fly off the handle with people when they told him something he didn't like hearing. Though she sometimes cringed inwardly when she heard herself deliver another little homily, and though Simon's eyebrows performed acrobatic feats of astonishment, she felt better for trying, rather than putting up with Simon's moods to his face and complaining about him behind his back, which was how everyone else seemed to behave. She could sense that he did take notice, even if he didn't appear to, and began to feel that he might have a grudging admiration for her as a colleague, in the way that she got things done in the office and around the Estate without putting people's backs up. It wasn't all straightforward but Shula perse-vered. She seemed to be able to find and to bring out in Simon a less prickly, less defensive and more human side. The family were still surprised when she asked if she could ask him to a barbecue at Brookfield.

'Of course, dear, if you like,' said her mother, looking puzzled, as if Shula were asking Beelzebub himself to break bread with the Archers.

'Do you have to?' groaned David. 'I was hoping to enjoy

myself.'

The evening was horrendous. Within minutes of his arrival, Simon and David managed to row over something to do with the Estate machinery, and Simon left practically before the charcoal had heated up. Shula was furious.

'Simon was my guest and he should have been treated that way,' she said accusingly to David. 'What did you have to discuss Estate business for?'

'What on earth else have I got to talk to him about?' retorted David.

Inside she knew she was cross not just on Simon's behalf but because her whole family would feel that they'd been proved right after all. Shula might have tried to redeem him but Simon Pemberton was an unpleasant and antisocial boor with an innate sense of superiority and a chip on his shoulder about happy families. What a combination.

Guy knew. He knew what Shula — whether consciously or unconsciously — was trying to do. He knew she was trying to rehabilitate Simon and he knew, as someone who had lost two members of his family, that the experience might not be entirely one-sided. At the beginning of September, with his wedding to Caroline a week away, he sought Shula out and asked her if she would keep an eye on Simon throughout the day. Shula knew his relationship with Simon had become more strained than ever and Guy was terrified that Simon might say or do something to spoil Caroline's happiness. Shula's reaction was more complex than she expected: more than anything else she felt irritated and indignant on Simon's behalf. She liked Guy, but he seemed to have such a low opinion of his son. Surely Simon wouldn't do anything as childish as to misbehave at the wedding? It seemed to her that Guy and Caroline interpreted Simon's resentment about the wedding as just that, whereas Shula felt that he was using his unease about Caroline as a way of getting at his father. But then ... perhaps she was herself becoming too partisan, seeing things only from Simon's perspective, when there were whole vistas of complication between him and Guy which she could only guess at. And she of all people wanted Caroline's wedding day to be perfect. Like hers had been. It was only when Guy had gone that she realised that he might have had her best interests at heart too, in giving her something to keep her occupied. She wondered if Caroline had suggested it. How complicated. How silly. Everyone going around trying to protect everyone else, trying to spare their feelings. But of course she and Mark had got past all that. In the last few years of their marriage they had been able to be totally honest with each other, without any need for subterfuge or mixed messages. It was a rare honesty. She would never find it again. But if she handled it right, she might be able to create something similar with Daniel.

For all Guy's worry, the wedding day went like a dream — at least, that's what Caroline called it. Caroline, slim as a wand in her designer outfit and Guy, proud beside her in his new suit, exchanged vows and rings in a civil ceremony at Lower Loxley. Then fifty or so relatives and close friends moved through for lunch before the blessing at St. Stephen's mid-afternoon. Jack Woolley's wedding present to Caroline, whom he regarded as a second daughter, was an evening party at Grey Gables to which most of the village was invited. Shula had a nervous moment when Simon took the stage but all he did was to thank Jack and to urge people to keep eating, drinking and dancing. Most people muttered and clucked their approval but it wasn't lost on Shula and nor would it have been on Caroline, she knew, that Simon could not bring himself to refer to 'the happy couple' or to ask everyone to toast their health.

Next day Bert and David helped to move some of Caroline's things from Grey Gables to the Dower House, which Shula had promised she'd oversee. Simon was there too. He and Shula were on their way to look at a piece of woodland which badly needed thinning out.

'The view from this window. You wouldn't get a better one anywhere,' said Shula as they waited in the sitting room for Bert and David to finish unloading.

'Then I'd better make the most of it while I'm here,' said

Simon crisply. 'I'm hardly going to be dropping in for the odd cup of tea any more. Don't want to interrupt the happy couple.'

'Oh, Simon,' said Shula. 'That's silly. Can't you just be glad for them?'

But Simon could not. And when he finally called at the Dower House after Guy and Caroline had returned from their honeymoon, on Shula's instigation of course, he would have to find them kissing on the doorstep.

'They've only just got married,' said Shula, pouring tea. She had invited Simon to call in at Glebe on his way back to Leamington. She didn't quite know why — because she felt sorry for him? Because he'd asked her to lunch and she hadn't wanted to go? 'It's a very special time.'

'I'll take your word for it,' he said shortly.

'You can.'

Simon really opened up then. Before it had all been a cover-up, absurd clichés about second marriages like Caroline being a gold digger (Caroline, who was Lord Netherbourne's niece!) and the fuss about the flowers at Lower Loxley, the white lilies, his mother's favourites, he said, which he saw as an insult to her memory. Now he talked more honestly than he ever had before about his mother and about Caroline — as he saw it — taking her place. His pain was visible.

'It's as if she's totally forgotten, wiped out, as if she was never there. I'm the only one who remembers her.'

'I'm sure that's not true,' said Shula urgently, needing to believe it herself.

Simon snapped himself out of it then, apologising for getting so maudlin and embarrassing her when really he was the one who was embarrassed. Instead he picked up Daniel, who had been crawling about on the rug, and joggled him about a bit, then carried him over to the window and raised him above his head. Daniel shrieked with excitement, his little hands parting the air and his chubby legs, ending in their comical corduroy bootees, kicking like a cross-Channel swimmer. Shula couldn't stand it any longer.

'Simon, could you go please?'

'What?' Simon lowered Daniel to rest in the crook of his arm and Daniel jiggled impatiently, shorthand for 'Again! Again!'

Shula stood up, knocking the low table as she did so, and rattling the tea cups.

'I'm sorry. Could you go?'

Simon shrugged helplessly, confused.

'Shula, what's the matter? What have I done?'

Shula held out her arms for Daniel and Simon passed him across.

'Please,' she said. 'Just go. Now.'

He wasn't to know it was her wedding anniversary.

It was just such a difficult time. First there had been Guy and Caroline's wedding, and seeing them so happy. Next week it would be Elizabeth and Nigel's first anniversary. There was bound to be supper at Brookfield for that, then it would be her mother's 65th birthday and a huge party. All these family occasions, where everyone else was in couples. What am I turning into? she thought reproachfully as she bathed Daniel later that evening. Some bitter old stick who can't bear anyone else to be happy? But she knew that wasn't the truth. It was only that all these occasions accentuated her feeling of alone-ness, of being the outsider looking in, unmatched, uncoupled, uneven, odd. Daniel beat the water with the flat of his hands, pleased with the effect.

'Hey, someone's splashing! Who's splashing?' Shula asked him. 'Is that you? Is that Daniel?'

'Da,' said Daniel firmly. 'Da-da.'

And then this afternoon. Simon, who was so good with Daniel, standing there in the window where Mark had always stood admiring the garden, stood with a drink when he came in from work, stood and taken her in his arms after the first I.V.F. attempt had failed and they'd both soundlessly wept. Profiting from Shula's lack of attention, Daniel brought his tug boat down with a smack on the surface of the water. A jet spurted up and caught Shula in the eye.

'No, Daniel, naughty,' she said, more sharply than she'd intended.

Daniel's gummy grin collapsed and he looked uncertain.

'Oh darling, Mummy didn't mean to shout. Time to come out now, anyway.'

She lifted him from the bath and wrapped him in his hooded towel, dabbing at his feet, drying between the tiny toes. His thumb went into his mouth. It was nearly bedtime. She knelt by the bath and hugged him close. She felt his breathing settle. He smelt heavenly. His hair stuck up fluffily in front where she'd rubbed it with the towel. In a minute she'd dry him properly and blow raspberries on his tummy and put him to bed clean and powdered in the cot she'd chosen alone, in the room with the Beatrix Potter frieze which Mark had never seen. It was so unfair. It shouldn't have been Simon holding Daniel. It should have been Mark.

Next day she was consumed with guilt. Of course she'd been upset but she shouldn't have taken it out on Simon, particularly when he had shown himself at his most vulnerable. She didn't know how she was going to face him. It wasn't even as if he was her boss. He was actually Rodway's client, which made the relationship even more delicate. What if he said he didn't want her working at the Estate any more? But she should have realised that wouldn't be his reaction. If it had been she could have fought against it, explained, even. Instead, when he came into the Estate office, he exhibited in that typical, well-bred, English way, something a million times worse than out-and-out anger — reserve. Shula babbled something about having had a difficult day and it being near Daniel's bedtime. She could tell that he didn't believe her and was as hurt by her inability to tell him the truth as by the original rejection — but how could she tell him? He'd never known Mark, he'd had nothing to do with that part of her life. She just couldn't. And no one else was going to tell him, were they? Sadly she saw all the ground she'd gained with Simon slipping away.

But someone did tell him. When they'd been getting on better, she'd invited Simon to her mother's 65th birthday party and he duly turned up, bearing a lavish book on Thai cookery. Shula had always known it was going to be another evening to be got through, anyway, with a stiff smile and a glass of orange juice (wine would only make it worse) and his presence was just another couple of pounds on the cross she had to bear. She lurked in the kitchen most of the time, excusing herself to check on Daniel if Simon came within view. Somehow she got through the evening. Next day Simon told her that he knew the real reason why she'd asked him to go. David had told him.

'I'm sorry ... ' she began, apologising as much for the deception as anything else.

'There's no need to apologise,' he said warmly. 'I know what you must have been thinking and I do understand. Really I do.'

She was so relieved. She collected Daniel from Brookfield that evening and sang along to his nursery rhyme tape in the car. Daniel was at first surprised, then pleased, and kept time by thumping his feet against the seat. Simon did understand. She knew he did. She should have known he would. She should have trusted him with the truth. After all, they were in the same position — he on the outside of his family, she on the fringe of hers. They had both lost someone they loved: his alone-ness was a mirror of her own. And if she was honest — really, really, honest, the sort of honest Mark had made her be — then wasn't the reaction she'd had when she'd seen Simon, literally, in Mark's place at Glebe, a little bit to do with the guilt at having let Simon into her life at all, at having started to feel something, whatever it was, again, after all this time? It was no longer a simple case of 'I want Mark back' though she did, and always would. It was, perhaps, starting to be a case of 'I want some-one. Someone who will understand me like Mark did and will for-give what I can't change and with whom I can be myself again'. So was that someone — Simon?

He wasn't due in Ambridge the following week: they'd got the auditors in at Leamington. It was enough for Shula to know that they were back on speaking terms — she certainly wasn't expect-ing the enormous bouquet which arrived at the Estate Office early in the week. Ruth was there at the time. Blushing, Shula opened the card.

'They're from Simon, she explained to Ruth then read on, her voice less sure. 'He wants me to go out for dinner with him tomor-row night. At Botticelli's.'

'Botticelli's?' queried Ruth, intrigued. It was the most expensive restaurant in Borchester. Shula sighed. It was all moving too fast.

'I don't think I can go,' she said.

'Oh, go on,' said Ruth. 'Why not?'

Shula shook her head. She couldn't begin to convey what she was feeling.

'Oh, Ruth, it's all too complicated. I just don't think ... it's too soon — and even if it wasn't ...' She would have to turn him down. She just hoped he'd understand — again.

At home, the flowers filled three vases. She put one in the sitting room, one in the hall and a perfect single rose by her bed. She rang Simon to thank him — and to explain about dinner. He hadn't got long because he was meeting a customer for a drink but he said he understood.

'Some other time, then,' he said.

'Er ... yes,' said Shula. What else could she say? In the end she'd gained nothing but time. And not much of that either. On Friday he turned up at the Estate Office.

'I knew if I didn't come in person to say I was taking you out tonight I'd get the same brush-off I got on Tuesday.' He smiled. 'I've booked a table at Botticelli's for eight.'

'Simon ...'

'If you don't come, heaven knows who I'll have to invite. And you know perfectly well how much the wrong company can ruin a good meal.'

He was at his most persuasive. In the end Shula had to give in. There was only one problem ...

'I doubt if he'll wake up, but if he does, there's a bottle in the fridge—'

'Shula, stop worrying.' Kate and her boyfriend Roy Tucker had offered to babysit for Daniel. They wouldn't have been Shula's first choice but then the invitation to dinner had rather taken her by surprise. She took a deep breath.

'Sorry, I'm sure you'll cope,' she smiled.

'Of course we will,' said Kate. 'You go and get changed.'

That was a point. What had she got to wear to dinner at the smartest restaurant in Borchester with Simon Pemberton?

In the end she wore the sapphire silk shift she'd worn to Caroline's wedding. All her other smart clothes were black and tonight she didn't want to wear black somehow.

She knew from the start that it was going to go well. Everything had so mitigated against the evening — his unexpected invitation, her initial reluctance, the struggle to find a sitter — that it just had to. Simon was at his most charming, more expansive than she'd ever known him. It was as if a switch had been thrown inside which made him approachable, human — even fun. He made her laugh telling her about Kurt, one of his German suppliers, and the trip he'd made with him down the Rhine; about his first, disastrous brush with filo pastry; a bit more about his passion for rock climbing. You honestly wouldn't have believed it was the same man who put the fear of God into Susan Carter.

Back at Glebe Cottage, when Kate and Roy had gone and she had checked on Daniel, Shula came downstairs to find Simon sitting on the sofa, perfectly relaxed. She made instinctively for the armchair, but Simon patted the sofa beside him.

'Come and sit down beside me,' he said.

Shula sat, suddenly defenceless. Something tugged at her insides.

'He looks so like Mark when he's sleeping,' she said.

'But it's not the same,' he said.

Shula looked down at her hands in her lap, pleating a fold in her dress over and over.

'He can't put his arm round me and give me a cuddle.'

'I can,' he said softly. 'Is that nice?'

'Simon ... '

Shula panicked and went to pull away.

'Come on,' he urged, pulling her gently back towards him. 'It's what you need.'

'I don't know ... '

She looked at him. His eyes were kind.

'I do,' he said, 'and I'll tell you what else you need ... '
He leaned forward. She could feel his breath on her face.
'This,' he said. And kissed her.

Shula couldn't sleep. She knew it was ridiculous. She knew she'd be exhausted the next day and she'd got to go into Borchester to look at proper shoes for Daniel: he was so nearly walking. Yet here she was, like a teenager, grinning to herself and reliving the moment and tossing and turning. He'd only kissed her, for goodness' sake. It didn't mean anything. Of course it meant something. It meant something because she'd wanted it to happen. All the time at Botticelli's she'd been looking at his face across the small table, shadowed in the candlelight, watching his hands as he snapped a breadstick, noting the fringe of dark hairs under his cuff — all the time she'd been wondering if he would kiss her and she knew how badly she wanted him to.

The excitement and the delight got her through the long wakeful night. Adrenalin got her through the next day. It was only on Sunday, after she'd put Daniel down in the afternoon, that the doubts started to creep in. What had she been thinking of? If she was saying that, after eighteen months of loss, she was ready, tentatively, to take up her life again, did it have to be with Simon? Was he really the right person, or was he just there? Was it a good idea even to think about getting involved with someone who was so difficult — no, let's be honest, so disliked? What on earth would Caroline say? And David and Ruth? And her Mum and Dad?

Shula wandered out into the garden. It had been raining earlier and there was a tangy smell of wet earth. The lawn needed pricking over and feeding. She should be potting up her bulbs for Christmas. Instead she dropped down on the wooden seat against the back wall of the house: the overhanging thatch had protected it from the worst of the rain. Daniel's room was right above her so she'd hear him when he woke. Daniel ... Anyone she started to see would become a part of Daniel's life, too. As he became more aware of the people around him, that was another thing she couldn't take lightly. If she got involved with Simon, with anyone for that matter, it would have to be a proper commitment. She didn't want anything casual. It wouldn't be right for Daniel. It wasn't right for her. What would Simon want? She didn't know much about his past romantic history. He'd been involved with someone called Helen, she dimly remembered, when he'd first come to Ambridge, but that had finished. Had they been together long? Or was she the latest in a long line? She sat there until Daniel started to coo from his cot in the room above. By the time he did she had decided. She couldn't live her life by pulling back all the time. She'd had enough false starts and setbacks with Simon. She would go with whatever happened.

She was on pins for the whole day on Monday, even though he'd told her he'd be in Leamington. And when, at the end of the day, she heard what was unmistakeably his car arrive, her heart gave such a thump it almost pitched her forward onto her desk. He was very chirpy, kissed her on the cheek, said he'd had a lovely time on Friday night. She was the one who didn't know how to handle it, feeling safer when they were talking about business. That's when he let it slip about not wanting to leave too many loose ends before he went.

'Planning a trip?' asked Shula. 'Is it anywhere nice?'

'Well, I'll be picking up some tackle in Dusseldorf and then it's over to Dubai,' he replied, engrossed in a file.

Shula swallowed.

'Dubai? As in the Middle East?'

'It's the only one I know of.' Simon snapped the file shut and chucked it back on Susan's desk. He beamed at Shula.

'That's a long way,' she said carefully.

'It is quite, isn't it?' he agreed.

It transpired he'd be away for two months.

Shula was devastated. She'd completely misread the situation. So he'd kissed her. Well, what was that in the 1990s? Evidence of a lifetime commitment? He'd obviously just been being friendly and she'd let her imagination run away with her and turned it into something else. All day she was quiet. Simon noticed, kept trying to draw her out of herself but she'd gone beyond help. Her fear of what she might already have given away and the possibility of the humiliation that she'd been saved from burned in her like a flame.

Even when he gave her a lift home she couldn't make herself tell him why she minded so much about his trip. But it was all so confusing. If Friday hadn't meant that much to him and he could go away without a qualm, why was he so persistent in trying to tease out what was upsetting her?

Daniel picked up on her edginess and was tetchy himself. He pushed away his nighttime bottle and grizzled. Exasperated, Shula gave him a spoonful of Calpol and put him down, closing the door firmly on his sobs. Five minutes, that was all she needed, then she'd go back to him. There was a knock on the front door. Now Daniel would wake up properly and she'd never get him off. She listened at the foot of the stairs. By a miracle he'd gone quiet. She went to the front door and opened it. It was Simon.

'Look,' he said, when they'd gone through to the sitting room, 'If I've done anything to upset you, I'm sorry.'

Shula sighed. What was the point?

'No,' she said, 'It's probably me. I'm probably just being silly.'

He spread his hands.

'Shula, what?' he said gently.

She'd lied to him about her anniversary. She'd sworn that she wouldn't do it again.

'I ... it's just ... this trip. You going away. I mean, on Friday ... I thought we ... look, why didn't you tell me?'

He looked faintly puzzled.

'Well, I don't know. I expect it didn't occur to me.'

'Simon, you're going to be away for two months. How could it not have occurred to you?' She paused. She wanted so much to believe him. 'I'm just wondering where all this leaves me.'

He took a pace towards her.

'Where would you like it to leave you?' he said softly.

Shula took a step back.

'This is very difficult for me,' she said, almost pleading. 'It's been a long time since I've ... '

'I know,' he said, holding up his hand to stop her saying any more. 'Look, this thing in Dubai, it's only for two months. You're surely not going to tell me that something as insignificant as that is going to get in the way of us, are you?'

So. He said he hadn't told her on Friday that he was going away because he didn't want to mix business with pleasure. He thought of her as pleasure. He'd used the word 'us'.

He didn't stay long. He had to get back. He'd already been half way down the motorway when he'd turned round because he'd known something wasn't right. Oh, he was hopeless. The first man she might allow herself to feel something for since Mark and he kept his life in strict compartments, getting him to talk about feelings was like pulling teeth, her family and her best friend couldn't stand him ... And what did *she* think about it all?

She couldn't sort it out. All next day she was distracted. She wasn't sure whether she'd see Simon again before he left and if so, whether it would be in the office in front of Susan or whether he'd call on her at home. At the end of the day, when he hadn't shown up, she asked her Mum if she could hang on to Daniel while she went for a walk. She said she needed to clear her head. She went straight to Lakey Hill. She stood on the top, where she'd stood hundreds, thousands of times before, buffeted by the wind. Below, the village lay in its accustomed pattern, fields folding round lanes, trees, buildings. So little had changed. Well, the bungalow had been built, and the barns been converted, and Brian had put up a spanking new grain silo but, really, Ambridge was the same as ever ...

'Shula?'

'Simon. What are you doing here?'

He'd done nothing but surprise her in the last couple of days. He told her he'd asked at Brookfield and had realised there was only one place she'd come for a walk. She was touched he'd remembered.

'Are you pleased to see me?' he asked.

Of course she was.

'I suppose,' she said.

'I see, we're playing hard to get now, are we?' he said wryly.

'No,' said Shula truthfully. 'We're playing not sure of what to do.'

'Let me get this straight,' he said. 'You're worried that your feelings for me are going — '

'No, not my feelings,' she interrupted. 'I'd just about worked out what my feelings were.'

'Until yesterday, you mean. And then you started worrying about what I was feeling, yes?'

Or not.

'Yes,' she said.

He came closer, close enough to take her in his arms.

'I promise. You don't have to worry.'

He leaned forward to kiss her but she drew back. It would just be too much. She felt so churned up and confused — if he kissed her she'd cry and then she'd have to try to explain to her Mum what she didn't fully understand herself and it would all be too much, and she'd cry again. She really just needed to be on her own. She told him so and Simon seemed to understand. He knew he couldn't push her any further.

'I'll phone as soon as I get there,' he called as he disappeared down the hill.

'OK,' she called after him.

Faintly, through the wind, she thought she heard him call that he'd miss her.

'What?' she shouted.

'I'll miss you.' This time it was clear.

'Bye,' she called. And said to herself: 'I'll miss you too.'

It was starting to get dark: the sun had long gone behind the trees in the west. Since she'd come out, the lights had gone on in the bungalow, around the cow sheds, in the kitchen at Brookfield. Lakey Hill held no fears for her in the dark — she could have found her way down it blindfold. How odd that Simon should have found her on Lakey Hill. Was it significant? She smiled to herself. She didn't know. She honestly didn't know. She thought he was sincere in what he said: when she was with him she *knew* he was sincere. The important thing was that she was prepared to give him a chance. She knew that after having been so careful with herself for all this time, having gauged her reactions, eked out her emotions, she was ready to take the risk. And tomorrow, after work, she would take Daniel to the churchyard and talk to Mark about it. She stayed just a little longer as the darkness deepened. Then with one last deep breath she began her journey back. Back to Brookfield — to her home, her child and her future.